Dear Reader,

I don't know about you, but I'm absolutely thrilled *pink* to see a reissue of this four-book series! By now you have read the first reissue, *Morgan's Legacy*; that was the first two books of this series. Now here are the other two, *Morgan's Rescue* and *Morgan's Marriage!*

Originally, I'd penned *Morgan's Mercenaries: Love and Danger.* As you well know, no family ever escapes "life" and all its drama, intensity, hardships and triumphs. Up to that time, nothing of much import had happened to Morgan or his family. I knew I wanted to write, one day, about his children (*Firstborn,* Jason's story, is coming out in June 2004!), and in order to write about them, readers had to know a lot more intimate details about th~~e~~ family I'd presented.

Because Morgan live~~s~~  it spills over into his ~~~~ everyone. In *Morgan's* ~~~~ Morgan is rescued. Th~~e~~ will create further tens~~ion~~ ~~~~ and hurdles or each character to overcome in the later years. In *Morgan's Marriage,* I wanted to look at the aftermath of the terrible tragedy that befell them. How does it affect a marriage? How do you handle a terrible wound and begin to try and heal from it? I hope you enjoy *Morgan's Rescue* and *Morgan's Marriage.* The books to come are going to be about their children, so be watching for them! As always, I love hearing from you.

Warmly,

Lindsay McKenna

And don't miss these additional titles by

LINDSAY McKENNA

MORGAN'S LEGACY
February 2004

FIRSTBORN
coming in June 2004

DAUGHTER OF DESTINY
coming in July 2004

LINDSAY MⷜKENNA

MORGAN'S
HONOR

Published by Silhouette Books
America's Publisher of Contemporary Romance

SILHOUETTE BOOKS

MORGAN'S HONOR

Copyright © 2004 by Harlequin Books S.A.

ISBN 0-373-21882-6

The publisher acknowledges the copyright holder
of the individual works as follows:

MORGAN'S RESCUE
Copyright © 1995 by Lindsay McKenna

MORGAN'S MARRIAGE
Copyright © 1996 by Lindsay McKenna

CONTENTS

To my readers, who love Morgan and his family
as much as I do.

MORGAN'S RESCUE

Chapter 1

Pilar Martinez stood quietly before her old boss, who frowned at her from behind his massive desk.

"Pilar," Hector Ruiz said, opening his short, pudgy hands toward her, "I know you will not want this assignment." He sighed, then sat a little straighter in his well-padded executive chair. "As your old friend, I asked you to come into Lima today to see me. To talk of this problem—together."

Pilar moved to the leather wing chair that Hector was gesturing for her to make herself comfortable in, her low-heeled shoes making no sound on the thick maroon carpeting. How long had it been? She mused as she sat, crossing her legs beneath the skirt of her pale pink business suit. Ten years ago, she had stood in this same office, a young woman whom everyone said belonged back in her native village with her family, not in the governmental halls of power.

Pilar studied her old friend and mentor. Hector had been like a father shadowing her life then, protective of her youth and naïveté as the daughter of the Spanish ambassador—a Castilian nobleman—and a Quechua Indian housemaid. Unlike most of Peruvian Society, Hector had held no prejudice against her as a mestiza. Instead, he had treated her with unfailing kindness despite her mixed-blood ancestry, and for that she would be forever grateful.

Now, she noted, perspiration shone on Hector's wrinkled brow. Though he was short and fat, Hector possessed a certain vanity about his appearance. He liked jewelry, and several heavy gold and diamond rings studded his stubby fingers. His suits were of the finest fabrics and craftmanship yet they managed to hang on him poorly despite every effort by his tailors to correct their fit. His shoulders were simply too round and slumped, no matter how much padding the tailors added. He looked a little as if he were wearing football pads, Pilar thought with a secret smile.

"It has been a long time," she agreed softly, smoothing her skirt's silk fabric across her thighs. She took the white leather purse from her shoulder and placed it in her lap, draping her fingers across it, as she smiled at Hector over the expanse of his desk. The huge mahogany piece dwarfed him, but Pilar knew that the rule in Peruvian business—and even more so here in the halls of the country's government—was that the importance of the person was related directly to the size of the office and the desk within it. As if for extra insurance, a gold pen set shone conspicuously from its place on the gleaming desk top. Behind Hector framed color photos of his family, ten in all, lined a shelf. Many diplomas and certificates of accomplishments adorned the rich mahogany walls, and the windows overlooking Lima provided an appropriately impressive backdrop, framed by wine damask drapes. Everything about Hector's office testified to his power.

"Too long," Hector agreed, then nodded at the approach of his secretary. "Ah, here is Manuela Gomez. She brings us good, rich coffee and some cookies."

Pilar turned slightly to see Hector's secretary, now in her fifties, enter the sumptuous office, a silver tray in her hands. Manuela was tall and thin, her black-and-gray hair drawn back severely into the chignon at the base of her neck that Pilar recalled from years ago. Ever conservative, she wore a dull gray business suit with tasteful pearl earrings and a simple choker of pearls. The secretary studiously avoided Pilar's steady gaze as she carefully placed the silver tray on Hector's desk.

"Thank you, Manuela," Hector said with a smile as he lifted his steaming cup. "Come, Pilar, have a taste. The finest coffee in Peru."

Hector seemed unaware of Manuela's cold, fleeting

look as Pilar reached for the bone-china cup, but Pilar didn't miss the implied judgment in the other woman's eyes. Evidently the passing years hadn't softened Manuela's feelings about a mere mestiza being treated royally in her boss's office. The secretary made an about-face, much like a well-schooled military officer, and left as quietly as she had come. Forcing herself to shift focus, Pilar settled the saucer in her left palm and picked up the delicate cup, savoring the black coffee's fragrance. She took a small sip.

"There is nothing like a good cup of coffee," Hector said happily, reaching for a chocolate-covered cookie. "Here, Pilar, help yourself to some of these. You're as thin as a rail. I think you take after your mother."

She smiled a little at Hector's flattering reference to her beautiful mother, thankful again for his lack of disdain toward her heritage. Instead, Hector treated Pilar with the warmth and respect due any old friend. "Thank you, but I have just had lunch."

"So," Hector said with a sigh, leaning back against the tan leather behind him, "after your husband Fernando died, you are the manager of the finest Paso Fino breeding farm in Peru? I hear your horses take the blue ribbons no matter where you show them. That is quite a compliment to you as a trainer."

She bowed her head slightly. "Working with horses suits me well, Hector."

"It's your Incan blood," he said, waving the cookie expansively in the air. "You were always quiet and gentle—like a deer, I thought when we first met. I have heard at some of the embassy parties about your taming of that rogue stallion, El Diablo— and that you are the only one who can ride or handle him. He's earned quite a reputation in the horse circles. I was with the Sepulvedas the other night at a dinner for our president, and they were complaining loudly how you swept the championships, gathering all the major awards with that black devil.''

''Perhaps the Sepulveda family, with their wonderful Paso Fino breeding stock, has gotten too used to winning everything?''

Chuckling indulgently, Hector lifted the cookie toward her in a salute, then popped it into his mouth. ''Mmm, this chocolate is the best. These are my favorite cookies. Are you sure you won't have any?''

Laughing lightly, Pilar said, ''Hector, if I ate those, I would not fit into my riding clothes!''

He grinned affably and leaned forward for another cookie. ''Very well, I will eat one for you, then.''

Despite his cheerful banter, Pilar felt the tension building in her. It wasn't anything obvious, just the familiar tightening sensation that had so often served as a red flag to warn her of danger. But Hector was not dangerous. No, if anything, he'd saved her life a number of times in the past and acted as something of a paternal figure. She'd not seen him in several years, since her most-recent service to her country, but because of the horse circle she was in, she'd heard news of him at the parties she was forced to attend from time to time. Of course, Hector never forgot her birthday, in late May, and she never forgot his mid-December one. They always exchanged cards and gifts. And Pilar would always love him fiercely for his unflinching loyalty to her—despite her blood.

"Well…" Hector sighed, eyeing the last cookie on the silver tray. "I must say no to the last one. I'm trying to lose some weight. My doctor says my cholesterol level is too high, and I must cut out fat. Did you know that chocolate, the rich gift of the cocoa bean, is very high in cholesterol?"

"That's why I don't eat much of it," Pilar said, quirking her eyebrows at him.

With another sigh, Hector sipped his coffee and set it aside. "Even my wife, Carmellita, is making the chef produce low-fat meals for me." He wrinkled his nose. "Of course, we are invited to so many embassy parties that there is still good food to eat."

Her mouth stretched into a full smile. "Hector, you always find a way to get what you want."

Looking pleased, he laced his fingers across his protruding belly. "Yes, I do, Pilar."

"One of your skills."

He nodded. "I'll take that as a compliment." He paused, his face turning suddenly serious. "But now we must talk of business."

Pilar's stomach tightened another notch. "Yes," she murmured.

"You were a part-time undercover agent for us off and on for many years, Pilar, and your work was al-

ways above reproach. I considered you my best female agent.''

Heat rose from Pilar's neck to her face at the glow
in Hector's dark brown eyes. She knew he would
never make such a statement lightly. ''Thank you,''
she said.

''You gave us three years of superior service.
When your father died, it was hard on you—as it was
for all of us who wept at his loss. And of course I
know there were, ah…let us say, extenuating circumstances for your leaving government employ.'' He
frowned and looked up at the ceiling. ''I was pleased
when you agreed to help us three years ago, when
Enrique Ramirez captured two of Morgan Trayhern's
men.'' He rolled his head to the left and pinned her
with a dark gaze. ''Without you to help lead Jake
Randolph and our special team into Ramirez's fortress, their rescue could have been a disaster, Pilar.

''Maybe,'' he continued, waving his hand in the
air, ''there are people here who would dispute that,
but I don't. You were the reason for the success of
that mission. You know the jungle, and you know
Ramirez, because your village exists in his shadow.
You knew Ramirez's trails and activities and were
able to identify his thugs. Some may hold up their
noses at your Incan blood, Pilar, but I never have.
You have the sixth sense that good agents must possess. I think your mother's blood running through you
has contributed as much as your father's to your be-

coming one of our finest agents. I do not take lightly what you bring to our table, Pilar.''

''Thank you, Hector.'' It was unlike him to be so lavish with compliments. Instead, like her mother's people, he tended to believe actions spoke louder than any words could. Pilar realized he must have a great favor, indeed, to ask of her.

''You came out of retirement, and your job as manager of the Paso Fino farm to help us then, and I was greatly relieved when you said you would.''

''Only because of you, Hector, and you know that.''

''Yes, yes,'' he murmured, offering her a fatherly smile. ''And I appreciated your loyalty to me. Our government has worked with Morgan Trayhern quite often over the problems of cocaine from the coca fields in the mountains sent north to the United States.''

''Yes, I know.'' Her mother's village, which made its living by agriculture, had nearly been coerced by Ramirez's thugs to turn away from their usual crops and grow coca for the express purpose of producing cocaine. Had it not been for the elders, including her influential grandmother, Aurelia, the village might have fallen for Ramirez's cajoling and trinkets. Instead, it was one of the few communities in the mountainous region that had not been gobbled up by the man.

Hector took out a linen handkerchief and mopped

his perspiring brow. "Pilar, you are like my own daughter, you know that?"

Her stomach tightened even more. "Hector, you said the same thing to me three years ago when Morgan Trayhern's men were captured by Ramirez." She placed the cup and saucer back on the silver tray.

"Yes, yes, I did." He carefully refolded the handkerchief and placed it in his back pocket. "What I tell you now is to be held in total confidence. Do you understand that?"

"Of course," Pilar murmured. She clasped her hands on top of her purse. Hector's expression had become pained. "What is going on, Hector? I don't think you looked this worried when Trayhern's men were captured. It must be very bad."

"It is, it is, Pilar." He stood up and lumbered around the desk, his gaze never leaving hers. "You are like a daughter to me, Pilar," he repeated, "and God in Heaven knows—" he raised his hand in testimony "—I don't want to ask this of you. You have always been so loyal and honest. You are young and beautiful, with a lifetime stretching before you. I hate to even talk of this incident, but I must. I fear you are the only one who can help us."

He leaned against the edge of his desk, very near her chair, his voice lowering with feeling. "You know that our government interfaces on all levels with the United States. We have worked with their FBI, their CIA, DEA and so on, over the years. Now we have military specialists from the army and Marine Corps down here helping our troops wipe out the cocaine connections. And you know that Morgan Trayhern's people were asked to participate in the defending of certain villages near Ramirez's mountain fortresses." He looked at her intently. "You remember meeting Morgan?"

Pilar nodded somberly. "Of course, Hector."

"He is a man of immense integrity. Like you and me, Pilar."

"Yes, he was. I liked him immediately."

"His word is his bond," Hector agreed. "I could always count on Morgan to be honest. He never played word games or hid a secret agenda as so many of the other government people we deal with do. Do you recall that after you helped free his men from Ramirez's prison, he sent a huge donation to your village as thanks?"

"I won't ever forget it," Pilar said, closing her eyes in thought. She had met Morgan Trayhern at a party at the American embassy a month after his men had been freed. He'd asked specifically to meet her, to thank her personally for her help in leading the troops successfully through the hazardous jungles and mountains to Ramirez's hideout. Morgan's intensity had impressed her. Never had she met a man so profoundly loyal to the people he employed. The depth of his concern for them, unmatched even by Hector's warmth and caring, had shaken her.

Morgan had toasted Pilar in front of all the officials, generals and ambassadors, openly acknowledging her help. And she had stood, champagne in hand, blushing and longing to run away. She had never liked the limelight, but Morgan had gently wrapped his hand around her arm—as if he knew she might bolt—and raised his glass, his voice ringing with emotion as he gave her the lion's share of credit for the mission's success.

Later, he had pulled her aside and asked if she would consider working for Perseus. Pilar had been honored, but her days as an undercover agent were over. After the pain of the events that had first caused her to leave her country's service at twenty-one, she'd sworn never to resume that role, so she had turned Morgan down. Never would she forget his probing gaze as he'd silently studied her—as if he could look inside her head, inside her heart, and know what she was thinking and feeling. Only one other man had ever affected her that way. But with Morgan she had felt none of the panic or anxiety that the other man had aroused, only the burning focus of his care and perception.

Morgan hadn't been daunted by her lineage, either. In fact, he'd applauded her Indian blood. One of the reasons she had taken the mission in the first place was because of the Eastern Cherokee heritage of Wolf Harding, one of the two men captured by Ramirez. And she'd told Morgan the truth about that decision. It didn't matter whether Wolf was North American or South American, they shared the same blood. Morgan seemed to intuitively understand her reasoning.

When he'd asked what he could do to thank her, Pilar had been dumbfounded. No one had ever asked that of her before, so she'd had no words for him. Morgan had placed his hand on her shoulder and said he would think of an appropriate way to repay her courage in laying her life on the line for his people. Two weeks later, Pilar had been back at work at the horse farm when she'd received a check from Perseus for twenty-five thousand dollars. An accompanying letter from Morgan explained she was to use the money for her village in whatever way she felt was needed.

And every year since then, a check for the same amount had arrived. Pilar took the money to the council of elders of the village, which included her grandmother, and in three years, the local children had a schoolhouse and a teacher. Books had been bought, classes organized, and now a vocational school was being built to serve the entire region, where Indian children could learn not only to read and write, but other marketable skills as well. All thanks to Morgan Trayhern's unending generosity.

Pilar opened her eyes. ''What do you want of me, Hector?'' she asked steadily.

''It concerns Morgan.''

''Oh?''

''Yes.'' He sighed. Again, he took out his handkerchief and mopped his brow. ''Something very bad has happened,'' he muttered. ''I'm afraid Ramirez and Garcia have conspired to kidnap Morgan from his home in the United States and to take his wife, Laura, and their son, Jason, as well.''

Pilar was instantly on her feet. ''Oh, no!'' Her purse slid off her lap. Shaken, she leaned down and retrieved it. ''When did this happen, Hector?''

''Not long ago.'' He shrugged lamely. ''We were contacted immediately, and my office has been working feverishly to help Perseus with its efforts to locate them. The good news is that Laura was found at Garcia's estate on Nevis Island, in the Caribbean, and Jason, their small *niño,* was found in Maui, Hawaii.''

Pilar's stomach tightened into a knot, and she pressed her palm against it. ''*Dios,* Hector. Are they all right? What about Morgan? Have they found him? Is he dead or alive?''

He held up his hand. ''One question at a time, Pilar.'' He wiped his brow. ''Laura was rescued first, and now I've received word that Jason is safe, too. The Pentagon just intercepted a satellite message, and they've been able to confirm that Morgan is being held at Ramirez's stronghold near your village.''

Pilar's stomach screamed with pain, and she swallowed against a dry throat. ''Oh, no....'' She inhaled sharply. ''He's alive?''

''We don't know.''

''Knowing the snake that Ramirez is, Morgan is alive but very badly tortured,'' Pilar said bitterly, pressing a hand to her forehead. ''Not Morgan Trayhern. Of all people, Hector. He is a good man. A man with a generous heart.'' She sank back into her chair, glad for its support.

Hector moved to her side and patted her shoulder gently. ''I know, Pilar. I know. I'm aware of his generosity to you and your village. I don't know too many men in this world with such strength of loyalty to others. It grieves me badly in my heart of hearts to know that Ramirez has him hostage.''

Shutting her eyes, Pilar tried to stop the anguish threatening to rise from her stomach into her throat. ''He's such a fine person,'' she said in a choked voice. ''You saw what Ramirez did to the two men we rescued?''

''Yes,'' Hector murmured heavily, moving back to his former position against the desk. ''The Indian almost died. Ramirez is a monster when it comes to drugs and torture methods.''

''Ramirez hates Morgan,'' Pilar whispered, looking up at her former boss. ''He even threatened to come into our village with his men and kill all of us. He did that to another village near us.''

''That is why you are here, Pilar,'' Hector said in a low voice. ''I must ask for your help once again. I need you to lead one of Morgan's finest operatives to the fortress. We are afraid if we go in with special troops, a second time, Ramirez will kill Morgan. Ramirez will be expecting us to use the same tactics. He knows we will try to rescue Morgan if we locate him. Luckily, right now, we believe Ramirez has no idea that we have done so.

"That is where you come in, Pilar," continued Hector, settling more heavily against the solid mahogany. "We want you to go back to your village. Don the clothes of your people and go undercover, saying you're the daughter of a farmer from one of the villages Ramirez controls. They don't know everyone from those communities, so you should be safe enough in that regard. Lead this agent to Ramirez's fortress. A special team in several helicopters will wait well outside Ramirez's sight and hearing."

"What do you want me to do then, Hector?"

"We want you to penetrate the fortress, Pilar. Find out where Morgan is being kept. If he is alive or dead."

"And then this special team will fly in and take him out?"

"Yes." He frowned. "This mission will be much more dangerous for you, Pilar. Last time, you led a contingent of troops to the fortress and stood back while they made the assault. This time it is different." He gave her a keen look. "Your life will be in direct jeopardy. There will be no immediate and assured rescue if you get into trouble. But you'll be going in with one of Morgan's most trusted mercenaries. Two against Ramirez. The odds are not fair, I grant you, but if we are to have a prayer of rescuing Morgan, we must do things differently and surprise Ramirez completely. I'm sure he will be expecting troops as last time and will have prepared accordingly.

"Many people from these villages serve as his eyes

and ears, as you know. You must have as little contact
with anyone as possible. If you must talk to people,
tell them this white *Norte Americano* has hired you
to take him into the jungles to carry on his botany
work. Morgan's mercenary will pose as a biologist
from Stanford University in California, and you as his
guide. The local people will accept that explanation.
Scientists are always coming to our country for such
reasons.

"You are to make your way through the jungle and
into the mountains to his fortress, *El Nido del Águila,*
the 'Eagle's Nest.' Enter the fortress and find Morgan.''

Pilar wrinkled her nose. "Any woman entering *El
Nido del Águila* is a target, Hector. You know that.''

"Yes, yes, I do know it. But someone must get in
and verify that Morgan is there.''

"This plan is very dangerous, Hector,'' Pilar said
with great deliberation. "I have a daughter to raise. I
cannot just throw responsibility aside without serious
promise from you—from the government of Peru—
that you will care for her monetarily if I am killed.''

He stared at her. "Then you will take this assignment?''

"Only because Morgan is involved. Hector, I do
not want to put my life on the line. My daughter,
Rane, is seven years old, and she is my world—'' Her
voice broke. "I know my grandparents will care for
Rane while I take this mission. But if Ramirez catches
me, I have no doubts about what will happen to me,

Hector. I have seen his cruelty. If he even suspects that I'm a government agent, he will drug me and wring the truth out of me. He will rape and kill me, then send his men to my village to kill everyone. He will kill Rane and my grandparents. I have seen the devastation he can wreak.''

"The government of Peru has already signed papers on your behalf, Pilar. I told them that if you took this mission, generous monetary provisions had to be made for your daughter and village.''

"Yes," she said, studying Hector. "I won't do it otherwise. I can't...."

Hector moved around his desk, pulled open a drawer and produced a legal-size document. "Here, read this. If you agree with the provisions, Pilar, then sign it.''

Her hand trembled slightly as she took the heavy, official-looking document. In it, the Peruvian government promised to protect her family. A stipend of one thousand dollars a month would be provided for Rane until she was eighteen years old. Rane would be sent to the university in Lima to get a degree, with all expenses paid. Permanent troop protection would be offered to the village, should Ramirez find out where she had come from. Her grandparents would be placed in a protection program and kept safe.

Pilar studied every clause carefully. Finally she looked up. "I want Rane to have a full scholarship to Harvard University, Hector. If Ramirez discovers my real name and connection, the government is to take Rane to the United States. She is to be provided three thousand dollars a month until she graduates, with payments to stop once she gets a job. She will be given a new name and identity. I know Ramirez well enough to know he would try to track my daughter down and kill her out of revenge.''

"It will be done," Hector promised, taking the document and quickly writing the new clauses into the contract and initialing them. "Anything else?"

"I want my grandparents to receive a monthly check from the government of Peru for five hundred dollars until the day they die. Just because they're placed in a protection program doesn't mean they will be cared for. Government people could dump my grandparents into some small town and leave them without a way to survive.''

"Very well," Hector murmured, again writing hastily. He looked up and handed her the document. "Sign, please."

Pilar took the pen. She stood and placed the document on the polished surface of Hector's desk, her stomach quivering with fear. If it weren't Morgan Trayhern's own life at stake, she would never take this mission, risking her beautiful daughter, the child created out of pure love. But she owed Morgan. Scribbling her signature, she realized the enormity of her decision.

"There...." she murmured, handing the document back to Hector. "It is official."

"And legal." Hector placed the document aside. "I will make sure that all these things are done should you be killed, Pilar." He opened his hands. "But of course we will do everything to prevent that from happening in the first place. We will do our best to ensure contact with you via radio. The special troops assigned to this mission are the best we have. And one of Morgan's best mercenaries will be at your side."

Pilar sat down. "You must be speaking of Jake Randolph, then. Remember? He was with me when I led the troops to the fortress before."

"Er…no, it isn't Jake. He's at Perseus, running the company in Morgan's absence. It is another man.…" Hector pulled a file toward him and quickly opened it. "Ah, yes. And this is so fortunate, Pilar—you have worked with this man before."

Frowning, Pilar said, "I've worked only with Jake Randolph from Morgan's company."

"No, no, you misunderstand." Hector beamed happily and held up a color photo. "You must remember Culver Lachlan? He used to be with the CIA. You two worked together for three months and—"

Pilar gave a cry, standing up so swiftly that the heavy chair she was sitting in was nearly knocked over. Her fists knotted and she stared, frozen, at the face looking back at her from the photo.

Hector frowned. "Pilar? What is it? You look as if you're going to faint. *Dios,* are you all right?" He quickly dropped the photo and rushed around the

desk. Slipping his hand under her elbow, he helped
her back into the chair. "Come, come," he coaxed,
"sit down. There...that's it." He straightened and
gave her a confused look. "Pilar, you look as though
you've seen a ghost. What is it? Surely, you remember Mr. Lachlan? He was the last agent you worked
with before you had to quit." He patted her shoulder.
"Pilar?"

Tears rushed to her eyes as she sat rigidly, only
vaguely aware of Hector's attempts to comfort her.
Oh, no, no...how could this be? Could fate be this
cruel? Her mouth had gone dry and her throat constricted. Tears blurred the world around her as she
struggled to control her rampant feelings. *Culver.*
How she had tried to put him out of her heart and
mind. *Culver Lachlan.* The name sent a bittersweet
river of feelings coursing through her, including a terror, and anxiety in her stomach that nauseated her.

"*Dios,* Pilar, let me get you a glass of water. You
look so pale. Stay still. Stay still and I will be right
back...."

She barely heard Hector leave her side. All her focus, all her rage, sadness and guilt were aimed at the
photo lying on his desk. It had been years. Eight long
years... Pressing her cool, trembling fingertips to her
brow, Pilar tried to rise above the rush of emotions
released by the unexpected sight of that photo.

Alone in the office, she stood on wobbly knees.
Leaning across the desk, she forced herself to take the
photo and turn it around, though her fingers seemed

to burn where she touched it. *Culver Lachlan.* His name went like a knife to her suddenly aching heart. Eight painful years of trying to forget. How could he suddenly be thrown back into her life?

Suddenly panicked, Pilar acknowledged with a horrible realization that by signing those papers, she had been stuck not only with the mission, but with Lachlan. She forced herself to look at the photo. He was a giant of a man at six foot five, brawny and strong as his Scottish ancestors before him. He was square jawed, with a thick, bull-like neck, broad, powerful shoulders and a barrel chest. He was built as stoutly as the finest Paso Fino. Solid. Hard. Dangerous. Oh, how dangerous he had been to her young, vulnerable emotions! Though he'd been only twenty-five at the time himself, but he'd been far from innocent to the ways of the world as she had been.

Much as she wanted to, Pilar couldn't forget the imposing shadow Culver had cast on her life. But the man in the photo looked different from the Culver she remembered. Here was a hardened warrior with a face like armor itself, the pale blue eyes devoid of emotion.

Jerking back her hand, Pilar stood hypnotized by the photo, wanting to wrench her gaze from it, but helpless to do so. Her heart was pounding like that of a frightened animal relentlessly pursued by a jaguar. She saw a coldness she'd not seen before in Culver. His mouth... She quivered internally, recalling his mouth upon her own, hotly, swiftly taking hers, stealing her breath, stealing her very soul with those scalding, spiraling kisses. Now that mouth had become a thin, harsh line, no longer revealing any softness.

"Pilar?" Hector came rushing back into the room with a glass of water, the liquid slopping onto his hand in his hurry. "Here. Drink this...."

She sat down and accepted the glass as Hector hovered anxiously, wringing his hands. He was breathing hard, and she felt bad to have caused him such distress. After sipping the water dutifully, she handed it back to him.

"Th-thank you, Hector. I will be all right now."

"Are you sure? I thought you were going to faint, Pilar."

"This agent, Lachlan..."

"Yes?" Hector set the glass down on his desk, near enough for her to reach it if she wanted to. He circled the desk and sat. "What about him?"

"Do—" In spite of herself, her voice broke. "Do I have to work with him?"

"There is no one else. Is there a problem here, Pilar? I thought you would be overjoyed to know that an agent you had worked with undercover before would be helping you again. You already know each other, and he seemed to like you. I recall he did try to contact you after that mission. You're a team already, Pilar, and I believe it will serve you well."

Pilar felt torn as never before to divulge the shaming truth to Hector. But the look of fatherly anxiety on his face stopped her. She could tell no one. Not even him. Only her grandparents and Fernando, her now deceased husband, knew the truth. Not even Rane knew—nor would she ever know. Pilar's throat ached with tension from holding back unshed tears. She wanted to weep violently, like the sudden thunderstorms that popped up and rolled across the hills above the jungle, sweeping everything clean. But if she cried, Hector would only worry more.

"Pilar?"

"It's all right," she managed to whisper. Picking up the glass of cool water again, she sipped it.

" You do not trust this man?"

"I...trust him...."

"What then?"

"Are you sure he's with Morgan's company?"

"Very sure. Jake Randolph called me personally to tell me he was available. Jake, too, felt it was a good thing you two had worked together before."

Touching her throat, Pilar whispered, "And he wanted to come on this mission knowing I would be his partner?"

Hector shrugged dramatically. "Jake and I did not talk about that. He just said that Lachlan was available and would take the mission."

"But he's been told I'll be on it?" she persisted.

Hector began to relax a little, some of the tension draining from his features. "Of course, Pilar. He was briefed as much as you have been."

Faintness rimmed Pilar's vision, but she fought it

off. The desire, heartbreak, rage and anguish refused to be stilled within her, and she felt like a volcano erupting inwardly. Only the cool solidity of the glass clenched between her hands gave her some semblance of sanity in that moment. Pilar couldn't believe Culver would go on a mission with her. Not now. Not ever again, after what had happened.

"Wh-when will he arrive?"

"Tomorrow afternoon at three. We'll pick him up at the Lima airport."

"And where do you want us to meet?"

Hector sighed and brought out a large manila envelope stamped Top Secret. "Only one other person and I know the contents of this envelope, Pilar. I helped formulate the plans contained within it, including specific and detailed instructions of anything you need to know. This mission has the strictest degree of secrecy because we know there are moles on Ramirez's payroll.

"Please be very careful with the contents of this envelope. Read it where no one will disturb you. Provisions have been suggested for Rane while you are gone, and we will make sure your employer has no inkling of why you're leaving for two weeks. We've arranged to have one of our agents call the farm and ask them to fly you to Argentina to pick up a mare that will be bred to El Diablo. The owner will think you are in Argentina, preparing the flight for the mare. Of course, we'll have a mare show up at the farm when you return to maintain your cover."

"Good," Pilar whispered as she nervously touched the thick, heavy envelope.

"Here," Hector said with a frown, handing Lachlan's photo to her. "Put it in there with the rest."

Woodenly, she did as she was instructed. "Are you sure he knows he's going to be working with me?" she couldn't resist asking again.

Hector gave her a strange look. "I'm positive. Jake Randolph said he would brief Lachlan immediately after our phone call. I told him I would try to talk you into taking this mission." He touched the phone at his right hand. "As soon as you leave, I'll call Jake to tell him you've signed the contract."

"I see." Pilar took a deep, unsteady breath and got to her feet. She gripped the edge of the desk for a moment, reorienting herself.

"Pilar," he said worriedly, "is there something I should know? You are acting strangely, and it isn't like you. Is there a problem with this agent? I personally went over his file from the CIA and Perseus. He has an impeccable record and was given the highest marks when he left The Company. You will see that for yourself, though." He pointed to the envelope beneath her left arm. "His complete dossier is in there for you to peruse."

Alarm spread through her. "And what about me? The information on me?"

Hector shrugged. "He will be given the same."

Alarm became panic. "What of my family?" *What of Rane?*

"All the usual information."

Her heart plummeted. Would Culver know? Would he suspect? He couldn't. He just couldn't. Pilar tried to focus on her legs, willing strength into her wobbly knees. "Very well, Hector, I'm going to go home."

"Good," he said, getting up. He came around the desk and threw his arm around her shoulders briefly. "Be careful, Pilar. I know you are an excellent agent. And you have much to live for. You've got that beautiful daughter...."

Tears flooded her eyes as she hugged the older man affectionately. "I'll be very careful," she whispered. "Just knowing you're behind me, Hector, gives me hope."

He released her and looked at her worriedly. "This is one mission we cannot fail. I know the walls have ears. I pray to God I have taken every possible precaution to ensure the safety of you and your family."

Pilar nodded, sniffed and turned away. If she didn't leave, she was going to cry in earnest. For herself. For the fear she felt about the mission. As she walked to the door to let herself out, she knew she had to tell her grandparents what was happening. Even though the mission was classified, she had to get Rane to the safety only they could provide.

As she walked down the long, polished hallway, Pilar hoped Hector had already provided those outlets on her behalf. He knew how much family meant to her. She'd already lost her mother and the two men in her life she'd loved with a fierceness that defied description. Her father had passed away. And Culver? He'd probably thought she was dead. Or wished she was. She knew he would never forgive her. Not even after eight years.

Her hands felt damp and cold as she stood waiting for the elevator that would take her to the first-floor lobby. It was January, the beginning of summer in South America. Although Lima was the country's largest city, and its capital, it wasn't nearly as large as New York or Buenos Aires. Still, people in impeccably tailored business suits traversed the halls as she stepped from the elevator and headed toward the revolving glass-and-brass doors. Pilar hated the city. It was her Indian blood, she knew. To her, cities meant congestion, chaos, pollution and stress—people hurrying and scurrying everywhere.

Catching a taxi outside the complex, she directed the driver to take her to the train station, from where she would head south, out of the city. Rancho Verde was a mere hour away from all this craziness, but right now, Pilar longed as never before for its peace and open spaces. She felt suffocated in the cab, even though the windows were down, allowing the warm salt air of the Pacific to waft through, lifting strands of her shoulder-length hair.

What was she going to do? How would Culver react to her? She tipped her head back against the seat and closed her eyes. She could almost feel his hatred. His anger. Could she blame him? No. But then, he never would have understood, either. He could be stubborn, immovable and highly opinionated. He had walked into her life like a tank blasting away, and she had been soft and malleable in response. And then things had gotten out of hand. Completely.

Sighing, Pilar pressed her hand against her brow. What was she going to do? She had signed a contract she had to fulfill. And she *wanted* to fulfill it, because Morgan deserved her help. But how was she going to do it with Culver at her side? She would be terribly distracted, she knew. And distraction could get her killed. Rane would be in danger, too. What if Ramirez found out the truth of her identity? Her precious daughter's life would be on the line as much as her own—as would her grandparents'. *What was she going to do?* And how, with Culver's glowering, menacing presence, was she going to hold herself together long enough to rescue Morgan?

Chapter 2

Culver is coming. Culver is coming. The words echoed through Pilar's thoughts with each beat of her thoroughbred mare's galloping hooves. Desperate to do something—anything—to quell her growing anxiety, she had placed a jump saddle on Honey, a lovely, seventeen-hand-high chestnut, her favorite mount at Rancho Verde. But as she and Honey circled the largest of the horse farm's pipe-enclosed training arenas, Pilar's mind refused to stray from the coming meeting.

The day was warm and slightly damp, with the tang of salt in the air. The Pacific Ocean was less than a mile away, and humidity tended to settle in the lower elevations. Rancho Verde was a dream come true—

the largest horse farm in Peru, immaculately kept by
the Antonio and Cecelia Navarro family—and Pilar
longed to find her usual peace of mind through work.
But it was three o'clock, and she couldn't escape the
knowledge that Culver would even now be landing at
the Jorge Chavez Airport in Lima. Hector would be
meeting and briefing him, then, according to her orders, she was to meet him at seven tonight at Hotel
of the Andes, one of Lima's finest four-star palaces.

Honey snorted as she cantered slowly, guided by
Pilar's sensitive, gloved hands. Riding brought Pilar
a sense of freedom she otherwise never seemed able
to achieve—except in visits to her grandparents' village. A black, velvet-covered hard hat protected her
head in case of falls as she put Honey through her
paces over the two-to-three-foot jumps. But Honey
was so steady that Pilar never worried about that possibility. The arena was quiet, for the afternoon and
early evening here were considered siesta time, and
no one worked. Only Pilar couldn't rest. She hadn't
slept well last night, either, her dreams entwining with
haunting nightmares from her shameful past.

The sky was cerulean blue, with a few white wisps
that reminded Pilar of Honey's flowing flaxen mane
as they cantered about the enclosure. Tall trees, grown
scraggly from the frequent winds off the ocean,
hugged the arena, and a cooling breeze chased away
the worst of the early summer heat. The hacienda itself, constructed of pale yellow stucco with a red,
Spanish-tile roof, was situated below the training

grounds in a small vale. From their higher position, the various arenas for the jumpers overlooked the surrounding, tree-covered hills and Pilar could see the sparkling deep blue of the Pacific in the distance.

She guided Honey with her legs and a slight change of weight on the saddle as she took three jumps in a row. Each time the mare gathered and collected the energy in her hind legs, Pilar felt as if she were on a powerful, living spring. The big, easygoing mare trusted Pilar implicity, sailing effortlessly over another two-and-a-half-foot jump.

A combination jump, consisting of a pool of water and a four-foot barrier, was next, requiring Honey to stretch to her maximum length as well as jump ''big.'' Just as Pilar steadied the mare for the exercise, the back of her neck prickled. A red flag. Why was she sensing danger? She had little time to assess the warning as she lifted upward, knees jammed tightly into the rolls of the saddle, riding easily on the horse's withers as they approached the combined jump. Honey's front legs rose and she soared like the Andean condors that floated over her grandparents' village. For a moment the mare seemed to have wings like Pegasus. As Honey landed solidly on the other side of the jump, Pilar gently pulled on the reins.

Squinting against the western sun, she looked toward the buildings that housed the tack and stables. Her hands were wet, the gloves slightly slippery on the double reins as the mare came to a halt. The animal's ears went instantly forward—toward the same area Pilar was studying. The prickling sensation at the back of her neck was a sure sign of trouble, Pilar knew. That internal warning system—which her mother had attributed to her spirit guardian, a jaguar—had saved her life a number of times when she'd worked undercover. So now she strained to see past the blinding sunlight to the stable area.

Nothing moved. As expected, the farm help were enjoying siesta. A few horses hung their heads out of their roomy box stalls and looked around, but none were snorting or appearing alarmed. One of the older dogs, a black-and-white mongrel Pilar had rescued from Lima long ago, moved with a limp down the breezeway between the stalls. Frowning, Pilar lifted her hand and touched the back of her neck. Rubbing it, she again swept her gaze along the long, rectangular barn area. She saw no one. But she felt someone watching. Watching *her*.

Compressing her lips, she gathered up the reins. Perhaps if she ignored the sensation, it would go away. Maybe it was merely anticipation over having to meet Culver tonight. Her stomach had been on edge ever since Hector had dropped his bombshell. And her heart…well, her heart felt as if Culver's own massive, powerful hand was relentlessly squeezing it. After all, what was she going to say to him? That she was sorry? It seemed such a lame, weak word at this point. Blowing out a breath of air in exasperation, Pilar tried to return her focus to Honey and the remaining jumps, but the sensation of being watched refused to go away. Danger was present—and it was very near.

Culver Lachlan stood just inside the breezeway of the stables, watching Pilar Martinez ride a magnificent chestnut jumper. He scowled as he eyed her, struggling to control those wild feelings that had first erupted in him when Jake had ordered him to take this mission. Pillar was like hot butter in a skillet, so effortlessly did she move in rhythm with her horse. It was obvious she loved to ride. And Culver remembered all too well seeing that same pure joy on her face a long time ago. A joy that he'd— *Stop it,* he ordered himself harshly. *Stop remembering. It won't do any good. She left you when you were down for the count.*

But no matter how much he wanted to hate Pilar for what she'd done to him, Culver couldn't bring himself to feel it. The voice inside his head coldly announced that she had used him for her own means, gotten what she wanted and abandoned him.

Well, what the hell had he expected, anyway? She was a woman, and the women in his life had always been as unstable as C-4 explosives. He'd never had good luck with them. Still, Pilar had seemed different. His gaze never left her as she rode at a canter around the arena, taking the jumps with ease. Even at this distance, Culver could see that the twenty-two-year-old ingenue he'd fallen hopelessly in love with eight years ago had become a woman, blooming with the full-blown beauty of a mature rose compared to the sweeter, less-complex bud—and still able to take his breath away.

Was Pilar's ebony hair still long? He couldn't help but wonder. Were her eyes still those of the jaguar that roamed the Peruvian jungles? She had the most arresting eyes Culver had ever seen. Her Incan heritage made them almost black, but Culver had found out quickly that he could determine Pilar's emotions by watching for sparkles of real gold in their depths.

Over the three months they'd worked together, he'd learned to love watching those huge, luminous eyes, slightly tilted, again by her Incan heritage, shift from near black to a rich, golden brown. His heart twisted in his chest. How deeply his feelings ran—even now. It was stupid, he knew. He was thirty-three years old—old enough to know better. *Face it,* he reminded himself cruelly, *she was a young college girl out for a fling.* She hadn't wanted commitment. She'd wanted the high adventure and pulse-pounding sensuality of combining passion with life-and-death work.

Shifting his weight to his other booted foot, Culver rested his shoulder against a large, wooden support post and absorbed the sight of Pilar as she rode. Memories came flooding back—so many of them painful. Why had she run out on him in his darkest hour? All he'd wanted was Pilar at his side. He'd been scared, seeing his whole twenty-five years of life flash before his closed eyes. Yet as soon as they'd made it to the hospital, she'd disappeared. The last memory of Pilar he had was of her running alongside the gurney as the ambulance attendants raced with it toward an operating room. He'd been bleeding to death. Pilar had been crying, gripping his limp, nerveless hand. Her long, luxurious hair had been damp and twisted into strands, the expression on her face one of sheer terror, and those lips… Culver groaned. No one had a mouth quite like Pilar's. Full and almost heart-shaped, it had drawn him like a hummingbird to a rosy bloom filled with sweet nectar.

With a sigh, Culver crossed his arms over his chest. It was agony to be here. God knew, he'd fought Jake about this assignment. He wanted no part of teaming up with Pilar—not after what had happened. How could he trust her? His heart certainly couldn't. After he'd nearly died in that hospital, he'd tried many times to contact her. And to what end? Hector would merely say Pilar was undercover and couldn't be contacted, and eventually Culver had gotten the message. After all, even undercover agents came off the job to rest once in a while.

Pilar's canary yellow breeches showed off hips and long legs as slender as he remembered. At this distance, he couldn't see her face clearly, but the outline of her form was unmistakable, and unwillingly he acknowledged the tightening in his lower body at the memory of her. Culver drew in a deep, ragged breath and closed his eyes. How he'd tried to forget the feel of her warm, sleek body against his. Forget her small, delicate hands restlessly roaming his chest, his shoul-

ders, eliciting firestorms as she caressed him, her eyes
big in wonderment....

"Stop it!" he snarled aloud. He turned, hoping no
one had heard him, but the breezeway was empty. An
old, limping dog approached him, wagging its tail.
Angry at himself for allowing the vault of memories
to spill out from beneath his steel control, Culver
leaned over and patted the dog's head absently.

He had no time to waste. He had to let her know
he was here. It was the last thing Culver wanted to
do—face the sight of rejection in her eyes. He'd never
really cared what anyone thought of him until Pilar
came along. She was different, exotic—like the heady
fragrance of the orchids that laced the jungle trees.
And when she'd opened to him, he'd believed he'd
met the woman who could fulfill him on every con-
ceivable level. Like an orchid stretched fully into
bloom, she had given herself to him, allowing him to
inhale her dizzying fragrance.

To this day, Pilar haunted his dreams. He still had
torrid, sensual dreams about her touch, the way she
looked at him, that caressing smile that shot through
him like hot sunlight, letting him know he was the
center of her world. Well, it wasn't so. He'd stupidly
made the assumption that Pilar felt about him the way
he did about her. Culver had never fallen in love with
anyone before Pilar—or since. Maybe that's why she
was always in his heated, humid, jungle-like dreams
like some ethereal fog that would reach out, tease
him, and yet as he tried to grab it and embrace it,

would dissolve upon his contact. Or, maybe the silent, dangerous jaguar who owned the jungle.

Anxiety riffled through him. Humiliation. Desire. He felt all those things as he decided to step from his hiding place and walk to the pipe fence where Pilar could see him. How would she look at him? Hector had said she knew he'd been assigned as her partner for this highly dangerous mission.

As he pushed away from the beam and straightened, Culver felt the weight of worry press down on his broad shoulders. A terrible anxiety was building in his chest. No matter how angry or hurt he was about how Pilar had treated him, he didn't want her placed in a situation where she could be killed. As he stepped out of the breezeway into the sunlight, Culver knew in the depths of his aching heart that he would still step between her and an oncoming bullet—as he had once before. He walked slowly toward the arena.

He felt a certain satisfaction in knowing she didn't realize he was here. Pilar was at the other end of the arena, having just finished a series of jumps. She had brought the thoroughbred from a canter to a walk. As Culver placed one booted foot on the fence's lowest railing, he saw her dismount. Frowning, he watched her intently. At five foot three, she was short next to the giant horse she rode. He laughed to himself, remembering their height difference. The first time Pilar had seen him, her dark eyes had widened enormously and she'd said in Spanish, "You must be a giant from a special place on earth."

Her low, breathless voice had sent tingles through him. Pilar had never met someone from Scotland, and the awe combined with curiosity in her gaze had made him feel special and powerful. At the time, Culver had been expecting to work with a hardened veteran woman agent. Instead, he'd found this wild, exotic orchid bud preparing to burst open to the world at large, and he'd wanted to be the one to watch each of her beautiful petals unfold, to reveal the honeyed depths of her womanhood.

Culver shook his head. In the eight years since, he'd waited for the memory of Pilar to disappear. But as he stood at the fence, watching her pat the thoroughbred, he realized with a terrible, sinking feeling that every emotion he'd had eight years ago was just as brilliantly alive within him today, burning fiercely and without apology. Running his fingers through his short dark hair, he wondered what he would say to her. Blazing anger paralleled an aching need.

Something happened. Culver felt it before he actually saw Pilar react. She had been petting the horse, praising it, when suddenly she turned on her booted heel and looked down the length of the arena—toward him. His heart thudded once in his chest to underscore, even at this distance, the intensity of her gaze. How he wished he could see her expression. Culver shook his head. To hell with it; the time had come. Bending down, he climbed between the rails. Sand and sawdust covered the arena, and his rough-out boots sank into the mixture as he straightened to his full height and squared his shoulders.

Pilar gasped, her hand contracting on the reins. She had to be seeing things! But she wasn't. Her eyes widened as she realized Culver Lachlan was walking down the arena—toward her. Her heart skipped a beat as panic set in. Her breathing became ragged. *Culver!* The word shot through her like an arrow—striking straight to her soul. An ache began to pool in her lower body with memories of Culver's strength and incredible tenderness as he moved deeply within her, branding her his for all time.

Tears raced into her eyes, but just as quickly, Pilar forced them away. Culver must not see her cry. He must not know how she really felt. Her hands grew sweaty as she stood by the horse, rigid with an un-settling mix of anticipation, fear and need. As he walked slowly toward her, so much came careening back to her. The sound of his laugh, low and deep, like the reverberation of a medicine drum. His pale, sky blue gaze, which sent heat jagging through her like bolts of lightning teasing the jungle canopy above her village during a storm.

The color photo of Culver she'd studied was no match for the real thing. He was still a giant to her, built sturdily, of good strong bone, as he used to say. How many times had she lain against him? Felt the weight of him upon her like a warm, secure blanket? No feeling in the world matched that of Culver on top of her, his body a shield. He always felt more

stable, more solid than she. Pilar gulped as each step
brought him closer. What was she going to say to
him? What *could* she say? He'd never understand nor
forgive her for what she'd done. Worse, if he knew
the whole truth, he might try to take from her the one
thing that mattered most in the world.

Culver was not conventionally handsome. He'd
once said that his face was carved from the rugged
granite cliffs of his Scottish home. But Pilar adored
those craggy features. Now crow's-feet marked the
corners of his eyes, and slashes on either side of his
mouth gave new depth to his face. His cheekbones
were high, like her own, but his face was square, with
a hawklike nose that reminded her of the harpy eagle,
a huge aggressive white eagle that plummeted like a
dive-bomber through the Peruvian jungle to snatch a
monkey for its dinner.

Pilar tried to steady herself, but it was impossible.
Already she could feel strength ebbing from her with
each wild heartbeat. Culver's eyes looked merciless.
Pilar knew from experience that a deep, dark blue
meant he was angry, while they became lighter with
happiness. Right now they were a stormy cobalt, and
the set of his mouth frightened her. How warm, exploring yet powerful that his mouth had once been
against hers. As big as he was, when Culver kissed
her, he'd taken her gently, inviting her to surrender
herself to him. Then his kiss would deepen, becoming
hotter and more frantic, until their mouths clung together with passion.

Shakily, Pilar removed her hard hat, and the black hair she'd coiled on top of her head spilled in a cascade about her shoulders. It was nowhere near the length it had been when she'd been Culver's lover. But right now, it seemed as if the eight long years between then and now had not occurred at all. Pilar felt pinned by his gaze as he moved ever closer. She trembled inwardly with a violence that frightened her. Oh, to be touched by him in that special way once more! How many nights over the years had she tossed and turned, aching to feel his strong hands caressing her damp skin as if she were a high-strung thoroughbred in need of a gentle touch to soothe her fractiousness?

Pilar's mouth grew very dry as Culver closed the distance. Only belatedly did she realize he was wearing Levi's, rough-out boots and a short-sleeved, white cotton shirt that outlined his magnificent chest and shoulders. There was nothing weak about Culver. He was macho in a way few men would ever be, in Pilar's opinion. As always, his skin was darkly bronzed, a tough shield, seemingly capable of challenging any harshness the world had to offer. A lock of dark hair tumbled across his lined brow, which was covered by a light sheen of perspiration in the summer heat.

One of the many things Pilar had come to love about Culver was his loose, elastic gait. His athletic build was his heritage, he'd told her. He came from a line of warriors who'd repeatedly challenged the kings of England. So many nuances from past con-

versations jammed Pilar's spinning senses as Culver
came to a halt no more than six feet away. She felt
the hot, angry rake of his gaze, like a wildfire burning
from her black leather boots up across her thighs and
abdomen, over the gentle curves of her breasts. Then
his eyes locked with hers, and Pilar felt her lips part
as she stared back at him, seeing the good and the
bad, his weaknesses and strengths. Culver wasn't perfect by any means, and he had a nasty temper when
things didn't go his way. She strove to shield herself
from that anger now, fairly boiling in his dangerously
darkened eyes.

"You're early," Pilar heard herself say faintly.
Honey moved restively, as if sensing her confusion
and anxiety, and she turned and placed her gloved
hand on the mare's sweaty neck to soothe her.

Culver stared at Pilar, struggling to hold on to his
anger. When she'd removed her hard hat, her delicious hair had showered around her, blue black as a
raven's wing. The straight, shining strands framed her
small, oval face to perfection, while Pilar's dark eyebrows reminded him of the thin crescent of the waning moon, accenting her luminous eyes framed by
thick lashes. Her nose was fine and thin, and he knew
it came from her father's side of the family—the Castilian aristocracy. But her slightly parted mouth was
his undoing. Without a speck of lipstick, it was like
a ripe, exquisite fruit begging to be picked.

Culver gathered his raging feelings. "I wanted our
meeting to be private," he growled. How he ached to

step forward, reach out and caress her highly flushed cheek. Pilar's skin had a golden, dusky tone, heightened by the blush in her cheeks, which gave her an endearingly helpless look. But she was far from helpless, as he knew all too well. She was a government agent and a damn good one. If not for her quick thinking, tough mind and ability to focus, he wouldn't be standing here today. Pilar's face appeared soft and vulnerable on the surface, every expression there for the reading, but he knew she was hard beneath that exterior. Hard and cruel. Selfish. Self-serving.

The short-sleeved white blouse she wore outlined her curves to perfection. Culver wondered just how many lovers Pilar had had since he'd taken her virginity. Plenty, he told himself angrily. She was petite, slender and even more graceful in her movements than he remembered. Instead of being an equestrian, she should have been a ballet dancer, though her height might have been a detriment to that career.

Nervously, Pilar pulled off her leather gloves. "I was to meet you at seven," she protested weakly. Inwardly, she cringed. If she didn't do something, she feared she would burst into tears—or throw herself into his arms. And the expression on his face spoke not of forgiveness, but of bitterness and anger.

Culver deliberately placed his hands on his hips and slowly looked around. "Yeah, I know." Dammit, why did she have to look at him like that? He could see hurt reflected in her eyes—hurt and...desire? Yes, desire of all things. After what she'd done to him.

"You might as well know up front, Pilar, I didn't want to work with you."

Hiding the pain his words caused, she tucked the gloves beneath the brown belt that circled her waist. "I expected that. I asked Hector if he was sure you knew I was going to be the other agent." Pilar forced herself to look up at him. "I knew you wouldn't like it."

"No."

She gave a slight, pained shrug. "Well, what's important is Morgan."

"Is that why you volunteered for this? Did you have an affair with him, too?"

Stunned, Pilar stared at him. "What?"

"You heard me."

Pain gripped her heart. "I—uh, no, I had no affair with Morgan."

"Given the circumstances," Culver continued, "the thought crossed my mind. I know why I'm here. The man saved my life, and I owe him. But I wonder just what the hell you owe him to get you to agree to take a mission with me."

Anger erased Pilar's hurt. She glared at him. "You haven't changed at all, Culver. Not at all! You are the same pigheaded person I knew eight years ago!" She tugged gently on the reins, turning Honey to head her toward the barn.

"Hold on," Culver rasped, reaching out and grabbing Pilar's upper arm. Though careful not to hurt her, he put enough pressure in his grip to bring her to a halt. Her head snapped up, her eyes going black with fury.

"Don't touch me!" Pilar cried, jerking out of his grasp. *Dios,* why did he have to touch her? She backed away, breathing raggedly, and raised her fingers to the place his massive hand had covered. "Don't *ever* touch me again, do you hear me?" she rattled, her voice off-key. Tears stung her eyes, and Pilar forced them back. She saw contriteness come into Culver's eyes, but it never reached his rugged features or the set slash of his mouth. "Don't do that again," she whispered brokenly. "Not ever..."

Culver stood, breathing hard, his hands curled into fists at his sides. "Stop acting like I hurt you, Pilar. I didn't, and you know it."

Pilar tried to focus her spinning senses. Culver's contact had been completely unexpected—the only thing that could make her drop the shield she hid behind. He didn't realize how evocative his touch was, or that it made her want to surrender to him— all over again. Instead, he was taking her response just the opposite—as an indication that she couldn't stand his touch out of hatred or disgust.

Her heart swelled with anguish at that knowledge, and Pilar drew herself up to her full height. She allowed her hand to drop from the arm Culver had touched, but she was unable to keep her voice from trembling as she said, "We have to work together. I accept that. What I don't accept is you thinking you own me. You don't. And don't you dare touch me again. My reasons for helping Morgan are my own. Truth never needs a defense, Culver, and I don't have to spill my heart to you any longer.'' Pilar saw her words hit him like bullets ripping into his flesh. The pain showed in his eyes, no matter how impassive his face remained.

What they had shared long ago, she was discovering, was still just as vibrant as ever. A miraculous thing had occurred after they'd made love that first time on a luxurious carpet of grass near that pond. From that moment on, Culver had not been able to veil his true feelings from her.

Now Pilar read the pain in his eyes and regretted her words. The last person she wanted to hurt was Culver. She'd already hurt him more than anyone in her life, and she could barely live with that knowledge even to this day. Pain was something she'd known a great deal about, and she'd promised herself to avoid causing it to others, yet the very person she loved most in the world was the one she'd hurt the most. Pilar ached for Culver, wanting to take back her words but knowing she didn't dare. If she didn't erect some kind of barrier now, she would be lost.

''Fine,'' Culver growled. ''Let's get out of this sun and into the barn. We have a lot to discuss before I go to the hotel tonight.''

Nodding jerkily, Pilar brought her mare along with her. So much remained unsaid, yet she could say nothing. It was obvious Culver hated her for what she'd done. If he could not forgive her for that, he would never forgive her for the far worse transgression she'd made. She'd been so young then—and a product of the culture that raised her, despite her Harvard education. But how could Culver be expected to understand that—to know the full extent of the pressures brought to bear on her then?

Looking back now from her more-mature perspective, Pilar could see that the decision she'd made eight years ago might have been wrong—and in making that decision, she might innocently have committed a transgression far worse than the one that had originally caused her to flee from Culver's bedside on that awful night.

Chapter 3

Culver tried like hell to ignore the gentle sway of Pilar's hips as they made their way back to the barn's breezeway. He stood back and watched as she put the sweaty mare into cross ties and unsaddled her. Such anxiety showed in Pilar's dark, beautiful eyes. Still, he couldn't keep his gaze from dropping to her mouth—and couldn't prevent the heated memories of taking that soft, luscious mouth from rushing back to taunt him.

"Why didn't you wait and meet me at the hotel?" Pilar demanded breathlessly as they made their way to her office, a small house near the barn, after the horse had been put away. The sun was lower in the west now, the trees beginning to cast long shadows across the property. She pushed several errant strands of hair from her eyes.

Culver kept his gaze on her as she opened the door to the tiny white stucco house with its red tile roof. "I don't trust the Peruvian government. I flew in early, just in case."

Glancing up at him, unable to stop her inner trembling, Pilar moved quickly into the coolness of her sumptuous, yet homey office. Culver looked out of place in it—clumsily large compared to the delicate furniture the owners had installed for her. "Hector is someone you can trust," she said, hesitating at the kitchen entrance.

"I had my luggage sent on to the hotel," he said. "And I contacted Hector."

Her stomach wouldn't settle down. "I have things I must do."

Lowering himself to a Queen Anne couch, Culver shrugged. "Go ahead, then. I'll wait."

Pilar hesitated. His rugged features were unreadable as he surveyed his surroundings. She needed to *think,* but his presence made it nearly impossible. She got herself a glass of water from the apartment-size kitchen and took it into the bathroom with her. First, a cooling shower to wash away the grime of the day's riding. Then she'd be ready to head to her apartment in Lima.

Culver ordered his body to relax, with little success. He'd never dreamed he'd see Pilar again, and he knew he was still emotionally in shock. She hadn't

changed at all—except to become more beautiful,
more confident and more desirable, dammit. The college girl had grown into a stunning woman. Frowning, he thought of the anguish in Pilar's voice when
he'd pulled her to a stop. And it had been anguish—
real pain. My God, how much did she hate him, to
flinch from his touch like that?

Wiping his mouth, Culver looked around Pilar's
serenely elegant office. It was atypical for Peru, he
supposed. The furniture wasn't the dark, ponderous
Spanish style, and small plants lined the window,
where sheer, pale green drapes had been drawn back
to allow the north light to enter. The furniture was as
graceful and diminutive as Pilar, the couch and two
chairs leaving plenty of the floral, Victorian-design
carpet visible. The walls also had been painted a pale
green and were hung with prints of Amazonian orchids. He scowled.

On a bookshelf across the room, he saw several
framed photos. Pushing himself up, Culver moved toward them. A large gold frame held the photo of a
black-haired girl with light brown eyes, smiling for
the camera. She wore a pale pink dress with lace at
the collar, and a dark pink ribbon held her hair back.
Culver sensed something oddly familiar about the
child, who he guessed must be around seven or eight.
That smile. Culver's fingers burned as he replaced the
photograph on the shelf. It was Pilar's smile. A bitter
taste filled his mouth. Pilar's child. She had married,
obviously. Or had she?

A sickening feeling invaded Culver as he took in the next photo, where a tall, gray-haired man held the same child, Pilar next to them, smiling. Happy. Looking around, Culver wondered where this man was. If, indeed, Pilar was married to him. Divorces didn't go down well in South America. Women who tried to divorce their husbands could end up dead in the perverse macho traditions of the culture. Violence against South American women was a common, everyday occurrence. How had Pilar gotten away unscathed?

Then Culver laughed bitterly at himself. Pilar had gotten away from him, hadn't she? He'd been the one mortally wounded by their relationship, after all, not her. Setting the second photo back in place, Culver noted sounds coming from the hall then heard the shower running. A crazy urge to shed his clothes and join Pilar in that shower was nearly his undoing. Somehow, he had to get a tighter grip on his emotions. He would never have believed he still had this much feeling left for Pilar.

It had hurt so damn much when she'd cried out like that as he gripped her arm. She was the last person on the face of this earth he wanted to hurt—even now. Quirking his mouth as he wandered into the kitchen and got himself a drink of water, Culver decided he was crazy. Pilar had hurt him, not the reverse. He'd loved her, and she had wounded him—forever.

Returning to the living-room sofa with the glass of

water in hand, Culver tried to be patient. Jet lag was pulling at him, and he was exhausted by the events of the past forty-eight hours. Suddenly the couch seemed so inviting that he put the glass aside and stretched out. Closing his eyes, he told himself that he was going to rest for only a moment.

Pilar dressed hurriedly in a dark blue cotton shirt-dress—one of a few simple outfits she kept in the closet at her office. She belted it with white leather, then slipped into comfortable white sandals. Her briefcase was packed. Where they were going, she wouldn't be doing much paperwork. An hour had passed since Culver had blasted back into her lonely world, and her heart was still beating out of control, underscoring her surging emotions. Oh, why had he touched her? Memory of his roughened, caressing fingers moving across her body made her stop what she was doing and take a deep, unsteady breath.

Culver appeared older, more mature, naturally, but also harder. The look he'd given her, so cold and unfeeling, was one she'd never seen from him. Pilar knew she deserved it, and accepted it with a confirmation of her guilt. It would serve neither of them for him to know the full truth. *Ever.* Turning, she picked up her briefcase, shut off the light and walked down the hall toward the living room.

A sudden sound stopped her—and stirred a familiar chord deep within her. Snoring. It was Culver snoring! Her mouth curved tenderly for a moment. Whenever Culver slept on his back, he snored. How many times had he awakened her with his snoring? But with a nudge from her hand, he'd turn onto his side without waking and the snoring would stop. The memory was warm, filled with love. Pain flared on the heels of it. How many years had she slept alone? How many times had she awakened during the night and reached out for Culver's comforting presence, only to find him a figment of some dream?

Releasing a little sigh, Pilar told herself to get moving. She had much to do before they left Lima. As she stepped quietly into the living room, she saw Culver's long frame draped across the couch. He was asleep, his thick arms crossing his chest, one leg dangling over the end of the couch, the other sprawled out next to it. In sleep, he looked less harsh. Less threatening, Pilar realized. She knew she should wake him, but something begged her not to do it just yet.

As if an invisible cord tied her to him, Pilar moved even closer, to within a few feet of the couch. Culver slept deeply, his snoring ragged. No longer were his lips pressed into a dark slash of accusation. This mouth was the one she remembered, the one she'd kissed hundreds of times in their short, torrid months together in the jungle. For the first time Pilar remembered Culver's smile, and the feeling it inspired in her, as if the sun itself were smiling down at her.

As he slept, an errant lock of dark hair had curled slightly on Culver's now-smooth brow. No longer was he scowling. How wonderful he looked while sleeping! Pilar stood, feeling her heart tear open as she absorbed his less-threatening pose. The ache to reach out and nudge that strand of hair back into place was powerful. Swallowing hard, she moved to the end of the couch. She couldn't touch him. She mustn't. She could never kiss that wonderful mouth again.

"Culver?" His name came out so softly that Pilar thought it couldn't possibly awaken him.

Instantly, Culver sat up, his reflexes slow with grogginess. As soon as he saw Pilar, he froze. She stood hands clasped in front of her, in a tastefully conservative blue dress. Her hair was sleek, falling to a slight wave just below her shoulders—a magnificent cape to frame her oval, dusky features. Culver frowned and rubbed his face savagely.

"I must have dozed off," he growled thickly.

"The flight to Peru is long," Pilar whispered, a catch in her voice. Automatically, her fingers had risen to rest against the base of her throat as she stared down at him. The white cotton shirt was stretched to its limits across his broad back and shoulders as Culver sat, his hands draped across his knees. She tried to smile, but didn't succeed. "We need to get going."

"Yeah," he rumbled, pushing himself to a standing position. How lovely Pilar looked in the simple, yet businesslike dress. Well, wasn't she a businesswoman? Somehow, her wilder side and love of horses didn't jibe with what she wore now. Then he saw the edge of a dark leather thong, mostly hidden by the collar of her dress.

"You still wear that jaguar amulet?" The words were out before he could stop them. He saw the shock on Pilar's face.

"Why…yes, I do." Nervously, she fingered the leather thong. Had Culver forgotten nothing about her? Maria, her mother, had been a jaguar priestess to her people—a woman of great healing power and authority. The jaguar ruled the jungles, respected as much as it was feared by the Quechua people. When Pilar was born, she had been given the amulet, a small leather pouch that contained the hair of a jaguar her mother had faced in the jungle and mesmerized with her song of power. The jaguar had allowed her to take hair from its coat, proof that Maria had met a jaguar and, more importantly, lived to tell about it. The Indians respected anyone who assumed his or her power from an animal protector. Pilar had grown up knowing the jaguar was her spirit guardian, watching over her as long as she wore the medicine bag.

Culver managed a grimace. "I haven't forgotten much at all," he admitted thickly, as if in response to her unspoken question.

Pilar forced herself to move, to reorient back to the present. "Come on. My car is in the garage."

"Let's take my rental car."

Pilar agreed with a nod, deciding it wasn't worth arguing over.

Culver moved to her side and picked up her briefcase.

"You don't have to do that," she protested.

"I want to." He gave her a look that warned her he wasn't in the mood for arguments.

Opening the door, Pilar hurried through and locked it behind Culver. "I'll drive," he said firmly, walking toward the barn area, where he'd parked the large, dark green Buick in the shade. He and small cars didn't get along, Culver acknowledged as he put Pilar's bag in the trunk and managed to fold his bulk into the luxury car. It was still siesta time—five o'clock. The sun was hanging very low in the west, and the verdant slopes of the mountains were spectacular as they drove down the long dirt road that would eventually take them to the highway.

"Once we get to the hotel, we'll talk about our plans to rescue Morgan," he said, glancing at Pilar. She sat stiffly in the seat, her hands clasped tightly in her lap.

"Why not now? The hotel could be bugged."

He shrugged. "I thought you said you trusted Hector."

"I trust *him,* but the government has moles. He said that himself."

"It's a thought," Culver murmured, slowing down for a Stop sign. The four-lane highway into Lima wasn't busy at this time of day. Most people stopped work and rested for siesta, and Culver had always thought it a good idea. After all, who was worth anything brainwise after two or three o'clock on any given day, anyway? The South Americans had it right on this one. He pulled onto the highway and accelerated. Turning on the air-conditioning, he said, "This mission is dangerous. You know that."

"No one knows it better than I do. Ramirez has killed people at our village because we wouldn't bend to his demands."

"He's a sadist," Culver growled. He gave her a worried look. "I told Hector I didn't like his plan of sending you into Ramirez's fortress alone to locate Morgan."

"I don't like it, either, but it's not an option, is it? Who else can do it? They certainly won't let you in." She opened her hands to convey her helpless feeling.

His own hands tightened on the steering wheel. Culver was nearly oblivious to the natural beauty surrounding them. The blue Pacific shimmered off to their left, since Lima occupied prime beachfront property. But Culver's heart was centered on Pilar and her wonderful low, breathy voice. As she leaned forward slightly, the cascade of her hair hid her expression, and he longed to reach over, push those thick, silky strands behind her delicate ear.

"How someone as murdering and black as Ramirez has survived this long is beyond me," he said grimly. "The last time I locked horns with that bastard was when I was with you, eight years ago."

Pilar felt faint. Was Culver going to bring up their past? She prayed he would not. She wasn't sure she could stand it. "He continues to be the most powerful drug lord in Peru," she said in a halting voice. "His methods haven't changed. He still prefers rape and tortures.''

Culver felt anger. "I don't know if I can let you go into that compound...."

At his harsh tone, Pilar twisted to look in his direction. Culver's face was set, his mouth a hard line. "What do you mean?"

He shrugged, his voice taut. "No woman deserves that sort of treatment. Not even you."

The coldness of his voice shattered her. Pilar turned away, pretending to look out at the landscape flashing by. The implication in his tone was clear: she deserved something—something bad—for leaving his side when he'd been near death. Knotting her hands in her lap, she held back any response. Even if Culver knew the whole truth, he wouldn't understand.

"I saw a couple of pictures in your office," Culver muttered. He glanced at her profile, clean and somehow innocent. "Who are they?"

A lump formed in her throat, and Pilar felt herself go cold with fear. Moisture sprung to her palms. "They..." She struggled to breathe. "They are my daughter and my husband."

"I thought so."

The syllables were like shards of glass being ground into her flesh, hurting her as nothing else could. It hurt to breathe. It hurt to even be alive in that moment.

"When did you get married?" Culver hated himself for asking. It was none of his business, but he had to know.

"Uh...eight years ago." Pilar squeezed her eyes shut, the anguish too much to bear.

"What's his name?" he demanded harshly.

"Fernando."

"But you still use your last name, Martinez. Why?" He felt the pressure of anger and betrayal in his chest. Eight years ago, he had loved Pilar, while she'd had this man on the side, hidden from him. She had lied to him with her body, with the kisses and looks he could have sworn were for him alone.

Touching her brow, Pilar whispered, "Fernando died of a heart attack two years ago. I—I took my name back at that time."

"And the girl? She's yours?"

A knifelike pain stabbed her heart. "Yes, Rane is my daughter."

Compressing his lips, Culver stared straight ahead. He heard the tears choking Pilar's voice and wondered about them. Could she possibly feel any remorse over what she'd done to him? The picture congealed before him, and Culver realized he'd been some kind of lovesick fool to have fallen in love with Pilar. She had been two-timing him. He was sure Fernando hadn't known about him, either.

It was on his lips to ask her why she'd done it. How she could have. Culver would have bet his life then that Pilar was not only an innocent, but completely honest with him. *Face it,* he told himself, *you*

took one look and it was all over. He'd fallen as
surely as if someone had struck him with a sledgehammer. In truth, Culver knew little about Pilar.
They'd had the CIA mission to complete, and their
days had been spent on guard, with only occasional
nights of torrid embraces whenever they could feel
safe enough. They hadn't made love all that many
times due to the danger that had always surrounded
them. And Culver vividly remembered each of those
melting experiences. Any other woman's kisses paled
in comparison to the rich depth of those he'd shared
with Pilar. He'd shared his soul with her. She'd sold
his soul to the devil.

Tears flooded into Pilar's tightly shut eyes as she
kept her face carefully positioned so that Culver
wouldn't suspect the depth of her heartbreak. Even
now, despite what she'd done to Culver, he seemed
protective of her. He'd stepped in front of her and
taken a bullet meant for her eight years ago—and had
nearly died in the process. She'd left him in the hospital. Alone. Her lips parted, the lower one trembling
as tears wet her lashes before she forced them back
once more. How long she could hold their destroyed
dreams and shattered hopes at bay, Pilar did not
know.

Finally, their approach to Lima claimed Culver's
attention. Driving in the frantic traffic of Peru's capital always felt like dodging stampeding bulls. The
Hotel of the Andes was one of the finest in Lima, and
as they drove up to the elegant entranceway, a porter

in a light gray uniform met them, opening Pilar's door with a flourish. The young man smiled and welcomed her. Nodding, Pilar climbed quickly up the white marble steps, with many tourists, mostly North Americans, bustling around her.

Gripping her shoulder bag, she reminded herself to stay on guard. They were government agents and therefore potential targets. She gazed out at the thick traffic clogging one of Lima's main arteries, the avenue in front of the hotel. It was seven o'clock; siesta was over. Those who had rested through the afternoon's heat were back at work. Sometime between ten and midnight, everyone would eat dinner. Pilar wasn't hungry in the physical sense, but as she looked at Culver, she felt like a sponge, dried out by lack of emotional sustenance. Somehow, simply gazing at Culver's imposing, implacable figure fed her renewed life.

How long had she felt depressed? Pilar was stunned to realize she'd been living beneath a dark cloud ever since she'd left Culver. She'd thought she'd recouped, moved on. Certainly Rane had provided a bright patch in what she now could see as an otherwise dreary world. As Culver walked toward her, she could see him looking around, all his senses on alert, as hers were. He had the look of a condor, with his regal power and watchfulness.

Culver fluidly moved up the steps toward Pilar. Without thinking, he started to reach for her arm, to lead her into the hotel. At the instant panic in her eyes, he dropped his hand.

"Come on," he muttered, stepping through the door.

The lobby was spacious and sumptuous, with sparkling crystal chandeliers highlighting the thick gold carpeting and white marble surrounding the registration area, where three clerks, dressed impeccably in the gray uniforms, waited. Pilar stood quietly at Culver's side as he checked himself in under the assumed name printed on his passport: John Kensington. Pilar smiled to herself at the inappropriate plainness of the name for someone with such an imposing presence.

Once registered, Culver shook his head at the porter and lifted his suitcase in his left hand. He looked at Pilar. "Come on," he said.

Pilar walked at his shoulder to the elevator, feeling a different type of tension around Culver as the doors slid open and they stepped aboard. He pushed the button for the fifth floor and they began to ascend.

"I don't like this place," he growled, watching the numbers light up in sequence as the elevator rose.

"Hector thought it would be safe."

He sent her a derisive look. "You keep saying that."

She glared at him. "He's been like a father to me. He's always been there for me."

With a nod, Culver watched the doors open, then looked both ways down the hall before easing out of the elevator. "Stay behind me," he ordered.

Pilar was mystified by his sudden caution. She was about to protest when she heard the slight click of a door opening behind her. Turning, she saw a man with a submachine gun step into the hallway from one of the rooms.

"Look out!" she shrieked, shoving Culver to one side.

Culver jerked around, his eyes narrowing. Two men in business suits charged out of a room not more than a hundred feet from them. Pilar was in front of him, her body a shield for his. Damn her! Dropping his suitcase, he grabbed her shoulder and hauled her toward the exit door fifty feet away, fingers tightened on the soft fabric of her dress as he literally threw her ahead of him. What was wrong with her, putting herself in the line of fire?

Bullets pinged and snapped around them as Culver ducked and ran, pushing Pilar ahead of him. The machine guns had muzzle suppressors, muting the sound. Bullets stitched an angry path beside his feet, and Culver dug his toes into the thick carpet, hurtling forward, sending Pilar crashing against the wall. She cried out as she hit it, but Culver was already shoving the exit door open. Twisting, he jerked Pilar past him and into the stairwell.

"Run!" he roared between ragged breaths.

Still stunned from the impact, Pilar staggered backward, then caught herself. She saw the terror in Culver's eyes. Sagging against the cold, concrete wall, she dug in her purse and produced a small handgun.

"Give it to me!" Culver yelled, holding out his hand, his shoulder against the door. At any moment, the henchmen would be upon them. "Get out of here. Run down to the first-floor exit!"

Pilar tossed the gun to him, turned and started down the stairs on wobbling legs. Her breath was coming in sobs as she reached one landing then another. Though her hand was clenched on the cool metal railing, she nearly fell when she heard the rattle of gunfire above her. Where was Culver? Her mind spinning, Pilar realized she had to get to the rental car. It was still in front of the hotel, she was sure; but were the keys in it or had Culver pocketed them?

She heard sudden heavy footsteps descending behind her. Culver. Or was it? Panic pushed her rapidly down the final staircase to the exit door and freedom. Gasping, she spotted the Buick and ran toward it.

A car's brakes screeched as Pilar ran in front of the vehicle. The driver honked and cursed, but Pilar ignored him as she reached the rental car and jerked open the driver's-side door. Yes! The keys were still in the ignition! Getting in, she started the engine. Where was Culver? Was he hurt? Dying? *Oh,* Dios, *please, get us out of this alive....*

Pilar backed the car out just as Culver burst from the exit door. She honked, and he halted, turned and ran toward her, gun in hand. As he leapt into the passenger side, she jammed her foot on the accelerator, nearly ripping the door from his hand as he slammed it shut.

"Get down!" he roared, his hand suddenly on the back of her head, pushing her below seat level. Bullets popped through the window, showering them with glass.

Peering out, Pilar yanked the car into the traffic, weaving and accelerating at the same time. She was aware that Culver's hand had left her hair. He had twisted around, looking out the shattered rear window.

"Keep going. Keep going. I don't see them."

As much as she hated Lima because it was such a big city, Pilar had grown up here, and she knew every back alley and side street. She drove relentlessly, making sudden turns to avoid red lights. For nearly an hour, they wove their way through the city, until finally they were out in the country once more, the lights of Lima behind them.

Pilar had been trembling for half an hour. Wind whipped through the damaged rear window, chilling her taut nerves. She could feel Culver's tension as if it were her own. Her mouth dry, she managed to say shakily, "I think we've lost them, don't you?"

Culver glanced at Pilar in the dusk. "I think so," he said, noting how pale she looked with the wind whipping her hair wildly around her face. He could see small rivulets of blood near her temple where flying glass must have struck her. Her lips were parted, her eyes huge with terror. Without thinking, he reached over and stroked her cheek, wiping at the blood. "You're hurt...."

Pilar gasped as Culver's rough fingers touched her, sending electric tingles racing across her skin.

Jerking back his hand, Culver cursed richly. He hadn't meant to touch Pilar. She'd made it all too clear that she wouldn't welcome it, and now that same look was on her face, making him feel like hell.

"I—I'm okay. It's just a scratch. Are you okay?" Pilar whispered tremulously.

"I'm fine," he snarled. Relaxing for the first time, he said, "It looks like your friend Hector screwed us royally."

Gasping, Pilar darted a look at him before returning her eyes to the road. As darkness fell, the traffic around them became very light. "What are you saying?"

"That Hector gave us up to Ramirez's men."

"No!" Pilar cried. "No, that is impossible!"

"Do you have a better explanation of what went on?" He glared at her.

"Not right now. But we need to stop. I need to call Hector."

"Call him?" Culver couldn't keep the derision out of his voice. "You want to call him so he can run a trace on where we are and finish us off?"

"Listen to me, Culver, Hector is *not* our enemy!"

"Yeah, and at one time I thought you loved me, too."

Pain sheared through Pilar, so unexpected and shattering that she braked and pulled the car abruptly off the road onto the berm. Turning toward him, she rasped, "I can't help the past, Culver. I live in a hell because of it. But that was then, and this is now. We must call Hector. He's our only contact in the government. Without him, we're alone, and we're going to need coordinated help if we have a prayer of rescuing Morgan. You know that!"

Culver was breathing hard, the air seeming to sear his lungs as he held Pilar's raw gaze, taking in the anguish that burned in the depths of her eyes. Her voice was raspy, and as a flash of headlights momentarily illuminated her, he thought he saw tears glistening in her eyes. No, it was impossible. The seemingly innocent college girl who had played him for a fool would hardly be crying now.

"Look, the Peruvian government is riddled like buckshot with moles," he said in a low, guttural tone. "You know that and so do I. Hell, that's what damn near got me killed eight years ago, Pilar. Or have you conveniently forgotten that, too?"

Pilar felt as if he'd slapped her. "Stop it! Stop it! I have forgotten nothing, Culver. Do you hear me? *Nothing!*" She was sobbing for breath. Fists clenched, she rattled, "I know our government isn't trustworthy. But Hector is!"

"We should head out to your village in the jungle," he snapped. "Leave Lima, Hector and everything else behind."

"I can't do that."

"Why the hell not?"

"Because," Pilar rasped, "my daughter is at my

apartment in Lima. I *must* go back, Culver. I can't leave her there.''

Culver raised his eyes heavenward. ''For God's sake, why didn't you tell me that?''

''I was going to leave you at the hotel and go pick Rane up.'' Pilar swallowed hard, her voice sounding worried. ''Culver, what if they know where Rane is? They could take her hostage....''

''Then where the hell were you headed just now?''

Pilar felt as if she were being physically assaulted, his words raining on her like blows. ''I was going to take you to my village, to my grandparents' hut. You'll be safe there.''

His mouth compressed. ''And then what? You were going to drive back to Lima alone for your daughter?''

She smarted beneath his glare. ''Yes.''

Culver swore and sat back.

''I know you don't want to be here. I know you don't want to do this mission with me.'' Her voice cracked. ''I was just trying to make it easier on you—''

''Easier?'' He turned, gripped her shoulders and shook her. ''What the hell's easy about this? Nothing. Not a damn thing. But you aren't going back into that snake pit without me. You hear me? Next time, talk to me—let me know what's going on in that head of yours. I'm not a mind reader, Pilar, as you well know. I thought I knew you at one time, but I don't. I never did.'' He released her and his mouth flattened. ''I thought I knew you...but I've learned. So from now on, you tell me what you're thinking, dammit.''

Swiping at the small trickle of blood on her cheek, Pilar drew in a deep, unsteady breath. ''All right, I'll tell you what I think. I have to go back to Lima and pick up Rane. I think we should try to call Hector from a pay phone somewhere after we know she's safe. Then we'll take her to my grandparents in the village, where she'll be protected.'' Her skin seemed burned where Culver had gripped her, but she felt herself drawing an odd sort of strength from his action—and the need to protect her that still seemed to run deep in him.

''Don't tell Hector where we are or where we're going. Most of all, we have to keep your daughter out of this. Taking her to the village is a good idea.''

Shaking in earnest, Pilar raised her hands and struggled to steady her emotions. ''Rane is so young. What if they've taken her? I've tried so hard to protect her, to—''

''Okay,'' Culver said harshly, unbuckling his seat belt, ''move over. I'm going to drive. Don't worry, we'll get your daughter. She'll be fine.''

Pilar eased her hands from her face and looked at him. She had expected Culver's expression to be harsh and emotionless, but it was anything but. His narrowed eyes gleamed with an unexpected tenderness that she had thought she'd never see again. ''Y-yes,'' she whispered, opening the door. ''You drive.''

Chapter 4

Pilar tried to gather her strewn emotions as Culver drove steadily back toward the lights of Lima. It was ten o'clock—dinnertime for most of Lima's residents—and traffic had once again become light. Taking a handkerchief from her purse, Pilar wet it with her saliva and tried to wipe away the remnants of blood on her temple and cheek.

Nearly all of her attention was centered on Rane—getting her out of Lima and to some semblance of safety. Just having Culver in the car with her steadied her frayed nerves somewhat. She stole occasional glances at his rugged profile, which reminded her of the Andes—relentlessly harsh yet beautiful, suggesting a stoic loneliness. The tight line of his mouth revealed that he, too, was worried. They hadn't spoken since night had fallen, the darkness like a cocoon in which to hide their thoughts and feelings.

Culver broke the silence as they once again approached Lima. "Tell me the best way to get to your apartment."

"We should probably take an indirect route, using small side streets," Pilar suggested.

"I'm in agreement. We don't want to risk being seen by one of Ramirez's men again."

"You think it was his men who tried to kill us?"

"No question in my mind." Culver shot her a glance. Beneath the streetlights, Pilar's face appeared taut and colorless. She had wiped away the telltale blood at her temple, but her eyes were wide, and he could see terror and anxiety in them. Even now she was beautiful. They'd almost been killed. He could have lost her. His heart squeezed in pain at the idea. No, he didn't want to lose her. Despite all she'd done to him, she still managed to look innocent—and vulnerable—as if life hadn't hardened her as it had him.

Culver digested those discoveries about Pilar. Her hair was windblown, in mild disarray around her soft, oval face, and she seemed untouched by the unfolding events except for her concern for her daughter. On that point, Culver agreed with her. No child deserved to be caught in the cross fire between adults. Pilar's daughter was too young to protect herself, and her safety had to come first, before their own.

Pilar began giving him directions as they entered

Lima. "It's an apartment east of the city. My house-keeper, Alexandra Somoza, lives there with us," she explained as they wound their way through quiet back streets tightly lined with houses.

"Good, then Rane has someone to take care of her."

"Yes," Pilar whispered unsteadily, "she does."

"So you think your grandparents' village is the best place for her?"

"It's safer there."

"Why not leave her with Hector?"

Pilar heard the derision in Culver's voice and met his eyes momentarily. "Hector would put her in a safe house if I wanted, but Rane is sensitive, and I know she would be frightened. No, I want her with people who love her. She's used to going out to the village on weekends with me. My grandparents love her dearly. They will see to her safety."

"There's a possibility Ramirez or the mole inside the government knows exactly where your grandparents live."

"I know that." Pilar touched her aching temple. "It's a risk I have to take. I don't see a better option."

"We can't take her with us."

"No!" Pilar didn't mean to sound so alarmed, but she couldn't help herself. "Rane has been protected all her life. She knows nothing of what I once did for a living. I want my daughter to be able to sleep at night without nightmares."

"Did you have nightmares after you quit your job as an agent?"

Pilar avoided his sharp look. A lone car passed them as they moved down a curving side street. "I have them to this day, sometimes," she whispered.

"Part of the trade."

"Isn't it, though." Pilar gave Culver more directions, then murmured, "I don't know how you continue to be an agent."

His smile was cutting. "I was about to turn in my resignation to Jake when this thing began to unfold," he admitted. "I've had it. All I want is to get back to the land, where I belong."

"You talked of wanting to live with my people at one time," Pilar reminded him quietly. Culver had confided in her during their three months together that he'd fallen in love with her village and the jungle. She glanced at him shyly. "What would you rather be doing?"

Culver shrugged, never losing his awareness of passing automobiles. "I'm not sure. Some of my ancestors were Scottish seafarers who sailed the world, so I think it's in my genes to travel. But we always had an anchor, a homebase to come back to after wandering." His mouth flattened. "I guess that's what I'm missing most now—a home."

Pilar absorbed his words. This was the first time Culver hadn't treated her coldly. He was more like his old self, the person she remembered from so long

ago. "I...never knew much about your background—
before."

His laugh was sharp. "Yeah, we didn't spend too
much time doing background checks on each other,
did we?"

Heat rushed into Pilar's face at his words. They had
been thrown together on a makeshift CIA mission,
and the moment their eyes met, they'd both felt the
undeniable electricity. The ache to touch Culver, to
find out what it would be like to kiss him, had become
almost an obsession to Pilar that first month. Once
some of the danger eased, they had come together like
the sudden thunderstorms that gathered so quickly
and unexpectedly over the Peruvian jungle. Pilar had
never forgotten that first time—nor any of the times
they shared. Those memories were the stuff her
dreams were made of. Even now.

Culver saw how his comment had hurt Pilar. She
had turned her face away, pretending to look out the
window, but the shame in her expression was clear,
arousing an anger directed mostly at himself, but also
at her for her ability to affect him at the deepest levels. What they'd had, while it lasted, was the best
thing he'd ever experienced. He no longer knew what
Pilar would call their coming together, but for him, it
had been love. Pilar had brought her virginity, her
innocence to him, had walked trustingly into his arms,
her eyes guileless. And he'd taken her that humid
jungle night, surrounded by the aphrodisiac fragrance
of orchids clinging to the surrounding trees. To this

day, Culver could not separate memories of her from the heady, exotic scent of those rare flowers. Nor did he want to.

"Turn here," Pilar said in a choked voice. "We can park a block down on the right."

"I don't want to stop in front of the apartment," he warned. "They could be waiting for us."

"We're two blocks away."

Culver nodded, respecting Pilar's intelligence as an agent. Despite her overriding fear for her daughter, she was keeping a cool head. "I thought your skills might be a little rusty, but they don't seem to be," he murmured, braking and pulling into a parking space in the block she'd indicated.

"I am rusty, as you put it," Pilar admitted as he shut off the engine. Gathering up her purse, she unsnapped her seat belt. "I can use all the help you can give me."

Culver nodded and looked around the quiet, darkened neighborhood. "This is one of the wealthy sections of town, if my memory serves me," he said in a low tone.

"Yes, it is."

"I'm glad you did well for yourself, Pilar."

His words cut her to her soul. Compressing her lips, she opened the car door as she said, "Fernando was one of the finest, most gentlest men I have ever known. He cared for us. He protected us." She choked back the rest as she glared over at Culver, recognizing the jealousy in his darkened eyes.

"I cared for you, too. I protected you. But I guess that wasn't enough, was it?"

Pilar wanted to cry at the pain in his voice, but now was not. the time. "It's the past," she cried softly. "Let it go!" Leaving the car, she hurried down the sidewalk, her hand in her purse, touching her pistol. If only she could shield herself from Culver's angry sniping as easily. She knew she had it coming, and she felt helpless to protect herself.

As she climbed wrought-iron steps that she knew led to an alley that would take them to her apartment building, she felt Culver's presence. Glancing over her shoulder, she saw him approach soundlessly, his strides much longer than her own. His face was set and unreadable, but she could sense the anger throbbing around him. Well, he had every right to be angry.

"Take it easy," he growled, coming up to her side. "Slow down." His gaze moved ceaselessly, casing the street as they walked. Many areas weren't lit by the sparse streetlamps and he and Pilar stuck to the shadows. Large apartment buildings rose on either side of them, and small trees lined the boulevard, with a few concrete benches at bus stops. Culver longed to reach out and touch Pilar's arm—just in case. Matching his stride to her much-shorter one, he remained on her streetside.

Pilar tried to check her panicked pace. Culver was right. She would look out of place and could draw attention to them if Ramirez's men were watching.

Her shoulder brushed Culver's arm, and she jerked away, inhaling sharply. Touching him was like tapping into a secret compartment hidden in her heart, revealing a glowing coal from the past that refused to die, reminding Pilar of all she had forfeited.

"Is there a rear entrance to this place?" Culver asked in a low tone.

"Yes, this way." She turned onto a narrower sidewalk lined with tall bushes that offered perfect cover. She led him to a door the janitor used.

Culver stepped ahead of her. "Give me your gun."

She pulled it out of her purse and handed it to him. The small pistol looked like a toy in Culver's hand. He motioned for her to stand back, away from the door. So many of the ingrained habits of being an agent were flooding back to her. Never directly approach any door—approach from the side so you won't be hit if someone begins firing through it from the other side. Her heart took up a staccato beat as Culver pressed himself against the wall next to the door. With his left hand, he pushed it open, then stepped inside. She was amazed by his agility, despite his size.

"Come on," he said harshly, signaling for her to hurry inside.

Few lights illuminated the building's basement, but Pilar could see enough to lead Culver to the freight elevator. "This will take us up to the tenth floor, where my apartment is." She stepped in, Culver following closely.

He shoved the pistol into the waistband of his jeans and pressed the button. "Ten. Is that the top floor?"

"Yes." Pilar wrung her hands in worry. Was Rane safe? What would they find? She pressed her hand against her eyes.

"She's going to be okay."

Culver's thick, low voice was as comforting as a touch. Pilar dropped her hand and looked up at him. "How did you know?"

His smile was one-sided. "It may have been eight years, Pilar, but I haven't forgotten much about you."

In that moment, as the elevator slowly rose, Pilar realized how badly she'd needed to hear something kind from him. She let out a breath of air. "I'm so worried about Rane...."

"My gut tells me she's okay. Just relax." Suddenly Culver ached to reach out, slide his arm around Pilar's small, tense shoulders and pull her against him. He knew he could give her solace. Just as quickly, he wondered if he was crazy or if jet lag was affecting his senses. Much as he wanted to be angry as hell at Pilar, his heart had other notions.

As the elevator slid to a halt and the doors opened, Culver again went on guard. The hall, with walls of highly polished mahogany, was empty at this time of night. Everyone must be inside, eating. As he and Pilar moved soundlessly down the corridor, Culver could smell various meals being cooked, and his stomach growled. Despite the danger, he was hungry. But food would have to wait.

"The next door on the left," Pilar whispered, coming alongside Culver. Unable to help herself, she hurried ahead, her key in hand.

"Wait," he ordered, holding out his arm to stop her. He empathized with Pilar's anxiety but wasn't about to allow a lapse of security because of it. Ramirez's henchmen could be waiting just inside that door, submachine guns ready. He saw no sign of forced entry or anything else to indicate a struggle. Slipping the key into the door, Culver turned the brass doorknob quickly and stepped into the apartment.

Pilar was on his heels. Everything looked fine. She could hear her housekeeper, Alexandra, moving about in the kitchen. Her heart dropped with relief, and she looked over at Culver, who was tense and alert, the pistol raised.

"It's all right. I hear Alexandra. It's fine...." She shut the door, locked it and tried to pull herself together.

Her fifty-year-old housekeeper poked her head around the corner as Culver slipped the pistol back into Pilar's purse. "Ah, there you are! Rane and I were wondering what had kept you so long at the rancho." She halted and observed Culver. "And who is this?"

Pilar almost smiled at her housekeeper's sudden imperious attitude—like a guard dog spotting a stranger on her territory. "This is Señor Culver Lachlan. He's—"

"I've got a mare to breed to El Diablo," Culver

said, interrupting Pilar. Above all, he didn't want their cover blown—not even to the housekeeper. The woman had steel gray hair piled atop her head, and her thin face was pinched, but her dark brown eyes looked kind.

"Er…yes," Pilar said, hurrying across the simply furnished living room. "Where is Rane?" She had to see for herself that her daughter was really alive and well.

Pointing toward the kitchen, Alexandra said, "In there refusing to eat her vegetables, but eating the noodles as if she's famished."

Culver began to relax a little. He watched Pilar hurry across the room and disappear through the swinging kitchen door.

Alexandra smiled primly. "*Señor,* would you like a meal? You are *Norte Americano,* no?"

"I am," he said, easing away from the door. "And yes, I'd like to eat, but—Señora Martinez and I are in a hurry."

"Oh?" Alexandra raised her thin, almost-nonexistent eyebrows.

"Business," Culver said. "But I will take you up on a cup of good Peruvian coffee, if you have some."

"Black?"

Culver grinned a little. No one drank good coffee with cream or sugar down here, he knew. "Yes, black."

"*Bueno.*" Alexandra swept a rangy arm toward the

couch. "Please be seated, Señor Lachlan. I will serve you in here."

Culver nodded. As the housekeeper disappeared into the kitchen, he took a better look around the condo. Either Pilar was making very good money or, more likely, she had married into money via Fernando. A photo of the man graced the mantel of the alabaster fireplace, along with a photo of Rane. Culver forced himself to look at this important part of Pilar's life, then quickly turned away.

Fresh flowers of all varieties filled an antique pitcher on a Queen Anne table in the center of the living room. The furniture was all Victorian and very feminine, without a trace of a man's presence anywhere. Sheer ivory-colored drapes covered the windows, flanked by thicker curtains in a print featuring pink rosebuds and greenery. Culver noticed some toys strewn about near the couch and a red rubber ball against the wall. A doll, very old and obviously very loved, sat on the couch itself.

Everything about Pilar's apartment spoke to him of serenity. He wasn't surprised. Wasn't that one of the many gifts she'd given him? Pilar had always been a calming influence on him simply by her presence, he acknowledged as he slowly sank onto the couch. Absently, he picked up the doll. It had a brown Indian face and long, black yarn hair twisted into two braids. Its clothes were straight out of an Indian village—colorful, simple and utilitarian. Culver handled the doll with reverence, noting it had weathered many

years of active loving. The little girl had probably had
it for her entire seven years of life.

Culver heard the sound of a child's delighted
laughter. Then, for the first time since his return to
Peru, he heard Pilar laugh. His chest constricted and
his hands tightened around the doll momentarily.
How he missed that breathy, earthy laughter. He
could close his eyes and see her laughing, joy glistening in her eyes, her luscious mouth curved upward
to show even white teeth. When Pilar laughed, it was
without reserve—the laugh of a woman in touch with
Mother Earth.

As the recurring ache squeezed at his heart, Alexandra marched back in, a silver tray in hand, arranged
with coffee and several small sandwiches and cookies. "*Señor,* you must eat something before you go.
Señora Martinez insisted. She has taken Rane to her
bedroom to pack some clothes. She said she would
be out very shortly." The housekeeper set the tray
down and poured him the coffee with a flourish.
"Now, you must eat."

Culver smiled. "*Gracias, señora.*" Alexandra
flushed a little at the genuine enthusiasm in his voice,
then turned and headed back to the kitchen. Culver
wasted no time eating all four of the sandwiches, surprised at his appetite. The coffee was hot, rich and
fragrant, and it warmed his inner chill. The pleasant
refreshment reminded him of another thing he'd loved
about Pilar—her thoughtfulness toward others. She
was such a dichotomy. How could she be so kind, yet

leave him near death in a hospital and disappear from his life without so much as a word? With a shake of his head, Culver picked up one of the cookies.

He had just finished his second cup of coffee and the last of the cookies when he heard a child's giggling. Twisting around on the couch, he saw Pilar, now dressed in a white cotton blouse, jeans and flat, brown leather shoes, appear with her arm around her daughter. Worry marred Pilar's expression, although she was smiling—no doubt for the child's sake. Rane was a tall, slim little girl. Culver was surprised at how tall she was for her age. She had her mother's huge eyes, but in a much lighter shade of brown. Her hair was rich and black, pulled smoothly into braids that hung down her narrow chest. Rane's eyes danced with laughter, and Culver thought for an instant how much the daughter resembled her beautiful mother.

"Rane," Pilar said, resting her hand gently on her shoulder, "I want you to meet Señor Lachlan. Culver, this is my daughter, Rane." Nervously, Pilar searched Culver's face, watching a gentle smile break the hard line of his mouth as Rane, with her typically bold and friendly ways, walked up to him.

"You have my dolly," she said, pointing to it.

"So I do," Culver answered, smiling. He leaned over and handed Rane her doll. "I think you take her everywhere with you."

Rane tilted her head. "How could you know that?"

"She looks much loved."

Rane giggled, turned and ran back to her mother, throwing an arm around her and hiding her face.

Pilar smiled and placed her hands on her daughter's head and shoulder. "It's all right, sweetheart. Culver won't hurt you. He's a *Norte Americano.* Remember, I showed you on the map where he lives?"

Rane peeked at Culver. "He's a giant, Mama! He's so big!"

Culver smiled a little more broadly. "I guess I am."

Pilar colored fiercely and knelt down, smoothing her daughter's fine hair away from her brow. "Now, listen to me, Rane. We are going on a trip, the three of us. Señor Lachlan is going to take us home to see Grandmother Aurelia and Grandfather Alvaro. Won't that be fun? You'll get to see Grandma's chickens and pigs again."

Rane eased back and became suddenly serious. She wrinkled her nose. "Mama, can I ride the donkey? Last time you said I was too little." She stood back and pointed to her legs. "See how I've grown? My legs are longer now. Can't I ride the donkey?"

Culver watched the joy in Pilar's eyes as she conversed with her daughter, vivid proof of her love. The child was friendly, open and enthusiastic, but looked as if she was going to be much taller than her mother when she grew up.

"Perhaps," Pilar cautioned as she straightened. "I will leave it up to Grandma to decide whether or not you can ride that old, bossy donkey. You wouldn't want to fall off, would you?''

Rane pouted and walked over to the couch, not far from Culver. ''You always say I'm too small, Mama.''

''Wait,'' Pilar said with a sigh, ''and someday soon you will grow up big and tall.''

Rane turned her head toward Culver. ''Like Señor Lachlan?''

Wincing inwardly, Pilar whispered, ''Exactly like Señor Lachlan.''

''I'm ready if you are,'' Culver said, rising.

''I've got our bags packed.''

''Thanks for the food. I was hungry.''

Pilar felt herself melting in response to the genuine warmth glowing in his eyes. ''I grabbed a sandwich myself as we packed.'' She held out her hand. ''Come, Rane.''

Rane galloped like a frisky filly around the coffee table and grasped her fingers. ''Let's go, Mama! Hurry! I want to see Grandma and Grandpa!''

Culver asked in a lowered voice, ''Have you told the housekeeper anything?''

''Only that we'll be visiting another an Argentinian horse farm to look at a mare, and we'll be gone for two weeks.''

''She knows Rane will be at the village?''

Pilar grimaced. ''No, I told her she would be with us. When we use one.''

Culver nodded his approval. If Ramirez realized

Pilar was part of this mission, his goons could come
in here and scare information out of the old housekeeper, putting the girl in jeopardy. He saw the pleading look in Pilar's eyes to say nothing more in front
of her daughter. "Okay, let's get going. I'll bring the
luggage."

Pilar sighed softly. Rane was sound asleep in her
arms. They had taken Pilar's second car, an older
Volvo, and had made it two hours out of Lima, on
their way to Tarapoto, without further mishap. Overhead, the night sky sparkled with stars. This stretch
of road was devoid of other cars, and she relaxed
almost to the point of dropping off to sleep herself.
Culver had taken advantage of the thermos of coffee
she'd brought, drinking it steadily to stay awake.

"It won't be long," she promised him softly as she
rested her hand across Rane. Her daughter was so
lanky that her small, sock feet rested against Culver's
massive thigh, but he didn't seem to mind. In fact,
Rane had gravitated to him. Pilar wasn't surprised.
She had gravitated to Culver, too.

"Good," he rumbled, rolling his shoulders to release the tension accumulating in them. "I'm dead on
my feet."

"I know you are," she said, giving him a worried
look. The sudden intensity of his gaze at her words
caught her by surprise. Just as abruptly, he turned his
attention back to the road ahead. They were now

climbing into the hills, far from the Pacific. "I don't know how you do it. I never did...."

"What?" Culver saw such peace in Pilar's face now that her daughter was safely in her arms.

She sighed softly. "I was always amazed at your untiring spirit. You never seemed to give out or give up." Pilar laughed a little and looked at him with tenderness. "Remember? I was always the one who had to rest. You were always ready to push on."

"Yes, I remember." Culver felt his heart beat hard in his chest at her intimate look. Pilar had a way of making him feel he was the center of her universe when she talked with him. He felt that way now. Bitterly, he reminded himself it was a facade—just part of the pretty packaging of Pilar Martinez.

"I'm scared this time, Culver."

He wrenched himself out of his self-pity. "What?" He glanced at her once more, and saw that her face was drawn with worry.

"I'm scared as never before." Pilar gazed lovingly down at her sleeping daughter and gently caressed her hair. "I have an awful feeling about this mission. I have from the start. Ramirez is evil. He has no heart in his chest. He kills as naturally as we breathe."

Culver checked the urge to reach out and touch her sagging shoulder. "Maybe," he said huskily, "you have more to lose this time around."

"Rane is my life," Pilar admitted in a broken whisper, as she studied her daughter's sleeping face. "She's taught me so much about giving and taking

love. She has helped me heal in so many ways. I'm
sure she'll never realize all she's done for me, and it
doesn't matter.'' Her hand stilled on Rane's small
shoulder. She saw the expression on Culver's face.
His eyes had softened, as had the set of his mouth.
When he realized she was watching him, his features
hardened again. Pilar wanted so badly to tell him how
sorry she was, but it would do no good.

Instead, she said, ''Tell me about your home in
Scotland, Culver.''

''You didn't know much about me eight years ago.
Why is it important now?''

She felt the cutting edge in his low tone. He refused
to look at her, and she was glad for the cloak of darkness that hid her reaction to his biting words. ''You
talked of wanting a home,'' she persisted. ''Are you
going to return to Scotland?''

''My grandparents live there—I have relatives in
Scotland and England. But my folks live in Colorado.'' His mouth twisted. ''I guess the Rockies were
as close as they could get in the U.S. to the Scottish
moors and mountains. I like isolated places with lots
of trees, and I like people who work with the earth
and respect it.''

Tentatively, she asked, ''Do you have brothers or
sisters?''

His hands tightened on the steering wheel. A part
of him was wary of Pilar's attempt to weave more
intimacy into their relationship. She was so persona-
ble, but where did the right to know and the right to

privacy begin and end? With Pilar, the boundary was all too blurred. "I have four brothers and one sister, Mary."

"And does she live in Scotland?"

"No. In Durango, a small town in southern Colorado, near my folks."

"Is she married?"

"Yes. She's got two kids."

Pilar smiled a little. "Then you're an uncle."

He nodded. "They're good kids. Mary's divorced, but she has custody of them, and Bob, her ex-husband, sees them on weekends." He wanted to ask about Pilar's marriage to Fernando, but decided he'd rather not know. Why stab his heart with another ice pick? Was he a masochist or something?

Pilar stroked Rane's arm gently and watched her sleep. It was on the tip of her tongue to ask if Culver was married. Had he found someone, as he so richly deserved to do? Someone who could care for him the way he was capable of caring? Pushing a strand of hair out of her eyes, she released an unsteady breath. Just being this close to Culver made her ache with desire. Despite the harshness of the intervening years and circumstances, she wanted him now as she had the first time their eyes had met. Pilar didn't fool herself this time, however. She would never allow Culver to know she still wanted him. They lived in very different worlds. The two could never truly meet and bond. Her world wouldn't allow it.

"We'll be in Tarapoto in about forty minutes," she

said into the silence. Looking at her watch, she saw
it was three in the morning. Darkened jungle hugged
the two-lane highway now, silhouetted against a
starry sky.

"Good, because I'm ready to keel over from lack
of sleep."

"How long has it been?"

"A good thirty-six hours."

"Do you want me to drive?"

"No, you have Rane on your lap. Don't wake her."

"If I talk, does it help you stay awake?"

His mouth quirked. "Yes, talking helps." And God
help him, he had so many questions he wanted to ask
Pilar. "I remember one time you saying your father
had royal blood?" He glanced at her.

Pilar stirred. Talking might help keep him awake,
but she wasn't completely comfortable being the target of his attention. "My father was an aristocrat from
Spain—an ambassador to Peru."

"And he married your mother, Maria?"

"Yes...Mama was a Quechua medicine woman."
She opened her hand and studied it. "I was an only
child and very much loved."

"I imagine," Culver said, "you lived a life of luxury." A lifestyle he couldn't have given her at
twenty-five.

"Yes," she agreed. "I grew up at the consulate in
Lima, surrounded by servants. Later, my papa sent
me to America for college."

"And you went to Harvard," he confirmed, remembering.

Pilar nodded.

"Was it hard moving back and forth between North American society and this one?"

She sighed and nodded again. "You know how it is down here in South America. At Harvard, I didn't have to endure the kind of prejudice I experience here. People can be cruel. Manuela, Hector's assistant, for example, hates me."

"Why?"

She heard the dismay in his voice, and it gave her the courage to tell him the story. "Because I'm mestiza—what you might call a 'half-breed' in the U.S. You see, Manuela comes from a rich family of pure Castilian lineage. When she saw me leaving Hector's office one day shortly after I became an agent, she turned to a friend and said, 'Imagine mating a fine Paso Fino stallion to a donkey from the barrios of Lima. What you get is her.'"

"The bitch."

Pilar felt the grating anger in Culver's voice. "The words cut me deeply," she admitted, surprised by his response in her defense. "I guess I should have been used to such remarks by then, but I could never seem to harden myself in that way. I tried to hold my head up and keep my shoulders squared, as my mother counseled me. She was a housekeeper at the consulate when she met Papa. They fell in love, even though everyone said it was wrong."

Culver nodded. He was familiar with South American prejudice. A woman was considered the property of her husband. A daughter's entire fortune and life was tied to the man her father chose for her to marry. "Are your parents still around?"

Pilar felt sadness overwhelm her. "My wonderful Papa died when I was twenty-one. It was one of the worst days of my life. He died suddenly, of a heart attack. He was only sixty."

"And your mother? What did she do without the shield of your father between her and Lima's rich?"

Pilar smiled grimly. "She fled Lima and moved back to the village where she was born. Without Papa's powerful presence, Mama didn't want to stay where she wasn't welcome. Five years later, she died suddenly, without warning. Now," Pilar whispered, "all I have left are Grandmother Aurelia and Grandfather Alvaro."

"And you got out of your career as an agent when?"

Squeezing her eyes shut, Pilar managed to say in a strained tone, "I joined at twenty-two, as soon as I graduated from Harvard. I was part-time in only three years. I—I quit after our mission."

Culver heard what was not said. She had married Fernando, a man twice her age—probably chosen by her father for her when she was ten or twelve years old. Fernando was a man of obvious wealth and station. Well, Culver couldn't fault Pilar for that, could he? She was mestiza, considered an outcast by the well-to-do of Lima with their aristocratic Spanish blood. Her father had been rich, and she wouldn't marry below her station, even with her half-breed blood. No, old Fernando had been a far more appropriate suitor than Culver had been. Hell, he'd been a twenty-five-year-old CIA agent with five thousand dollars in savings, no aristocratic breeding and without the sort of future prospects Pilar had wanted.

Bitterly, he acknowledged a certain understanding of her decisions. Looking at Rane, her beautiful daughter, he figured Pilar must have had at least had six years of happiness before her husband died.

"If something does happen to you," he said, "will Fernando's family take care of Rane?"

Shaken out of her state, Pilar stared at him. "Fernando?"

"Yes."

She frowned and gave him a questioning look.

Culver motioned to the girl. "If you die, will your husband's family take care of Rane?"

"Oh…yes, they will."

His eyes narrowed. "You aren't sure?"

"Well," Pilar stammered, flustered by the question, "of—of course they will."

Culver was puzzled. Why should such a simple question make her so rattled? Pilar wasn't the kind of woman who was easily shaken. But she had a characteristic habit of pushing the hair from her eyes when she was nervous, and she was doing that now. Why?

It didn't make sense, but Culver was too damned tired to try to figure it out at the moment. All he wanted was a mat on the floor of a hut and a good night's sleep.

Chapter 5

Culver barely stirred. Somewhere in the distance, voices were speaking Quechua. Children were laughing and playing. A rooster very near let loose with a raucous crowing to where he lay. The smell of woodsmoke permeated his exhausted senses and he became aware of the hard earth beneath him, the blanket woven of llama wool folded under his head as a pillow.

Something warm and soft met his hand as he stretched his arms and yawned. Culver pried open his eyes, his groggy brain slowly recalling his mission. On the heels of that realization came the memory of arriving at Pilar's grandparents' village about four this morning. They had been shuffled off to a small thatched hut with little preamble, though Culver remembered meeting Aurelia, Pilar's grandmother, who had led them to the hut.

He recalled Pilar's surprise and panic at having to share the floor of the hut with him. What had she thought he was going to do? Make love to her? This time at least he'd been too bone tired to be wounded by her rejection of him. Instead, he merely stumbled into the hut, lay down in the far corner on a mat and drew up a blanket for a pillow. Almost instantly, he'd spiraled into badly needed sleep.

What was he touching? The gloom in the hut was nearly complete. A blanket hung across the entrance, with only a fine line of sunshine peeking around its edges. As his eyes adjusted, he realized with a start that it was Pilar who lay so close to him. She was still asleep, he saw as he eased up onto one elbow. The soft light stealing around the blanket washed lovingly across her form.

Pilar lay on her back, her hands clasped near her breasts, a blanket drawn up over her. How beautiful, how achingly desirable she looked. Culver couldn't help himself as he leaned over and threaded his fingers through the tangled black hair near her face. The hut's dim lighting accentuated her Incan ancestry, from her high cheekbones to her broad, unmarred brow. She was thirty-two years old, yet, he marveled, she had changed very little from the time he'd first known her. Maybe it was her ageless Incan blood.

Her hair spilled like a dark flow of moonlit water across a small pillow beneath her head. The strands felt like warm silk, just as he recalled. His fingertips tingled as he eased the strands back to get a better look at her face. Her skin was dusky and velvety soft. Did he dare touch her? How badly he wanted to. Culver wanted to do more than that. Her lush lips were parted, begging to be kissed.

It would be so easy to lean over and graze those lips. His lower body tightened with hungry need. With undeniable memory. Culver allowed his hand to rest lightly against the crown of Pilar's head. Belatedly he realized that Rane, who had slept in Pilar's arms last night, was gone. Having no idea of the time, he guessed that the girl had long since awakened and was probably out happily running around with the village children.

His gaze moved back to Pilar. How small and innocent she looked in sleep. Last night, they'd nearly died, yet as her breasts rose and fell slowly, she looked supremely untouched by life. Culver's fingers moved as if they had a life of their own, lightly stroking her silky hair. All he had to do was lean over and place his mouth against hers. The driving desire almost shattered his massive control.

Pilar murmured in her sleep and rolled onto her left side. The blanket slipped, revealing her shoulder. Her white blouse was wrinkled, but Culver didn't care. Pilar could wear the most expensive of gowns or nothing at all and she still looked just as beautiful in his eyes. Her hair tumbled gently downward, caressing the curves of her face and slender neck. Her hand

stretched outward, connecting softly with Culver's
chest, his skin tightening instantly where her fingers
rested. He marveled at her reaching out for him, even
in sleep. Then he scowled. Probably for Fernando, not
him. It hurt to be realistic about it, but Culver strove
to be ruthlessly honest with himself. It didn't pay to
be an idealist, as he knew from hard experience. Pilar
had taught him well.

Her breath was shallow and moist against his skin.
He'd shed his shirt last night in the heat of the hut.
Now her breath tickled strands of hair on his chest.
Her fingers lay slightly curled against him. *So innocent.* The words, the feeling, flowed through Culver.
In sleep, Pilar trusted him. Taking in a deep, ragged
breath, he recalled as if it were yesterday how Pilar
used to sleep in his arms—peaceful as a newborn
baby. She'd felt completely safe, protected by him.
Even with the danger that had swirled around them,
she had slept quietly in his arms.

They had had each other, he realized, sadness blan-
keting him as he studied her small, delicate hand. An
automatic trust had sprung up between them, and it
had translated into the abandon with which they had
made love. He released a long, painful breath as he
stared down at Pilar. What could he have done differently to keep her? How many times had he asked
himself that question? What had he done wrong to
chase her away?

It was true that he wasn't rich or aristocatic. As he
studied Pilar, he tried to be sensitive to the plight of

a South American woman. The husband was the autocratic ruler here. Marriages knew no equality. Women became so much chattels, allowed no life of their own, no hopes or dreams outside their kitchens and the raising of large broods of children. A husband was considered macho if his wife had many children, for that showed his sexual prowess. And the concept of machismo included making the wife bow to the husband's needs and demands.

Culver sighed. He'd lived in South America off and on for a decade now, and he'd often been disgusted by the way men treated women. Among the Quechua, women were respected as equals, so they didn't suffer as the rest of South American women did. It was a Spanish problem, not an Indian one. Intellectually he could understand that Pilar had been no less trapped by the male-dominated environment than any other South American woman. Her only hope was to marry someone rich and affluent and thereby escape some of the worst of the daily drudgery. Money would provide the services of a maid and housekeeper, and among the rich, families tended to be smaller.

Culver knew how intelligent Pilar was. He'd always respected her savvy—a combination of her American Liberal-arts education and her deeply rooted Incan heritage. Still, how could she be expected to come back to this village with her royal blood and marry a dirt-poor farmer? She lived precariously between two opposing worlds.

Leaning over, unable to help himself, Culver

lightly touched Pilar's arm, the skin firm, warm and velvety beneath his fingers. So she had married some old man for his money. Fernando had probably been promised Pilar, anyway, falling for her blazing beauty and youth. How could Culver blame her for finding her own way to avoid the cultural quagmire that threatened all women down here? His mouth tightened. Maybe that was why he had such a hard time staying angry with her.

"Mi querida," he whispered near her brow, as he had once called her so often. *My darling.* She had always been his darling—a beautiful, rebellious survivor of a woman.

Pilar stirred. She heard Culver's deep voice rustling like leaves nudged by a breeze. Her dreams were lush. Fulfilling. He was touching her, moving his roughened fingers slowly up and down her arm. His breath feathered across her brow and cheek as she heard the endearment, and her heart opened like a flower starved for sunlight as his mouth pressed lightly against her hairline. She loved her dreams, for in them, she could be with Culver again, laughing, playing and loving without the burden of the terrible price they had paid.

A slight moan came from within her as she felt herself being eased onto her back. Culver was with her, and that was all she needed. His hand was warm and supportive on her shoulder, and she felt him trace her collarbone. Something was wrong with the dream, though. She was wearing clothes. Usually in her dreams, she was naked and standing beside a deep, dark blue pool with rich green grass beneath her feet. Culver was naked, too, drawing her into his massive arms, smiling down at her with that predatory smile that made her blood sing with anticipation.

"Mi querida...."

Where did dreams end and reality begin? Pilar could feel his lips bestowing a series of small, moist kisses on her forehead. Each touch of his mouth sent a delicious tingling sensation from her head right through her to her very core. The dream felt so real. More so than ever before. Somewhere in the background, she heard a rooster crowing. Something wasn't right. Pilar dragged herself out of her deep, languid sleep. As she began to surface to awareness, she realized she could still feel Culver's hand on her shoulder, caressing her, and his lips continued to trail along her temple.

She slowly lifted her lashes. Though still caught up in the remnants of sleep, her vision blurry, she could smell Culver's naturally musky scent. No dream had ever been this real. A small, startled gasp escaped her, and she groggily looked upward—into the burning intensity of Culver's light blue eyes. He studied her in the intervening silence. Her breath caught. He was so close, so close.... Wildly aware of the gentle pressure on her shoulder, she felt as if she were drowning in the desire she read in his eyes. His expression was no longer hard or distant. No, this was the man she

had once known so intimately. His lips were parted,
his vulnerability clear.

Pilar's body throbbed as if in a fever state. The
ache within her grew with each wispy, ragged breath
she took as she stared wonderingly up at Culver. He
wanted her, with a raw, naked need. She wanted him
no less. Dizzied by his nearness, by the power of him
as a man, Pilar lay helplessly snared within this embrace, her skin still tingling where he'd kissed her
brow. Only inches separated them. Would he kiss her
lips? Pilar saw the intent in his eyes as his gaze
shifted to her mouth. She felt his grip on her arm
tighten further. How badly she wanted his kiss. If
kissing Culver would make her world right, Pilar
would have surged forward those few inches and
kissed him first.

Then, through the flimsy hut walls, Pilar heard
Rane laughing with the wonderfully joyous freedom
of a child. *No.* Her own tough reality came rushing
back like a shower of ice water. She couldn't kiss
Culver, though every cell in her body screamed out
for his mouth's caress. If she did, she would be lost.
Her carefully constructed world, which she'd worked
so hard to keep in place, would shatter like a crystal
glass beneath the blow of a hammer.

"Please..." she whispered unsteadily, "please
don't kiss me, Culver...." Instantly, she saw his eyes
narrow dangerously, anger replacing the desire. His
hand drew back from her shoulder, and inwardly, she
wept for the loss of that cherished sense of effortless

intimacy. His mouth tightened once more into a hard, uncompromising line. Regret tunneled through Pilar as Culver shifted away and sat up, his legs crossed.

How masculine he looked with his magnificent chest and shoulders exposed. He had the beauty of the deadly jaguar—lethal power mingled with an oddly heady promise of letting her feel that strength, become part of it. Pilar knew Culver's magical sway over her could kill her, too; as surely as jaguar. What little was left of her wounded heart couldn't stand the pain of sharing with him and losing him. She'd barely survived the first time; she didn't have the strength to survive him again.

Bitterly, she sat up, the colorful wool blanket spilling into her lap. She hurt for Culver, knowing her words had injured him. She reached her hand toward him.

"I—I'm sorry, Culver. I wish...I wish so many things were different...."

Culver sat, stunned by her rejection. They had been so close to kissing each other. So close to touching once more. He saw the regret on Pilar's still-drowsy features. Her hair was tousled wildly around her face, and he ached to pick up a brush and stroke those silky strands, taming them back into place. How many times had he dreamed of brushing Pilar's hair? Feeling those strands slide between his fingers, so full of life and shining like a raven's wing? Too many, he angrily reminded himself. Why the hell had he tried to kiss her when she'd made it all too clear that she no longer wanted him?

"It won't happen again," he said harshly, forcing himself to his feet. The hut was gloomy and he looked around for his shirt, finding it crumpled up in the corner on one of the woven mats that covered most of the hut's dirt floor. He saw that blankets covered the windows as well as the door, accounting for the murky lighting. He leaned down, jerked up his shirt and threw it across his shoulder.

Pilar got to her knees, trying to fight off the sleepy confusion that still held her. "Culver, it's not what you..."

He glared at her as he stalked to the entrance and jerked open the blanket. "I said it won't happen again. Let it go, Pilar."

Even after he'd stridden angrily away, Pilar remained kneeling, devastated. Rubbing her hands against her arms, she bowed her head and fought back the sobs that threatened to well up from deep within her. It hadn't been a dream. But how had she ended up on his side of the hut? The dwelling was very small, the type an elderly person lived in alone, but last night, they'd been dizzy with exhaustion. Her grandmother had brought them to the nearest empty hut. Pilar was grateful for her grandparents' care. She remembered Aurelia placing a blanket over the still-sleeping Rane after Culver had gently placed the girl on one of the mats.

Pilar had lain on her side, facing her daughter's

back. She vaguely remembered Culver lying down on the opposite side of the hut, but that was all. She looked slowly around the place now. How had she managed to get over here, to his sleeping mat? Stymied and a little frightened of the evident strength of her own subconscious, she realized Culver had remained where he'd slept. At some point, she knew, Rane had awakened and left the hut, but Rane had had the benefit of a much better night's sleep than they, since she'd slept in the car all the way from Lima. Looking down at her watch, Pilar saw it was nearly ten in the morning already. Her heart ached with longing for Culver. She had to apologize to him. At least if he had been the one to come to her side of the hut... But no. It wasn't his fault. It was hers—again.

She heard the sound of Rane's laughter, once more, this time mingled with the deep rumbles of Grandfather Alvaro's somewhere nearby. Rousing herself, Pilar knew she had much to do today. First, she would go for a swim in the small, beautiful pond ringed by rushes where the villagers sometimes bathed. Being in her mother's village always made her feel safe. Pilar knew she wasn't—not with Ramirez's fortress a mere twenty-five miles away—but the serenity of her people still created that sense of security, deserved or not.

Easing to her bare feet, she stretched fitfully. She picked up all blankets they'd used, folded them carefully and stacked them in a corner. She savored the familiar scent of woodsmoke as she left the hut. Blinking in the strong sunlight cascading down through the trees, she looked around and spotted Grandmother Aurelia leaning over a tripod cooking pot, stirring the contents. Dogs and children were playing here and there throughout the tiny village of barely a hundred people. The elderly remained close to their huts, the women working on llama-wool weavings and the old men sitting and talking nearby.

The air was fresh and clean here, the humidity high. Touching her usually straight hair, Pilar smiled, knowing it would soon become wavier in the damp air from the nearby jungle. The village was situated just above the jungle, on the slope of a mountain. Below them a thick, dark green canopy stretched to the horizon. Down there, Pilar thought with a shiver, lay Ramirez's fortress. Down there, too, somewhere beneath the shining foliage, Morgan Trayhern waited for his rescuers.

Abruptly, Pilar blocked the automatic images of Morgan being tortured. Thinking about it wouldn't help Morgan, it would only weaken her with fear. She saw Aurelia straighten and look over at her. Her grandmother's dark brown face was lined with age, but the kindness of her smile and the love shining from her eyes soothed Pilar's battered heart. She lifted her hand in greeting, then hurried toward the edge of the village to prepare herself for the day.

Culver sliced through the pond's icy water, each stroke like an explosion, releasing a little more of his anger and hurt. He swam naked, rinsing away the grime of the past forty-eight hours. His feet touched the pebbled bottom and he stood. Closer to shore, sand lined the floor of this oval-shaped pond, fed by icy streams from the craggy Andean mountains that towered over the village. Culver's skin roughened with goose bumps as he walked to the edge of the pond. Though it was midmorning and summer, the air was still cool at this elevation. Scooping up a handful of sand, he scrubbed his body with it. Nothing cleaned like sand, and as he washed, unbidden thoughts sprang to mind of that other pool—one he and Pilar had discovered somewhere deep in the jungle northeast of Lima. They had scrubbed each other's backs with sand much like this.

Muttering a curse, Culver wondered why he couldn't staunch the relentless cascade of memories about Pilar and himself. Leaning down, he sluiced off the sand, his skin feeling vibrant, warm and tight from the scrubbing. To get at his feet and legs with the refreshing sand, Culver took a seat on the grassy bank, noting the herd of llamas, in all colors and sizes, feeding below on one of the verdant hillsides. The village was perfectly situated between the mighty Andes, their snow-covered, granite peaks thrusting to the heavens above, and the humid jungle, close enough for the villagers to gather its rich array of fruit and nuts.

Yes, this village was a virtual Shangri-La, in Culver's opinion. The only fly in the ointment, he thought as he sat on the bank, scrubbing his feet, was Ramirez's fortress in the lush jungle below. He looked up into the deep blue sky, accented with long strands of thin, white gossamer clouds. More than once he'd entertained the thought of living here—but that had been eight years ago, with Pilar the woman he would have shared this tranquil farm life with. He knew some of his friends might think him crazy, but others, like Jake Randolph and Wolf Harding, understood his need to sink his roots deep into the earth and revel in a simpler, more natural existence. The sun warmed his damp back, and he smiled. It was a perfect day. Well, almost.

Sighing, he rinsed off his legs and got out of the water. Shaking his arms and hands, he allowed the slight, playful breeze and the sunlight to dry him. He knew he'd miss this coolness once they entered the jungle. Frowning, he retrieved his jeans, sat on a fallen log and pulled them on. His hair dripped with water and he pushed the damp strands back off his brow.

A sound caught his attention, and he snapped his head toward the well-worn path the villagers took to the pond. His heart thudded. Pilar stood uncertainly, a towel in her hand. The expression on her face told him she was as surprised as he was. Scowling, he said, "Come on, I won't bite."

He reached for his shirt and shrugged it over his shoulders as he watched her walk hesitantly toward him. The path ended at the pond, near the log where he had left his socks and boots. Pilar looked so soft and innocent as she picked her way delicately along the trail. Culver wanted to look away, to ignore her. Impossible. She was barefoot! He allowed the corners of his mouth to lift momentarily. Here, she was free to be her natural self. The villagers never wore shoes unless they had to, and he knew Pilar disliked them. It was her Incan blood longing to be free of such civilized confinement.

As she drew near, he saw the wariness in her eyes. Could he blame her? No. Feeling foolish, Culver hurriedly tugged on his boots and tied the leather laces into double knots.

"The water's cold but fine," he said gruffly, looking up as she halted in front of him.

Pilar nodded. "Culver, I owe you an apology—"

"You owe me nothing," he snarled, getting to his feet. He shoved the tails of his cotton shirt into his Levi's, with angry movements.

"I do. Please," she begged softly, holding out her hand, "hear me out."

He glared at her. "Why should I?"

Pilar held his glare. "Have we moved so far apart that we can no longer talk? I remember—"

"That's the past," he snapped. Putting his hands on his hips, he said in a low, vibrating voice, "It's the past, and that's where you want to keep it, isn't it, Pilar? God help me, but I don't have the control I wish to hell I did when it comes to you. This morning

was a mistake.'' *A terrible mistake.* His mouth flattened as he saw his words landing like fists, their
impact clear on her vulnerable features. Angry at his
lack of control, he snarled, ''Let's just make the best
of this, okay? I don't like it any more than you do,
Pilar. I'm human, too, dammit, in case you don't remember.''

Pilar stepped forward, touching his arm. As her fingers curved around Culver's powerful bicep, she felt
a vibration go through him and saw the shock register
in his eyes at her unexpected gesture. For a moment,
the hardness and anger in them dissolved. ''Please,''
she begged in a raw voice, ''I know I'm hurting you
by being around you. I don't mean to, Culver. *Dios,*
if there was anything I could do to stop the pain I
give you, I would....''

Helplessly, she held his narrowed gaze. He stood
like a magnificent bronze statue of a hero, proud,
wounded, yet holding his head high, tolerating her
hand on him. It took everything Pilar had to keep
tears from streaming down her face, but she couldn't
keep the sound of them out of her voice as she spoke.

''It was my fault back at the hut. I—somehow, I
rolled over after Rane got up. I should have stayed
on my own side, Culver. Please, forgive me. I don't
blame you for what happened this morning. It was
my fault. Do you hear me?'' Trying to steel herself
against the suffering that had come into his eyes, Pilar
forced herself to release his arm. When she did, it
was almost as if Culver suddenly sagged before her.

The rigidity went out of him, like a punctured balloon deflating.

"I don't blame you," he said hoarsely after a moment of tense silence. "I shouldn't have touched you, even if you touched me."

Pilar's eyes widened. "I touched you? In my sleep?"

Culver grimaced and looked above Pilar's head, studying the Andes's snowy peaks. "I made the mistake of touching your hair, that was all. You turned toward me and your hand fell against my chest."

Pilar dragged in a breath. "I see...."

He gave her a sad smile, the anger bleeding out of him. "I'm sure you do. You always did, Pilar. Maybe it's that jaguar blood of yours trying to entrap me— mesmerize me like before. I don't know."

Pilar's hand went to the small medicine bag that hung around her neck. "Do you think I did it on purpose?"

"No, of course not. You were asleep." Culver raked his fingers through his drying hair. "I don't blame you, Pilar. You're looking at me like some lost lamb. Stop it! I can't roll back the past, and neither can you." Frustration tinged his voice as he gazed at her. "The past is the past. It's over and done. Destroyed."

"Yes," she whispered faintly, closing her eyes, unable to stand the terrible grief shining in Culver's eyes.

"Hell," he muttered, "take your bath and meet me

back in the village. We've got a lot of planning to do before we head into that jungle.'' Turning on his booted heel, he strode down the path.

Breathing raggedly, Pilar opened her eyes and watched Culver stalk off. Even wounded as he was by her decision, he treated her with respect. A South American man would not have tolerated her behavior as he had, though a Quechua man would. Culver was a good man. An honest one. A man with a large and forgiving heart. Much like Fernando. Pushing her hair back from her face, she sat down on the log to undress.

The day was exquisite, but Pilar felt raw. Her heart was weeping. She could feel it pounding in her chest as she removed her blouse with trembling hands. As she closed her eyes to her feelings, she saw Culver's face—proud, fierce and defiant, yet with a tenderness burning in his eyes that made her want to weep for what they had lost. And it had all been her fault. Hers alone.

Chapter 6

Culver was busy setting their army-issue, two-way radios onto a special frequency when Pilar came back to the village. It had been brought in by a CIA helicopter from Lima—one that Hector did not know about. Rane, curious seven-year-old that she was, sat companionably near him in the dirt, watching him solemnly. She was a living, breathing miniature of Pilar, as far as Culver was concerned.

In front of him, on a clean blanket, was spread the array of state-of-the-art equipment they would take into the jungle with them. Don Alvaro, Pilar's grandfather and village shaman, well into his nineties, sat opposite them on a wooden chair, rocking slowly back and forth, his dark brown eyes flicking from

Culver to the equipment and back to his great-granddaughter.

"You need these machines?" Don Alvaro finally asked in broken English.

Culver looked up. "Yes." The tall, thin old man was weather-beaten, his tobacco-brown skin, stretched tight across high cheekbones, and deep lines at the corners of his eyes attesting to his time working the corn and potato crops on the terraced hillsides. Yet he emanated the aura of power befitting his role as leader of the village.

"You challenge Don Ramirez, eh?"

Culver's hands stilled over the radio he was holding. How much had Pilar told her grandparents? Very little, he hoped. He wondered if she'd told him they were going to try to rescue Morgan. She must have. He chose his words carefully as he continued to assemble the radio.

"We're here on a secret mission, so I can't say much."

"Ahh," Don Alvaro murmured. His face stretched into a shining smile as he caught sight of Pilar walking toward him. "She walks like the jaguar she was born to become, does she not?"

Culver scowled, barely glancing in Pilar's direction. She was drying her hair with a thin white towel, the long black strands shining in sunlight dappled by the trees among which the village had been erected, to provide a modicum of summer shade, as well as protection against the winter's rainy weather.

"Yes, she's a jaguar all right," he muttered.

"You know," Don Alvaro continued pleasantly, gesturing toward Pilar, "that my wife, Aurelia, performed a special ceremony for Pilar's parents in order to bring her spirit into being." He beamed. "Once in every generation, if you are from a jaguar medicine clan, a special spirit child is brought forth to carry into the future all our knowledge, experience and ceremonies." His smile grew tender. "Pilar is our great hope."

"She doesn't live with you. How can she help your people?" Culver thought of her job at the horse farm and wondered how often she came back to the village, and if she was aware of her responsibility.

Chuckling, Don Alvaro slapped his knee. "You have lived among us many years, my friend. Surely you know that we are shamans?"

Culver placed the radio headset before him on the blanket, and Rane handed him the plastic bag containing the second unit. She smiled brightly up at him, and he couldn't help but smile a little in return. The child was innocent, and she came from Pilar's body— a body he had once loved.

"I know among the Indians you have medicine people," he answered slowly, again glancing to check Pilar's continued approach. She had draped the towel around her shoulders, the white creating a dramatic contrast with her dusky, golden skin and black hair. Culver knew she wasn't even aware of her ethereal beauty, which must have any number of men falling at her feet in adoring admiration. And her lack of vanity only added to the depth of his unwanted feelings for her.

"We are not ordinary people," Don Alvaro corrected, rocking in the chair. "Shamans are different. We travel to the other worlds. We fly to the past, work with the present and can see into the future. Medicine people heal with herbs, ceremony and songs. We do a great deal more." He lifted his hand. "Pilar possesses such skills. She can fly because she is a priestess to the jaguar."

"Really?" Culver looked up at the old man, not certain how to take his confidently spoken statement.

"Mmm, but my granddaughter is afraid to embrace her power. Aurelia tells me to be patient with her—that in time she will become one with her gifts."

"And when she does, what will happen?" Culver attached the mike to the headset.

"She will be able to move at will into the other worlds and help others. She will become a healer, which is her true calling in this lifetime."

"Not a horse manager?"

Chuckling indulgently, Don Alvaro said, "My son, her destiny was decided long ago." He gestured to the sky. "The moon and stars were right. The energy came, and life was breathed into my daughter's womb. Pilar was sent to us with a purpose. She rides horses and works at a rancho, but it is temporary." He frowned. "I am afraid there is great danger ahead of her, though. She is coming to a fork in her life path. If she chooses wrongly, she will leave us forever.''

The calmly spoken words got Culver's instant attention. He stopped assembling the second radio, and narrowed his eyes speculatively on the old man. Don Alvaro had sunk back into the creaking old rocker, a sad look on his face as he studied Pilar. Culver believed that shamans possessed magical, inexplicable qualities. As a CIA agent stationed in Lima, he'd met such a shaman once, who had taken him to a jungle clearing and given him a drink called *ayahuasca*—the vision vine. He remembered heaving his guts out, time after time, while the shaman whistled and sang for hours on end. Finally, Culver had lain on the damp jungle floor, caught up in a series of vivid images....

Culver sat apprehensively with a group of six other CIA agents in an oddly open area in the middle of the jungle. Don Gonzalez, the shaman who had promised to induce a vision of the future, had given him a blanket to sit or lie on. The moon was full, and it was near midnight, the jungle producing a virtual symphony of sounds around them. Because he'd experienced many things and had traveled the world in his twenty-four years, Culver treated this ceremony with deference, willing to approach it with an open mind. Don Gonzalez squatted in the middle of the circle of men mixing the "vision vine" herb in a bowl, whistling and singing.

The other agents, all Peruvians, sat solemnly, their

legs crossed, their attention on the old shaman. Don Gonzalez's white hair shone like a startling halo around his head, the luminescence of the moon powerful in this meadow in the midst of the moist, fragrant jungle.

To Culver's surprise, the old shaman brought the ayahuasca first to him. His bony hands thrust the nondescript wooden cup toward Culver.

"Drink, my son," he urged.

Taking the cup, Culver stared down into the dark brown liquid.

"All of it," the shaman commanded with a flourish of his hand.

Without hesitation, but with some misgivings, Culver pressed the rim of the cup to his lips and drank. Surprisingly, the liquid was sweetish tasting and thick. As he finished gulping it, he saw the shaman's black eyes sparkle.

"Tonight you will meet your destiny," was all Don Gonzalez said as he moved away to refill the cup for the next recipient.

At first Culver became violently ill, his spasming stomach muscles contorting his body. As again and again he was sick with great shuddering heaves, he worried that he'd been poisoned. But gradually his body calmed, and he began to have the urge to lie down. He'd heard many things about ayahuasca, *and the Peruvian agents swore by it. Culver noted the reverence with which the other agents, his friends,*

*treated the experience. He knew shamans' powers
were held sacred here.*

*The shaman began to whistle and sing again shortly
after everyone had drunk from the cup, three of the
other men getting sick as Culver had. The singing
seemed hypnotic, and Culver finally gave in to the
urge and lay down on his back, staring up at the sky.
A warmth began to permeate him, starting in his toes
and working slowly upward. In his mind, he knew it
was impossible—at midnight, the jungle would be
growing cooler, the inevitable, shroudlike fog appearing between the layers of tree canopy that covered its vast reaches. Still, the sensation of warmth
was pleasant and lulling. The Shaman's singing was
rhythmic, and soon Culver felt himself drifting into a
state of deep relaxation.*

*Whatever it was, this altered state felt good.
Warmth crested like small ocean waves toward the
top of his head. As soon as it entered his skull, he felt
a terrific whirling sensation, as if he were being
sucked into a powerful whirlpool. The shaman's singing changed, growing higher pitched, and Culver felt
his body changing with it, lengthening here, shortening there. Beneath his closed eyelids, lights began
to flicker like blinking dots of sparkling color. At first
they had no form, but soon they began to coalesce.*

*The lights throbbed, gathering intensity and pur-
pose, and Culver felt a power radiating from the
golden glow as it slowly took shape. He watched,
mesmerized, as a female jaguar formed from the light*

*and walked out of the radiance down a jungle path.
Culver felt her incredible power and purposefulness
as she trod silently on the huge pads of her feet. Her
coat glowed like the sun, the thick, black crescent
markings speaking of her silent, deadly power.*

*He found himself standing on the same jungle trail,
directly in the path of the jaguar. Culver knew he
should feel fear, for he'd seen a jaguar kill a man
once. This cat was thickly muscled, low to the ground
and unquestionably deadly. But as he awaited her approach, an incredible calm filled him. When she saw
him, she halted about six feet away. Lifting her magnificent head, she studied him in the building silence.*

*Culver felt hypnotized by the jaguar's intense gaze.
Suddenly, her nearly black eyes turned gold, the black
becoming a mere pinhole in the center. As soon as
that happened, he felt himself being pulled forward,
hurtling toward her at a terrific rate of speed. He
started to scream, but it was too late. Everything went
black. At first he felt cramped, almost suffocated, but
as he adjusted to the darkness, he felt the powerful
beat of a heart against him, then the thick bone of
curving ribs. In that moment, he realized he was inside the jaguar. Somehow, he'd become her! He was
the jaguar. The power he felt was unlike any other
he'd ever experienced. This feeling was wild, prime-
val—untrammeled animal power of the highest degree—and he felt the jaguar's confidence as she began walking again with her languidly graceful gait.*

Somewhere in his distant mind, Culver remembered

what the natives had often told him about the jaguar: how she would hypnotize her chosen prey simply by looking at it with her mesmerizing eyes, pulling its spirit out of its body, rendering it incapable of movement. And that was how he'd felt when she'd looked at him with those stunning eyes—paralysed.

Darkness fell over him again, and Culver felt himself being propelled out of the jaguar. In the next moment, he was back in his own body, staring at her on the jungle path. The jaguar switched her tail, blinked slowly at him and turned away, dissolving into the glistening clouds she'd originally come out of. He stood watching the golden clouds as they began roiling, shifting in new and different ways.

The face of a young, beautiful woman appeared. She was laughing and dancing naked by a dark green pool surrounded by grasses, and wild, colorful orchids hung from nearby trees. She was the jaguar, Culver somehow knew, but in human form. Her hair was long, almost to her waist, and shone like sparkling moonlight on water. Her graceful arm movements reminded him of the hula dancers of Hawaii. Her body was slim, untouched and virginal, and each sway of her hips stoked a fiery heat building in his loins. He no longer cared if she really was the jaguar. He moved toward her, wanting to mate with her, wanting to expend this deep, animal feeling that possessed him, that he had become.

When she turned and saw him, she laughed, the low, throaty purr of a jaguar greeting her returning mate. Her eyes were ebony, shining as brightly as a thousand full moons. Her lips curved in welcome, and she opened her arms to him as he approached. Walking into them, wrapping his around her, feeling the moist, sensuous heat of her body collapsing joyfully against his made him growl—like a jaguar. He guided her down onto the thick, luxuriant grass and found himself naked beside her. Wherever she touched him, purring, her fingertips roaming searchingly across him, tiny, volcanolike fires seemed to erupt. He'd never ached for a woman this way before. He was tied in knots of fire, wanting to bend double with the pain of his need.

Her eyes danced with joy and she began to kiss him from his chest downward. He lay on the carpet of grass, its cool dampness a stark contrast to the branding heat of her lips as they reverently caressed his skin. He wanted her on a primal level, and yet, as she stroked him, rubbing sinuously against his body, he felt that something sacred was taking place between them. Culver had never experienced the hunger of desire combined with the sort of spiritual fire that seemed to surround them. Sex was sex. Or was it?

As the jaguar woman moved on top of him, allowing him to enter her, he felt a terrific shift within him on so many levels that he had no words for it. He could merely feel, with a purity that was much more than sex. Whatever power this mystical woman possessed was something so sacred that he'd never, in all his life and travels, encountered it before. He felt

*tears leaking from beneath his closed eyes as he rev-
eled in the juxtaposition of animalistic need and purity in their consummation—two separate souls being
brought into a sacred oneness that left him in awe of
their magical coupling.*

*The golden clouds enveloped him, and suddenly the
woman was no longer beside him. The clouds roiled
again, turning dark and threatening above him as he
lay naked and sweaty on the grass. Lightning bolts
ripped from the churning sky, striking him in the
chest, in the region of his heart. Blackness engulfed
him, and he felt himself tumbling wildly through the
storm's grasp like a leaf ripped from a tree during
one of the jungle's powerful afternoon thunderstorms.*

*Though he was being buffeted by the clouds and
lightning, Culver felt a horrifying sense of loss. Never
had he felt such grief and such a soul-deep depriva-
tion. The sense of abandonment, of being torn from
the woman who had made him feel whole, became a
well of grief tunneling through him, making him gasp
for air.*

*Culver was gasping, his heart pounding, sweat run-
ning off his brow in rivulets, when he felt a hand on
his chest. His eyes flew open. Don Gonzalez was
squatting over him, his bony hand laid gently over
Culver's heart. The shaman studied him in silence.*

*"You have walked the path of the jaguar people,"
he said in a low, gruff tone. Removing his hand, he
took a wooden bowl and flicked droplets of water over
Culver. "You have taken on the power of the jaguar.*

It is very dangerous, but it can bring the rainbow, too. The jaguar is our most powerful spirit guide. Many pursue that power, and most are killed by it. You are a Norte Americano, *and you are ignorant of her ways."* He nodded and slowly stood as he continued to sprinkle the water.

The water cooled Culver, and his heartbeat began to slow and grow steady again. His breathing went from rasping gasps to deeper lungfuls as he felt himself return to the here and now, no longer caught up in the vision vine's storm.

"You will discover the power of the jaguar, my son. Once you know it, it will be up to you to integrate it into yourself." Don Gonzalez set the bowl aside and came and squatted once more by his side. *"It is female energy—the most powerful on Mother Earth. We are her children. All of us."* He waved his finger at him. *"You will meet a woman who is a jaguar priestess to our people. If you love her, you will become her."*

Stunned, Culver lay, still caught up in the remnants of the winds of ayahuasca. What was real? What was not? His body vibrated with the memory of what he'd experienced, with the jaguar and then with the beautiful, virginal maiden.

"And if I don't love her?" he croaked to the shaman.

Don Gonzalez smiled benignly. *"No man can resist the offer of jaguar medicine. She embodies all of the positive and negative of the feminine, my son. She is part seductress, part destroyer. You will experience both. The question is will you survive? And if you do, what then, I wonder?"* His smile increased knowingly. *"I have seen shaman apprentices actively hunt jaguar medicine, only to be killed by a jaguar in the jungle. They are found, torn apart and partially eaten."* With a shake of his head, he murmured, *"You come by the medicine honestly. Those apprentices who pursue her are in search of egotistical power, not the integration of the power to create a more-balanced human being."* His eyes sparkled. *"You achieved that state, that integration. Now that you know this feeling of wholeness, you will search for her, and when you find her, you will mate with her as you did in your vision. Then—"* he opened his hands and looked to the sky above *"—only the Great Mother will know your destiny."*

Culver felt cleaner and lighter. Despite the many times he had vomited, then felt caught in a dizzying inner tornado, he felt amazingly good—almost buoyant. "And can I integrate this power?"

With a shrug, Don Gonzalez said, "If the jaguar came to you, yes."

Culver looked deep into the man's dark eyes. Somehow, he knew Don Gonzalez already had knowledge of his eventual success or failure, but the old man wouldn't reveal what he knew. "And if I don't?"

"Then the jaguar goddess will destroy you." He touched his own chest, where a necklace of colorful macaw feathers rested. Tapping his heart, he said,

"Jaguar medicine is about integrating the female energy within yourself. It is an inner marriage. It is also the journey to the fullest opening of your heart. No other medicine tests you this strongly. It asks that you open your heart fully, with trust. You must stand completely naked and vulnerable to the jaguar. If you do not, you cannot accept the unconditional love she will offer you. There is no chance for he who hesitates, my friend. Trust. Stay receptive. Remain vulnerable. This priestess is still far away. You will meet her in the summer—a year from now, north of Lima. She will save your life."

Culver shook his head sharply, emerging from his powerful memory into the bright sunlight of Pilar's village. At the time of his vision-vine experience, he had silently laughed at the shaman's prediction. However, when he'd met Pilar, it had been at exactly the time and place the old man had predicted. But Culver hadn't had any idea Pilar was destined to become a jaguar priestess until just now, when Don Alvaro had mentioned it. He absently continued assembling the radio, scowling. "Does Pilar know she's a priestess?"

"Of course. That is why she wears her spirit guardian's hair in the medicine bag around her neck. It is a sign of her destiny."

Pilar came up to her grandfather smiling in greeting. Leaning over, she kissed the old man's parchment-thin cheek. "I see you have met Culver?"

"Yes," the patriarch said, gesturing for her to sit

in another rocking chair not far from his own. "Sit, *mi nieta*," he said, using the Spanish words for "my granddaughter."

Pilar saw the scowl on Culver's brow increase. Should she sit? Or should she disappear and leave them alone? Don Alvaro's long, strong fingers wrapped around her wrist, tugging her toward the rocker. Hesitantly, Pilar sat. Rane beamed at her.

"Mama, look! Culver said I could help him. Look at these radios! I've never seen anything like them."

Pilar held her daughter's light brown gaze, and her heart ached at the sight of her sitting so close to Culver. If he minded her daughter's presence, he didn't show it. She saw him look at Rane, his features softening. A vague hint of a smile played at the corners of his compressed lips. A fierce longing for Culver swept through Pilar, and an odd ache centered in her womb.

"Culver knows a great deal about mechanical things," she told Rane softly. Pulling the towel off her shoulders, she carefully folded it and placed it on the fallen log beside her rocking chair.

"He has been showing me so many things!"

Pilar caught Culver's gaze. He seemed amused by Rane's spontaneity, but how could anyone not be swayed by her daughter's sunbeam beauty and loving nature? No one could remain impervious to Rane's heart-centered love. But then, Pilar reminded herself, Rane had been created out of the heat and passion of the greatest love in her life, so it was not surprising.

"Perhaps," Don Alvaro said to Pilar with great seriousness, "we should have a ceremony before you leave to attack Don Ramirez's fortress in the jungle?"

She nodded. "Yes, I would like to receive the blessing of you and Grandmother Aurelia before I leave." She glanced at Culver. "Do you want to partake of a *ayahuasca* ceremony?"

He shook his head. "No way. Once was enough."

"You have tasted the winds of *ayahuasca?*" she asked, surprised.

"Yes. A long time ago," he said rather abruptly.

Pilar studied him in the intervening silence, feeling the tension radiating around him. "You don't have to take the drink with me. You can take it alone, if you don't want me around. I understand."

Culver's head snapped up, his eyes narrowing on her. "It has nothing to do with you being there or not."

"Do not push him, *mi nieta.*" Don Alvaro patted her arm gently. "You leave tomorrow morning, no?"

Culver's mouth tightened, and he glared at Pilar. "Just how much have you told them about our mission? We're on a strictly need-to-know basis, in case you didn't realize it." He knew he was snapping unnecessarily, and he hated himself for sounding so petulant. He saw Pilar's face mirror hurt from his verbal assault.

"I've told them nothing, Culver."

He stared at her. "Sure," he said mockingly. This was the first time Pilar had lied to him so openly.

Usually her lies were subtle as a jaguar noiselessly stalking her prey through the jungle. Her blatancy angered him.

Her lips parting, Pilar stared at Culver, then at her grandfather. "Listen to me, Culver," she said in a low, firm tone. "My grandfather is a shaman. So is my grandmother. You have lived in Peru long enough to know that they possess a knowing far beyond our own. My grandmother told me last night when we arrived that they had been expecting us. They travel in the other dimensions, the worlds of the past and future. They know what is happening around us."

"Really?" he said condescendingly. "Then ask them the outcome of our little jungle hike. Is Morgan alive? Will we successfully rescue him?" He snorted. "Better yet, ask the old man if either of us will survive. On second thought, I can answer those questions myself. Do you know what the likelihood of survival is on our mission? About ten percent. Which means we've got a ninety-percent chance of buying the farm. I don't need a shaman or an *ayahuasca* ceremony where I heave my guts to find out that answer."

"Don't you dare make fun of my grandparents! Just because they're shamans from a culture you don't accept or believe in doesn't take away from what they know!"

Rane got up and moved away from Culver. She slid into Pilar's lap and linked her long, slim arms around her mother's neck as she rested her head against her shoulder. Pilar tried to control the feelings

in her voice, aware that their argument was upsetting
Rane. "For your information, people who drink *ayahuasca* during a ceremony for a valid reason do not
have to heave their guts out. The cleaner a person is
inside, the less vomiting he or she experiences."

"I see," he growled, placing the radio back in its
protective plastic. "So I'm not clean inside. Well—"
he looked straight at her "—you're the jaguar priestess around here. Go ahead and go to your grandparents' ceremony. I'm staying out of it."

Tabling her anger, Pilar gaped at him. "Jaguar
priestess? What are you talking about?"

"Oh, come on," he drawled acidly as he leaned
over and picked up a revolver, preparing to check it
over and clean it, "You know damn well what I'm
talking about."

"No, I don't!"

"Pilar, you keep surprising me, you know that?"
Culver pulled the safety off the Beretta and studied
the weapon critically. "Here you are a jaguar priestess for your people, and you never told me. In fact,
you said so little about your real parentage—"

"At the time, it wasn't important," she snapped.
No, at the time, she thought ruefully, they'd fallen
into each other's arms, loving hotly, without regret or
apology.

Culver's mouth twisted into an ugly line as he
broke down the revolver piece by piece to begin oil-
ing it against the jungle's humidity. "A hell of a lot
of things weren't important except surviving."

Stung, Pilar held Rane more tightly, feeling her daughter tremble at the amount of anger in their exchange. She stroked her long, dark hair, flowing loose around her shoulders. All her life, Pilar had worked to keep her daughter from the violence of the world. Rane sighed and closed her eyes, nestling her face in the curve of her mother's neck. She relaxed, and Pilar was grateful. Too bad her touch didn't have the same mollifying effect on Culver; but too much bad blood had passed between them, Pilar admitted. She could hardly blame him.

"My grandparents have been telling me for as long as I can remember that I had a special responsibility to fulfill with my life," she explained in a low, controlled tone. "But I wasn't aware until you just told me that it was as a jaguar priestess." She glanced at her attentive grandfather, who she knew was listening with his heart. He didn't know much English, but from experience, Pilar knew that the revered shaman could understand on another level exactly what was being said. "That is something I will have to speak to them about now, on top of everything else that is going on."

Culver gave her a questioning look but said nothing. Out of long habit, he began applying oil to the gun's dark metal. Pilar sounded so convincing. If he hadn't learned so painfully, firsthand, of her ability to deceive, he would have believed her statement. She looked sincere and a little in awe of the information

he'd given her. Hell, she was just good at lying, he
told himself angrily.

"We've got enough to worry about right now," he
snapped. When he saw Rane flinch at the tone of his
voice, he softened his words. "You do whatever you
want to prepare for our little hike tomorrow morning.
But I know that vision vine is hallucinogenic, and
you'd damn well better not meet me tomorrow in a
drugged state."

Glaring at him, Pilar whispered tightly, "I would
never jeopardize your life like that and you know it!"

"Really?" Culver allowed the sarcasm to drip from
his voice. "You've got a funny way of looking at
things, then."

"What are you talking about?"

"You've already killed me in a hundred different
ways."

Stunned, Pilar drew in a sharp breath, pain shooting
through her hammering heart. She felt Don Alvaro's
fingers move in a caressing motion on her arm.

"*Mi nieta,*" he murmured, "there is much to do
before you go. Leave Rane here with Culver. You
will come with me, eh?"

Blinded by agony, Pilar nodded. Easing her daughter from her lap, she set her in the chair and asked
her to stay behind. Rane nodded and curled up in the
chair, rocking it slightly with one slim leg. Unable to
look at Culver, Pilar helped her grandfather to his
feet. He took the twisted, dried jungle vine he used
as a cane and leaned heavily on it.

As they walked slowly through the sprawling village, protected beneath the trees' stretching limbs, Pilar tried to steady her breathing. Her heart ached without relief, and as she gently steadied Don Alvaro with a hand around his upper arm, she said unevenly, "I don't know why this happened, Grandfather."

"What?" he inquired, looking down at her kindly.

"My being teamed up with Culver again. I—I thought he was out of my life—forever. I never expected him to walk back into it." She rubbed her heart with her hand. Combating tears, she whispered brokenly, "I still love him so much. I've hurt him so badly...."

"*Niña*, child, you carry both his and your own burden in your heart. It is very hard to carry one's own grief, much less another's anger and hurt, eh?"

Sniffing, Pilar fought back tears and pressed her head against his thin shoulder as he slowly wound his arm around her and drew her against him. "Y-yes, it is, Grandfather."

"Perhaps," he said, looking toward the hut where he'd lived all his life, "when you drink of the ceremonial cup this evening, the winds of *ayahuasca* will speak to you in a vision that will make the way more clear. Perhaps—" he smiled at her gently "—your heart will be healed of the many burdens it has carried. alone for so long. The secrets you carry are heavy, *mi niña*."

Pilar stared up at her grandfather for a heartbeat. Her grandparents were wise, and she allowed her panicked soul to find peace in his liquid, brown gaze, a soothing of the violent ache in her heart. Shamans were wonderful healers, she reminded herself.

Pilar recalled one of the many stories her grandparents had told her when she was a child sitting in the hut at night, about how one had to undergo a near-death experience before receiving the calling to become an apprentice shaman. Since shamans traversed all the dimensions, they could not be afraid of such travels. Only those who had died could be admitted to these other worlds, and shamans were able to make such journeys and live to tell about it—because they themselves had died and returned to life.

Don Alvaro brought Pilar into the hut where Aurelia was kneeling, grinding corn on a heavy, flat stone. Nearby, a small fire of coals was ready to cook the tortillas she was preparing for them. "Pilar knows of her path as a jaguar priestess," he said as he sat down in his favorite rocking chair, crafted from scraps of mahogany.

Aurelia stopped her grinding. "Eh?" She looked at Pilar, who took a seat at the rough-hewn table. Light from the four windows filtered in, accentuating the shadows. "Well," she said busily, returning to her grinding, "we knew she would learn of it soon, anyway."

Pilar ran her fingertips across the table's worn surface. "Why didn't you tell me?"

Aurelia sighed, sifting the corn flour into a small

pottery jar. Wiping her hands on her colorful red-and-black skirt, she slowly rose from her arthritic knees. "In order to become a priestess, you must almost die." Aurelia halted in the middle of the hut and stared at her granddaughter. "You have not had that experience—yet."

"Once you had lived through the experience—passed to the other world and returned—" Don Alvaro added softly, "we would have told you. Then you would already have understood the death experience, and what we do as shamans." Opening his hands, he said, "The journey you and Culver take tomorrow will place you in a life-and-death situation. You will have many choices along the way, *mi niña*. We pray for you. And for him. We pray that you return to us alive, but we cannot yet know if that will happen."

Aurelia came over and patted Pilar's slumped shoulder. "*Mi niña,* the life path of a jaguar priestess is the hardest of all." She smiled a little and touched her large, ample breast. "I serve the jaguar goddess myself. The first half of my life was filled with tests involving life and death—my own and others'. By the jaguar's grace, I passed them and lived to work in her service as a *shamanka*," she said, using the term for a female shaman. Her worn, plump fingers rested against Pilar's hair. "Your heart carries many burdens, my little one. We ache for you as you do yourself. But a *shamanka* cannot heal others unless she knows what it is like to suffer in many areas as a human being. How can she understand another's pain if she has not traversed that path herself? So you see, it is necessary, this painful process we undergo, to become worthy of the jaguar goddess's attention.''

Shaking her head, Pilar looked up into her grandmother's round, brown face. She felt such peace and love radiating from the old woman that she opened her arms and slid them around her grandmother's ample waist. Closing her eyes, she buried her face against Aurelia's softness. The feel of her grandmother's still-strong arms encircling her gave her courage and dissolved some of the lingering agony in her heart. ''I'm so scared,'' she whispered. ''I've hurt Culver so much. I don't know how I'll get through this mission with him. Being around him is like holding my hand in a fire. I hurt all the time, Grandmother. Sometimes I hurt so much I can barely breathe.'' Looking up, her eyes bathed in tears, she said brokenly, ''Sometimes I wonder whether, if I quit breathing, the hurt would finally go away....''

''Ah, *mi niña,*'' Aurelia scolded softly, framing Pilar's face with her work-worn hands. She leaned over, her features bare inches from Pilar's as she held her granddaughter's gaze. ''The jaguar goddess is hard on us, I know. And the love you carry in your heart for this *Norte Americano* is a blessing and also a curse to you. Is that not what being a *shamanka* is all about? You stand with one foot in this world, your other foot in the many other worlds. How can you know pain if you do not know pleasure? How can you know love if you have never loved fully? Your heart and soul were given to Culver. We do not question his love for you, nor yours for him.''

With her thick, callused thumbs, Aurelia caressed Pilar's smooth cheeks. *''Mi niña,* this is your final test before you can approach the jaguar goddess and ask her blessing to become an apprentice. This mission will be a test for you in every way.'' Her voice dropped to almost a growl as she said, ''Whatever you do, my little one, you must walk with an open heart. Do you hear me? Do you understand? Even though this man throws arrows of anger and hurt, you must not close your heart to him or anything around you. To do so is to fail this test. Be receptive. Continue to love without anger, guilt or shame.''

Pilar's eyes widened at those words. Looking into the wise, velvety depths of her grandmother's eyes, Pilar knew the old woman was aware of the shameful secret she'd carried eight years. Choking on sudden tears of gratitude, Pilar whispered, ''I understand, Grandmother.''

Aurelia smiled, her entire face radiating with a loving glow. ''Tonight, we will hold an *ayahuasca* ceremony for you, to beseech the jaguar goddess on your behalf to protect and watch over you and this *Norte Americano.*''

''Thank you,'' Pilar whispered. ''I want to pray for Morgan Trayhern, too, Grandmother. If anyone needs prayers, it is that brave man, not me.''

Chuckling indulgently, Aurelia released Pilar and

planted a swift kiss on her brow. "You make the jaguar spirit happy with such unselfish love for another, *mi niña*. That is why I pray strongly that your walk with death will not be final, that you can place your feet on the rainbow bridge, but also come back from it—back to your people. That you can give your heart again, without the clouding of the past as before."

Surrounded by the comfort of her grandparents' love, Pilar felt her burden easing. They had been her nurturing support for so many years—since the deaths of her parents. She realized that she hadn't visited them often enough or long enough in the past eight years. Her stays had generally been limited to weekends, two or three times a year, and Rane always cried when they had to fly back to Lima. Well, didn't she want to cry at the thought of leaving, also? Looking around the simple thatched hut, and at the kind intelligence in the faces of her grandparents, Pilar felt a new stirring in her heart.

"If I survive this mission," she said in a tremulous tone, "I want to come home. I want to come back here and live with you. I've missed family so much—more than I've realized until now. And Rane needs the love and support you have for her. She needs to know her people, the source of her soul and blood."

Aurelia glowed in approval as she stood in the doorway. "We pray it will be so, *mi niña*. Nothing would give us more happiness than to have you here at the village with us. You will begin to apprentice with me and learn the ways of the *shamanka*.''

Sadly, Pilar whispered, ''I've been so blind, Grandmother. You were here all along. Why didn't I realize that? Why did I have to spend two years in Lima alone after Fernando died, trying to raise Rane by myself? I've suffered so much by doing that. You know how our society looks down on a woman and child without a man. I have endured name-calling and accusing looks, as if I should apologize for living when my husband is dead. They insisted I should remarry, but my heart belongs to just one man…and I can never have him again.…''

''Be patient, *mi niña*,'' Aurelia soothed. ''Though the spirit of the jaguar is harsh upon us, she is also bountiful in rewarding those who pass the trials she sets before us. Be patient. Perhaps all your dreams can be fulfilled.''

Pilar got up, smiling brokenly. ''I have no more dreams, Grandmother. They died when Culver almost died—for me. I don't live for myself. I live because of Rane. She deserves a mother, someone who loves her fully. I don't want to be yanked out of her life as my mother and father were from mine.''

Frowning, Aurelia murmured, ''We must pray very hard tonight.''

Pilar left the hut, following her grandmother down the mountain. Aurelia was in her early eighties, spry despite her weight and age. The trees became thicker as they got farther from the village. Pilar knew without being told that her grandmother was going to a special spot where the *ayahuasca* vine grew wild. The day was warm, the sun shining brightly through wisps of clouds.

Pilar knew that her grandparents had seen death many times. Ramirez and his men had slaughtered more than thirty people from their farming village in the past twenty years, and there wasn't a family in the region completely unaffected by his atrocities. She also knew the chances of surviving the mission were small, as Culver had so coldly pointed out. As the breeze playfully lifted and twisted strands of her hair around her face, Pilar regretted so much.

Chapter 7

It took every vestige of Pilar's control to hide her tears when Rane stretched her slim arms up around Culver's neck. As he bent to say farewell to her, her daughter's eyes were wet with tears. Culver had crouched and taken her into his arms, holding her tightly against him. He wore a heavy pack on his back and had to balance it during Rane's unexpected embrace.

"Keep Mama safe," the little girl sobbed against his neck, her face pressed against him. "Don't let her get hurt. I love her. She's all I have left. Take care of her, Culver."

Culver patted Rane's narrow shoulder tenderly. Unexpectedly, tears dampened his own eyes as he

held her small form to him. This morning when he'd
gotten up from the hut where he'd slept alone, he'd
been in a foul humor. He'd grimly expected Pilar to
be late for their agreed-upon 0600 meeting at the edge
of the village. And he hadn't expected Rane to be
waiting at her side, gripping her hand as if letting go
would be releasing her to her death. The look on the
child's usually joyous face softened his feelings, melting away the angry defenses he'd erected in his heart
earlier this morning.

Rane's hair was soft and smelled freshly washed,
hanging loose all the way to her narrow hips. She had
placed a small pink orchid in her hair, attaching it
awkwardly with a bobby pin, the delicate flower accentuating her innocent loveliness. Placing his hands
on her shaking shoulders, Culver eased her a few
inches away from him. The child sniffled and, with
trembling hands, tried bravely to scrub her eyes free
of tears as she looked up at him. Such emotion
showed in her light brown eyes that he managed a
small smile for her benefit.

"It's going to be all right," he said, defying his
own hard-and-fast rule about not underplaying the
danger of any given mission. Gently taming errant
strands of hair back from Rane's damp cheek, he
placed them behind her tiny ear. At seven-and-a-half,
she wore petite diamond earrings that made her look
even more feminine.

"M-Mama says you're a w-warrior from long

ago,'' Rane stammered between sobs. ''She s-says you saved her life once before.''

Culver's gaze flicked to Pilar, standing a few feet away. Another lie. ''Well...'' he hedged, ''our lives were saved because we worked together like a good team.'' Actually, Pilar had saved his miserable hide. That was the truth of the matter. Still, deep within himself, Culver could understand why Pilar had turned that particular fact around to offer her fearful daughter solace. He saw tears glittering in Pilar's own eyes, her hand pressed to her mouth as if to stop a sob struggling to break free.

Culver leaned over and kissed Rane's damp, pale cheek. Throwing caution and his conservative training to the wind, he said, ''Listen, your mama underwent a sacred ceremony last night and it will give her protection. She's going to be all right, Rane.'' He hoped to God his words would prove true.

Hiccuping through her tears, Rane reached out and touched his recently shaven cheek. ''Y-you promise?''

Culver hung his head, avoiding the child's innocent eyes. How the hell could he promise such a thing? Her small hand, so delicate and soft, rested against his cheek, holding the same kind of warmth he'd always noted in Pilar's. Pilar came from a family of healers, and he'd guessed that was behind the heat radiating from her hands, so he wasn't surprised Rane possessed the same warm touch. *Oh, what the hell.*

"Yeah, Rane, I promise I'll bring your mama home alive. How's that?"

Instantly, Culver saw Rane's expression change. She was like a chameleon, in a sense—just as Pilar was. Culver knew Peruvian *shamankas* were known as "shape-shifters," able to turn themselves not only into animals, but into other human forms as well. Rane obviously possessed the rudiments of that ability, he thought, as he watched her small face lighten, her eyes glow brightly with relief and hope.

"Oh," she cried, flinging herself back into his arms and wrapping her own as tightly as she could around his neck, "thank you, Culver. Thank you!" Excitedly, she tore from his grasp, touched the orchid resting in her hair, then worked for several moments to free it. "Here, I want you to take this with you. Grandmother says I have orchid medicine. She says that if I give a person an orchid, he will be healed and protected. I want you to be safe, too...." Rane became somber as she leaned over and eased the small bloom into Culver's left shirt pocket, which she studiously buttoned so the flower couldn't be lost on their trek.

"There," she said seriously. "I will go to my altar that Grandmother helped me set up in our *casa*, and I will pray for you, too."

Reaching out, Culver caressed Rane's hair. "Now I do feel safe," he said to her in a husky tone. The love shining in the child's eyes rocked him. Rane tilted her head, watching as he straightened and rearranged the heavy pack straps pulling at his shoulders.

"It's time to go," Pilar called gently. She caressed Rane's hair, leaning down one last time to hug her daughter tightly, before releasing her. Out of nowhere, her grandparents appeared. Though they were both old, their features worn by life, Pilar saw the gentleness glowing in their weathered faces. A fog hung just above the jungle, and the humidity was high. She fought tears again as Rane ran to stand between the aged couple. A ragged breath escaped her as she gazed at her family. Chances were good that she would never see any of them again.

Her heart nearly broke with grief. What would happen to Rane? As Pilar looked over at Culver, she saw that his expression remained tender from the child's unexpected attention. Rane had magic in her touch, but then, her heart was pure and she was innocent, and Pilar knew how easily Culver responded to that combination. Once, she had been like that.

"Come on," he rasped gruffly as he passed her on the well-beaten trail leading down the slope toward the jungle.

Raising her hand, Pilar tried to smile at Rane, but didn't succeed. Turning quickly, she fought back tears and blindly followed Culver's huge, striding form down the trail. Some of her anguish eased as they left the upper world of sunlight, clouds and villagers and entered the darkened labyrinth of the jungle. The heavy humidity enveloped Pilar, and instantly she began to perspire as she struggled to maintain her balance with the heavy pack jostling against palms, vines and other encroaching plant life. It almost seemed as if the plants were wishing them well, patting them, reaching out in their own way as the two humans trod ever deeper into the jungle. A blessing of sorts for a successful journey, Pilar hoped.

Hurrying to keep up with Culver, Pilar sensed how upset he was. Because of Rane's unexpected request? Probably. She certainly knew that he didn't want to be here with her. The trail continued to descend along the slope of the hill, and here and there, Pilar could hear droplets tapping from one leaf to another as the thick fog condensed. Above her, the opaque white mist floated like a billowy canopy over the entire region. But it was usual for fog to embrace the jungle until about ten each morning.

About a mile into the jungle, the trail widened enough to allow two people to walk easily side by side. Culver turned and looked expectantly at Pilar. Her skin had a sheen of moisture on it, and her eyes were dark and focused. He saw the stubborn set to her mouth and instantly wanted to kiss her—kiss her until she melted against him. The errant thought was an unwelcome interruption to his own focused attention, and he scowled as she drew to a halt a few feet from him.

"Are you doing okay?" he asked. The packs they wore would provide everything they needed for the next four days. Ramirez's jungle fortress was a two-day trek deep into the heart of Amazonia.

She smiled briefly and wiped the perspiration from her brow with a red kerchief she took from around her neck. "Yes."

"You're not acclimated to this."

"Neither of us are," Pilar said, looking around in admiration at the towering trees, draped everywhere with dark green vines thick as cables. In a way, they reminded her of giant, beautiful spiderwebs. The screeching howls of monkeys preceded them, warnings to friends of human trespassers in their environs. "I'm glad I have Incan blood. I can feel my body shifting, rebalancing to this heat and humidity."

Culver nodded and placed his hands on his hips. "I hate the jungle."

"Why?"

"It's hot and uncomfortable—and I feel like I can't breathe."

She smiled softly. "We have always said that the jungle is the womb of Mother Earth. The moist darkness is fertile. Everything lives and grows here, just as a baby grows inside a woman's body."

Culver was struck by the symbolic beauty in Pilar's words. "I've never thought of it in those terms." He wiped the sweat from his face with the back of his hand. On his hip, he wore a holster and the black Beretta he'd cleaned yesterday. Pilar wore no obvious weapons. Her cover, after all, was that of a *shamanka* guide for a U.S. botanist. Her hair, pulled back into a single, thick braid that curved across her shoulder, was wavier than usual from the jungle's moisture. How clean and clear her golden skin looked, Culver thought. How shining her eyes, with their hints of an inner, secret joy.

"What are you so happy about?" he demanded abruptly as he gazed around them.

"I had forgotten how much I love the jungle." Pilar gestured overhead to an old, thick rubber tree. In its distorted, twisted limbs hung a huge purple-and-white orchid. "Look above you, Culver."

He twisted to look in the direction she indicated. The orchid, one of a string of blooms, hung within his reach. Lifting his hand he gently broke the stem and captured seven blossoms at once. Lifting them, he inhaled their heady fragrance.

"Here," he muttered, handing them to her. "A string of jungle pearls for your neck."

Shocked at his unexpected gift, Pilar reached out and took the slender, bending stem, heavy with flowers. She saw the burning look in Culver's eyes and felt as if he'd reached out and touched her. Cradling the orchids in her hands, she stared up at him. "Thank you...."

Culver gave her a cutting smile. "You always reminded me of an orchid," he grudgingly admitted. *Open, vulnerable, giving and feminine.* "Wear them. You can really play the part of guide to this ignorant *Norte Americano* plant specialist." Turning on his heel, he continued along the now-level floor of the jungle.

Quickly stringing the orchids around her neck, where they rested between her pack's straps and her chin, Pilar inhaled their aromatic fragrance. Dizzied by this surprising gift, she hurried to catch up. For every stride Culver took, Pilar had to take two. But she managed to move to his side. She felt him look down at her, felt his scowl. Too bad if he didn't want her at his shoulder. Still, she noticed he checked his stride slightly for her sake. Puffing a little, she twisted to look up at him.

"In my next lifetime, I'm going to be born tall, with long legs like yours," she teased.

Culver gave a slight smile. Glancing over, he saw that the color of her eyes had lightened. Pilar was happy. The realization struck directly at the heart he was so desperately trying to protect from her dazzling smile, soft voice and tender looks. "Short people do have their problems," he admitted. Right now, they should be safely out of range, for the most part, of Ramirez's men. Because the fortress was hidden so deeply in the jungle, Culver knew from experience that Ramirez didn't post many guards. But several hit men frequently took on the guise of villagers from the small settlements that ringed the fortress. He and Pilar couldn't know for certain if a villager was friend or foe. He did know that it was safer to speak in English, because many of the Indians and some of Ramirez's men didn't know the language.

Chuckling, Pilar nodded. "Small but mighty. Look at Grandmother Aurelia. She is barely five feet tall, yet she's one of Peru's most powerful *shamankas.*"

"Speaking of that, how did the ceremony go last night?" He eyed Pilar and saw her face suddenly close up. Her lips, once parted, became compressed, and Culver sensed a dread in her. In spite of himself, he worried about the vision of the future she might have received and its potential accuracy. He watched as she pushed hair from her forehead—another sign of nervousness.

"It will be," she said carefully, "a difficult mission."

"Difficult being another word for disastrous?"

Pilar opened her hands. "My death is near."

Culver jerked to a halt. He stared down at her. "Death?" His voice came out strangulated, filled with disbelief. How could Pilar stand there, calmly accepting such a thing? Then he remembered how shamans had to traverse between life and death for their patients in order to heal them. Death for them was not the fearful experience that the Western World saw.

Combatting tears, Pilar smiled brokenly at Culver. Gone was the flinty look in his eyes. She saw his sudden anguish on her behalf. "I feel that is why Rane was so upset this morning. Even though she wasn't at the ceremony, she knows...." With a sigh, Pilar whispered, "I don't want to leave Rane, Culver. My parents died early, and I know the pain of it. I don't want Rane to experience that.'' She shrugged out of her pack and laid it aside. As she rubbed her shoulders, she said, ''After the ceremony, early this morning, I talked with my grandparents about my vision. They agree that I could die a physical death. It's part of my final test to take on the spirit of the jaguar. Anyone who is invited to the jaguar medicine must have a near-death experience. Whether I survive depends on many things, some of them outside of myself.''

Cursing softly, Culver lowered his pack to the ground in turn and sat next to Pilar on a damp log near the trail. She was only inches away. It was inconceivable to him that she could die, yet he knew that going up against Ramirez could easily guarantee both their deaths. Was he prepared to die also? Staring at Pilar's serene face, Culver knew the answer was a defiant no. Maybe she was already lost to him in some ways, and they could never recapture what they'd had, but he couldn't stick his head in the sand about the lethal possibilities of this mission. As angry and hurt as he was by Pilar's actions in the past, he emphatically didn't want her to die. The admission softened his attitude toward her.

''I know enough about the vision-vine ceremony,'' he began stiltedly, ''to know it's not just a bunch of hallucinations.''

Pilar nodded and sighed. ''That's why I undertook the ceremony.'' She clasped her sweaty hands together. ''When you nearly kissed me the other morning, I thought I was dreaming," she continued softly, unable to look at him. "I wanted you to kiss me. I felt like a parched plant on the high desert plateau of the Andes, with your kiss like life-giving moisture." She felt a flush rise from her neck into her face at the admission. Culver's intense inspection felt like the heat of a fire upon her.

"Last night, I saw so very much. I saw Morgan...." She lifted her head and gazed at him. "Ramirez has been torturing him brutally. They have given him drugs to drain information from him. He is like a robot, from what I can see. He is alive, but not in his body. Do you know what I mean?"

"Drugs disconnect you, Pilar," Culver agreed harshly. "Damn. I knew Ramirez would do that to him. But you say he's alive?"

"Yes, I saw in my vision where he is. They no longer guard him within the compound. Morgan sits on a small bunk in a tiny room on the second floor of the *casa*. He sits staring into space, unmoving. I saw his shadow—the part that is invisible yet gives us life in this physical body—lying beside him on the floor."

"What does that mean?"

"That he is slowly dying."

"He's probably been drugged so many times that he's toxic," Culver muttered. "That son of a bitch!" He tightened his hands into fists as he referred to Ramirez.

Sadly, Pilar touched her necklace of orchids. "He

may not survive, either. My vision—'' she waved her hand in the air ''—became murky, and I saw us dead. In another phase of it, I saw Morgan alive, but I was dead. In another, we both barely survived the mission.''

"How do you interpret that?" Culver knew that shamans under the influence of an altered state created by the vision vine often saw the future broken down into different paths a person could take. One thing he'd learned from shamans in Peru—alternate realities represented choices. What the person chose would manifest physically. Desperately he wondered which choice Pilar would opt for. In his heart, he knew she would struggle toward life, for Rane. But bullets didn't choose who they would kill, and Ramirez would murder them without a second thought.

"Choices," she whispered brokenly. "I'll have the choice to live or die." Rubbing her hands on the thighs of her jeans, she said, "I want to live, but I don't know if that's enough to ensure it."

"What can make the difference between you living and dying?"

Pilar held his agitated stare. "Love."

Her reply haunted Culver. He twisted around on the log, placing his long legs on either side of Pilar, unable to stand the suffering in her face any longer. Driven by hunger and need, he raised his hands and framed her face. How soft and pliant her skin was. Looking deeply into her now-golden eyes, he saw her lips part. The invitation was there. He felt her suddenly tense, and with his thumbs, he caressed her high cheekbones.

"Mi querida," he whispered thickly as he leaned down. For an instant, Pilar tried to pull from his grasp, but then, miraculously, he felt her surrender to him. His heart soared with that knowledge as he closed his eyes just as their mouths touched. How long he had been without her! The tentative grazing of her lips sent a sheet of fire raging through him, from his heart downward. He tasted the saltiness of her lips, and then she opened to him, like the fragrant orchids grazing his cheek as he took her mouth more deeply.

The jungle's humid heat swirled around him as he tasted the nectar of Pilar's lips. When she fearlessly returned his searching, tentative kiss, fire jagged through him, and he felt rather than heard her moan of surrender as she leaned forward, her breasts brushing against his chest. Her arms lifted and moved across his shoulders, and her fingers slid up his neck into his hair. Her touch was as fiery and beautiful as he remembered.

Hungrily, he slid his mouth against her wet, full lips. She was a thick, waxy orchid, opening to him, presenting him her natural, heady fragrance and offering him her nectar as a woman. Her ragged breath fanned his cheek. Her mouth was pliant even as it plundered his own questing lips. He couldn't get enough of her, and his fingers tightened on her face, drawing her more deeply against him. The feel of her breasts was enticing as her fingers ranged over his head, then slid across his face, as if rememorizing every detail.

Culver wanted more. Much more. Tilting her head, he dove his tongue deeply into her mouth, where it tangled with hers in a sliding, molten heat, spiraling crazily toward that door deep within him that he'd kept carefully barred and locked ever since that day Pilar had left him so abruptly. Her moan was like a jaguar's purr, and his pleasure at the sound thrummed through him as if he were a drum being played by her honest need. Her fingers explored his craggy features, outlining his thick eyebrows, caressing his eyelids as softly as butterflies, then moving tenderly down his cheekbones to stroke the hard granite of his jaw.

How much he'd missed all of this. As he dragged Pilar into his arms, Culver pressed her tightly against him, one large hand cradling her back, holding her as close as he could without actually entering her. Volcanic heat exploded through him as her small hand moved downward, sliding beneath his shirt and over his collarbone. As their hurried breathing mingled, Culver's heart thudded without relief. He tunneled his fingers urgently through her bound hair, rewarded by the feel of it loosening beneath his insistence. The ribbon holding the thick, luxurious mass eased, and the strands came cascading down over his hand and arm. The orchids' fragrance combined with her natural, earthy scent. Culver had never felt more alive than when she was in his arms, making exquisite love

to her. He'd never felt the devastating, numbing—
death of the soul as he had when she'd left him.

In some dim corner of his now barely functioning
mind, he began to understand on a new level the concept of the worlds a shaman traverses in his or her
inner journeys. Pilar was his life and death. As her
mouth crushed against his and they clung wildly to
each other, he felt reborn, as if all his dying grief had
been transformed in that instant when she had surrendered willingly to him once again. He cared about
nothing at this point except Pilar, and the dreaded
possibility that she might be torn from him again—
this time, by one of Ramirez's bullets.

The jungle's heat, the slickness of their caressing
hands reminded him of the giving of life. Pilar had
been right—the jungle was the womb of Mother
Earth. And Pilar was *his* life. His destiny. Culver realized he had known it on some inner level all along,
but had been too bitterly afraid to admit it even to
himself. Now she was here in his arms, exchanging
intimacies he had only dreamed of.

Thunder rumbled warningly overhead. Vaguely,
Culver acknowledged it and knew that pouring rain
soon would strike the jungle canopy with fury. Tearing his mouth from Pilar's, he stared down into her
golden eyes. His fingers trembled as they tunneled
into her hair on either side of her precious face. The
words, *I love you,* nearly burst from him, but Culver
stopped himself. He knew the folly of opening the

depths of his emotions to Pilar. Last time, she'd abandoned him at his darkest hour of need.

Wrestling to contain the feelings rumbling through him like the approaching thunderstorm, Culver gripped Pilar's shoulders and rested his brow against hers. He felt her hands flatten against his chest, felt their burning warmth seem to sear through the damp cotton of his shirt. Though aching as never before to love her fully, completely, he forced himself to release her—and saw a matching desire for him in her eyes.

Pilar's long-ago rejection had left him believing she would never want him again. The discovery that she did was bittersweet. Nothing could come of him giving her his heart again. He simply wasn't willing to risk it. The pain was too great for him to endure a second time. It would kill him.

''It's going to rain,'' Culver muttered thickly, pushing himself to his feet. Stumbling like a drunken man toward his pack, he absorbed all of his reeling emotions. He felt as if he'd consumed the fury of the coming storm: an incredible tension raged between the longing to lose his soul to Pilar again and the need to prevent that very tragedy. Thunder rumbled again. The storm was within three miles, the rain less than fifteen minutes away.

As they resettled their packs on their shoulders and headed more deeply into the jungle, Pilar struggled with the gamut of emotions Culver had released with his powerful, unexpected kisses. Though sunlight overhead was dispersed by the canopy of trees, occasionally an actual beam of light would find its way to the damp, leaf-strewn jungle floor. Most of the time, the light was dappled and in constant motion, like the patterns of light reflected off a mirrored ball hanging above a dance floor. Clouds were moving in, though, and Pilar watched as shadows began to encroach on the sun-speckled jungle. The storm was approaching, but it was nothing to match the storm she was experiencing within her. Her lower body ached with a burning memory she couldn't seem to banish, of Culver, deep inside her, moving with her, showering life into her just as the rain sated the thirsty jungle.

Pilar walked silently at his shoulder, and a rush of relief flowed through her. Thank God Culver had broken their kiss. He had more sense than her errant body did. She knew all too well the supreme danger of giving herself to him. At this point, without an exploration of the full truth of what had happened, it could only cause him pain.

No, Pilar told herself, shaken by the thought, she wasn't willing to risk the possible consequences of opening herself up to him and telling him everything. She just couldn't. She had too much to lose.

"It's funny," Culver muttered eventually, the sound of his voice instantly deadened by the thick vegetation around them, "I thought I knew what dying was all about when you left me. I grieved as if you were dead. Now you tell me you might die, and I'm feeling it all over again, only worse."

Pilar didn't dare look at Culver. She heard the uncertainty in his roughened tone, and without thinking, she reached out and blindly wrapped her fingers around his big, thickly callused hand. It was a hand that had loved her to oblivion, to a special world of love and light she had never experienced before—or since. He halted abruptly at her touch, and she tightened her grip on his hand as she turned to face him. The expression on his face was heartrending. Instantly, Pilar released his hand, afraid of invoking more pain by her presence.

"I owe you an apology, Culver," she began, her voice unsteady. "I—I...my world was pulled out from under me when you were wounded. You were so close to death. I didn't think I'd reach help in time to save you. I know it happened eight years ago, but at times, it seems like yesterday." Pilar touched her damp, white cotton blouse. The thunder sounded another warning, much closer this time, the jungle vibrating with the booming rumbles. She looked up at the canopy and then back at him. "I can still feel how I felt then. The terror. The grief."

Culver looked at her strangely. Why was she telling him this? "But you didn't have to leave me, Pilar. Why did you run? I remember you at the hospital, holding my hand, crying and praying out loud for me. But when I regained consciousness, you were gone. The doctors didn't know where you were. The nurses

didn't know—'' His voice cracked. "I wanted to die
when you didn't return. I couldn't understand why
you left me. You saved my life, then just disappeared.
Why?''

Biting down on her lower lip, Pilar looked away.
"*Dios,* Culver, I—I wish I could tell you, but I
cannot.'' Abruptly, she remembered hearing him say
casually, not long after they met, "Oh, sure, I love
kids.'' They had stopped to help a small girl crying
outside a village, she recalled. "But I'm a long way
from being ready to settle down with children of my
own.''

"Hector said you were pulled undercover again,''
he was saying now, his mouth flattened. "A Q-
clearance mission. I knew from CIA experience that
if someone goes Q-clearance, I might as well ask a
brick wall for information. Hector refused to tell me
anything more. Two weeks in that hospital, and I was
transferred by plane back to the States. I tried,'' he
said, frustration ringing in his voice, "through Hector
to reach you. But he gave me nothing.''

Wincing, Pilar nodded and closed her eyes, unable
to stand the anguish in Culver's gaze. "*Mi querido,*''
she whispered faintly, "I didn't want to leave you,
but something…came up. Something only I was able
to handle.'' She opened her eyes, Culver's rugged
features blurring before her. "I'm so sorry, Culver. I
didn't mean to wound you that way. I had no inten-
tion…'' She opened her hands helplessly. "I wish I
could heal your pain. I see you still carry the injury

in your heart, the grief and anger toward me.'' Her voice broke, she was so close to tears. ''Can you ever forgive me, Culver? If I am going to die, I need to know you will forgive me for abandoning you at the moment of your greatest need. Can you?''

Culver's throat constricted. Reaching out, he cupped her cheek. How soft and firm her skin was beneath his fingertips as he grazed that velvety slope. She'd called him ''my darling.'' The sweetness of the words soothed him like a healing salve, easing the ache in his heart. He saw tears swimming in Pilar's eyes, saw her valiant attempt to force them back. The girl he remembered from so long ago would have burst easily into uncontrollable tears, and he would have pulled her into his arms, rocking her as she cried, soothing her tiny kisses and caresses.

How badly Culver wanted to do just that. For the first time, he began to understand the depth of Pilar's own anguish over abandoning him. He had thought she didn't care, but he'd been wrong. So very, stupidly wrong. Now he continued to stroke her cheek with his thumb, seeing the magic of his touch as her large, cat's eyes changed to glorious gold. Joy coursed through him, sharp and breathtaking, avalanching his old grief, which at long last began to dissolve.

All he had to do was take one step forward, drop his arms around her small form and pull her against him. He saw the unmistakable need in Pilar's eyes. Yet, as she held herself rigidly, he knew just as surely that she didn't want his embrace. Before, a simple kiss, a loving touch would have eased her pain. But back then, life had been simple between them. Joyous. Bitterly, Culver dropped his hand from her cheek and sighed.

"I forgive you, Pilar. I guess I had already forgiven you a long time ago, if you want the truth." He felt an immediate lightening in his chest, as if merely speaking those words freed him of so much of the ugliness he'd carried. Anxiously, he watched Pilar's face, to see if his words would have an equally healing effect on her. Never had he wanted anything more for her.

Pilar took in a deep, cleansing breath. "*Dios,* thank you…thank you…." She stepped away from Culver, feeling suddenly dizzy—and at the same time an uncontrollable need of more contact with him. But she didn't dare give in to it. He'd wanted to kiss her again—she'd seen it so clearly in his eyes. And she'd wanted him to. Breathing raggedly, Pilar turned and began walking as fast as she could down the trail. *Culver forgave her.* She'd seen the sincerity in his darkened eyes. Heard it in the grave tone of his unsteady voice. So much of her guilt and shame was miraculously dissolving around her as she moved swiftly through the jungle.

Raindrops heralding the approaching storm began to plunk loudly against the highest canopy of leaves more than a hundred feet above them. The three levels of trees in the jungle's distinctive canopy would absorb most of the storm's fury, Pilar knew. Still, the gentler droplets cascading off the leaves of the lowest trees would soak them thoroughly soon enough. Where was Culver? Pilar slowed and partially turned, to see him walking a good hundred feet behind her, his features alert, his gaze constantly shifting like personal all-terrain radar, on the lookout for trouble.

The many shadows had lengthened as the sunlight was doused by dark gray clouds, which were illuminated occasionally by brilliant bolts of lightning. By dusk, the combination of darkness and fog would make this storm-ridden scene seem bright. They had about four more hours of daylight, Pilar figured. She turned and resumed walking, this time at a more reasonable pace. Rain continued to explode against the upper canopy, and lightning zigzagged above them, creating sudden, eerie shadows. As she'd known it would, water began to drip steadily, quickly soaking her hair, face and clothing. Eventually, as the trail twisted and turned, Culver was again at her side, and Pilar gathered the courage to steal a quick glance at him. His mouth was no longer pursed, as if to stop a wave of pain, and the look in his eyes, though sharpened, no longer had the frozen quality that had so dismayed her.

Somehow, a small miracle of healing had occurred between them, she realized humbly. The kiss they'd shared had broken open the old, infected wound. And her reaching out to touch him and ask his forgiveness had somehow allowed him to find that forgiveness in his heart. A new light shone in his eyes, and his very gait had changed. Pilar couldn't define it exactly, though she sensed a great weight had lifted from his too-long-weary shoulders. She bit her bottom lip. If only she had the courage to tell him the whole truth of what had happened eight years ago.

Chapter 8

Culver prodded the small fire with a twig. Near dusk, they'd made a lean-to of huge, thick palm leaves. He'd dug a deep hole, and Pilar had started a fire. Luckily, a snake had slithered across their path earlier, and he'd killed it, so chunks of meat were now roasting in the flickering flames, slowly turned by Pilar. The two of them had been soaked to the skin by the thunderstorm, and though the rain had long since stopped, Culver knew their clothes would never completely dry in the perpetually high humidity.

They sat close together, as the lean-to's tiny dimensions dictated. After adding a few more still-damp twigs to the fire, Culver glanced at Pilar. Her hair was in mild disarray about her face, framing her haunting, jaguar's eyes—eyes that had communicated to the depths of his soul with just one look. The taste of her kiss still lingered hotly in his memory. Her cheeks were high with color, and he sensed she hadn't forgotten it, either.

Darkness was falling. Culver watched as the thin smoke rose and caught in the palm-leaf roof above them, swirling and separating until only slight wisps escaped the shelter. No one should be able to detect their presence—at least for tonight. Tomorrow, Culver knew grimly, was another situation altogether. Tomorrow, by nightfall, they would reach Ramirez's fortress. With every mile closer, the danger to them increased exponentially.

"Did you ever marry?" Pilar asked softly. She looked up from the skewer of meat she held over the fire. Culver's eyes sharpened on her, his expression quizzical, and she realized he probably hadn't expected her to ask personal questions of him. Yet, to salve her own conscience, she needed to know. If she died, she wanted to know what had happened to Culver in these intervening years.

He gave a one-shouldered shrug and prodded the fire with a stick. "No. You married," he added, his voice flat, filled with resentment.

"Yes, I married Fernando."

"Were you...happy?"

Unable to bear his burning gaze, Pilar looked down at the fire, continuing to slowly turn the meat. "Fer-

nando was a dear friend,'' she whispered tremulously.
''He…was generous.''

''Rich?'' Culver didn't mean for his voice to sound
hard. He wanted to know of Pilar's past. He saw how
his spat-out query had struck her. She winced, unable
to look up at him.

''Yes, Fernando was rich.'' With obvious effort,
she lifted her chin and eventually met his gaze. ''He
was rich from the heart, too, and that was why—well,
why I agreed to marry him.''

It wasn't unusual in this culture, Culver knew, for
an old man to take a young wife. He was sure Fernando had been more than satisfied in the bargain.
Too, marriages here were often arranged, though he
had a hard time picturing that for Pilar, with her independence. His mouth compressing, he asked, ''Was
Fernando a friend of your father's?''

''Yes, he worked at the Spanish consulate as assistant to my father. They were the closest of friends.''

''I see.'' So it had been an arranged marriage. Culver stared down at the dark brown leaves and twigs
that covered the ground beneath them. Pilar's father
had undoubtedly betrothed Pilar to Fernando when
she was a young girl of ten or eleven. The agreement
would have been that when she reached a certain age,
they would marry. Had that age been twenty-one?

His mind raced with these potential new answers
to his old questions. By South American custom, Pilar
would have had to give up her independence and
marry Fernando whether she wanted to or not. Culver

had crashed into her life when she was twenty-two. And he'd taken her virginity, no question of that. Virginity was a virtue highly prized by South American men.

Perhaps Fernando had demanded Pilar's hand in marriage when she'd come off their mission. Though Pilar was independent by the standards of a South American woman, her Quechua blood also made her a product of her culture. She couldn't operate completely outside it and survive. Her fling with him had been exactly that—a wild, untrammeled instant out of time. Her opportunity to explore her curiosity about a man's touch. Maybe Pilar hadn't meant to give him her virginity. Maybe she'd been as carried away by the moment as he had—to her later regret.

Culver wasn't sure if Pilar had ever loved him. She had been young and naive. He'd had enough women over the years to know that that much hadn't been an act. And she definitely had been a virgin when she'd come into his embrace. Perhaps Pilar had fallen in love with him—the sort of girlish, romantic love that was lucky to last beyond two or three months.

He knew his own feelings had been deep and real, more than a passing infatuation. Though, to give her credit, he'd been so overwhelmed by the intensity of his emotions at the time that he hadn't stopped to think about long-range plans. He'd felt then as if life stretched out forever before them. Serious decisions had seemed miles away, so he hadn't talked of love and marriage. As he glanced at Pilar's sad features now, his heart twinged with that old, never-forgotten love. Pilar's fault in this might have been nothing more than youthful ignorance, he realized now. He'd been the sorry fool to love her honestly, to the depths of his soul. Pilar hadn't had the experience to recognize what he was giving her—and what it meant to him. How could she? Fernando might have gotten her body, but had he touched her soul? Culver knew that when he and Pilar had kissed back there on the trail, he had tapped into her soul as surely as he had eight years ago.

Now she was a widow with a child, but far too young in South American society to get the usual widow's respect. And men of this hemisphere probably were threatened by her independence, money and full-time career.

"Where did you go after you went home to North America?" Pilar asked, breaking the thoughtful silence that lay between them. Around them, monkeys were howling and screaming to one another. As the insects of the night began their songs, it were as if a musical surrounded them, soft and nonintrusive to the web of good feelings spinning between them as they huddled in the shelter of the lean-to.

"I recuperated in Bethesda, Maryland," Culver said slowly, rolling a twig between his thumb and forefinger, studying it critically in the coming darkness. "After that, I was sent to Europe to work undercover in Spain."

Pilar smiled softly. "My father's home."

"Yes. I was stationed in Madrid."

Sighing, Pilar met and held his tender gaze. "I have always wanted to go to Spain, to see my father's hacienda, to visit where he was born. I heard so many stories, growing up, about how he used to escape from his nanny and ride the countryside around Madrid on his Andalusian gelding. His nanny, who was in her fifties, was poor at riding and would take him out only occasionally."

"So you have your father's love of horses." Culver suddenly felt aware of how much he didn't know about Pilar. Their time together eight years earlier had been concentrated, passionate and dangerous, leaving little time for talking or in-depth exploration. Now he savored this moment more than he'd ever have thought possible. They were safe. They were alone and without interruption. Stretching out so that his legs curved behind her, his head resting in the palm of his hand, he studied her in the failing light.

Pilar chuckled slightly. "My father said I had the blood of a caballero—a horse person—in me from a very young age."

"Did he take you riding as a child?"

"Often. I loved it. He bought me a Pampas pony from Argentina—a Spanish mustang—and I took lessons at a riding academy in Lima when I was six." Smiling wistfully, Pilar said, "My father made a point of riding with me each Saturday. It was our time together, and I loved it." She sobered, looking out into the grayness. "I loved him so much. I miss him even more now—his counsel, his wisdom...."

Fog was developing at the lowest level of the canopy. Culver watched it disinterestedly as he absorbed the tremor in Pilar's tone. Her eyebrows knitted as she leaned over the fire, tending to the skewer. One of the positives of South American culture, he thought, was the connectedness of families and how close extended families remained, whereas in the U.S., the family unit had, for all intents and purposes, been dissolving rapidly.

"When Fernando died, did you feel alone?"

Pilar twisted to look at him. How peaceful Culver seemed, stretched out like a jaguar at rest. But he was lethal—to her volatile, vulnerable emotional state— as never before. "I felt like a ship without a rudder," she admitted. "I was in Lima, alone. My parents were dead, and I was an only child. The sole family I had left was here in the village—my grandparents. My father's family lives in Spain, and when Fernando died so suddenly, I thought briefly of moving to Madrid to be near them. I...I needed someone at that time...."

Pilar didn't tell Culver she'd needed him, though it was true. It would have been cruel to say so. She fully realized what her decision to leave him at the hospital had cost him, and she didn't wish ever to inflict that kind of injury again. From that perspective, had their kiss been good or bad? She wasn't sure. It certainly had opened up a kaleidoscope of memories and yearnings she'd thought she had put to rest over the years. Evidently she hadn't.

"What stopped you from moving to Spain?"

With a shrug, Pilar picked at a rectangular piece of white meat with her fingers, delicately pulling a strip off and tasting it. Their meal was done. Picking up two small palm leaves to serve as plates, Pilar divided the meat between them. As she handed Culver his share, she said, "I cannot ever ignore my Incan blood, my ancestry as an Indian. Moving to Spain would be like dividing my soul from my body." She looked out at the jungle lovingly. "This is my soul, Culver. Here, in the forest, the womb of Mother Earth.

"My grandmother has helped me see the wisdom of staying, in terms of looking deep into my heart and understanding that my power, my strength, comes from the soil I was born on." She pulled a piece of snake meat apart and ate another bite.

"Because you are a *shamanka* jaguar apprentice?" he wondered aloud, chewing a bite of the snake, which tasted like fresh, grilled chicken.

"In part, yes." She smiled a little. "As a *shamanka,* I would always have the capacity to walk in many worlds simultaneously, Grandmother said. Some know me as manager of a horse farm. Others as a competing rider at horse shows. I am a socialite to others, a rich widow, a woman without a husband. Then to others, I am a mestiza—or an undercover agent." She looked up, a smile playing on her lips. "Or a *shamanka* apprentice."

"You wear many hats," Culver agreed. For him, she was a friend, lover and confidante—the woman he wanted to make his wife. The only woman. Pilar would never know that, however, he thought, and an incredible sadness blanketed him.

"Since Fernando's death two years ago, I have tried to come here more often, but I see now it has not been often enough. Rane needs family, and she has no one in Lima or at the rancho. She needs to know the love, support and guiding wisdom of her great-grandparents." Her smile dissolved. "I need them, too," she added in a whisper.

"I imagine," Culver said in a low tone as he finished his portion of the snake meat, "you need them more than ever."

With a little laugh, Pilar said, "I have been seriously thinking of quitting my job as rancho manager and moving to my grandparents' village."

Culver's eyes narrowed on her. Pilar had been educated in the U.S., at Harvard, sent abroad to get the best possible education, as was common for the children of rich families in Lima. She had a degree in economics, and her father had once planned for her to go into the family business in Spain, a manufacturing concern. But with his early death, none of that had transpired.

"What would you do in a village with no electricity? No modern conveniences?"

Laughing gently, Pilar finished her meal and plucked some of the damp leaves just outside the lean-to, using them to wash her fingers. "You may be shocked to hear that I prefer the light of the sun and moon to electricity. So what if we have no indoor plumbing? We have a spring-fed pond where I can wash at the end of each day, in pure water, without chemicals, unspoiled by the hand of man. The vegetables my grandparents raise are healthful, grown without pesticides in rich, composted soil." She shook her head gravely. "No, Culver, I find life in my grandparents' village calling me strongly. Rane would have a family there—and I could be with her, guiding and teaching her in so many ways that haven't been possible in Lima. City life deadens one's heart, disconnecting us from the sacred unseen that lives and breathes around us." She held his dark, thoughtful gaze. "I know you understand what I am saying."

"I feel it," he agreed in a roughened tone. "And I don't disagree. City life is a big disconnect from the country—from so many things. I never thought I'd hear myself say it, but I could actually see myself living in a village like your grandparents'. I'm ready to give up my high-risk merc life. Maybe it's going to extremes, but I'd like to experiment with something simple in a way that's not available in the U.S. anymore."

Pilar absorbed his words, heartened by his obvious love for the village life that was so important to her. She shivered. "I was never so glad to leave Lima as right after Fernando's death, when I went to visit my grandparents. I hated the hypocritical aristocrats who, once Fernando wasn't there to protect me, again looked at me as if I were less than them because I was mestiza.''

''Your mestiza blood is the royal blood of Incan kings,'' Culver said. ''It's nothing to be ashamed of. It's something to be proud of.''

Pilar opened her hands in a helpless gesture. ''It's one more reason to get Rane back to the village. I want her to reconnect with her Incan roots. I didn't have that choice, growing up, and I see the struggles I've had, reaching back to that deep instinctive part of who I really am. I want Rane to dig her small fingers into the rich, black soil. I want her to laugh in a thunderstorm and feel the cool drops of water refreshing her. I want her to lose herself in the beauty of the Andes and the caressing moisture of our beloved jungle.'' She stopped, realizing she was babbling. ''I want so much for her....'' she whispered.

''You want for Rane what was denied you,'' Culver said gently. He saw tears glittering in Pilar's eyes, and in that moment realized how alone she had been all her life. It was true, her father was a powerful and rich Spanish diplomat, but her blood was in the Incan soil of Peru. And because Pilar's mother had been trapped in a society that did not honor women or their needs, he was sure Pilar hadn't been allowed to go home—to the spiritual home that he knew her grandparents' village was for her.

''Yes,'' Pilar murmured, feeling tired and very old.

She sifted some of the dark, moist soil through her fingers, using it to douse their fire in its deep pit. "Rane is the light of my heart, my only future," she began, her voice raw with emotion. "I do not want her family ripped away from her as mine was. I want her to know the love of a man and a woman. If she can't have a father, at least she can have a grandfather." She squeezed her eyes shut, fighting back tears. "Rane reminds me of myself so long ago. I felt so lost growing up, but now I know why. Something deep within me is driving me to leave Lima and come back here, to my roots."

Culver nodded and stretched out, using his arm as a pillow. He could no longer see anything beyond Pilar's silhouette, but that didn't matter. He reached out, his fingers coming to rest on her bent, tense back. "Come on, lie down here beside me," he entreated huskily. "You're tired. You've been through a lot in the past couple of days...."

Dashing the tears from her eyes, Pilar acquiesced. Culver's hand felt steadying. If she was going to die on this mission, for her last night on earth, like a greedy miser, she wanted to gather to her as much as she could of that thing that was most important to her—time with the only man she had ever loved. Culver made it so easy for her to lie down beside him and stretch her length against him. Her back fit against his chest, and where their hips met, she felt an instant ache.

But it could not be. She dared not love him—even

if it was for the last time. Exhausted emotionally, she felt Culver place his arm beneath her head.

"Here," Culver whispered thickly, positioning his hand against her hair and guiding her head to his shoulder, "lie on me." A sigh escaped him as Pilar fitted her head and shoulder against him. They were far enough apart to allow the humid breeze to move between them. It was simply too hot to lie pressed together, though that was exactly what Culver wanted with every fiber of his being. He wanted to tear the clothes off her small, beautiful body and press into her until they breathed each breath together, and their hearts thundered in that mystical, powerful union he so ached to experience again.

The terror that Pilar might die filled him as he felt her tired body surrender to him. He sensed a fine tension running through her as he placed his hand protectively on her upper arm. The night beings—crickets and frogs—sang to them as he closed his eyes and inhaled Pilar's unique fragrance. Little by little, she began to truly relax, as if sinking not only into his light embrace, but into the arms of Mother Earth herself.

Somewhere in the distance, Culver heard thunder rumbling as if to warn him of the coming daylight— and the coming danger Pilar would be in. Was there any other plan possible, rather than sending her into Ramirez's fortress? Culver racked his brain as the night deepened around them and a vague fog shrouded them, muting the night creatures' sounds.

One thing was certain: if he were to walk into Ramirez's fortress, they'd blast him out of existence in a hail of submachine-gun fire.

Pilar's soft breath caressed his outstretched arm, which she lay on like a pillow. The heavy strands of her ebony hair were silky against it, and the velvet of her cheek was soothing. Stabilizing…

Culver jerked awake. He must have fallen asleep, but he didn't remember doing so, because his mind had been crawling with possibilities of how to keep Pilar safe. Somewhere above the canopy, a full moon shone, and as he looked over her small form, the jungle around them appeared luminescent and otherworldly. Fingers of fog drifted among the dark shapes of a huge variety of leaves. He shifted his awareness to Pilar. Sometime during the night she had turned over, and her face now pressed into the hollow of his shoulder, her limp arm curved across his torso. Her small breasts moved with each slow breath she took.

Culver's eyes filled with tears as he pulled away just enough to gaze down at her sleeping features. Her lips were parted, her lashes dark fans against her cheekbones. Innocence radiated from her. Her hair was curling from the humidity, curving around her oval face. How could he ever have been angry with her? Culver felt he understood better now why Pilar had left him. He could accept her explanation, knowing the cultural bounds she had to survive within.

With his finger, Culver lightly traced the winged arch of her eyebrow, following it down the slender curve of her jawline to her neck. Her skin was damp from the humidity, and he felt the slow, constant pulse at the side of her neck. What a brave, courageous heart she had, Culver thought. For no apparent reason, the image of Rane's face hovered before him. The child had her mother's oval face and Incan features, from her large, slightly slanted eyes to the voluptuous, bowlike mouth. Yet Culver saw her father in her, too—a mouth that was more set, more stubborn than Pilar's, and her eyebrows weren't wing-shaped. He saw other differences, too. Her skin tone was lighter than her mother's. Culver hadn't thought about that much, because many Castilian Spanish were light skinned.

Rane's eyes were much lighter brown than Pilar's, though they possessed the same jaguar gold in their depths. He smiled a little. That kid was going to break many a young man's heart when she grew up. Yes, she was a heartbreaker just like her mother, though she'd be taller and more sturdily built than Pilar. He recalled the photo of Fernando, and how slender and light framed the man had been. Where did Rane get her build? he wondered. Pilar's bone structure had always seemed fragile as a bird's despite her strength and tenacity.

Perhaps Rane had gotten genes from some long-ago relative on Fernando's family tree, someone who had been larger and more broad shouldered, as she was. Judging from her height now, Culver guessed she would be five-eight or five-ten by the time she

was a young woman, and those proud shoulders and
that erect carriage would work in her favor.

Pilar whimpered in her sleep, pulling Culver out of
his thoughts. The sound wasn't loud—more like the
soft, frightened cry of a child left alone in the dark.
Gently, he caressed her hair, shoulders and back to
soothe away whatever was scaring her. Within moments, the small wrinkles that had gathered on her
broad forehead disappeared.

How easy it was to love her. Culver smiled tenderly. Just one touch took away her fear. And God
knew, she had reason to fear. Worriedly, he lifted his
head and stared out at foggy, moonlit landscape. His
mind again touched on the possibility of Pilar dying,
and instantly he recoiled from the thought. He'd just
found her again. He couldn't lose her so soon. Then
he laughed harshly at himself. Pilar wasn't his to
have, any more than he could reach out into the neb-
ulous moonlight and capture those ethereal strands of
fog.

Too much from the past still stood in the way. Pilar
hadn't said she wanted him back, and Culver knew
her well enough to realize she would have said it if
it were true. No, her destiny was elsewhere; he wasn't
part of her life's picture. Oddly, the realization didn't
pain him as much as before. The kiss they'd shared
had been as much healing as it had been a sensuous
reminder of their shared past.

Culver sensed it was near dawn—perhaps another
hour till daylight. Their night in each other's arms

was nearly over. Their only night. An ache centered in his chest. He could die today, too. They both could. As he lay on his side, absorbing every detail of her lovely face into his heart, he wished for so much.

When he'd met Pilar at that embassy ball, she'd stood there in a white silk gown that lovingly outlined every contour of her body, and the powerful urge had struck him to take her, love her and plant the seeds of children in her—that this could be the woman to settle down and raise a family with. Never had Culver entertained such thoughts before meeting—Pilar. Gently, he caressed the crown of her hair, knowing she was a true earth mother. Though she was small, her hips were naturally wide, and he knew she'd be able to carry babies well. Many babies. Their babies. Slowly, unwillingly, he began to recall that first time they'd made love, a month after their embassy meeting....

"I want to bathe," Pilar said. She stood on a grassy bank by a shallow green pool they'd discovered. Above her, a narrow waterfall splashed into the pool with a constant, soothing sound.

Culver nodded and studied the area. "I think we're safe here," he told her gruffly. Pilar wore a short-sleeved, khaki blouse and slacks, with a brown leather belt cinching her slender waist. Though her clothing was masculine by South American standards, it took nothing away from her powerful femininity. That shined through, Culver decided, whether she was in a clinging white silk gown at an embassy ball, as when they'd met, or dressed for this dangerous mission, where they played a deadly tag with cocaine growers in the mountains north of Lima.

Culver saw the relief in Pilar's face and allowed a partial smile to form on his mouth. They were both hot, dirty and stressed to the limit. For a week, they'd been chased by Ramirez's soldiers. But now it looked as if they'd gone deep enough into the jungle to lose them. Culver knew the respite was temporary, but they desperately needed time out for a good night's sleep and a chance to recoup.

"Turn around," Pilar ordered, her lips curving in a shy smile.

Reluctantly, he did so. His loins ached with need. Being around Pilar was an exquisite torture he could barely endure. At twenty-five, he'd thought he knew everything about the wiles and ways of women from his CIA travels around the world, but he'd been so very wrong. Pilar's sultry golden gaze made him feel like a wildfire out of control.

Hearing a splash, he turned automatically, an unconscious agent's reaction to the slightest sound after a month on the run from men who would kill them without hesitation.

Too late. Pilar stood in the center of the emerald pool, her wet hair gleaming in the afternoon sunlight that dappled the sparkling surface. His mouth went dry and his heart started a slow pounding that this time wasn't due to fear.

Pilar was naked, her lithe golden body gleaming with the water that ran off it in rivulets as she lifted her hands to slick back her nearly waist length hair. When her lashes lifted and her gaze met his, she froze, standing like a statue, her hands still in her hair. Her lips parted. Culver groaned, the sound coming out in an animal-like growl. Somewhere in his spinning senses, as he devoured her with his gaze, he recalled the old shaman telling him he'd meet a jaguar priestess north of Lima who would steal his heart. Well, right now, Culver would gladly sell his soul to the devil himself to have her.

Though everything in his training forbade it, it was as if an invisible force was pushing him forward. He held Pilar's startled gaze as, piece by piece, he dropped his clothing on the bank. It was as if some strange spell had come over him. Was it her huge golden eyes rimmed with sable brown that held him captive? Culver no longer cared. All he knew in that suspended moment out of time was that Pilar was his; they belonged together. She was his mate, his destiny.

Culver heard a splash and realized he'd stepped into the cool water of the pool. White sand glowed beneath his feet as he waded toward Pilar, their eyes still fixed upon each other. This time, he knew, he was helpless to stop himself. A new and urgent desire to make Pilar his once and for all overwhelmed him. The water deepened as the sand sloped gently downward. Pilar stood in waist-deep water, her small, uplifted breasts taut, the nipples full and hardened.

Slowly, very slowly, she allowed her fingers to ease from her hair. Culver's eyes narrowed and he felt his body respond powerfully to her femininity. Culver was young, and strong and handsome as he walked toward her. With each step he took, he was mesmerized by the flow of her thick black hair rippling around her shoulders and breasts. His heart pounded wildly in his chest, and he saw her lift one hand and barely touch the top of her breast as she waited breathlessly for him.

It seemed so right to him—her waiting as he waded slowly toward her. He saw the intent in her golden eyes, which captured and held him prisoner. Oh, how many times had he ached to kiss her? As the dappled light moved across his tight, hard body, Pilar's lips parted in anticipation. Yes, this was right. So very, very right. No longer did Culver allow years of training to whisper that loving this woman was forbidden. From the moment he'd met her at the ball, he'd known Pilar was destined to hold a special place in his life.

Culver knew that Pilar lived in two worlds: Quechua and Spanish. And between two religions— Catholic and shamanic. Perhaps that was why this felt so right. She was South American; he, North American. All her life, Pilar had experienced opposing lifestyles and philosophies. It seemed fitting that her first time loving would be with a man who was not of her world.

As Culver halted mere inches from her and reached

out with his right hand, Pilar closed her eyes and waited. He knew she didn't know how to love a man— only whatever she might have heard from other girls on her university campus. It didn't matter. Now she waited for his touch—for that coming together he'd dreamed of since their fated meeting in Lima.

As his palm grazed her wet hair, a small gasp escaped her lips. Culver's fingers trembled imperceptibly as they ranged downward toward her shoulder, where the thick, ebony mass lay, then curved across her left breast.

"I'll be gentle...."

His growled words seemed to ease the fear of the unknown he'd seen banked in her eyes. His touch proved galvanizing, provocative. Pilar swayed, seeming dizzied by the feel of his lingering fingers on her sensitive skin. Barely opening her eyes, she looked at him. Despite her innocence, he could see a kind of knowing in her gaze—probably due to her shamanic upbringing, he realized.

Without thinking, for being around Pilar seemed to erase his conscious mind and open his heart, he reached out and took her small hand, placing it on his chest. His skin tightened instantly at her touch, and he froze momentarily as Pilar boldly allowed her gaze to move upward, to meet the need he knew must be burning in his own eyes. He was barely aware of the light splashing of the waterfall behind them, of the melodic call of the birds and monkeys. All that existed in his world at this moment was Pilar.

He was going to kiss her. She was a novice at the ways of men and women, and Culver saw momentary anxiety in her eyes, as if she was afraid she might disappoint him. As her other hand came forward and touched his skin, her fingers automatically ranged upward, and Culver felt as if the sun itself was touching him. A new level of understanding seemed to come to life in her expression. He dipped his head to take her mouth, to ask her to surrender to something beautiful within her, and suddenly all the anxiety disappeared from her eyes. In its place, he saw a wonderful look of primal, heated desire, so essential that Culver groaned. Pilar raised up on her tiptoes and lifted her chin to meet him halfway.

As Culver's mouth settled on hers, he felt her tremble. In one smooth motion, he lifted her off her feet and up into his arms. Their mouths clung together as she lay warmly against his bulk. She'd closed her eyes, her arms automatically wrapping around the thick column of his neck as he waded back out of the pool with her. Culver lay Pilar on the soft carpet of grass, aware only of the natural way her supple body settled next to his. She was on her back, and he moved above her, his callused hands framing her face as he began in earnest to teach her how to kiss him.

He kept his mouth tender and cajoling, and her lips parted beneath his gentle assault. He tasted her power as she tasted him, the ragged moisture of her breath flowing across his face as he eagerly returned her tentative, exploring kiss. Her nipples tautened against him as the wall of his chest met her rounded breasts. He sank more heavily against her, and as he deepened the kiss, Culver's senses spun out of control. A low moan, like the throaty growl of a jaguar, reverberated in Pilar's chest as Culver's hand captured and followed the curve of her breast. Automatically, she strained upward, and Culver realized hazily that while she might not know exactly what she was asking for, her body knew.

He encircled her breast with his fingers and felt her skin tighten deliciously. Tearing his mouth from hers, he allowed his lips to settle on that hard, straining peak. Pilar uttered a small cry of surprise and pleasure. Automatically, she threw back her head and pressed herself against him. Her fingers opened and closed spasmodically against his thickly bunched shoulders as he suckled her, and a white-hot sensation bolted downward through him. Reaching out to her, he slid his fingers between her ripe, curved thighs, which parted willingly to him.

The world ceased to exist for Culver. He knew only the feel of Pilar's untutored mouth on his, the softness of her inner thighs. His breath became ragged, and he felt a silent plea from her as he slowly began to ease his fingers into the velvety inner folds of her womanhood. Oh! The pleasure was golden, hot sunlight falling wonderfully upon him. Her thighs parted farther, of their own accord, and Culver felt the depth of her need. No longer did he worry about taking her virginity or what her future husband might think. She had captured his soul and willingly offered herself to him in return.

Each stroking sensation of his fingers brought another shattering cry of pleasure from Pilar. As she moaned and twisted in his arms, pressing herself wantonly against him, a pressure began building like the power of a volcano within him. He heard her cry out his name, felt the reverberation of her voice move through him like the deep tone of a shamanic drumbeat. Moisture and warmth combined, and moments later Culver heard Pilar utter a small cry of surprise, felt her whole body tighten in an exquisite trembling that moved him to awe. He growled her name, but saw that her world in those moments consisted only of heat, light, intense pleasure and her gasping breaths. She clung to him, her form bowed tightly against his, hungrily absorbing the continued pleasuring of his fingers as he brought her to an exquisite fulfillment she'd never known before.

Moments later, Pilar opened her eyes and looked dazedly up at him. Culver's face was mere inches from hers, and at the sated, dazed expression in her luminous gaze, he felt alive as never before, all his senses intensified. He breathed in her exquisitely feminine scent, his body trembling as if the last of his control was disintegrating.

"You're like those orchids," he rasped, leaning down and caressing her lips. "A beautiful, opening orchid." He stroked her again, and she moaned, her lips—more sure now—needy upon his. Smiling to *himself, Culver was thankful he'd had enough control to allow her the gentle discovery of her first orgasm. She was trembling with pleasure, and he felt her thighs open again in silent invitation. There was only one way to do this, to welcome her into the world of a man loving his woman. In one sure motion, he rolled onto his back, moving Pilar on top of him, positioning her legs across him so that the moist wetness of her womanhood made direct contact with him. He groaned as he felt her featherlike weight settle provocatively upon him. Gripping her arms tightly, he felt his lips draw away from his clenched teeth as her womanly heat bathed him.*

The sultry look on Pilar's face as she settled upon him included surprise and joy. Culver watched her expression closely as he gripped her slim hips and slowly began to ease her back and forth across his hardened member. Her lips parted, and he saw her eyes go gold again with utter pleasure. "Enjoy me," he growled. "Take me into you as much as you want...." This way, he knew, he would not hurt her. This way, she'd have a chance to adjust to him naturally, as her own desire dictated. He continued to rock her back and forth, feeling her hands move of their own accord across his torso and chest. She seemed lost in a world of intense pleasure, and Culver felt the hot explosion within his knotted loins moving closer. He didn't know how much longer he could control himself.

When Pilar leaned forward then eased back, Culver

growled. Her silken depths were hot and tight. He felt her hesitate, felt her body begin to accommodate him—felt the veil within her that told him unequivocally that she was a virgin. Moving his hands upward, he caressed her straining breasts and captured her nipples between his thumbs and forefingers. Instantly, she gasped, and her hips moved in a primitive knowing. Culver increased the intensity of his contact, pressing up against that wall within her. He knew she was feeling pressure as well as some pain. Stretching upward, he put one hand on her back and brought her forward, his lips capturing one of her nipples.

As he suckled her, he felt her melt against him. He curved his other hand along her lower back and hips and drew her close, feeling the veil break within her. A small cry escaped her lips and he teethed her nipple, transferring her attention from the discomfort below to the pleasure above. Pilar had frozen momentarily as he'd pierced her virginity, but as his lips and tongue continued their ardent attention at her taut nipple, she sighed like a contented jaguar and lowered her head till her forehead rested against his hair. Realizing her pain was gone, he released her nipple and, sitting up, brought her legs around him so that she could sit on him. The look in her eyes was one of cloudy pleasure, the last remnants of pain quickly dissolving as he moved his hips to bring that pleasure full circle.

Framing her face, he took her mouth, deeply. Irrevocably. Thrusting his tongue into her hot, liquid depths, he allowed it to tangle with hers. Her hands clenched at his shoulders and she surged forward like butter melting upon him. He felt her body accepting him, and to his great joy and intense pleasure, she began to move her hips in a rocking motion, her movements so evocative that at last they snapped his massive control. The tantalizing friction within her hot tight confines was too much for even him to bear. Groaning deeply, he helped her move against him and heard her gasp, this time with the luxury of pleasure.

The scent of orchids teased his flared nostrils, heavy and fragrant even as the velvet of her body encircled him, holding him a willing prisoner. With each rhythmic movement, Culver felt himself hurtling toward an explosion he could no longer contain. He gripped her hips hard and felt the volcanic release surge through him and into her. She cried out, and he growled her name, his arms wrapped tightly around her slender form. He felt as if he became a jaguar in that moment, and she, his eternal mate.

Culver's eyes closed, and all he could do was hold her tightly, rigid with such a white-hot pleasure such as he had never tasted before. The oneness with her that spun through him at that moment was unlike anything he'd experienced in his life. They were no longer man and woman. They were one being of light and energy, and Culver understood for the first time in his life what love really meant. It meant losing himself completely in his mate—a giving over, a wonderful surrendering of not only his physical body, but

*of his heart and soul as well. In those split seconds
after his release, he felt two things. One was that he
wanted Pilar to be pregnant with his child—a child
created out of their intense coupling and the love he
held for her. The second was that Pilar was his mate
for life. No other woman could ever hold his heart as
she now held it, gently within the confines of her own
heart and body. No one....*

As he picked up a strand of her hair and tested its
pliancy between his thumb and index finger, Culver
shook his head. If Pilar had known how many times
he'd almost broached the subject of marriage, she'd
no doubt have laughed at his foolishness. Always before, Culver had taken his time with a woman, set his
own pace. And never before or since Pilar had he
been so smitten. They'd made love three more times
in those long-ago, dangerous days. And although he'd
loved her, he'd never said the words. But this time
he had a chance to make unerringly clear exactly how
he felt about her.

Yes, they could have made some beautiful children
between them, and God knew, these children would
have been well loved. He'd been willing to give up
his traveling for her—for them. Raised in a loving
household of eight, Culver knew the strength of the
family unit. His parents had loved him and his siblings well and continuously, and he'd wanted to experience that with Pilar through children created out
of the fires of their own love.

Now that idea—once so certain—was a dust-covered dream, buried deep in the vault of his heart, with no chance of resurrection. But dammit, he wanted—no, demanded—a second chance. Culver laid the strand of hair gently on the side of Pilar's face and watched it bend to the contours of her bone structure. He didn't dare think of the future—or the past. Only the present was alive now. Very possibly, they had no future at all, beyond this day and evening. By nightfall, they would have arrived at the fortress. From then on, each breath they took might be their last.

A gut-wrenching cry started deep within Culver as he continued to stroke Pilar's cheek. Life was so unfair. Of all the people who deserved to live, Pilar was foremost. She wasn't a bad person, just a woman caught in a culture that didn't respect her as a human being. They could have had so much together had she not run back to Fernando to fulfill her marriage obligation.

The fire in Culver's loins throbbed like a pulsating drumbeat begging to be released—by her. Pilar knew she might not survive this day. She had already kissed him. Might she consent to make love to him? His heart beat hard at the errant thought. As he laid his hand on her shoulder, his fingers lightly kneading the flesh beneath her blouse, he decided he was going to find out.

Chapter 9

Just as Culver leaned forward to place his mouth tenderly against Pilar's, he heard the heavy whapping of helicopter blades moving rapidly in their direction. Instantly, he gripped Pilar's shoulder and shook her awake.

"Let's get out of here," he rasped, practically dragging her out of the shelter and into his arms. He saw the confusion in her sleep-ridden eyes as she gripped his shoulders to steady herself.

"What?" she asked thickly.

It was still dark, but Culver's eyes had long since adjusted to the gloom. "A helicopter," he said in a harsh whisper, pulling her away from the lean-to and into the jungle's cover. He put his arm around her waist holding her close beside him as they crashed through a tangle of vines and over brush.

Fear gushed through Pilar as she clung to Culver for balance. He was like a bulldozer, knocking down small trees and plants as he lunged forward. In her barely functioning mind, she knew the helicopter could be one of Ramirez's. Keying her hearing, she tried to shake away the hand of slumber. She had been sleeping deeply, better than she could recall in a very long time—but then, she'd been in Culver's arms. She'd felt safe. Protected.

Even now as she stumbled along, sometimes tripping over exposed roots in the darkness, she felt protected. Culver wasn't wearing his shirt, and she felt the power of his muscles as she hugged his waist.

The helicopter drew closer, the *whap, whap, whap* of its blades punctuating the dense fog still lying like a blanket over the treetops.

"Here," Culver grunted.

Pilar felt herself being hauled up beside a huge rubber tree. He flattened her against the tree's smooth bark and moved protectively in front of her, shielding her with his body. Her face was pressed against his naked chest, the hair tickling her nose. She heard the powerful pumping of his heart, felt the strength and warmth of his body as he leaned forward to completely shield her from any possible view as the helicopter moved ever closer.

Pilar wanted to struggle, but it was useless. Culver was looking upward, his eyes narrowed, his eyebrows drawn in concentration. Now she was experiencing the warrior side of him, a side she'd known so well eight years ago. By shielding her with his body, he was making himself a potential target. Her mouth went dry as the sound of the helicopter continued to reverberate through the jungle. While the fog absorbed some of it, the humidity accentuated the vibration, so that Pilar could feel the resonation through the trunk of the tree she was pressed against.

Fear mingled with concern for Culver. If it was one of Ramirez's helicopters—and who else besides the Peruvian army had them out here?—it could mean a team of drug runners was being flown in. Or the aircraft could be intending to land at the fortress and take millions of dollars worth of the white powder known as cocaine to some distant drop point.

Pilar's hands rested tautly against Culver's waist. Perspiration made her palms slick against his skin. She looked up as the vibration and noise heightened, and Culver automatically pressed her more closely against the tree. What if Ramirez's pilots saw them? Did the aircraft possess the infrared technology necessary to detect them by their body heat alone? Real fear choked Pilar, and she struggled to breathe.

The helicopter roared overhead, probably two or three hundred feet above the canopy, skimming the edge of the fog. Culver let out a ragged sigh of relief as the chopper continued its trajectory toward the east. Easing away from the trunk of the tree, he could barely make out Pilar's stricken features in the growing light of dawn. Terror showed in her eyes and in her parted lips. Her hair lay in disarray around her face, and automatically he smoothed several strands away from her eyes.

"It's okay," he rasped unsteadily. Stepping away from the tree, he kept his hand on her arm, because she seemed as if she might fall. Pilar touched her brow and gave him a grateful look as he guided her away from the tangled roots of the tree to a flatter area.

"I never expected a helicopter," she confided breathlessly.

Culver frowned. "Makes two of us." Shaking his head, he added, "I got too relaxed. I should have been expecting something like this. Though we're on the periphery of Ramirez's fiefdom, I should have been more alert."

"No," Pilar whispered as she turned and faced him, her hands resting on his forearms. "You couldn't have known, Culver."

"Maybe not." He absorbed Pilar's upturned features. Her clothes were wrinkled, clinging to her curves in the humidity. How hauntingly beautiful she looked. His mouth twisted tenderly as he reached out and caressed her hair. "You look so beautiful...."

Where had that come from? Culver cursed himself for allowing the intimacy to escape. For an instant, he thought he saw Pilar's dark, fear-filled eyes turn tender with longing—for him. But just as quickly, she hid her reaction to his words, to his touch. Bitterly, he forced his hand back to his side.

"Come on," he growled, "we've got to get packed up and go. We're going to have to be careful today. Really careful."

Still trembling from his unexpected caress, Pilar had to force herself not to step closer to Culver. Right now, she wanted to kiss him—and love him. Her heart bled with the truth—that he could never want her as she needed him. Culver might have forgiven her, but Pilar knew that the past now lay buried permanently between them. Not even a man of Culver's generous heart could be expected to forgive her for the dark secret she carried.

Following him back to the lean-to, Pilar gently put to rest her heart's overwhelming longing for him— for a future together. After all, today could well be the last day of her life. She was going to absorb each moment with Culver and enjoy him on every level she could. And he wouldn't even have to know.

"We'll stop here," Culver said. It was midday, and in about three hours they would reach Ramirez's fortress. The jungle was thick around them, and the path they followed had probably been made by wild pigs. More than once, Culver had spotted jaguar spoor along the trail. The big cats probably waited patiently in the twisted, gnarled limbs of a rubber tree over the path, then dropped silently down upon whatever unfortunate pig or other animal passed by below.

Pilar shrugged out of her pack and placed it beside a fallen log, which she gratefully used as a seat. Culver joined her, sitting about six inches away. They hadn't spoken much today. They knew that small villages were situated all around them, and hunters could be out combing the jungle for meat, or women might be looking for roots and berries nearby. The jungle was so thick that unless one knew exactly what to look and listen for, a person could easily pass within ten feet of another and not be noticed. Consequently, they had kept verbal communications to a bare minimum, relying on hand signals when necessary.

After taking a refreshing drink of water, Pilar passed her canteen to Culver. She watched as the container nearly disappeared within his huge, callused grasp, and he tipped his head back to drink. His neck was thick and strong, his Adam's apple bobbing with each gulp. His face was bathed in a sheen of sweat that accentuated his rugged features, and dark strands of hair lay plastered against his brow. As he finished drinking, he looked directly at her, and Pilar felt herself melting inwardly beneath his pale blue gaze as he studied her in the intervening silence. A tingle spread deliciously through her as his careful look seemed to caress her face, lingering on her mouth, then moving down to embrace her breasts. But he turned away abruptly, frowning, and capped the canteen.

Wiping his mouth with the back of his hand, Culver reached inside his knapsack. Drawing out a holstered pistol, he strapped it about his waist. The time was upon them. He eased his leg over the log, straddling it so that he faced Pilar. Tension was evident in the set of her full lips and the worry she couldn't hide in her expressive eyes.

Taking her hand and easing her around so that she, too, straddled the log facing him, Culver gave her an intense look. "From here on out, things are going to get dicey," he said softly.

"I know," Pilar whispered, her voice barely audible. She tightened her fingers around Culver's strong hand. He seemed so confident, she thought, and she felt so helpless.

"I may not get to say too much from here on out," he murmured in a low voice. He lifted his head and surveyed the jungle around them critically. Swinging his gaze back to Pilar, he continued in a roughened tone, "Dammit, I wish this wasn't going down. I would much rather walk into Ramirez's snake pit than send you. I know it's not possible, but that's what I wish, Pilar." His hand tightened on her slender one. "Whatever you do, don't take chances." He stared at her hard. "I want you alive. Do you hear me? *Alive.*"

Looking away, Culver fought the tears that pricked the backs of his eyes. When he spoke again, his voice was raw with undisguised emotions. "I know there's a lot of pain and hurt between us. Eight years ago everything seemed so simple. We met, we...loved each other." He wanted to say, "We fell in love with each other," but he didn't. He had no idea any longer whether Pilar had seen him as her only fling before submitting to a marriage cast for her since childhood, or if she had truly loved him as he had her. The point was moot now anyway, wasn't it?

"I just want to say I'm sorry I took my anger out on you, Pilar. I understand better why you left me. I can even accept it...." His mouth flattened and he gazed into her luminous, tear-filled eyes. "You've got a beautiful little girl. Rane's the spitting image of you. I guess the main thing I hope for out of this is that you survive to live your dream of taking Rane back to your grandparents' village to grow up."

Pilar wanted to sob. She could see glittering moisture in Culver's eyes. Understanding just how hard it was for him to say these things nearly ripped her heart in two. But she didn't have the time to discuss things as she might want to. How could Culver ever really know why she'd left him? Just talking out loud was a risk to their lives right now, and she knew it.

Gripping his hands in hers, Pilar leaned forward, her voice soft and trembling. "Promise me one thing, Culver. I swear I'll never ask anything of you again—only this."

Shaken by her quiet intensity, he stared at her. "What is it?"

Swallowing against a lump forming in her throat, Pilar whispered, "Promise me that if I die, you will take care of Rane. Care for her as if she was your child.... *Dios,* this means so much to me. Take her back to the village and live with her and my grandparents. I know what I'm asking of you, but you're the only one I can trust with this. Love Rane and be her father in my absence. She needs a father.'' Her voice cracked with desperation as she said, ''Promise me you'll do this, Culver? For Rane, if not for me?''

Anxiously, Pilar searched his stoic expression and saw the tears gathering in his eyes. Up until this moment, she'd had no idea how much sway she still had with Culver, but she saw it now. His expression grew vulnerable at her pleading, and she was thankful. Nothing was more important than this last request. Pilar knew she might have ruined her own chances, but Rane had a whole life stretching out in front of her. With Culver's guiding hand, beneath his care and nurturing her daughter would blossom.

Looking away, Culver fought the tears. He'd never cried in front of anyone before. For some unknown reason, Pilar's request touched his aching heart as nothing else ever had. He felt her fingers gripping his, sensed her anxious gaze on his face as she waited for his answer. Agreeing could mean leaving his job as a mercenary and living in the village for at least a decade of his life. His gut wrenched, and he felt a powerful attachment toward Rane coming to life within him. He had no explanation for the feeling, but it was undeniably there, vibrant and alive. As alive as his love for Pilar.

Culver's heart twisted in his chest. Part of him wanted to go into denial and tell himself that of course Pilar would survive this mission and fulfill her dream for her daughter on her own. Another part of him—the hardened realist—recognized that she could very easily die. Meeting Pilar's gaze once more, he saw pain, love and hope burning in her guileless, golden eyes. How could he deny her anything? Even this?

"All right," he rasped, "I promise."

All the tension bled out of her, and she sank back, her shoulders sagging. "*Dios!* Thank you, *mi querido*. Thank you...."

"There's a possibility I'll get killed, too, you know."

Pilar nodded. Battling her tears, she covered her face with her hands momentarily. "I know," she rattled hoarsely. Allowing her hands to drop from her face, she looked up and absorbed Culver's vulnerable expression. How could she ever have doubted that he would fulfill her last request? Blindly reaching out, she wrapped her arms around his massive shoulders and pressed her cheek against his. "Th-thank you, *mi querido*. I will never forget your love for me. I...I promise you that." Swiftly, she kissed his lips, tearing her mouth from his and moving away before he could react. The burning desire that flamed instantly in Culver's eyes made her tremble. Pilar wanted nothing more than to love him fully. Completely. But their time was up.

"We must go," she said unsteadily as she stood. "It is time...."

* * *

Ramirez's fortress was large. Culver hunkered down beside Pilar as they watched the movements of the guards at the wrought-iron gate to the hacienda-style home, situated in a clearing in the jungle. The pale pink stucco seemed out of place amidst the greenery. A dirt road, rutted deeply with the tracks of four-wheel-drive vehicles, led to the fortress, connecting it to surrounding villages.

Dusk was upon them. Night would fall within half an hour. They had been crouching here for the past two hours, timing the guards, noting the vehicles that come and went. Several men, dressed like farmers, wore bandoliers of ammunition across their chests and carried submachine guns.

During the hours of waiting, Pilar's heart had settled down. The fear that had swept her like an ocean tide had eased a bit. She had changed into the costume of a village woman—a dark blue, cotton skirt hanging to her ankles, a white blouse and bare feet. She had braided her hair and put on several native necklaces. To anyone passing by, she was simply another Indian from one of the nearby villages.

Pilar wasn't sure how well Ramirez's guards knew the villagers. It would be impossible to recognize them all, she hoped; she would be taking that chance when she walked up to the gate. Though only the guards and Ramirez's staff lived within the fortress, food and water were supplied daily by villagers. She hoped the guards would see her as just another housekeeper come to fulfill part of her village's expected duty to Ramirez.

If they did doubt her, she could be taken prisoner at that point and interrogated—just as Morgan had been. But then their mission would fail.... No, she had to get into the fortress, confirm that Morgan was alive and make her way back to Culver, who would alert his contact, Major Mike Houston.

The Peruvian Special Forces helicopters would come flying in like the cavalry when Culver called. But first Pilar had to get back into the fortress at three in the morning, when the guards were at their least alert, and the household would be sleeping as well. It would be up to her to free Morgan and lead him out of the enclosure.

The plan had many ifs, Pilar acknowledged, but it was their only chance of saving Morgan. Well, first things first. She had to get inside the fortress. Nervously, she adjusted her blouse and looked up at Culver. Wordlessly, he gripped her and swept her into his arms. The breath escaped her in a near gasp of surprise as she felt herself pressed against his hard, male body. Tilting her chin, Pilar parted her lips and knew he was going to kiss her one last time.

Her eyelashes drifted closed as she felt Culver's breath wash across her face. She ached for contact and wasn't disappointed. His lips brushed hers with a demanding force. This kiss, she realized, was one of claiming, telling her how much he loved her—still. Lifting her arms, she slid them around Culver's neck, pressing herself wantonly against him as his mouth plundered hers and she drowned in the resulting splendor. His lips branded hers and she felt his tongue enter her, stroking her, letting her know she was the only woman for him.

Their breathing grew ragged as Pilar offered herself upon the altar of love. Culver tasted male, the saltiness of perspiration mingling with the sweetness of a mango he'd recently eaten. Hungrily, Pilar returned his ardor, and wanting to leave him indelibly touched by her lips, as proof of her unspoken love for him. Finally, tearing her mouth from his, she gripped his arms to steady herself. Her knees felt like jelly, and she was gasping for air as she met the full intensity of his narrowed, predatory gaze.

"I must go...." Abruptly she turned, hurrying away from him, because if she didn't leave that instant, she knew she'd burst into tears of grief, of loss. Oh, if only she could turn the clock back those eight long years and have a second chance at her tragic decisions. But, it was too late. Shifting her focus to the danger that lay ahead, she hurried through the jungle, moving swiftly and silently toward the edge of the clearing that held the fortress.

She did not look back. She didn't dare. Gripping her skirt, she raised the material above her knees and leapt to avoid small roots blocking the path before her. Her heart was pounding with fear as she saw a large, meaty guard moving lazily back and forth in front of the main gate. She prayed to the spirit of the jaguar to give her the cunning she needed to gain entrance.

Culver crouched, well hidden by the jungle. His mouth still tingled wildly in the wake of Pilar's heated response to his kiss. His body throbbing with unsated desire, he watched her approach the guard. It was so dark now that he couldn't see more than their silhouettes. Whatever Pilar was saying, the guard did not lower his deadly submachine gun from his shoulder. Blinking sweat out of his eyes, Culver held his breath. Would the man let her by?

They'd noticed a lot of activity—frequent comings and goings of villagers as night approached. Culver wondered if Ramirez was having some sort of feast or celebration. He'd also heard some singing, guitar playing and shouts coming from inside the compound. Now he saw Pilar lift her skirt and twirl in front of the guard. Despite his anxiety, Culver noted the elegant grace of her movement. At last the sentry lifted his arm and pointed, and Pilar disappeared through the wrought-iron gates.

Swallowing hard, Culver looked down at his watch. It was nine o'clock. Relief swept through him; she had been given access to the fortress. But she still had so many barriers to clear. Would she find Morgan? Would someone blow her cover? Keying his hearing, he heard several shouts, followed by laughter, the sounds happy and celebratory rather than threatening. Several jeeps drove up carrying armed guards. More

of Ramirez's goons, Culver thought as he watched
them being waved through.

His mouth dry with worry, Culver eased his bulk
down until his knees sank into the damp carpet of
decaying leaves near the huge rubber tree where he
hid. He had no way to know if Pilar got in trouble.
Though they'd brought state-of-the-art technology
with them, she couldn't chance wearing a mike and
radio. She must do nothing to rouse the curiosity of
the guards. Never had Culver prayed more than he
did now—for Pilar. He was relatively safe in comparison. If she was discovered, she'd be taken immediately to Ramirez.... Culver shuddered, unable to
follow that devastating line of thought.

Still, his mind veered this way and that, filled with
terrible fear for Pilar. Dammit, he should be protecting her. She shouldn't have to enter that pit by herself.
Yet he knew she was an excellent undercover agent
with an uncanny ability to camouflage herself, blend-
ing easily into her surroundings. She had jaguar medicine, he reminded himself as he rested his hands on
the taut fabric covering his thighs. Jaguars moved like
shadows in the jungle—undetected until the moment
they revealed themselves to freeze their victim with
a mesmerizing stare. Then and only then would they
pounce.

Wiping his mouth with the back of his hand, Culver
tried to keep his nervousness at bay. His mind swung
to safety measures he could institute if, God forbid,
Pilar should be taken prisoner. Unfortunately, he had

very few options. If the Special Forces came in, blasting away, Ramirez would counter with his army of loyal followers, and the fortress bristled with equal, if not better, firepower. Besides, Ramirez would likely put a gun to Pilar's head and blow her brains out even if they were able to breach his defenses.

Rane's face flashed before him—her delicate features and huge, light brown eyes with their look of innocence. Shaking his head, Culver wondered what in the hell that was all about, but he didn't have time to think it through. Pilar's life was on the line. How brave she was—courageous in a way few would ever be. Because Morgan had helped her and her people, she had boldly taken this mission—even knowing Culver would be her partner. That decision alone took guts, he admitted grimly. And he hadn't been kind to Pilar, either. Yet she'd braved his withering anger and had magically turned his fury back into burning desire. Her jaguar medicine again, Culver thought with a slight smile.

The Indians believed that jaguars could shape-shift into different forms, human and animal. Well, Pilar would need all of those talents and more to get to Morgan. So much could go wrong. What if Morgan was dead? Or so ill he was unable to leave the compound under his own power? Pilar could hardly carry him out on her own. Suddenly, Culver remembered Pilar's vision-vine ceremony. She had seen Morgan— like a robot, but able to move about. And without guards? Culver found it very hard to believe.

But he'd lived in Peru for five years, and he knew better than to laugh at mystical visions. Rubbing his jaw, his eyes narrowed, he continued staring at the entrance, praying for Pilar to hurry up and come out. Come out with good news of Morgan Trayhern.

Chapter 10

Pilar released a ragged breath of relief. Her vision-vine experience hadn't been wrong. She stood on the second floor of the hacienda, at the western corner, which was dark and hidden from the lights of the celebration taking place down in the courtyard below. Peeking through a small, barred window in a heavy door, she saw Morgan Trayhern sitting on a narrow cot.

Pressing herself back against the stucco of the hall-way, Pilar gulped, her heart pounding. Risking a second look, she watched Morgan for several moments, hardly daring to believe it was really him. Because of a huge shipment of cocaine successfully delivered to the United States, she'd been able to gather, Ramirez had ordered a party for his soldiers and the many people of the surrounding villages who collected and grew coca leaves for him.

It had been relatively easy to slip past the guard at the gate, who had looked at her with lascivious eyes. She'd told him she was one of the dancers for the celebration, and he'd easily accepted her explanation. Having memorized the blueprint of the fortress, Pilar had headed straight for the area where she believed Morgan was being held. Now she watched Morgan closely. His face was unshaven, his unkempt black beard slightly streaked with gray. He sat on the cot, his elbows on this thighs, his hands loosely clasped between his legs. His hair was long, unwashed and uncut, giving him a wild look. Obviously they had not allowed him to shower.

His clothes were threadbare and of the type a peasant farmer would wear. What bothered Pilar most, though, was the blank look in Morgan's usually intelligent gray eyes. His pupils appeared dilated, and she wondered if he was drugged. He sat motionless, staring into space, his face slack.

Suddenly she heard footsteps approaching up the stairs at the rear of the hacienda. It was one of the guards! The man wore a white cotton shirt with two bandoliers across his wide chest, a submachine gun resting on his left hip as he slowly climbed upward. Her heart pounding, Pilar realized she would be discovered. The black iron railing that enclosed the balcony leading to the second-floor rooms curved to an end a hundred feet away. Only one stairway reached it, and the sentry was on it.

Desperate, Pilar moved quickly to Morgan's door. Sliding her fingers over the knob, she twisted savagely. It opened! Not daring to believe her luck, she shoved the door open and slipped inside, praying Morgan would remember her, or at least realize she was friend, not foe. She knew drugs could distort a person's senses. Pilar had seen people turn paranoid—even against their loved ones.

She quietly shut the door and whirled to face Morgan. The window was open, and she could hear the guard's boots scuffing lazily against the red-tiled floor as he came closer.

Morgan didn't move. Pilar stared at him in utter disbelief, but he didn't so much as bat an eyelash at her unexpected presence. The guard drew closer. Pilar swallowed hard, her mouth dry, her heart pounding heavily in her chest. What if he came in to check on Morgan? She had nowhere to hide. The tiny room had no closets or bathroom.

Pilar didn't want to die. The feeling struck her so hard that a ragged breath tore from between her compressed lips. Her hearing keyed to the shuffling gait of the guard, and she pressed herself flat against the wall, out of view of the window. A sudden sound of metal striking the iron bars made her jump.

"Hey, gringo!" the guard snarled in Spanish. "Pig. You stink! Look at you. *Big Norte Americano* pig! You're filthy!"

Pilar's eyes widened tremendously as the guard ran what she thought must be the barrel of his weapon against the bars. She watched Morgan closely as he lifted his head at the sound. He stared at the iron bars, his face still completely blank.

The guard laughed loudly. "Gringo pig! You not only stink like one that has rolled in garbage, you look like one!"

Pilar's breath snagged. The guard cursed Morgan richly for another moment. Would he test the door? Rigid with fear, she waited.

The guard moved on, shuffling slowly on down the hall. Pilar sagged back against the wall, her knees limp with relief. Breathing raggedly, she waited again. The guard came back, racked the window bars once more with his weapon and left. Oddly, Morgan remained staring at the window, as if transfixed by it.

Anxiously, Pilar craned her neck and studied the window. Thin yellow curtains hung on either side of it. They were dirty, with holes here and there, but they could be drawn across the aperture. How long did she have until the guard came back? she wondered.

Moving slowly so as not to startle Morgan, she lifted her hand and carefully pulled the curtains across the window. There, it was covered. Breathing a small sigh of relief, Pilar moved over to Morgan and knelt in front of him.

"Morgan?" she whispered, her voice unsteady. She watched his eyes. It took nearly a full minute for him to respond to the sound of his name. First, she saw his pupils contract slightly. Then, very slowly, he shifted his stare from the now-curtained window to her.

Pilar sat quietly, hardly daring to breath beneath his cloudy gaze. Taking a risk, she followed her instincts and slowly placed her hand on his clasped ones, still hanging loosely between his thighs.

"Morgan? Do you remember me? I'm Pilar Martinez. You met me three years ago at the American consulate in Lima. Morgan?"

Pilar kept her voice low, and she saw him struggle with her words, as if he wasn't absorbing all of them. His face was an expressionless mask, as if he were more dead than alive. Pilar saw the lurid red spots running up and down the insides of his arms, from his wrists up to the raggedly cut off sleeve of his shirt—needle tracks indicating he'd been repeatedly drugged.

Worse, as she studied him more closely, she saw that his nose had been broken and had not been reset. It was swollen, with yellow-green bruises visible beneath his eyes. His mouth, which Pilar recalled as such a strong feature, was split at least four places on the lower lip, suggesting frequent beatings. She wanted to cry for him—for the pain he'd experienced at Ramirez's hands. The odor of his unwashed body assailed her nostrils, and she forced herself not to react as Morgan continued to stare blankly at her.

Pilar tightened her fingers around his scraped and

bruised hands. His knuckles were puffy. Wincing, she saw that his fingernails were missing.

"Oh, *Dios,*" she whispered, stricken. On the heels of her shock came the anger. She hated Ramirez. She hated his delight in inflicting intolerable pain. Pressing her brow against Morgan's knuckles, she fought her tears.

Choking back a sob, Pilar lifted her head and gently framed his bearded face with her hands. "Morgan?" She spoke slowly, in clear English. "Morgan, can you hear me? If you can, nod your head."

His head moved fractionally.

Pilar's smile was filled with relief. "Do you recognize me? Nod if you do."

He continued to stare at her, as if transfixed.

"Morgan, I've come to help you escape. Do you understand me?" The look in his eyes didn't change. Pilar tightened her hands on his face. "Morgan?"

With an effort, he pulled out of her imprisoning hands. "Who—is Morgan?"

Pilar's heart slammed into her ribs, and her mouth fell open as she stared at him in shock. "*Dios*...oh, *Dios*...." He didn't even know his name! The drugs had taken everything from him, she realized as she knelt in front of him—even his identity. Trembling, she touched his knees, barely covered by the threadbare fabric.

"*You* are Morgan," she said firmly. "I am Pilar, your friend." She spoke the words clearly and slowly and was rewarded by seeing his pupils contract slightly again. Pilar sensed a reaction in Morgan, but was unsure exactly what it was. Her mind whirled with options. With agony. No wonder the guards didn't bother to lock his door. He was more vegetable than human. This was Ramirez's way of getting even. She rose unsteadily to her feet.

Looking around, she realized she must leave. Memorizing the layout of the small, smelly room, she leaned over. Did she dare tell Morgan they would rescue him later tonight? Would he slip and say something to his captors, thereby putting them in jeopardy? Under the circumstances, Pilar sensed she should say little. She placed her hands lightly on Morgan's slumped shoulders, feeling huge, thick welts on his skin beneath the shirt. Looking more closely in the feeble light provided by the sole dim bulb hanging from the center of the ceiling, Pilar saw that his entire back was matted with yellow lymph fluid—the results of lashings he'd received probably a week or two earlier. Here and there, his shirt clung to the fluid.

Overwrought at the thought of his pain, Pilar whispered, ''Morgan, I will be back. Do you hear me? Nod if you do.''

He inclined his head slightly, his stare fixed on the window again. It was as if he couldn't see her, though she stood directly in his line of vision. Uttering a prayer, Pilar turned and carefully pulled open the curtains. Everything must be left as it had been before her visit so as not to arouse the guards' curiosity.

Listening intently, she heard the guitar music,

brassy horns and jangling tambourines from below. The merriment was proceeding nonstop, and the drunken shouts of the men and women would provide good cover for her escape. Moving to the door, Pilar opened it a crack and looked both ways. No one was in sight. Giving Morgan a final glance she felt her heart plummet. He was staring at the window, unmoving.

Slipping outside, she quietly closed the door and made her way swiftly down the darkened staircase. The fortress was surrounded by a ten-foot-high stucco wall. Thorny bougainvillea in many colors climbed the wall, providing an additional barrier. Pilar prayed she could find another way out of this place besides the main gate, though none was indicated on the blueprint. She needed to explore the possibility. Switching to the internal instincts that her Grandmother Aurelia called her "jaguar sense," Pilar left the staircase and became a shadow in the night.

Culver was chafing from inactivity and worry. Nearly an hour had passed and Pilar still hadn't returned. His mind spun with possibilities—all of them frightening—as the music continued to float out into the night around the fortress. Cars and jeeps came and went in an almost ceaseless stream of partygoers now. The guards at the gate were lax. At least he could be grateful for that.

Angrily wiping the sweat off his brow, Culver narrowed his eyes against the light emanating from the fortress and wondered what had happened to Pilar. A slight sound from behind him, so vague and indistinct that he nearly missed it, caught his attention. The night insects stopped their busy chirping and singing, and instantly, Culver went on guard, his pistol raised and ready.

To his disbelief, he saw Pilar emerge from the jungle's dark embrace to appear, almost magically, at his side. Was she a figment of his overwrought imagination? Stunned by her stealth, Culver wasn't sure. Reaching out, he wrapped his fingers powerfully around her extended hand and saw her wince as he crushed it in his to prove to himself that she was real. As he relaxed his grip, a gasp slipped from his tightened lips.

"You scared the hell out of me," he snarled softly as she knelt down beside him. "I almost blew your head off. I thought you were the enemy."

Gulping, Pilar nodded, then reached out and gripped Culver's left arm. He uttered her name, and she felt herself being dragged against him. Her body met his, and his arms swept around her. With a moan, she surrendered to his anxiety on her behalf, understanding his need to embrace her.

"God," he rasped thickly, his lips near her ear, "I thought you'd been captured." Culver crushed Pilar hard against him, until he could feel the birdlike beat of her heart against his chest. Breathing raggedly, he felt the words *I love you* threatening to escape from his lips, but now was not the time or place to speak of such things. Still, Pilar felt so warm and alive in his arms. He buried his face in her hair, never wanting to let her go, but knowing he must. But the fact that her arms had slid around his waist and she'd returned his viselike embrace told him much.

Reluctantly, he eased her away from him and looked down into her distraught eyes, seeing terror there.

"What happened?" he rasped, unwilling to release her completely.

"Listen to me," Pilar whispered as she held his hands in hers. "Morgan is heavily drugged." Trying to steady her own frayed emotions, she sat close to him, her head bent near his ear to give him the information. For the next ten minutes, she went over every aspect of her foray into the fortress. Culver's face tightened more with each passing moment. When Pilar detailed Ramirez's torture methods, he cursed under his breath.

Pilar divided her attention between their hiding place and the front gate of the fortress as she talked. "One good thing, though," she went on breathlessly. "I found a small wooden door on the west side of the hacienda. It was covered with bougainvillea." She held up her arms, marked with bloody scratches from easing her way through the thorny plants that nearly covered the entrance. "I broke the branches, but left them in place in case someone checks that area. I didn't see a path to it, so I know it's not used. The bougainvillea has grown over it, and the lock was rusty. I had to find a rock the size of my hand and hit it several times to get it open."

Gently, Culver skimmed his hand over her torn, bleeding arm. What a pity to mar her beautiful golden skin, like warm velvet beneath his fingertips. He examined her fingers in the darkness and realized the rock had cut them, too.

"Can we use the door?" he asked, encapsulating her hand between his.

Pilar nodded. Then, frowning, she studied the fortress. "There are at least two hundred people in there right now, singing, dancing and very drunk."

"That's good," Culver muttered. "I'm sure the guards would rather be partying than making their rounds."

"To a degree, they do make their rounds," Pilar said, feeling the healing heat of Culver's hand over hers. She saw the worry in his eyes at her small injuries—negligible in comparison to Morgan Trayhern's horrible wounds. "We should go in about three. By then, everyone will be drunk and exhausted. If they aren't asleep—"

"They'll be making love," Culver finished grimly. Ramirez's men were well known for their lusty capture of young women from the villages to satisfy their sexual appetites.

Pilar nodded. "I worry about Morgan. I don't know if he'll come with us, Culver."

"He'll come if I have to knock him out and carry him on my shoulders."

"You may have to."

"They're probably shooting him up with a mind-altering drug every six hours or so. That's why he looks like a robot," he said. "Maybe, if we get lucky, the drug will be wearing off by three." He glanced at his watch. It was one-thirty. "Morgan was probably injected shortly before you found him."

"Which would explain why he was so glazed and unresponsive."

Culver's mouth twitched. "Exactly." He reached for his pack. "I'm going to contact Major Houston now and start setting up the time frame for their landing after we get Morgan out of there."

Pilar sat back, suddenly drained by the danger she'd escaped. At any point, she could have been snatched by one of Ramirez's guards. Leaning against a rubber tree, she felt the dull ache of her arms from the many scratches the bougainvillea had inflicted. Closing her eyes, she honed in on Culver's deep voice as he made the necessary radio contact.

She drew her knees up, wrapped her arms around them and tried to relax. But her mind swam with the trials still to come. So much still could go wrong.

Just listening to Culver's voice soothed Pilar's taut nerves. Going into the fortress once had devastated her, and she felt overwhelmed by the thought of doing it again. But she had to—for Morgan's sake. In her mind's eye, she pictured Rane's small, oval face, and her heart wrung with terror. A suffocating feeling threatened to overcome her, and she felt death stalking her.

Forcing her eyes open, Pilar sat up. Culver's knee barely grazed her hip from where he was sitting. To a degree, the physical contact ameliorated the terror she felt not at the idea of dying, but at leaving Rane, who so badly needed a mother—and a father. She stole a look at Culver's hard, sweating features as he continued to trade information with Houston. He looked so capable, and strong—as if he could survive anything life threw at him.

Yet when his gaze rose from the map laid out between his legs to meet her eyes, Pilar felt a trembling heat feather through her and her fear dissolved. She stared back at Culver, not daring to believe what she saw. Love? But how could he still love her? Hope sprang powerfully in her heart, flowing through her like a rainbow appearing after the dark of a storm.

Pilar's emotions felt battered. Being around Culver had aroused a whirlwind combination of guilt, shame and agony. She hated to hurt anyone—it went against her nature. And to hurt the only man she'd ever loved was the greatest of all crosses to bear. Culver broke eye contact and focused again on the map as he answered Houston. Pilar felt bereft. Culver's kisses meant more than she'd realized, she thought as she sat absorbing the very special look he'd given her.

Or, she wondered as she felt an ache center deep in her body, had it been merely her imagination working overtime because she smelled the presence of death? She hung her head, closed her eyes and blamed herself for the lack of healing between her and Culver—a healing that could never occur until she told him the truth. The *real* truth. But how could she? She feared that he would instantly reject her, and therefore reject Rane. Or he might try to take Rane away from her, which would be even worse. No man would stand still and accept what she'd done. It was beyond her to hope that Culver could be so much different. She sighed deeply. It was an impossible, heartbreaking situation. If she had to, she would go to her death with acceptance, and with one sincere regret—that she'd withheld the truth from Culver.

Vaguely, Pilar heard Culver sign off. She lifted her head and studied his shadowed expression. She saw an aggression in the depths of his eyes that she knew must involve their coming plans. "What will happen?" she asked softly.

Culver put the radio away. It was 2:15 a.m. In half an hour they would attempt to rescue Morgan. Handing Pilar the black nylon harness she would wear, he said, "They're winding up the birds right now. Two gunships will be coming in, fully loaded with weapons and a squad of Peruvian soldiers. Major Houston is the advisor to the group. He can't actively participate, but he'll stay with the choppers and direct them by radio, if needed." After putting on an armored vest beneath his shirt, he slipped his own harness across his shoulders. Hand grenades were snapped to it, as well as extra clips of ammo stored in special pockets.

He strapped on the hearing device that curved around his ear; a black collar fit snugly around his throat so that as he adjusted the pencil-thin microphone against his lips, Pilar could hear him no matter how softly he spoke, and vice versa.

To his right calf, he strapped a large, wicked-looking knife in a black nylon scabbard. Looking up, he saw Pilar hesitating over putting on her own harness. She'd donned the armored vest over her white blouse; it would help camouflage her.

"I'm not wearing this," she said, allowing the harness to drop. Pilar saw the expression in Culver's eyes harden. "I can't kill, Culver. I—I never could...."

"What if we need extra grenades? Or more clips of ammo?"

Helplessly, she opened her hand. "I know you're right...."

"Wear it...just in case," he muttered. "If there's any killing to be done, I'll do it." His eyes narrowed speculatively on her. "I don't want you in the line of fire. Understand, Pilar?"

Shaken by his roughened tone, she swallowed against the lump forming in her throat. "I—I'm sorry, Culver. You deserve someone who can protect you as well as you can protect me...."

His smile was mirthless as he checked his Beretta, then holstered it beneath his left arm. "You've never been able to hurt a fly, Pilar. Don't look so guilty, okay? I know you can't fire that weapon."

Tears gathered in Pilar's eyes, and she nearly

blurted, "I've hurt you more than you'll ever know, *mi querido.*" Bitterness galled her as she watched Culver blacken his face, arms and hands. With no need for such camouflage because of her naturally dark skin, Pilar stood. Time was of the essence now. They were on a schedule. The helicopters would be in the air shortly, speeding toward them from an unknown point.

Pilar fitted the ear- and mouthpiece over her head, making sure the collar was snug enough not to slip. The tiny microphones would be their only means of communication. Licking her dry lips, she took the lead; she would show Culver the way to the rear of the fortress.

Damp leaves from the low bushes swatted her skirt and legs as she tried to focus and steady herself. She had to become the jaguar again—stalking silently through the jungle. Jaguars owned the night. They were the night in all its aspects. To become one with the jungle, the plants, the animals, the insects, the very ground her bare feet trod upon, was the challenge.

Pilar's need to focus began to override her aching heart and worries about Culver—and Rane. As she melted into the darkness around her, she felt a subtle shift in her consciousness that heightened her hearing, sharpened her vision and enlarged upon her ability to sift one odor from another. She was now the jaguar. Unerringly, she wove silently closer to Ramirez's fortress.

Soon they were on the western side of the complex. As Pilar slowed, reached out and encountered the rough, wooden door, she felt another subtle shift. What replaced her heightened senses was more emotionally devastating. She felt Culver nearby, the aura of protection bristling from him. People still sang and strummed guitars in the courtyard—not half as many as before, but enough to cover any slight sound they might make slipping into the fortress.

As Pilar turned and looked up into Culver's face, she had a wild desire to reach up and kiss him one last time. Oh, she would give anything to feel his masterful mouth against her, guiding her, consuming her until she became one with him again. It was a ridiculous urge, and she sadly turned away, knowing full well she didn't deserve such a final, parting gift from him. Instead, she draped her fingers across the old, rusty latch and gently pushed down. She heard a distinct click, and the door creaked open.

Chapter 11

Culver didn't know what to expect when they slipped undetected into Morgan's room. The chamber was dark, except for what little light danced into it from the huge bonfire still blazing below in the courtyard, and it stank of urine and vomit. At least a hundred of the harder-core celebrants were still going strong, and Culver and Pilar had managed to sneak up to the second floor of the hacienda undetected.

Pilar closed the door and quickly pulled the thin curtains across the barred window. Culver crossed the room, his gaze pinned on Morgan, who was lying down. Was he asleep? As he closed the distance, he saw the man slowly lift his head. Leaning over Morgan, Culver gripped the man's shoulder and whispered, "We're friends, Morgan. Don't make a sound. We're going to get you out of here."

Pilar pulled Morgan into an upright position. Every second counted. If they didn't get away from the fortress fast enough, the guards would hear the helicopters and realize something was wrong. She saw puzzlement on Morgan's bearded features as she crouched before him to study his eyes, her hands on his knees.

"Morgan? It's Pilar. Remember me? I was here a little while ago." Her voice was low and breathless, her heart pounding unremittingly. She saw confusion come to his cloudy gaze. He looked at her, then twisted to look up at Culver, who stood over him.

"No," he mumbled. "Who are you?"

Crestfallen, Pilar said to Culver, "His eyes are the same. He's no better or worse than the last time I saw him."

With a nod, Culver came around and knelt at Morgan's side. "Do you remember me? Culver Lachlan?"

Morgan stared at him. "No..."

"That son of a bitch...." Culver rasped as he straightened. Ramirez had wiped out Morgan's memory completely with some drug. Fury sizzled through him, but Culver quickly clamped down on it and gestured sharply to Morgan. "Come on, we're springing you from this pigsty. It's time to go home."

"Home?"

Pilar panicked. "Morgan, your home is in Washington, D.C."

"It is?"

"Oh, no," she whispered. "You're married to Laura. You remember Laura, don't you?"

Morgan shook his shaggy head. "I...don't know any of you." Forlornly, he looked around the room and then back at Pilar. "Who is Laura?"

Rising, Pilar bit back a cry of sadness. "You have two children, Morgan. A boy and a girl. Do you remember their names?"

Rubbing his brow with his filthy, bloodied hand, Morgan whispered, "I don't have any children...."

"Enough," Culver snapped roughly. "Pilar, check the door to make sure the guards aren't around. I'm going to get him on his feet."

Instantly, Pilar responded. Morgan was a big man, but Culver, built like a huge, powerful bull, was larger, and Morgan was pathetically thin, a mere shadow of his former self. Culver pulled his arm across his own shoulder and hefted him to his feet. With a groan, Morgan sagged against his rescuer's tall frame, his knees buckling.

"Try to stand," Culver ordered gently, steadying him. The drugs they'd given him had not only made mush of his brain, they'd affected his entire nervous system. Morgan was weak and uncoordinated.

"It's clear," Pilar whispered. She stepped out the door and opened it wide. Moving ahead, she heard the scraping of Morgan's bare feet on the tiles. Her heart pounding, she hurried to the stairs. Shadows from the firelight danced along the walls. Shouts and loud laughter drifted up to her, and guitar music provided more dissonance as she carefully made her way down the darkened steps to the ground below.

Turning, Pilar watched the corner of the hacienda and the men's progress. Morgan was only semiconscious, leaning heavily against Culver, who was practically dragging him down the stairs. Breathing hard, Culver tottered beneath his load, added to the weight of the equipment he wore. Anxiously, Pilar looked on, her palms growing sweaty. She had no weapon. If someone came around the corner unexpectedly, she could do nothing. Culver wouldn't be able to get to his own weapon because he was helping Morgan.

The drugged man groaned as Culver guided him toward the west wall and the small wooden door. Pilar brought up the rear, constantly on guard. Morgan's knees kept giving out on him, despite his pitiful attempts to walk.

"Pilar!"

She spun around at Culver's rasping command. Understanding that he wanted her to open the door for them, she hurried ahead. The bougainvillea scraped and cut at her arms as she waded into it. Breathing through her mouth so she wouldn't make too much noise, she groped about until her fingertips met the rough wooden door. She heard Culver's heavy breathing through the earpiece she wore. Scrabbling to find the rusty lock, she wished for more light.

"Hurry!" Culver snapped.

Pilar heard the crunch of branches behind her. Morgan groaned again, the sound one of raw pain. She was sure those whiplash wounds that covered his back were being opened. Frantically, she moved her hands over the door's surface. There! She jerked it open and the rusty hinges gave a loud creak of protest. It took all of Pilar's weight to open the door far enough for Culver and Morgan to pass through.

Once outside Culver propped Morgan against the now-open door. "Hold him."

She nodded and pressed her hands against Morgan's chest to steady him. She watched as Culver removed his submachine gun.

"Take it," he ordered. "Cover our escape."

Nodding jerkily, Pilar stepped aside and took the safety off the weapon. The steel felt cold in her trembling hands. She hated violence of any kind. In her undercover work, although it had been dangerous, she'd refused to carry a weapon.

Dividing her attention, she saw Culver heft Morgan under his arms and drag him away from the wall.

¡Hola!

Sucking in a sharp breath, Pilar whirled around. Her eyes widened. A guard stood tensely at the corner, his face etched with surprise.

"*¡Alto!* Stop!" he yelled, and jerked the submachine gun off his shoulder.

No! Pilar backed up and slammed into the wall.

She saw the guard's face turn ugly as he lowered the weapon, pointing it toward her. Culver was gone!

"You there! Stop!"

Whirling around, she lunged for the open door, hearing the instant spat of the weapon as she did so. Bullets whined around her as she reached the entrance, and wood exploded in splinters to her right. Stucco flew past her. With a small cry, she dropped to her knees and tried to get out the door, but a vine caught her foot and she tripped forward. *Dios,* no! Panicked, Pilar scrambled on hands and knees through the doorway.

A siren started to wail behind her. Gasping, she struggled to her feet. Ahead of her, Culver had put Morgan in a fireman's carry over his shoulder and was lumbering quickly into the jungle, she saw. Time. Culver had to have time to get far enough into the jungle that Ramirez's men couldn't find them. Jerking around, Pilar dropped the weapon and reached for the rusty latch. She heard more startled cries from the guards. They were coming her way.

Wrapping her fingers around the latch, she yanked the wooden door closed. Then, picking up the submachine gun, she sprinted across the small clearing toward the wall of darkened jungle that stretched in front of her. It represented safety. She'd lost sight of Culver, but she knew from their game plan which direction he would go. Besides, with Morgan on his shoulders, he'd be making noise and moving slowly.

Breathing hard, her bare feet digging into the moist

leaves and sandy soil, Pilar ran as hard as she could, the cries of the guards ringing out behind her. They sounded so close! Not daring to turn around and look, she lengthened her stride. Part of her wished she was taller, with longer legs to carry her away from the pursuing enemy more quickly.

"Stop!"

The command rippled through her, and Pilar winced at the fury in the male voice behind her. They were going to kill her, she knew. Running hard, gasping as she went, she dove into the jungle. Safe! At last she was safe!

Pilar didn't break stride. As if her feet had eyes, she felt each step across the lumpy ground. She keyed her ears to the crashing of foliage ahead that heralded Culver's awkward progress. Would he make it to the landing zone in time? Pilar knew Major Houston would wait there only five minutes. If he didn't see them, he'd have to order the two helicopters to lift off. To remain on the ground too long in Ramirez's backyard was folly. A single guard could shoot a helicopter to oblivion.

Bullets whined around her. Vines snapped; bark flew. Pilar hunched over and ran harder, her mind racing even faster. In another minute or so she would catch up with Culver. But he and Morgan needed protection, someone to stay behind and create a diversion to ensure their escape.

Increasing her precarious speed, she was struggling to catch up when she heard someone fall. Then Culver grunted. Her eyes narrowing, Pilar saw Morgan sprawled on the ground, with Culver nearby, rising onto his hands and knees. Rasping for breath, she sped to his side.

"They're after us!" she gasped as she helped him stand. Culver had fallen over a thick, exposed root. Anxiously, she turned to Morgan, who was slowly sitting up, a dazed expression on his shadowed features.

Culver grimly swung around. "It isn't far," he growled.

"I'll create a diversion."

"No!" He whirled, his eyes thundercloud black.

"Don't argue!" Pilar cried. Reaching out, she grabbed his arm. "*Mi querido,* whatever happens, take care of Rane for us, please...."

Culver opened his mouth to protest. Before he could say a word, Pilar had disappeared back into a jungle, like a jaguar on the hunt. Shaken, he got Morgan back up and across his shoulders. Groaning under the other man's weight, he could do nothing but head forward again. He heard the yelps of the guards, like bloodthirsty dogs, then a sudden spate of gunfire. Swinging around, Culver dove onward, toward the landing zone. He wanted to stop, to turn around and help Pilar. She was right, he thought bitterly; a diversion had to be created or the guards would recapture Morgan.

More gunfire sounded, off to Culver's left. Pilar was leading them on a wild-goose chase, and they were following her. Breathing heavily, his muscles aching from the load he carried, Culver forced himself into a dogtrot toward the clearing he knew was ahead of them, but his heart and mind spun back to Pilar. She was risking her life for them. Again. As she had before, long ago. She was so small and delicate, yet she possessed such incredible courage.

More gunfire erupted—heavier and more concentrated. Stray bullets whined past them, and Culver automatically cringed, tightening his grip on Morgan. They could just as easily be killed by ricocheting bullets. His heart ached with unadulterated fear for Pilar's life. *Oh, God, please protect her.* I love her. *I love her.* It no longer mattered that she'd run out on him. He needed her, even as he needed each breath of air he forced into his heaving, burning lungs.

Suddenly, the *whap, whap, whap* of helicopter blades caught his frantic attention. Honing in on the sound, Culver realized with a sinking sensation that they were behind schedule. *Five minutes.* That's all they had before Houston lifted off without them, thinking that mission a failure. His heart pounding, Culver lengthened his stride. Leaves swatted heavily at them, branches slapping his face, cutting and jabbing at him. Still, his mind swung to Pilar. Behind him and to the left, he could hear the gunfire, almost nonstop. What if she was wounded? Dead? The thought nearly paralyzed him midstride. Shaking his head, Culver hunched forward, the weight of Morgan nearly unbearable despite the man's emaciated condition. Culver's muscles screamed in protest. His knees ached with each footfall.

Morgan groaned.

"Hang on," he panted. "Just hang on."

Morgan's life for Pilar's. The thought was startling. Horrifying. Culver breathed heavily through his mouth. No. No. Pilar couldn't be dead—or worse, captured. She would catch up with them. She would be waiting in the clearing, signaling the helicopters. She had to be!

His thoughts skewing wildly, Culver lifted his booted feet higher, hoping to avoid the lethal tangle of roots. Each step felt as if he were lifting a thousand pounds of weight. Burning pain flowed up from his cramping calves, affecting his thigh muscles and shortening his stride. Clenching his teeth against the searing pain, he crashed on through the foliage. The sound of the helicopters was growing louder. At any moment, they would land. How far away was the clearing?

Sweat poured into his eyes, blurring his vision. Shaking his head in a bullish motion, Culver suddenly found himself at the edge of the huge, open space. The sky was just turning gray with dawn and he saw the black, silhouetted shapes of the choppers appear out of the night sky. Breathing raggedly, Culver turned around. Where was Pilar? Damn! Where was she? Anxiously, he scanned the jungle.

The helicopters would arrive within the minute. Culver shoved off on cramping legs toward the center of the clearing, where they would land. Morgan hung limply over his shoulders now, unconscious. The soil here was soft, and Culver struggled to keep his balance with his heavy load. Somewhere in the distance, above the powerful beating of the helicopter blades, another spate of gunfire broke the dawn. Pilar? Was she coming? She knew the timetable. She knew five minutes was between landing and lift-off.

The helicopters set down, their blades still whirling at full power. Culver saw the nearest chopper door slide open. The aircraft had no landing lights—nothing to give it away to the enemy. Tottering, his knees like jelly beneath the weight, Culver moved forward again and saw a man in tiger fatigues running toward him full tilt. It had to be Mike Houston. Culver felt his strength draining with each step he took. As the man neared, Culver recognized his old friend from Army Special Forces. Houston's square face was painted in green, yellow and black stripes, his expression hard and set as he reached out toward Morgan.

"Let's go!" Houston yelled above the roar of the aircraft. He hauled Morgan off Culver's shoulders.

Culver staggered as the weight was taken away. Two Peruvian soldiers grabbed Morgan and hauled him quickly toward the first helicopter. Culver felt Houston's steadying grip on his arm. Turning, he met the grim-faced major, who was near his own age.

"Mike, Pilar isn't here. She decoyed for us," he panted.

Houston turned on his booted heel and lifted a pair of infrared binoculars to his eyes. "I don't see her, Lachlan."

"Damn!"

Every muscle in Culver's body ached, but nothing more so than his heart. "She shouldn't have done it!" He swore loudly. Glancing past the major, he saw that Morgan was now safely stowed on board the chopper.

Lowering the binoculars, Houston faced him. "We've got three minutes."

Frustration ate at Culver. He couldn't argue with Mike. If they waited for her, they could all be killed. Ramirez's men had powerful weapons capable of putting the helicopters out of commission. Compressing his lips, he gazed at the dark line of the jungle. "She's in trouble."

"What?" Mike shouted, leaning forward.

Culver cupped his hands around his mouth. "I said Pilar is in trouble. I feel it."

Houston straightened. He glanced at his watch. "It's time to go, Lachlin."

Culver reached over and took the submachine gun that hung from Houston's shoulder. "No. I'm staying. I've got to find her."

Houston eyed him. "That's stupid. Ramirez's men are crawling all over this place."

Terror gripped Culver. "I'm staying behind, Mike. You've got Trayhern. Take off."

"Dammit, Lachlan—"

Culver waved him away. "Somehow, we'll make it out of here—together."

"You're crazy!"

"Maybe."

Houston traded looks with him. Rubbing his jaw, he said, "All right, if you can find her, contact me on the same radio frequency. I can't promise anything, but I'll try to talk the Peruvian government into giving us a chopper to come in and pick you up—wherever you are."

Gripping Houston's hand, Culver nodded. "Thanks, Mike."

"Just be damn careful," Houston warned, then he turned and trotted back to the waiting aircraft.

Culver moved quickly back into the jungle's cover. He knew the sound of the helicopters would bring Ramirez's men running. He had to take some swift tactical action to get out of the immediate area. When things quieted, and dawn broke, he would try to track down Pilar.

His stomach turned with nausea. Pilar was either dead, wounded or captured. Tears burned in his eyes, but he fought them. Moving swiftly, his legs aching in protest, he headed away from the clearing, but parallel to the fortress, which was at least a mile away. His hunting and tracking instincts moved to the fore. He would need every ounce of jungle skill he possessed to avoid capture. In the distance, he heard the helicopters already growing fainter as they headed out of danger.

Pilar? His heart lurched with dread. Sweat covered him. The foliage was damp from the night's fog, stealing silently around him, just above his head. His hearing keyed, Culver caught the sound of several men talking in excited Spanish to his right. Crouching down, he became invisible, swallowed up by the thick bushes. He listened carefully but, heard no mention of Pilar. They were crashing through the jungle toward the clearing where the helicopters had been. Good.

The moment they'd passed him, Culver eased to his feet and moved in the opposite direction. His mind spun. What had Pilar meant by "Take care of Rane for us"? *Us?* A strange word to use and he'd already promised, so why had she repeated it like that? Stymied, his terror for her very real, Culver pushed on. He consulted his compass every now and then in the dim gray light. Mentally fixing in his mind where the fortress was and which direction Pilar had headed, Culver kept his eyes trained to the ground.

Lucky for him, his father had been a hunter in the Rocky Mountains and had taught him tracking skills as a very young boy. Culver had developed the skill to an art form over the years, though these days his quarry tended to be two-legged enemies rather than some hapless deer or elk. As the sun rose and the light improved, he began watching for other signs— the telltale broken leaf or twig indicating someone had passed hurriedly through an area.

Was Pilar hiding in the jungle? Was she hurt?

Bleeding? The image made him wince. It was only then that Culver realized they should still be in radio contact. Kneeling, hidden by the foliage, he pressed his fingers against his throat, where the communication device lay.

"Pilar? Pilar, this is Culver. Come in."

He waited, his breath suspended. He knew that the state-of-the-art headsets they wore were waterproof. Capable of working under the ocean if they had to.

"Pilar, if you can hear me, say something. Anything…"

Slowly scanning the area, Culver waited tensely. Nothing. His mind ticked off the possibilities. Pilar could be dead, her body hidden by the jungle. She could be unconscious and unable to respond. Or—his heart instantly rejected the final possibility just as strongly—Ramirez's men had found her, stripped her of her military gear and taken her back to the fortress.

Wiping his smarting eyes, he digested the situation. Day was breaking and the fog was thinning. Lifting his head, Culver spotted a swath of jungle that had obviously been disturbed. Getting up, he eased in that direction, his gaze moving to the soft, moist earth.

His heart slammed into his ribs. He halted. There. Everywhere he looked, the foliage had been torn up, leaves bruised and twigs broken. The soil was marked by numerous bootprints. Bending down, Culver looked closer. His mouth went dry as he saw a small, partial imprint of a bare foot. Pilar. A fight had taken place here, no doubt about it. Looking around, he searched the underbrush for other signs that would confirm Pilar had been here.

Several bullets had gouged into the smooth, gray surface of a thick rubber tree. As Culver eased toward it, something dark on one large, exposed root caught his eye. Stymied, he knelt down, unable to identify the substance in the dim light. Reaching out, he carefully touched it, then lifted his fingers to his nostrils. The metallic odor was distinctive and unmistakable. Blood. His heart started a slow hammering as he bent down and continued to search around the roots. They had caught Pilar, he was certain. But was it her blood or someone else's?

Getting down on his hands and knees, Culver searched frantically for any other sign that might confirm whether Pilar had been truly captured. Running his fingers beneath some large, broken-off leaves, Culver struck something. Lifting the leaves away, he felt his eyes widened with dismay. It was the black throat collar of the communications device Pilar had worn. Sitting back on his heels, he picked it up and studied it grimly. And then his gaze caught something else. His lips parted as he stared at it for a long moment in disbelief. A sizzling arc of pain moved through his chest as he leaned down and retrieved it.

The small, dark brown bag on a leather thong dangled from his fingers. Pilar's medicine bag. He would recognize it anywhere. As he slowly turned it over, his breath snagged, and his eyes bulged. The rear of the bag dripped—with blood.

Chapter 12

Forty-eight hours had passed—the most hellish hours in Culver's entire life. For a long time the jungle had crawled with Ramirez's men, combing and recombing the area for evidence of more enemies. At least six helicopters had come and gone as Culver lay buried beneath leaves in the hole he'd dug under the roots of a particularly large rubber tree.

He overheard passing guards say that Ramirez had left the fortress and flown to Bogota, Colombia, until things settled down. But what of Pilar? What had he done with her? Culver's gut felt like he'd swallowed acid, and his heart wanted to explode with frustration and grief. He couldn't even be certain if Pilar had been wounded. One of the guards could have torn the medicine bag from her neck and let it land in someone else's blood. What he did know was that this waiting was slowly killing him.

Finally Culver got a lead, though the news was not what he wanted to hear. Some guards walked within fifty feet of his hiding spot and he heard them say that Pilar was wounded and being held in the fortress's small dispensary. Culver didn't know how badly she was wounded, but it was enough information for him to proceed with. A blueprint of the fortress was branded in his mind, so he knew the dispensary was next to the guards' barracks along the north wall.

At three in the morning, Culver made his move. By luck, he'd also heard two guards talking about an entrance to the fortress on the north side of the compound. His heart pounded with fear. If he were caught—if they were caught—it would mean death for both of them, and Culver couldn't stand the thought of seeing Pilar tortured. His mouth compressed into a thin line. No, if they caught him, too, he'd pull out his pistol and put a bullet in Pilar's head before turning the weapon on himself and doing the same. They weren't going to be carrion for Ramirez. Not if he could help it.

Pilar moved her head slowly back and forth on the perspiration-soaked pillow as she moved in and out of consciousness, the fever sucking away at her strength, at her desire to live. Culver's dark, hard face

appeared before her. So close. So real. Pilar blinked
to clear the stinging from her eyes. Oh, how many
times had she thought of him? Slowly, the tragic
events of eight years ago began to unfold in her hazy
mind like an old black-and-white film.

*"You are pregnant, Señorita Martinez," Dr. San-
chez said heavily, his brows drawn down in disfavor.*

*Pilar sat on the gurney, dressed only in a light blue
gown. Her thigh where the bullet had grazed her, had
taken ten stitches and was throbbing like fire itself.
But the pain that gripped her heart as the meaning
of his words washed over her erased the ache of the
injury.*

"What?" she whispered.

*He nodded his graying head. "You are two months
pregnant. You did not know?"*

Oh, *Dios!* Pilar *hung her head in shame as she saw
the doctor look significantly at her left hand, where
no wedding ring encircled her finger. She saw the
accusation in his eyes. She had committed an unpar-
donable sin as a South American woman, not protecting her virginity for marriage.*

*"I suggest," the doctor said abruptly, "that you
tell the father of your child and get something done
about it legally, señorita."*

*With those parting words, Dr. Sanchez turned on
his heel, leaving her alone in the coolness of the hospital room. Covering her face, Pilar tried to think.
The baby was Culver's. They had made love only four*

times in the past two months—moments stolen out of time.

A sob tore from her as she lifted her head and looked toward the door. Culver was in surgery. He could die. He had taken a bullet for her, and she'd watched him go down like a felled ox. Had it not been for the American army advisor with them, Culver would have died in her arms on that damp jungle floor. Instead, they'd called in a helicopter and flown him directly to Lima, fifty miles away.

She loved Culver! She loved him so much that the ache in her heart nearly overwhelmed her. Now, she was pregnant—with his child. Pilar knew he didn't want children right now. He'd made that clear on several occasions. What was she to do? Pilar couldn't bear the idea of taking a life that lived within her. As a shamanka in training, her whole focus was on helping people to live.

But what could she do? Even if Culver lived, how could she tell him she was pregnant?

The door to her room opened and closed quietly, and she looked up to see her father's oldest and dearest friend, Fernando. He was in his sixties, his hair silver. His dark brown eyes traveled to hers.

"Hector Ruiz called me, Pilar. How are you doing, my child? He said you were hurt." Fernando walked forward with a limp, leaning heavily on his gold-encrusted cane, his hand outstretched, his smile filled with concern.

Pilar hung her head. "Oh, Fernando, I am all right...." She began to sob.

"I talked to Dr. Sanchez in the hall," he said, gently patting her slumped shoulders. "He said your leg is injured. Is it bad?"

Tears blinded Pilar as Fernando took her into his arms and very carefully held her. Resting her head wearily against his shoulder, she began to tell him what had happened. Her words came out in torn gasps, until the ugly truth about her pregnancy had been revealed. Fernando, older than her father, had been like a kindly grandfather during her growing-up years. He'd been her father's inseparable friend, and since his own wife had died in childbirth long ago, he'd made Pilar part of his extended family. As she told him the horrible truth of her condition, Pilar eased out of his arms, trying to scrub the tears from her lashes.

"I don't know what to do, Fernando," she quavered. "I am with child. Culver's child. I—I love him, but I know he's not interested in having children— and we've never talked of marriage."

Gently, Fernando touched her hair, taming it to one side. "Does he love you?"

Sniffing, Pilar turned her head away. "We have been very close, but he has never said those words to me."

"Never?"

It hurt to say in a choked voice, "No."

"I see...." Fernando sighed.

Pilar felt the terrible weight of responsibility on her shoulders. "I will be castigated, Fernando. Lima society will ostracize me. I will be worse than a mestiza to them now. They will call me a whore. The whore of a Norte Americano.*" She shut her eyes tightly. "Oh,* Dios, Fernando, *I did not mean to get pregnant. I—it just happened. I'm so sorry...." She hid her face in her hands and began to cry in earnest.*

"Hush, hush, my child," Fernando soothed as he patted her shoulder. "I have a plan. It is a good one. Stop crying and listen to me."

Pilar tried valiantly to stem her tears. Lifting her chin, she looked into Fernando's kindly, weatherbeaten face. Although he was of the Castilian aristocracy and a millionaire, he acted neither part. He'd always been a quiet, kindly shadow in her life, loving her as the daughter he'd never had.

"Wh-what?" she asked in a whisper.

He smiled paternally. "I will marry you, Pilar. You will have my name and my protection. It is the least I can do for your father. He was my best friend, and I know he would feel shame upon his family name if this secret got out. He was a good man. And you are still a child. I do not fault you for what you did. I know how youth can be." He smiled a little and caressed her hair. "How far along are you?"

"Dr. Sanchez said two months."

"Ah, good. That is not too far."

"You would marry me?" she asked, stunned.

"To protect you, your baby and your father's good name, my child."

"B-but—"

"You know that I love you as a daughter, Pilar. I will care for you and your child. I will ensure your baby has a name." He shrugged a little and gave her a gentle smile. *"I know I am not long for this world with this old, leaky heart of mine. If I can do this for you, no matter how little time I have left on this earth, then I consider it an honor. I have never told you, but you filled a large hole in my heart by allowing me to be close to you. You loved me as if I were part of your family. This is the least I can do for you."*

Pilar's mind spun. Her emotions reeled. If only Culver wanted her! But he could die on the operating table. And even if he lived, he no doubt would reject her outright. Fernando's kind face blurred before her eyes as she struggled with the problem. *"I—I have made such a mess of things,"* she whispered brokenly. *"I love Culver so much, Fernando. He's lying on the operating table, gravely wounded by a bullet that should have killed me. I know he loves me—he must."*

"But he is Norte Americano, *Pilar, and a government agent. He may not survive this operation. What then? You have said he doesn't want children. He's never told you he loves you. Those are not good signs, my child. If we marry today, we can still convince people the baby is two months early when it is born seven months from now. But we don't have much*

time. No one will suspect your child belongs to Culver, Pilar. He does not need to know.''

Pilar's heart felt as if it was shattering with pain. Hot tears blinded her. ''I have failed so many people,'' she sobbed. ''I love him, Fernando. He's the only man I will ever love! I know in my soul he is for me. I saw it in his eyes, in the way he loved me.''

''My child,'' Fernando said heavily, ''I'm sure Culver cares deeply for you. How could he not? But enough to accept that you are pregnant? Do you think he will marry you in this condition? Even if he lives, he will not want you. What will his family think? Think clearly now, Pilar. You are a South American woman. His family are Norte Americanos. Would they accept you?''

Miserably, Pilar shook her head. ''I have sinned so badly, Fernando. Even God will not forgive me for what I have done.'' She lifted her head and sniffed. ''I do not deserve what you offer me.''

''Your life has been hard, Pilar. I saw you struggle as a young girl growing up. Your mestiza blood has caused you much pain and hardship. I do not wish you to stain your family's name before the rich and powerful of Lima. Let me marry you. I will never ask for a husband's rights. You will be a daughter to me, not a wife. My heart has room only for my dear Angelica, who died in childbirth with our baby girl. But I can be your friend. Let me help you....''

Fernando had married her that very evening in front of a priest at his church. And he had saved her family name and made good on his promise to treat her as his beloved daughter. Pilar knew he had done it for her father, and she was grateful. When Fernando passed on, he'd left a half-million-dollar estate and his name to continue his powerful protection. And no one, outside of Dr. Sanchez, who had never breathed a word and her grandparents, knew the truth.

Pilar tried again to force her eyes open. How many times in her feverish state had she hallucinated that Culver was here to rescue her? She knew the infection of her bullet wound was creating the dream—mingled with her deep longing to see Culver again.

A cooling hand settled on her brow. She opened her eyes. This physical sensation wasn't a fevered hallucination. The hand—Culver's large hand—moved caressingly from her sweaty brow to her cheek.

Her dry, cracked lips parting, Pilar watched as Culver leaned closer. His face was smeared with mud to camouflage his white skin. He put a finger to his lips in caution. Pilar gulped and nodded that she understood. How had he gotten here? Her mind gyrated wildly with questions, then suddenly blanked out from the fever. She wanted to laugh hysterically and sob with relief. Sudden fear gutted her: if Culver was here, he was in great danger.

"Pilar," Culver rasped close to her ear as he crouched down by the cot, his arm moving protectively across her, "I'm going to carry you out of here. Whatever you do, don't cry out. Just hang on. You hear me? I'll get you to safety."

His eyes glittered with a feral quality she'd never seen before. And she saw tears in his eyes, along with blazing anger. Since her capture, Pilar had received no medical attention for the bullet lodged in her left shoulder. Ramirez's last order before he'd boarded a helicopter for Bogota was to let her lie without antibiotics or medical intervention until she told what she knew of the raid. Pilar had refused to talk, but in some ways felt thankful for her injury. There were many worse ways to die at Ramirez's hands. So she had lain here, preparing to die....

Culver left her side and she heard him rummaging around. Then she heard glass breaking, and he was back at her side. He scrubbed the inside of her right arm with an alcohol swab, then she felt the jab of a needle.

"Antibiotics," he rasped.

Sighing, Pilar felt relief flowing through her. Culver had accurately read the situation. For the first time in days, she allowed herself some hope that she might not die. She closed her eyes.

Pilar felt Culver's hands sliding beneath her body. She still wore her same clothes, now mud caked and foul smelling. She felt Culver lift her as if she were a feather. Instantly, pain ripped through her shoulder, and Pilar stiffened in his arms. This definitely was no dream. Biting down hard on her lower lip to keep from crying out, she squeezed her eyes shut.

Her head lolled against his shoulder, and her face

pressed into the side of his neck as he carried her to the door. Pilar wanted to help him somehow, but weakness flooded her. Struggling to keep a hold on consciousness, she focused on remaining quiet. The guards had said she was dying and then had laughed at her. They had stopped coming to check on her, saying that in another twenty-four hours they would carry her out in a body bag.

Now Pilar felt the powerful beat of Culver's heart against her side. The warm jungle air flowed across her, a welcome contrast to the antiseptic odors of the dispensary. Pilar knew they were still in serious danger of being discovered, but she couldn't think about it. The last of her reserves had to go toward fighting to maintain a thread of consciousness and to not cry out in pain. Each soundless step Culver took tore at her wound. Pilar heard insects singing. Opening her eyes, she looked up. For once, the fog hadn't formed above the jungle. Miraculously, she saw stars shining softly in the ebony sky.

Just as quickly, they disappeared as Culver eased her through a door and back into the jungle's dense foliage. Her energy was leaking away with each step he took, and she felt his sharp, punctuated breath as he moved deeper into the leafy darkness. They still weren't safe, and Pilar knew it. But with Culver's arms holding her tightly, she felt beautifully protected, even as the last vestiges of her practical mind told her it was an exaggerated sense of safety.

At one point, Culver stopped and laid her gently against a tree trunk. Pilar watched him through blurred vision as he called Major Houston and asked for a helicopter to meet them at certain coordinates. Pilar struggled to speak, but couldn't form words.

"Hold still," Culver ordered gruffly as he pulled the stained and bloody blouse away from her left shoulder. His eyes narrowed at the sight of her swollen, purplish skin. "Those sons of bitches," he rasped as he gently replaced the material.

Pilar looked dazedly up into his fiery gaze. "Th-they said they would give me medical treatment if I told them everything," she managed to whisper. Her lips pulled into a grimace. "I told them nothing, *mi querido.*"

Culver touched her feverish face. "I know," he whispered thickly. "Hang on, Pilar. Just hang on. We've got an hour's hike to the LZ, where Houston will meet us."

Pilar barely managed to nod her understanding. Then, as Culver picked her back up, she felt herself floating out of her body. No longer was she in pain, and because of her shamanic training, she recognized that she had slipped into an altered state of consciousness. Culver's mouth pressed momentarily to hers as he lifted her against him. Weakly, Pilar tried to respond, but it was impossible. Still, his mouth was natural and strong against her lips, feeding her strength and energy.

Moving in and out of consciousness, Pilar was

barely aware of leaves swatting against them, splattering them with dew. At least it was clean water and how she'd longed, at first, for a shower. But, more than anything, she was thirsty. The guards had withheld even water. Her mouth was cottony, and she felt nearly delirious for moisture in any form. As Culver carried her through the dense jungle, droplets of water occasionally splashed on her lips, and she ran her tongue across them to absorb the precious liquid.

A siren began to wail.

"Damn!" Culver muttered, turning briefly back toward the compound. They had come nearly a mile. A guard must have discovered Pilar missing. The hunt was on. His arms tightened around Pilar's light body. Glancing down at her, he saw that she was unconscious again, her head lolling back across his arm.

His heart rate soaring with anxiety, Culver began to trot awkwardly with his load. Pilar moaned softly with each footfall, and he knew the jarring motion was hurting her. His fingers flexed, holding her even more snugly against him.

If the guards found them, they'd kill them. He increased his stride, lifting his boots higher to avoid tripping over roots. Leaves and branches swatted at him continuously, some of them cutting mercilessly at his face and arms. Pilar might die. The thought terrified him. He knew the bullet was still in her body. What if it was near an artery? This jostling could sever it, and she'd bleed to death in minutes.

The added sound of barking dogs made his skin

crawl. Ramirez's men had called in guard dogs to follow their scent through the jungle. Culver increased his speed. He had to run. Despite Pilar's thinness, she still weighed at least a hundred pounds, and the muscles in his back began to protest. Culver knew he had another twenty minutes before they reached the small clearing north of the compound. Would Mike get there in time with the helicopter? If he was late, Ramirez's men and dogs would catch them without question, and Mike, too, would be endangered.

His mind gyrated back to Pilar. He loved her. He loved her more than life. And still he hadn't told her. If she died, what would he do? How could he go on living? Culver hadn't realized how dark his days had been for those years without her, until she'd magically reentered his life, like rays of pure sunlight and fresh breezes filling a room too long closed away. He no longer cared about the past or her reasons for what she'd done. He'd forgiven her. All he wanted now was a second chance, and with each step, he prayed to be given it.

The baying of the dogs grew closer. He and Pilar were ten minutes from the clearing. Culver pressed her head and shoulders tightly against his chest as he ran, covering the ground in long, loping strides. He was grateful she had passed out, so she no longer felt the awful pain of her wound. Then, to his terror, he felt something sticky and warm trickling across his arm. He jerked his head, glancing downward. Pilar's wound was bleeding heavily.

From far in the distance, Culver began to hear the faint sounds of a helicopter speeding toward them. The dogs were closing in. Five minutes. Just five minutes to the clearing. The guards were firing wildly through the trees in a wide arc, though they couldn't yet see him. Bullets whined and gasping for breath, Culver hunched over, using his body to shield Pilar. He heard her moan, then cry out as he leapt over an exposed root.

"Hang on," he gasped, tearing through the foliage and brush like a madman. He felt her hand weakly try to grasp his shirt, without success.

Suddenly, Culver burst out into the clearing. He jerked to a halt, panting heavily. The helicopter was close, though he couldn't see it. The dogs were closer, too. Placing Pilar on the ground, he allowed her to lean against his body as he knelt beside her. Pulling out his radio, he contacted Houston.

"Roger, White Raven, our ETA is two minutes. Out," Houston said.

Culver shoved the radio back into the web belt around his waist. Anxiously, he looked down at Pilar. She had slumped against his left side, her head sagging wearily on his chest. Culver tried to steady his breathing as he glanced behind them. He pulled out his revolver, knowing that any minute now the dogs would find them. The vicious Dobermans were trained to kill. He'd have no remorse about shooting them.

"Culver..."

He leaned down, struggling to catch his breath as he placed his ear near Pilar's mouth. She was speaking softly, in delirious fragments.

"What is it?" he rasped, dividing his attention between her, the approaching aircraft and the howling dogs.

"*Mi querido*...you must know..." Pilar used the last of her waning strength to reach up and wrap her fingers into the damp cotton of his shirt. She saw the hard set of his jaw, saw the terror and anger in his eyes. "Listen..." she pleaded faintly.

Culver looked into her dazed eyes, filled with tears. "What is it?"

"Rane..." she forced out the name, feeling the fingers of oblivion pulling at her again, "Promise to take care..."

"Dammit, I told you I would. Now stop this, Pilar. You aren't going to die. I want you to hang on. I love you. You can't die. You have everything to live for."

Culver loved her. Though the words were distorted by her semiconscious state, Pilar clung to them, focused on them. She felt her fingers slipping nervelessly from the fabric of his shirt as she tried to hold his attention. "Rane..." she whispered faintly, "your daughter... Promise to raise her, *mi querido....*"

Thunderstruck, Culver stared down at Pilar as she sagged against him, unconscious. A trail of fresh blood gleamed like a dark river across her left breast and arm. Had he heard right? Rane was *his* daughter? So much was happening that Culver didn't have time to think clearly about it. He saw the dark shapes of two Dobermans hurtling toward them. Without hesitation, he lifted the revolver and fired off two shots. The dogs yelped and dropped dead to the jungle floor.

Holstering his weapon, Culver scooped Pilar into his arms. The helicopter was landing, its whapping blades like thunder pounding through the jungle around them. Bullets whined as Culver sprinted across the clearing, the wind from the blades buffeting him like the blows of a boxer. Any second now the guards would burst into the clearing, firing.

As the helicopter touched down, Culver saw the door slide open. Mike Houston had a submachine gun, and the gunner at the door had an M-60 machine gun. Both began firing over Culver's head into the jungle as he ran. Fifty more feet. Forty feet. Thirty. All he had to do was make it to the helicopter. He dug his toes into the damp jungle floor, smelling the fresh blood from Pilar's wound and the hot oil of the helicopter engine. Smelling death.

His breath tore from him in ragged gulps and his chest burned from exertion as he prayed that they would be allowed to live. His muscles were in spasms of torturous pain, but the anguish in his heart overrode in his physical discomfort. All that was important was Pilar. Just as he reached the helicopter, a spate of bullets peppered it. Ducking, Culver saw a medic just inside the helicopter, his arms outstretched. Mike Houston was on the man's left, the machine gunner on his right. In a supreme effort, Culver lifted Pilar up to the medic.

More bullets exploded around him. With a grunt, Culver leapt into the helicopter and rolled heavily onto the metal deck.

"Lift off! Lift off!" Houston thundered, jerking the door closed.

Culver swore violently as the helicopter broke contact with the earth. He was thrown against the bulkhead as the aircraft made erratic maneuvers to escape, but his attention remained focused on Pilar, who lay sprawled on the deck behind him. He saw the paramedic frantically working over her. Houston pulled Culver upright and handed him a set of earphones plugged into intercabin communication.

"What's her condition?" he demanded.

"Critical," Culver rasped, wiping the sweat off his brow.

"I'm a trained paramedic," Houston barked. "I'll help Sergeant Ernesto, who's a Peruvian army medic. Just stay out of the way."

Culver nodded, feeling helpless. With the two men bent over Pilar, he could see nothing. He sank against the bulkhead as the helicopter strained for higher altitude and safety. Suddenly a faintness flowed into him. His muscles were knotted with cramps in his back, legs and arms, and he was shaking badly—shaking from the fear of losing Pilar. As he tipped his head back, he squeezed his eyes shut, her last words haunting him: Rane was his daughter. Oh, God, now

it all made sense. Those four beautiful times they'd
made love, he hadn't worn any protection. They'd
been unplanned moments between violence and danger, and he and Pilar had come together out of a need
to reaffirm the life link between them.

Rubbing his face savagely, Culver felt hot tears
prick the backs of his eyes. The helicopters swaying
and bobbing had stopped and flew in a straight, steady
line toward Tarapoto. Pilar had become pregnant with
his child. With beautiful, ethereal Rane, who looked
so much like her mother. No wonder the little girl had
such light skin and eyes. Now that he thought about
it, Culver realized Rane's jaw was shaped exactly like
his. Picturing her, he began to see other small things
in her face and body that spoke of his indelible stamp.
She was going to be much taller than Pilar and
strongly built, like the men and women in his family.

His lips parted, and he felt tears trickle through the
stubble of his beard, squeezing between his fingers,
which were pressed hard against his face. Pilar had
had to disappear, he realized, once she'd found out
she was pregnant with his child. With a jab of pain,
he recalled telling her he wasn't ready for a family
yet. But in South America it was taboo for a woman
to be pregnant and unmarried. It was a sin of the
worst kind in this culture, and Culver saw more
clearly why Pilar had married Fernando—out of
safety for her child and herself. Lifting his head, he
saw Houston holding an IV above Pilar's still form.

The tears in his eyes blurred his view of the two men working frantically to save her life.

What if Pilar died? Oh, God, no. Not now...

Pilar must have thought he would spurn her—refuse to marry her and give their child his name. They had spent three months on that mission—most of it in danger. The sexual attraction between them had been explosive. Pilar hadn't had a chance to get a real grasp of him as a person, Culver realized.

The vibration of the helicopter moved through him as it flew swiftly through the night toward the small hospital in Tarapoto. Pilar hadn't known him well enough to believe he sure as hell would have married her and insisted on keeping their child.

Culver lifted his face, warm tears streaming from his eyes, no longer caring if anyone saw him. He'd made so many assumptions, all of them negative, and had held his anger against Pilar for all those years.

Agony ripped through him at the look of worry in Houston's eyes as the other man turned to him.

"It isn't good, Lachlan. She's lost too much blood. We're doing what we can to staunch it. Didn't they take the bullet out?"

"No," he croaked. "I gave her a shot of antibiotics back at the compound. Ramirez was going to let her die if she didn't tell him about the mission."

Grimly, Houston nodded. "Her blood pressure is very low, and she could go into cardiac arrest any minute. She needs a transfusion. Surgery."

A cry ripped from Culver as he scrambled from his

position on the deck of the aircraft. He made a wild grab for Houston's arm. "You save her life, you hear me?" he yelled, glaring into the other man's haggard face. "Dammit, save her life!"

Chapter 13

"Pilar is in intensive care," Major Mike Houston said tiredly in way of greeting as he gripped Culver's slumped shoulder. "I just talked to the surgeon."

Culver roused himself. He'd been sitting in the hospital waiting room for nearly six hours. In the ambulance, he'd sat with Pilar, her small hand swallowed up by his, and at the emergency room door, he'd made the surgeon promise to allow Pilar to hold her medicine bag in her hand. The surgeon had understood, placing the small object in her limp fingers.

"She's out?" he croaked, his voice thick with exhaustion.

Houston came around the chair and stood in front of him, hands on his narrow hips. "Yeah, I caught up with Dr. Juarez in the scrub room. He'll be out to see you shortly." The officer smiled a little. "You look like hell, Lachlan. Why don't you get a hotel room down the street, take a shower and hit the sack? You can't do anything here for her right now."

Scowling, Culver stood. The Special Forces major still wore his tiger-striped fatigues, and darkness showed beneath his eyes. Houston had stayed with him in the hospital, and Culver was grateful for the American's care and interest. Right now, he felt damned alone. Helpless. He hadn't slept in over sixty hours, and he swayed drunkenly on his feet.

"They got a shower facility here?" he demanded.

"Yeah, in the surgeon's quarters. Why?"

"Can you get me some clean clothes from somewhere?"

Houston gave him an assessing look. "Yes."

Rubbing his bearded jaw, Culver nodded. "Good."

"You're staying." Houston didn't phrase it as a question; it was a realization. With a shrug, he said, "I'll get my aide, Sergeant Javier, to rustle up some civilian clothes."

"Thanks." Culver's vision kept blurring. He had been sitting in that chair sweating for six hours. As badly as he needed sleep, he couldn't rest. His mind raced with thoughts about Pilar, Rane and himself. He so desperately needed to talk to Pilar.

"This woman," Houston began awkwardly. "She means a lot to you, doesn't she?"

Culver nodded wearily as he began to walk down

the polished tile hall toward the surgeon's scrub area, Houston falling into step beside him.

"I just got off the phone with Perseus. I thought you'd like to know that their aircraft is on its way to the U.S."

"Anything on Morgan's condition?" Culver asked. His feet felt as if they were weighted with cement.

"They've got him stabilized. They brought a flight surgeon with them, a woman doctor who works for Perseus. Arrangements have already been made to put Morgan in Bethesda Naval Hospital in Maryland."

"Did the flight surgeon say anything about his condition? You saw what he was like—a vegetable, with no memory of anything."

Houston nodded grimly and pursed his lips as they slowed down in front of the surgeon's area. "No...no change, I'm sorry to say."

"And he's got a wife and two kids," Culver muttered. "He either has amnesia or they've permanently wiped out his memory. The poor bastard."

Houston opened the door for him. "I feel for his family."

Culver agreed as he walked through the entrance and saw the surgeon changing out of his green operating clothes. Turning, he held out his hand to Houston. "Thanks—for everything."

Grinning a little, the major gripped his hand and shook it. "I'll be hanging around until things stabilize for you here."

Culver nodded gratefully. First he'd talk with the

surgeon, then he'd get a hot shower, shave and put
on some clean clothes. After that he'd sit with Pilar.
She wouldn't know he was there, but that didn't matter.

Culver awoke instantly when Pilar regained consciousness for the first time. He'd been sitting in an
uncomfortable chair next to her bed, his head tipped
back against the wall. Major Houston had a lot of
power in Tarapoto Hospital, Culver had discovered
very quickly. Ordinarily, visitors weren't allowed to
stay in intensive care, but Houston had seen to it that
he was allowed to sit with Pilar. The beeps and sighs
of machines surrounded him as he tried to shake off
the grogginess.

Culver had completely lost track of time. He'd nodded off while stroking Pilar's cool, limp hand. The
clock on the wall read 6:00 p.m., so he must have
slept a long time. Blinking away the drowsiness, he
focused on Pilar.

She lay with IVs in both arms, her shoulder heavily
bandaged beneath a light blue gown. Her hair, once
muddy and tangled, had been washed. Though it
hadn't been combed very well, the strands lay like
shining raven's wings about her pale face. Her once-
beautiful lips were badly cracked. Culver had been
told that more than anything else, Pilar had been de-
hydrated. At once he'd realized she must have been
denied water since her capture. He wanted to kill Ramirez for his inhumanity. But now the IVs fed her

life-giving fluids to help her body fight off the massive infection.

Culver turned to call for a nurse, but she was already there. His attention riveted on Pilar, who had begun to move her head slightly. She closed and opened her mouth, whispering something. Leaning closer until his ear nearly touched her lips, Culver strained to hear her words.

"Rane…Culver…"

Holding her fingers in his, Culver swallowed with difficulty. The nurse, after checking the monitors, seemed satisfied.

"Is she doing okay?" Culver asked.

"*Si, señor.* She is becoming conscious. I will get the doctor."

Relief swept through him. He leaned down and placed a kiss on Pilar's frowning forehead. "Hush, *mi querida,*" he told her. "Everything is fine. You're going to make it. You hear me? You're going to live. Rane is safe, and so am I. Just rest." He watched the wrinkles on her brow ease. Somehow, Pilar had heard him and responded. The knowledge shook him to his soul. Her thick, dark eyelashes stood out in stark contrast to her pale skin.

Lifting his hand, he began to caress her hair with gentle strokes designed to soothe her. Pilar wasn't moving much, but he could feel a shift in energy around her. And then he laughed harshly at himself; he was so deprived of sleep he wasn't sure whether he was dreaming or if this was real. Still, her small,

slender fingers in his hand provided a definite connection to reality. As Culver looked down at her, he
felt his heart open like a flower. Without thinking,
just following his instincts, he leaned forward and
gently laid his mouth on hers in a kiss designed to
breathe life and strength back into her.

"Eh, Señor Lachlan?" the nurse inquired.

Culver broke the kiss and looked up. The doctor
and nurse stood expectantly in the doorway.
"Oh...yeah, come and take a look at her, Doc." He
flushed a little as he stood up and stepped aside. "I
think she's going to make it. What do you think?"

It didn't take the doctor long to make his assess-
ment. He briefly studied the raw, swollen wound
briefly and had the nurse apply a new dressing. He
nodded his gray head when he took her blood pressure. As he lifted each eyelid to check her pupils with
a small light, he even had the ghost of a smile on his
mouth.

"You are right, Señor Lachlan," Dr. José murmured as he straightened and looked across the bed
at him. "Señora Martinez will live."

Joy swept through Culver, strong and overwhelming. He stared at the tall doctor. "She's going to
live?"

He smiled slowly. "*Sí.* You are a tough *hombre,*
eh? Maybe it was you being here that made the difference. Your love for her. Your prayers, perhaps?
Or—" he pointed to the small medicine bag that Pilar

still clutched in one hand ''—maybe the power of her jaguar medicine.''

Culver struggled to find words as emotions overwhelmed him. Pilar was going to live. Live! Gulping, he rasped, ''Or maybe all the above, Doctor?''

Tapping his chest, the doctor smiled wider. ''Many times I have seen people hover in the arms of death in this room. I see the families of these patients sitting in the lobby, praying for them. Prayer is very powerful, eh? Especially prayers of a loved one. No, I think your love brought her back to us. I do not take the medicine of the jaguar lightly, for I've seen it work, too. But there is nothing like the heart, eh?'' He gestured to the chair. ''*Señor,* you still need sleep. She has decided to come back and live with you on this earth. The nurse will show you to a room with a bed. If Señora Martinez awakens, I will have someone come and get you.''

Culver studied Pilar, who had sunk into a healing sleep. The bed sounded damned inviting. ''Yeah, I'd like that, Doctor. Thanks...''

Culver awoke on his own. Glancing sleepily at his watch, he realized it was six in the morning. Hoisting his feet over the side of the narrow bed, he sat up. A small knock sounded on the door and he looked up.

''Come in.''

A nurse poked her head in the door. ''Señora Martinez is awake and asking for you, *señor.*''

Instantly, Culver was on his feet. He still hadn't

shaved, but at least he'd showered and had clean
clothes. The nurse couldn't walk fast enough to keep
up with him as he hurried down the hallway toward
ICU. Dr. José was standing just outside Pilar's glass-
enclosed room, and he smiled as Culver approached.

"She is asking for you, *señor*."

His heart soared. Yet it pounded with dread, too.
As Culver reached the glass enclosure, his gaze swept
immediately to Pilar, who was sitting up in bed,
propped by many pillows. Her dark eyes looked almost black in her ghostly face. Yet when their eyes
met, Culver felt his heart mushroom with joy, leaving
him breathless. Entering the room, he closed the door
quietly behind him. Someone had brushed Pilar's
hair, and it shone like an ebony frame around her oval
face. The look she gave him was shy and uncertain.
Why?

Reaching her bedside, he took her delicate face between his hands. His eyes filled with tears as he
croaked, "Welcome back, *mi querida...*" Culver
leaned down and brushed his mouth against Pilar's
lips, feeling her soft response to his tender foray. It
was all he could ask for. Sensing her weakness, he
eased his mouth from hers and allowed her to lean
back against the pillows.

Pilar's eyes were luminous with tears as she stared
up at him. He saw that she had the medicine bag
gripped in her right hand, resting on her blanketed
stomach. Retrieving a chair, Culver brought it over

and sat down close to her. He laid his hand on her arm and discovered she felt full of life now, not death.

"How are you feeling?" he asked thickly.

Pilar sighed softly and studied him. "Very weak," she said, her voice rough from disuse. "I—I didn't think I would live."

"I know." His fingers tightened briefly on her arm. "A lot of people were praying for you."

Her throat constricted. "You stayed..."

He frowned. "Why wouldn't I?"

Pilar felt a panic cut through the calming effect of the painkilling drugs. "I thought I dreamed it—or maybe I did not...." She gazed at him. Culver's face was shadowed by several days' growth of beard, giving him a dangerous look. His eyes were bloodshot, his features haggard with exhaustion. His hair, too, was uncombed, and she longed for the simple strength to lift her fingers and tame some of those dark strands back into place.

"What are the tears for?" he inquired gently, taking his thumbs and wiping the moisture from her cheeks. "Pilar?"

Closing her eyes, she absorbed his grazing touch. Oh, how strong Culver was. "Did I dream saying it?" she asked brokenly. She felt his fingers drift away from her face and his hand move slowly up and down her arm, as if to soothe her. Pilar had no strength to protect herself from whatever answer he might give her. She thought she'd told him Rane was his child

But had she? Or had it been a fevered hallucination? Wearily, she forced open her lashes and looked up at him. The tenderness burning in his eyes would dissolve when she told him.

Gathering what little courage remained to her, she murmured, "Rane...is your daughter...our child...." She could barely hold his gaze. Trying to steel herself against the coming explosion, Pilar realized she was completely defenseless, with no way left to shield her raw emotions. Had she been brought back from the upper world by the jaguar goddess to tell him the truth? Was that why she had been sent back through the tunnel of light into her body?

Culver's lips parted, and he felt hot tears well into his eyes. He reached over and covered the hand that gripped the medicine bag. "I know, *mi querida.* You told me out in the jungle when you were dying. Don't you remember?"

His voice was rough with emotion and to Pilar's shock, she could detect no recrimination in Culver's eyes—only the tears that had begun to wind down his cheeks, disappearing into the bristles of his dark beard. Short-circuited, her senses spun. She *had* told him! "But...you are still here...." she whispered weakly.

Culver slowly stood, then leaned over and framed her face with his hands. Pilar looked so frightened, so unsure. He understood why. "Listen to me," he said rawly, his voice gruff with emotion, "I love you, Pilar. I love Rane. Nothing matters to me but the two of you. Do you understand?'' He blinked and looked up. ''I didn't want to lose you. When I got you to that chopper, all I could think was that Rane was ours, and that I didn't want you to die.''

Gazing at her, not caring that he was crying, Culver leaned down to caress Pilar's mouth. Her lower lip trembled, and he felt a sob catch in her throat as his lips gently took hers. In that golden moment, all he was aware of was her warmth, her softness and her incredible courage. Easing his mouth from hers, he stared deeply into her tear-filled eyes. ''Nothing matters except you and Rane. Do you understand me, Pilar? The rest of our collective worlds can go to hell. All I want—all I'll ever need—is you. Rane is ours— created out of our love.'' He took a deep, ragged breath. ''And God knows, I loved you all those years. I never stopped loving you.''

Culver didn't approach any other serious topics with Pilar for several days. She had lost consciousness shortly after his admission, and Dr. José was concerned that too much stressful emotion would cost her dearly in terms of surmounting the infection that had nearly taken her life. Culver agreed. Pilar was transferred to a private room, and Culver had a bed brought in for him. He slept nearby, and whenever she awoke, he did, too, as if an invisible cord connected them.

Pilar had a number of nightmares, and Culver was grateful that Dr. José allowed him to stay with her

twenty-four hours a day. Culver brought her books
and read to her. She hated television, preferring instead to talk with him about many things—but never
again did she broach the subject of Rane being his
daughter. Sometimes Culver wondered what was going on inside Pilar's head. Had she heard his admission? That he was willing to take responsibility and
become Rane's father? Perhaps she'd been too
drugged from the surgery to remember his words.

At times Culver wanted to say something, but recalling Dr. José's warning, he took the man's advice
to heart. Pilar, he discovered, had been badly broken
by her recent experience. She wasn't as strong and
resilient as he'd thought. But then, he ruminated as
he walked down the hall toward her private room with
a handful of orchids in a vase for her, Pilar had carried a heavy load for eight years by herself. Culver
ached to talk to her of all she'd been through, to share
with her his understanding of why she'd made the
decisions she had.

Maybe today, he hoped. It had to be Pilar's decision, though. As he knocked on the door, he smiled
to himself. Every day, Pilar grew a little stronger, and
despite everything, it was sheer joy for Culver just to
be with her. As he opened the door, he saw to his
surprise that she was out of bed. She wore a dark pink
cotton robe, her right hand deep in one pocket as she
stood with her back to him, looking through the venetian blinds.

When Pilar heard him enter, she slowly turned. Her

left arm was in a sling and she managed a small smile of welcome. "You were gone a long time."

Culver grinned roguishly and lifted the vase of purple-and-white orchids so she could inhale their heavy, sweet fragrance. "One of the nurses in ICU told me about this old woman, a jaguar priestess living just outside Tarapoto, who raises the most beautiful orchids in the world." He smiled down at Pilar and watched a rosy flush come to her pale cheeks. "Well? What do you think? Are they half as beautiful as you are?"

Touched, Pilar leaned over and inhaled their heady fragrance. The burning hope in Culver's eyes lifted her depressed spirits. Straightening, she caressed the thick, waxy petals. "They are far more beautiful than I am," she whispered. Pilar had never thought of herself as beautiful, though the way he looked at her made her feel that way.

Snorting, Culver slid his hand around her elbow and guided her to a wooden rocking chair near the window. "Your face could melt the hardest of hearts," he said. Pilar moved slowly, her balance not yet totally restored. As she lowered herself carefully into the rocker, Culver placed the orchids on the table next to her bed.

"It's good for you to get away from here for a while anyway," Pilar said. She loved the rocking chair because it reminded her of being rocked in her mother's arms when she was small. "You are built for the outdoors, not places that close in on you like this.'' She looked around the sterile room and then back at him. Culver took another chair and brought it over to sit down facing her. How much she enjoyed their quiet moments together. In the past few days he'd talked a great deal about himself and his family. She'd learned so much. He was sharing a side of himself she hadn't known, and it left her yearning for him, for his kisses.

Oh, how she'd missed his kisses! She could recall each one with burning clarity. But since she'd been transferred to this room, he'd oddly removed himself in that sense. Although he slept here with her, on his separate bed, and he held her hand or caressed her hair occasionally, he hadn't kissed her again. Pilar's spirit died a little each day, bereft of the feel of his healing mouth upon hers. She was so needy right now, but she didn't expect Culver to understand her physical need for his touch. She was like a battery that had run down, and his kisses recharged the very depths of her spirit, infusing her with light and hope.

Sighing softly, Pilar folded her hands in the lap of the cotton robe. It was time. She felt strong enough now to talk to Culver without sleep overtaking her as it had been doing, suddenly and without warning. The antibiotics had worked their magic, and she had come back from the arms of death, fully back in her body and in the present. Glancing up, she saw Culver watching her with a curious, burning gaze. Her lips parted, and the corners of her mouth lifted slightly.

''I'm afraid,'' she admitted, opening her hands and

giving a weak laugh. "I felt I understood jaguar medicine, but I do not. I felt it was about strength and power. It is more than that. It is about living honestly." Pilar held his caressing gaze. "When I met you, Culver, I felt my heart open and embrace you. I had dreams all during my young life of a man's face, and it was your face. I did not know the gift of the jaguar was to bring visions of the future to me until Grandmother Aurelia told me. It was then I confided my dreams of your face to her.

"She laughed and hugged me. She said that was the man who would hold my heart gently in his hands. I asked her how I could know when I was so young who was going to love me. Grandmother said there are many things we can never explain. But when I saw you, I felt my chest open up, like one huge orchid unfolding all its rich, beautiful petals."

Pilar studied her tightly clasped hands for a long moment, searching for the right words to convey her feelings. The silence stretched out between them, but without tension. Instead, she felt Culver's respect and interest in her words, in how she saw her world—and his. That assurance gave her the courage to go on.

"When you compared me to an orchid, I felt this cord strung between us." She lifted her hand and moved it gracefully from her solar plexus to his. "How could you know of my special love of the orchid people? You seemed to know so much about me, and I felt it was because you remembered coming to me in your dreams. I didn't know how a *Norte Amer-*

icano could do such things. In South America, it is common and accepted, but..." Pilar shook her head and gazed at him in awe. "We had three months together, *mi querido*. I was so young at the time. Young and thinking that my life was endless. I laughed at the danger around us. I jeered at the violence always nearby. And when you loved me that first time by the pool in the jungle where the orchids grew, I felt my spirit fuse with yours. I felt our hearts melt into one. I felt my womb expand with a warm, golden light, and I felt your life within me."

Pilar licked her lower lip and went on in a softer voice. "I did not know it at the time, but I was pregnant with your daughter, our child—Rane. A wonderful, joyous sensation emanated from my womb. I felt the pulse of life in there, and I thought it was because we had become one and loved without regret or shame." She laid her hand across her abdomen and smiled fondly in remembrance. "Each time we made love after that, I felt stronger, more sure of you and of myself."

Pilar touched her forehead and frowned. "And then you were wounded. I was so afraid you were going to die. I didn't know at the time that I'd suffered a small bullet wound in my thigh—it was no more than a stinging sensation. When they took you into surgery in Lima, the doctor examined me thoroughly. I was bleeding." She pointed to her thigh beneath the robe. "That was why he examined me. I thought it was my moon time, though I'd not had one for three months.

The doctor said no, the blood between my thighs wasn't moon blood, nor was it from the fleshy wound on my thigh.''

Pilar looked up, and her voice grew hoarse. ''He told me I was two months pregnant. He said I would lose the baby if I stayed on my feet, that the shock of the mission had started to tear the infant from the wall of my womb.'' Pilar covered her abdomen and rubbed it gently with her hand. ''I had never lain with another man. I knew you were the father of this baby who was fighting to survive. The doctor said I must go home, stay in bed and rest, or I would lose her.''

A ragged sigh escaped Pilar's lips as she looked up at the ceiling beyond Culver. ''I had no one. My parents were dead. What was I to do? I had only one friend, and that was Fernando. Hector called him, and he came immediately to the hospital. I told him that you did not want children right away, that you were not ready for them. And he asked me if you had said you loved me. I said no. He said it was a bad sign, and I could not disagree. I wanted my baby to have a name, Culver. I did not want her to suffer as I had, with mestiza blood. To be a child out of wedlock is a curse here. She would be called the child of a whore. I couldn't stand it. I wanted Rane to be able to overcome her mestiza blood and hold her head high. She would not have been able to do so with a mother who was pregnant and unmarried. Fernando convinced me you would not want me pregnant.'' Frowning, Pilar shook her head. ''Now I wonder

about that. At the time, I believed him. I was so confused that afternoon. I was in shock from your nearly
being killed. I was traumatized by my own bullet
wound, though it was small in comparison to yours.
And to be told I was pregnant..." Her voice wobbled.
"It was too much for me to cope with." She rubbed
her furrowed brow with trembling fingers, and her
voice lowered with feeling. "We were married that
evening, so that when Rane was born, I could say she
was premature, and no one would suspect she had
been conceived out of wedlock."

Opening her hands, feeling drained, Pilar held his
tender gaze. "Oh, Culver, I hated leaving you in the
hospital. But the doctors told me you would live. Fernando said it would be best never to see you again,
but I sobbed myself to sleep for weeks afterward."

Getting up, Culver slowly moved over to crouch in
front of Pilar and capture her hand. The stricken look
on her face was telling. "I don't know what I could
have done at that point, but I would have claimed
Rane as my daughter," he said.

Tears shimmered in Pilar's eyes as she studied him.
His voice was gruff with emotion, his hands strong
and steadying on hers. "You would?"

"Yes," he rasped, "in a heartbeat. I know how
people look upon unmarried mothers down here. Your
culture is very different from mine. In North America,
a woman with a baby out of wedlock isn't such a big
deal. Down here—" he scowled "—it's a damned

mortal sin. You're shunned by everyone, and the child is an outcast—forever.''

Wearily, Pilar rested her brow against his. "Oh, Culver, I wish I had known. I wish…''

"It doesn't matter anymore, Pilar,'' he whispered gently, releasing her hands and framing her face.

Tears streamed down her wan cheeks. "I—I remember you telling me you wanted a family someday, but not at that age. I thought you'd send me away, that you wouldn't want to be told the truth. I sobbed it all out to Fernando, and he felt, under the circumstances, that I should marry him to protect my family's name and my daughter's future.''

Culver bowed his head. "I was just blowing smoke at the time, Pilar. I never really meant what I said about not having a family. It just didn't occur to me you'd get pregnant. Everything seemed so natural between us that—that the possibility escaped me. I wasn't being responsible, and that was my fault—not yours. I was older, more experienced, and I should have seen that we took precautions. But I didn't.…'' He gazed into her swollen eyes. "Fernando married you because he was your friend, and he was giving you and our baby protection from this society.''

"Y-yes… We never laid with each other, Culver.'' Her voice shook with tears. "H-he never touched me. He was like a father to me, very warm, very kind. He loved Rane so much. He treated her as if she were his own child.''

Once again Culver wiped away her tears. "I'm just

sorry I didn't know, *mi querida.* This isn't all your fault, you know. I bear a heavy responsibility, too.''

Sniffing, Pilar said, ''I gave up hope at that point. I thought you would be ashamed of me. Of getting me pregnant. I didn't think you wanted me or our baby. As I got older, I began to doubt what I had done, but by then, it was too late. I knew your anger with me would be great if I told you the truth. I was afraid you might want to take Rane away from me if you knew. Oh, *Dios,* how could I ever have left you when you needed me? How could I have been so cruel to keep you and Rane from knowing and loving each other?'' She placed her hands over his and held his glistening gaze. ''I never loved anyone but you— ever. So many times as Rane grew up I wanted to tell her about you, about our love.... But I did not want to hurt her like that. She was mestiza; that was enough. I did not want her to feel even more different from society by being an outcast, too.''

''I understand,'' Culver said gruffly, leaning over and gently taking her mouth. Pilar tasted of wet, salty tears. He felt her moan, a slight vibration as she hungrily returned his gentling kiss, intended to soothe the pain she still carried in her heart. Easing away from her, he saw the gold flecks deep in her eyes again, for the first time since she'd been wounded. Her cheeks were suffused with pink, and hope thrummed strongly through him.

''I love you, Pilar. I never stopped loving you through all those years.''

With a little sob, she sat up, her hand pressed to her lips. "Y-you never stopped loving me?"

Culver crouched, one hand on her thigh, the other on the arm of the rocking chair. "Never."

"I have hurt so many people," Pilar whispered brokenly, and she covered her face with her hand, beginning to weep in earnest.

"Come here," Culver whispered roughly as he drew her out of the rocking chair and into his arms. Careful not to jar her wounded arm, he brought her fully against him and held her. The sounds coming from deep within her reminded him of the cries of a wounded animal. Pilar shook in his arms with each ragged sob. All Culver could do was hold her, rest his cheek against her hair and rock her gently in his arms. He felt the pain of the load she'd carried alone for so long. Guilt ate at him. She shouldn't have borne so much by herself. Culver shook his head. He'd been young, irresponsible and foolish. And look how much it had wounded Pilar—the only woman he'd ever truly loved. Could she forgive him? Could Rane? Bitterness coated his mouth as he held her shaking form.

Little by little, her sobs abated, and finally Pilar leaned against him. He took her full weight and kissed her hair. "I never knew I'd be sent back down here, Pilar, but I'm glad as hell now that I was."

Wiping her cheek with trembling fingers, Pilar said in a wobbly voice, "I was in shock when Hector told me I would be working with you." She eased away just enough to meet his warm gaze. "I was so scared,

Culver—afraid you'd realize my secret. I died inside when you first saw Rane. I thought you might see the resemblance and prayed that you wouldn't.''

Nodding, he ran his thumb lightly across her arched eyebrow and cupped his hand against her cheek. "You don't have to be afraid any more, *mi querida.* It's no longer a burden you carry alone. I'll help you shoulder the load from now on.''

Relief swept through Pilar. The moments spun between them as her mind cartwheeled over so many options. "I'm worried for Rane. She grew up thinking Fernando was her father....''

"Shh, one step at a time, sweetheart,'' he said huskily, drawing her against him. "First I want you to get your strength back. We'll stay in Tarapoto until then. Then we'll go back to the village. Rane is old enough to understand some things, Pilar. We'll let her know that I'm her father and that I had to go away for a very long time, and that Fernando agreed to take care of her in my absence.'' He stroked her hair gently. "When she's older and can understand more, she'll know the whole truth of the situation.''

Closing her eyes, Pilar pressed her face into his shirt. His arms were shoring her up, nurturing her. "I'm so tired, *mi querido.* So tired....''

Culver kissed her hair. "I know you are, sweetheart. Come on, I want you to go back to bed and rest. I'll be here. I won't leave you....''

Chapter 14

Pilar stood at the entrance to their hut and watched as Aurelia took Rane's small hand. Today she was going to take her great-granddaughter deep into the jungle to begin teaching her about the herbs that could save lives. All those who walked the medicine path were taught from an early age about such things, and Pilar was grateful Rane would have the chances that she had not.

Eight weeks had passed since her release from the hospital. Culver and she had been married by a priest in Tarapoto before leaving for the village. She gazed at the plain gold wedding band on her finger, still not daring to believe Culver was her husband. It was a dream she'd had for so long that she still didn't quite

trust it to be real. Aurelia's wise care and the love of
Culver and her daughter had worked miracles on Pilar's healing process. Moving her shoulder a bit, she
could feel stiffness, but it was no longer painful.

The morning was cool without being cold, the fog
suspended like white gauze between the second and
third canopies of trees. The village was just awakening, the timid light of early dawn making the fog
glow like a radiant ceiling above the huts. The calls
of the birds announced the break of day, their music
enlivening everything around them.

Pilar stood absorbing the beauty of her home. The
younger men were already in the fields above the village, working with hoes or shovels, while the wives
and widows hovered around cooking pots. The children were just coming awake, their sleepy faces evident as they stumbled from their huts, rubbing their
eyes. Dogs barked and played among the pigs, chickens and noisy roosters.

Pilar recalled that sometime in the night, Culver
had left her and gone outside. Then Rane had come
in from her own room and had snuggled into her arms
on the thick floor mat. Had Pilar dreamed that Culver
had then come back, kissed her on the brow and whispered he'd be back later? With a sigh, she savored
the quiet joy she'd experienced ever since Culver had
returned fully to their lives.

Each day, he went with Grandfather Alvaro to the
fields, to work with the men. He left very early in the
morning, when it was still cool, and returned around

noon to eat lunch. Then it was siesta time—they spent the hot, muggy afternoon snoozing outdoors in hammocks until early evening, when the heat dissipated. Culver then would sit with the men of the village, drinking a locally made beer, telling stories, laughing and talking about the events that made up the fabric of their lives.

Yes, it was a good life, Pilar thought. Culver would return to their hut for the evening meal, to eat with her and Rane. They always talked about the day's events in detail during dinner. Rane had accepted Culver as her father far more easily than Pilar had ever thought possible. Perhaps it was because Culver made sure his daughter was with him every day, in some way, and he listened carefully to her youthful, bubbly talk.

Fernando, Pilar realized now, had cheated Rane of much. Culver was not only interested in what Rane had to say, but he talked with her at length, respectfully, as if her ideas and thoughts truly counted. Fernando, bless him, had never held such conversations with Rane. Despite his love for her, she'd been a mere child to him, therefore incapable of serious discussions or worth the time it would take to answer the many questions she asked about things that caught her curiosity and attention. Culver, on the other hand, took great pains to explain carefully when she asked him a question. Pilar did not fault Fernando, for he'd been an old man, his heart giving him many problems. She'd understood when Fernando would wave

his hand and ask Rane to leave him alone, for her
daughter was an impetuous, terribly curious child.

But now Pilar's heart swelled with quiet happiness
as she moved out to the cooking pot. Culver had already made a grain cereal and added water and honey
to it. A blackened kettle was set high above the coals
of the fire. The dish was fragrant, and Pilar stirred it
gently with a wooden spoon. Her thoughts drifted
back over the past eight weeks. Each night had been
beautiful to look forward to. The people of the village
had built them a three-room hut, so that Rane had her
own room, she and Culver had a bedroom and they
shared the main room, where they ate and welcomed
their many visitors. When Culver had driven her back
to the village, the entire population had stood waiting
to greet them.

Pilar had cried as her grandparents embraced her.
Rane had clung to her, her slender arms wrapped
tightly around Pilar's skirt, her small head pressed
against her mother. Culver had stood back, tears in
his eyes. Pilar hadn't expected a new home, or the
warm, heartfelt welcome she received. The hut was
completely furnished with the items they needed to
set up a household, and the generosity of the people
made her weep with gratitude. And each night, Culver
would put Rane to bed, tell her a story, kiss her on
the brow, then come to their bedroom.

How Pilar looked forward to that. Because her
wound was still mending, he would not love her. She
understood, but she reveled in the feel of his powerful

arms about her, drawing her gently against him. And she waited in sweet anticipation for his mouth to settle on hers. How badly she wanted to love him fully!

Pilar was so caught up in her heated thoughts of Culver holding her and kissing her that she did not hear his approach. However, her other sense—the jaguar medicine within her—felt his presence. She was sitting on a log near the cooking pot, the bowl of cereal in her hand, when she felt him arrive. Her brain told her that was silly, since Culver would be out in the fields at this time of day.

But as she lifted her head, her eyes met his. He stood a little off to one side, watching her, tenderness in his eyes. The expression sent a thrill through her. Pilar felt heat suffuse her heart, then streak downward like jagged lightning hurled from the sky into Mother Earth. The look in his eyes told her of his love, of his burning need of her—in all ways. He was dressed in a loose, white cotton shirt, the sleeves rolled up to his elbows. In his hand was a hoe. The jeans he wore were threadbare, outlining his magnificent lower body. Like all the men, he wore thick leather sandals to protect his feet, and she could see he had been in the fields by the dark soil clinging to his feet.

His gaze touched her, silent yet evocative. Slowly lowering the bowl to the log, Pilar watched his mouth curve slightly in greeting. When Culver walked, he reminded her of the silent jaguar, who owned the jungle on his own terms. Culver possessed an incredible masculine grace, and the eight weeks of hard field work had somehow brought a level of relaxation to his movements. Where before he'd been tight, almost rigid in his walk, now there was a fluidity about him that was beautiful to watch.

"I thought you were in the fields," she said a little breathlessly as he approached.

Culver placed the hoe against the side of the hut. "I was."

Pilar's mouth curved as he came and sat down next to her. "Are you not feeling well?" She searched his face, darkly tanned from the sun that shone brightly on the slopes above the village, where the terraced fields lay. So much of the tension that had been in Culver's expression had disappeared. Although his face remained as rugged as the granite Andes, at the same time it mirrored a relaxed quality.

"I feel great." Culver studied Pilar in the warm silence that hummed between them. She had braided her thick hair as she did every morning. Then at night, he would unbraid it and brush out the silky strands. It was a special time for them. "We're going somewhere," he said enigmatically. "Aurelia has packed us a lunch." He reached over and caressed Pilar's cheek. "All I need is you."

Surprised, she gazed up into his light blue eyes and saw amusement in them—and longing. Her skin tingled deliciously where he'd barely grazed her cheek. "Where are we going?"

Culver's mouth stretched. "Now, if I told you that, it wouldn't be a surprise, would it?"

Her lips parted. "What about Rane?"

"Aurelia is taking care of her all day. They know we won't be back until dusk."

Pilar studied him. "You have planned this carefully, haven't you, *mi querido?*" She saw Culver flush.

"Somewhat..." he managed to say, trying not to smile.

A deep, throbbing sensation began in her lower body. The look he was giving her was one a man gives his woman when he wants to love her—fully. Without reserve. Without regret. She felt a secret heat coiling tightly within her as she began to understand. "You are taking me somewhere that is private?"

"Very private."

"I see..."

"I think you're beginning to." He flashed her a slight smile. "Don Alvaro told me about this place."

"Oh?"

"It's a secret. Only the men know about it."

"Ahh," Pilar teased, standing up, "one of those." The Quechua had places for men and places for women. Each gender had unique, special places to go for healing, for ceremony or for time to think, uninterrupted. She knew that wherever Culver was taking her this morning, no one would interrupt them. Today he would love her. The thought made her go weak with desire. How many times had she ached to fulfill him with herself, her body like an anguished candle incomplete without him as her flame?

"I'll go over to their hut, pick up the knapsack and be back," Culver told her, rising. He saw her cheeks flush, making her look even more desirable. Pilar wore a simple white blouse and a pale blue skirt that brushed the tops of her slender ankles. She was barefoot and looked so much a part of this beautiful land—as if she belonged here for the rest of her life.

"How soon will we be there?" Pilar asked as she walked with Culver down a very old, rarely used path through the jungle. They had walked for more than two hours into a portion of the jungle she was unfamiliar with. She knew of all the women's places, the sacred places where they went for their monthly moon time, to spend five to seven days singing, dreaming, weaving and being close to the Mother, but she did not know this path.

Culver squeezed her hand. "Not much farther, according to Don Alvaro." It was nearly ten in the morning, and the fog was burning off, allowing dappled sunlight, like droplets of golden rain, to shimmer and dance through the thick canopy above them.

Pilar saw the jungle thinning in front of them, and she felt Culver's hand tighten momentarily around hers as they stepped out of the wall of foliage. Her breath caught. There in front of them was a waterfall nearly thirty feet high, the water gushing over the black-and-white-granite rocks into a huge oval pool below. The water was crystalline—a deep emerald green so clear that she could see fish swimming in its depths. Around the pool, water lilies extended their white petals skyward like slender arms embracing the sunlight.

"Oh!" Pilar whispered, her fingers going to her heart. "This is like a dream!"

Culver looked around, appreciating the beauty of the pool. "Don Alvaro told me about this place right after we brought you home," he said as he led her forward. Thick green grass covered the rounded banks. "He said this was the pool where a young man brings the woman he loves. A lovers' hideout, where they can have complete privacy."

Pilar halted at the pool's edge and gazed up at Culver. Her eyes filled with tears as she absorbed his tender look. "This is so much like the pool where we first met and loved...."

"Yes, it is." Culver released her hand and shed his pack, then took out a large sleeping mat and spread it beside the water. The rush of the waterfall mingled with the melodic songs of birds and the harsher calls of parrots that flitted like rainbows within the jungle wall. Culver saw the tracks of many animals, and knew the pool was a main water source for many jungle inhabitants.

Leaning down, he picked up a bright red Macaw feather. "Here, this is for you...." He knew how Pilar loved the brightly colored feathers. She was weaving a shield of ones she'd found on her daily forays into the jungle. Now he watched the delight in her eyes as he handed her the long crimson plume.

"Thank you!" Pilar stroked the feather lovingly and watched as Culver crossed to a very old rubber tree that leaned over the pool. Stretching upward, he picked a string of pink-and-white orchids that hung from the trees like a small cluster of stars. The look he gave her as he settled the necklace of orchids around her throat made her feel faint with need.

"These don't begin to do you justice," Culver murmured thickly as he began to slowly unbutton her blouse. He saw her lips part as his fingers lightly grazed her flesh. Pilar wore no bra under the faded white cotton, and her nipples began to harden beneath the fabric as he opened it. His voice grew hoarse with desire. "I wanted to bring you here, *mi querida,* to love you. I wanted to have you to myself for just a few hours, to make you mine again."

Heat swept through Pilar's breasts as he slowly opened the blouse to reveal them. She swayed unsteadily. Gripping his arms, she whispered, "Yes... please, love me, Culver. I—I've waited so long... dreamed so long of this moment...."

His hands slid beneath the fabric, and she felt the calluses as his fingers cupped her straining breasts. His skin was toughened by long hours of work, powerful sunshine and unrelenting wind, while hers was soft, her flesh molding and fitting into his strong hands. Her fingertips dug into his upper arms, and her eyes closed as Culver moved his thumbs teasingly over her nipples. The sensation was electric. A gasp escaped her, and she felt his hands gently draw her forward until his mouth fitted hotly against hers, his tongue moving boldly into its depths. Breathless, Pilar raised her arms to his neck and sagged against his strong frame.

His mouth drew fire from her. Before this, at night in their bed, he had kissed her gently. Tenderly. But now, as he eased the blouse from her shoulders and worked the clasp on her skirt free, he was neither gentle nor tender. No, this kiss was hot and seeking. Pilar felt her skirt pool around her feet. When his fingers molded against her flared hips and traveled down her body, she felt her lingerie join the skirt. Then she stood naked, fitted tightly against his clothed form feeling his masterful hardness pushing strongly against her belly to let her know just how much he wanted her.

Without letting his lips leave her mouth, Culver picked her up and carried her to the mat, where he gently deposited her on her back. His mouth was rich, giving and taking. She felt the prickle of his recently shaved skin and dragged into her nostrils the scent of his body, slightly sweaty from the hard labor he'd performed in the fields earlier this morning. Her fingers frantically worked at the buttons of his shirt, and she ached to tear his clothes off so his naked body could mold and fuse with hers. Finally the shirt fell away, and with his help, his Levi's soon joined it. In one hot, burning movement, he settled at her side, one arm beneath her neck, his other hand ranging up and down her naked body.

The moment he pressed her fully to him and she felt his male hardness insistent against the apex of her thighs, Pilar moaned with pure pleasure. He tore his mouth from hers and lowered it to one hardened, up-lifted nipple. Pilar tipped her head back, her throat exposed in exquisite surrender as he suckled her. Simultaneously, she felt his callused fingers moving downward, sliding between her thighs and easing her legs open just enough to give him entrance. Her body seemed suspended, waiting for his touch. As he slid down into that moist crevice, she shuddered, and an electrical sensation bolted up through her as he eased his fingers between the folds of her womanhood.

Instinctively, she curved tightly against him, her breasts pressed to his chest wall, her arms rigid with tension around his neck as he stroked her with velvet intensity. Her thighs opened wider, of their own accord. The fragrance of the pink-and-white orchids surrounded her and mingled with his very male scent. He suckled her other nipple, and she felt herself spiraling out of control, heat gathering rapidly wherever he stroked her. The hot liquid of her body spilled across his searching fingers like nectar produced by the fragrant orchids that lay around her neck. As his mouth fitted commandingly across hers once more, Pilar cried out, and a white-hot bolt seemed to shoot to her very core. But her cry was absorbed into his mouth as his tongue plunged again and again into her.

Culver smiled to himself as Pilar surrendered entirely to his ministrations. Her mouth was as wet and hot as the opening to her womanhood. He eased his fingers away from her, laid his hand on her small, curved thigh and opened her even more—to receive him. Laying her back on the mat, his mouth still clinging hotly to hers, he rose above her, covering her with his larger body and feeling her shift languidly beneath him in welcome. How long he'd waited for this moment! Culver had dreamed torridly of this coupling for eight endless years, and now, unbelievably, Pilar was here beneath him, her body writhing restlessly goading him to take her, to brand her as his.

The ache in his loins was nearly unbearable as he grazed the slickness of her moist inner thighs. His lips pulled away from his clenched teeth. He didn't want to hurt her, knowing she'd not lain with another man in eight years. She would be small and tight, just as she had been the first time he'd taken her virginity at the sunlit pool. Her mouth was pouty, soft and provocative against his. Did she realize that she was disintegrating his control with each movement of her hips? A hiss issued from between his teeth, and he froze above her, but she did not freeze in turn. With one twist of her hips, she slid upward, enfolding him, inviting him in.

It was too much. Culver hadn't expected her to be so bold, so assertive. Beads of perspiration popped out on his forehead as he tried to control himself. His rigidity made him tremble as she continued her gentle assault upon him, undulating her hips in an ancient rhythm that further crumbled his restraint. Heat was building inexorably within him, and he knew he would explode at any moment. Blindly, he plunged into her silken depths, the tightness overwhelming. His fingers curved and followed the shape of her head, and he felt her hands settle firmly upon his hips, pulling him closer, inviting him more deeply into her.

Dizziness exploded within him and he became mindless. He became the male jaguar taming his female. The fragrance of the wild orchids mixed with the raw, primal odor of their bodies, all conspiring against him. Groaning, Culver took her deeply, hard—plunging into her again and again, a little farther with each thrust. Suddenly white-hot heat surged through him, exploding like the power of the sun itself. Gripping her fiercely to him, he froze deep within her, and in that moment, she moved her hips, sucking the blazing energy out of him and into herself. With each graceful, undulating movement, he felt the power bleeding out of him like the waterfall that thundered into the womb-shaped pool below.

Within moments, he was spent, and Culver groaned and relaxed onto her smaller form. Kissing her soft, pouty lips, he drowned in the honey of life contained within her mouth. Moving his hips raggedly against her softer, more-provocative ones, he felt as if he were dying and going to a heaven he didn't deserve. The richness and depth of their recaptured love had made this time even better than eight years ago. They had been forged by the fires of life, shaped by intense and powerful emotions, and their lovemaking had gained an exquisite facet that had been missing before. The moments, golden and molten, spun together like a beautiful spiderweb that had captured the dew of the night and was now being shot through with sunlight. A deep glowing heat throbbed within him as she milked the last of his power into the depths of her moist, receptive body.

The love he felt for her in that moment was so rich, so intense, that Culver nearly drowned in the beauty as he moved off her and brought her alongside him, remaining deep within her, his hand flattened against the base of her spine to hold her hips captive. She held him in turn, a tender prisoner of love within her. Her hardened nipples grazed his chest wall, and he felt her ease away. Tunneling her fingers through his hair, she guided his head downward until once again his mouth fitted over one of those straining peaks, and he suckled her. A fine tremor moved through her as he held her in his arms in that moment, and he felt Pilar become boneless in his embrace, felt her release a sigh of utter womanly fulfillment, at one with the man she loved.

Culver could imagine nothing beyond this moment, and having this brave, warm and loving woman in his arms again at last. As they lay, locked together, he felt himself hardening again within her, filling her with his love. He felt the renewed honey of her liquid confines bathing him as his strength returned. Her belly was soft against him, and as he lay there, suckling her, holding her tightly, Culver wanted to give her another baby—a second child formed and fashioned out of this exquisite love that had never died.

As her fingers ranged through his hair, sifting the dampened strands, he lifted his mouth from her hardened nipple and gazed deeply into her lustrous, half-opened eyes, burning jaguar gold with love for him. He had no words. His throat constricted with tears as he absorbed her gaze, her touch. He loved her fiercely, as a jaguar possessed his mate—ferocious and territorial. For he was certain now: she was his mate for life, and he'd gladly fight to his death to see that she was protected and cared for, and never became separated from him again.

Pilar's lips parted, slick and glistening from his kisses, the corners lifting tenderly. She raised her hands and settled her small, slender fingers on the sides of his face. The love shining in her eyes shook him to the depths of his soul, and for the first time, Culver realized just how much Pilar loved him—had always loved him. Her love was fierce, he discovered, and no less loyal than his for her. His smile was very male, very tender, as he leaned down and barely touched his mouth to hers.

"I love you," he whispered thickly against her lips. "Forever…"

Epilogue

Culver tried to contain his surprise when they arrived back at the village that evening. Major Mike Houston was standing near their hut deep in conversation with several of the village elders. Culver's grip on Pilar's shoulders tightened momentarily, and she gave him a worried look. No one had expected to see Houston again. Why was he here, in their village?

Grimly, Culver quickened his pace. His hand dropped from Pilar's shoulder and he captured her hand, squeezing it gently to convey his support.

"There you are," Houston said, looking up.

Culver sized up the Special Forces officer, dressed in his fresh, tiger-striped utilities, a dark red beret on his head. Houston's pistol was at his side, and his black jump boots gleamed with a high polish. "What's going on?" Culver growled, halting and holding out his hand in greeting.

Houston smiled a little, nodded deferentially to Pilar, then devoted his attention to Culver. "I've been waiting a couple of hours for you, Lachlan." He gestured toward the clearing near the village where a U.S. Apache helicopter had landed, fully loaded with weapons. "I decided to drop in and let you know that the Peruvian government has taken out Ramirez."

Culver's brows dipped. "Taken him out?"

Houston's face grew hard. "Remember the fortress where he kept Morgan?"

"Of course."

"It's been leveled. The government decided to go after the son of a bitch—" He broke off abruptly, giving Pilar a distressed look. "Pardon me, ma'am, I didn't mean to be so graphic...."

Pilar nodded. "I understand, Major."

Relieved, his mouth twitching with the hint of a smile, he held Culver's assessing gaze. "Ever since you two rescued Morgan, the Peruvian government has been working overtime to locate Ramirez. Our spies told us he'd returned from Bogota. We found out he was planning to completely destroy this village as an act of revenge." With a shrug, he said, "When I found that out, I suggested to the general that we ought to do a little leveling of our own first. Of course, the Apaches were flown by Peruvian pilots. I just went along as an observer." His smile broadened.

"Too bad you weren't there, Lachlan. You'd have been our cheering section. Those Apaches destroyed the army of choppers Ramirez used to ferry the cocaine in and out of the country. Not only that, but the chief was there and got caught in the cross fire."

Culver's eyes narrowed. "Ramirez is dead? How can you be sure?" The drug lord had the nine lives of a cat. Over the years, Culver knew, the Peruvian government had tried many times to capture him.

"I saw it with my own two eyes." Houston settled his large-knuckled hands over his narrow hips. "After the Peruvian pilots leveled the fortress, we landed and went in with a company of land-based troops to finish the job. Whoever had survived was taken prisoner at that point. We found Ramirez's body in some of the rubble near the hacienda. He was dead."

Culver saw the glitter in Houston's eyes and understood the officer's pleasure in finding the drug lord dead. He felt Pilar's reaction and looked down at her. She'd gone pale. Automatically, Culver placed his arm around her small shoulders and drew her gently against him.

Houston sobered. "One of the women from the village, who had watched the attack, came up to us. She asked for a pistol from one of the officers and he gave it to her. She and her daughter had been raped by Ramirez. She put the gun to the man's head and pulled the trigger. So I know he's dead."

"Justice," Culver muttered, "finally."

Houston nodded gravely. "I was telling the elders

of the village that they're really safe now. And so are
you. One of Ramirez's men spilled the beans. During
interrogation, he told us there was a mole in Hector
Ruiz's office—it was his secretarial assistant, Manuela. She's in jail awaiting trial.''

Pilar's eyes widened enormously. "Manuela gave
us away, then?''

Culver nodded. "We were attacked by Ramirez's
men at Hotel of the Andes,'' he explained to Mike.
"And I thought Ruiz had sold us out. I was wrong.''
He gave Pilar an apologetic look.

Houston's eyes narrowed speculatively on Culver.
"I understand you're going to stay down here and
make your home in the village?''

Culver nodded. "For now. We may decide to alternate years between the village and my family's
home in Colorado. We can have the best of both
worlds for our daughter that way. My parents want to
see Rane grow up, too.''

With a shrug, Mike grinned a little and looked
around. "Not a bad way to live, really. You've got
the sun for light, clean water from the Andes and
good volcanic soil to raise food.'' He smiled down at
Pilar. "And a good woman. Wish to hell I had one.''

"Someday, if you get lucky like me, you might,
Houston. Until then, you'll be another lone wolf.''

With a sigh, Houston took off his beret to wipe the
sweat from his forehead, then settled it back on his
head. "Yeah, I was afraid of that. One more bit of
information and then I'll leave you to your safe, idyl-

lic life here, Lachlan. I called Perseus the other day
to check on Morgan's condition."

"How is he?" Culver asked. The man had never
been far from his thoughts in the past two months.

"The same, I'm afraid. He spent eight weeks recovering in the navy hospital at Bethesda. The doctors
have written him off. Nothing they do seems to bring
back his memory. He doesn't know his name. He
doesn't remember Perseus. Worse—" Houston grimaced "—he doesn't recognize his wife, Laura, or
their two children. Helluva sad situation, isn't it? It's
going to be a pleasure to make a call to Jake Randolph. He's still running Perseus, and I can't wait to
let him know we've taken Ramirez permanently out
of the picture."

"How sad," Pilar whispered, tears in her voice,
"for Morgan and his family. What will his wife do?"

"I guess she's planning on taking Morgan to a special place he loves—a cattle ranch in Arizona. Morgan made friends with the rancher's son in Vietnam,
and the family has offered them a cabin on their property that's fairly isolated, so they can have time to get
to know each other again. Jake said that Laura's extended family will take care of their children while
they take some time off together. I think Laura's hoping that relaxing surroundings and getting him out of
that hospital setting will help jog his memory. Quality
time alone, you might say."

Pilar shook her head and pressed her hand to her
lips. "Oh, I feel so badly for Laura. How awful to be

with her husband, who once loved her and now sees her as a stranger. How hard it must be for her...."

Culver squeezed her gently. "We know from experience that love is never easy."

Pilar wiped the tears from her eyes as she absorbed Culver's tender, loving look. "No, it's not. But love, if it's true, will never die."

Houston sighed. "At least there's one happy ending in this ongoing mess. I've got to get back to Lima before they start wondering where the hell that Apache helicopter is." He smiled a goodbye to Pilar, then held out his hand to Culver. "Stay well and happy, Lachlan. Since I'm permanently assigned to Lima as a military attaché, let me know if there's anything you need, okay?"

Culver gripped the officer's lean, spare hand. "You bet I will. Thanks, Mike—for everything." With Ramirez dead, Culver knew, people of the region could breathe a huge, collective sigh of relief.

"I hear from Pilar's grandparents that they're hoping you're going to be a papa—again—real soon," Houston teased.

Culver had the good grace to blush. He looked down to see Pilar blushing, too. Automatically, she placed her hand on her belly in response, and the elders surrounding them chuckled indulgently.

With a hearty laugh, Houston clapped Culver on the shoulder and left, striding toward the waiting helicopter. Culver turned with Pilar to watch him walk away.

"I cannot believe all this," Pilar whispered as they saw Houston disappear inside the helicopter, the door shutting behind him. The blades began to turn slowly.

"What? About Ramirez?" Culver asked, his gaze on the helicopter, but his heart centered on Pilar.

"Yes. It's like a prayer that's been answered. He was such a monster, Culver."

With a sigh, Culver turned and led her toward their hut. The elders nodded, the group breaking up and heading to their homes for the evening meal. As the helicopter took off, the noise echoed against the slopes above the village. At the door to their hut, Culver turned and watched the dark green aircraft lift into the sky, hazy now as the sun rode low on the horizon. Pilar's arm went around his waist, and she leaned on him.

"Major Houston is a good man. I don't understand why a woman hasn't fallen in love with him yet."

Culver chuckled. "Sweetheart, Houston is a professional soldier."

"You are a mercenary. What is the difference?"

"Was," he corrected as he led her into the hut. Someone had left a vase filled with colorful wild orchids in the main room. The soft dusk light filtered through the windows, and Culver seated himself on one of the wooden chairs. Pilar took a seat on the straw mat at his feet and began to prepare the evening meal.

An incredible peace blanketed Culver. He had everything, he realized humbly as Pilar leaned against

his knee. Her legs were crossed beneath her skirt, her
bare feet hidden by the material. As he looked around
the simple hut, he realized he was the richest man on
earth. He'd seen the envy in Houston's eyes—for the
man didn't have a good woman to love and accept
him. Culver had recognized that look of longing, and
it made him feel damned lucky.

Reaching down, he caressed Pilar's hair. "Rane
will be here soon. Grandmother Aurelia said she
would bring her home at dusk, if you're worried."

Pilar looked up and smiled tenderly at him. She
tied off one long, thick braid with a scrap of red yarn.
"I am not worried, *mi querido*." She caught and captured his hand. Guiding it down to her belly, she
placed her two hands over his one large one. "Do
you wish for another child?" she whispered, holding
his burning gaze.

Culver gently ran his hand across her belly.
"Sweetheart, I want all the kids we can support. And
I'll love every one as much as I love you." He sighed
and sat up again, looking toward the opened door. In
the distance he could see Grandmother Aurelia and
Rane, hand in hand, coming across the clearing, each
carrying a sack filled with what he was sure were
many varieties of herbs. "I hope we have two more
beautiful daughters exactly like Rane and a couple of
strong, healthy sons to round out the family." He
shifted his gaze back to Pilar, thinking how radiant
and exotic she looked in that moment as she sat next

to his legs, her hands still pressing against her belly. "What do you want?" he whispered thickly.

"Just you—and our love that never died," she said softly, tears in her eyes. "Our babies, no matter how many, will always be babies of love...."

Gently, Culver leaned down and touched her mouth with his. Her lips were swollen from the power of his earlier kisses, so he was tender with her. "I'll love you, Pilar, forever...."

* * * * *

MORGAN'S MARRIAGE

Chapter 1

It was raining. Or was the sky crying? Laura Trayhern stood rigidly on the steps of the Operations building at Andrews Air Force Base in Washington, D.C., peering anxiously through the gray light of dawn. The Perseus jet bearing her husband, Morgan, trundled slowly toward them. It was February, but instead of snowflakes, cold raindrops fell.

As Laura stood huddled in her tan raincoat, her hands plunged into the deep pockets, a wool muffler encircling her neck, trapping her shoulder-length blond hair, she remembered Morgan telling about that rainy Virginia night seven years ago when he'd been summoned to a general's home. The dying man had sent for him, wanting to reveal the truth about cir-

cumstances that had sent Morgan into the clandestine
life of a traitor to his country. It had been the first
time in years he'd stepped back on American soil.

A shiver wound through Laura. If Morgan's situation had been desperate then, it could well be critical
now. How badly injured was he? Less than twelve
hours ago he'd been rescued from a cell at drug-lord
Ramirez's Peruvian jungle fortress by two very brave
and daring operatives. The woman agent, Pilar Martinez, who had entered the fortress to locate Morgan,
was missing in action. But her partner, Culver Lachlan, a Perseus employee and mercenary, had managed
to get Morgan out of that hellhole and onto a waiting
Peruvian army helicopter.

Now Culver was back in the jungle, searching for
his missing partner—and Laura was standing on these
cold concrete steps watching the Lear jet, bearing her
husband, rolling far too slowly toward Operations.
She tried to still her anxiety, but to no avail. Radio
silence had been maintained for the entire flight out
of South America, for fear of reprisal attempts by
Ramirez. But on board, she knew, was one of the Air
Force's best flight surgeons, Dr. Ann Parsons. Laura
and Morgan knew Ann well, and with the surgeon's
medical knowledge and special expertise working
with men and women traumatized in battle, Morgan
was in the very best of hands.

Still, she had no idea what kind of shape her husband was in. He was alive; the flight team had re-
ported that much by radio once they'd reached U.S.

airspace. Laura squeezed her eyes shut. She felt herself sway. A large hand settled supportively around her upper arm.

"Laura?"

She lifted her chin and looked up into Jake Randolph's weary, carved features. Since the fateful day that she, Morgan and their son, Jason, had been kidnapped by Ramirez, Jake had taken over the day-to-day running of Perseus for Morgan. And she could see the toll this worldwide marathon of searching out and rescuing them, with the help of three extraordinary merc teams, had taken on him.

"I'm all right," she whispered. But she wasn't, and she knew Jake could see it. Anxiety, rage, worry and sorrow—emotions writhed within her like agitated snakes. Her personal captivity had come at the hands of Garcia, Ramirez's right-hand man, who'd held her prisoner on Nevis Island in the Caribbean. The work of Morgan and his Perseus mercenaries had badly disrupted Ramirez's cocaine trade to the United States over the past year, and the drug lord had decided to get even in the most personal of ways. Luckily, Jason had been relatively well treated and hadn't been physically harmed during his imprisonment. Although emotional consequences were inevitable after such an ordeal, Dr. Parsons had assured her earlier that Jason, due to his age and resilience, would likely be the first to heal. Laura—and Morgan—could take much longer to come to grips with the personal nightmares they'd endured at the hands of Ramirez and Garcia.

"A few more minutes," Jake reassured her, leaving his steadying hand on her arm. "Do you want to wait in the ambulance for him?"

Laura noted the grudging lightening of the sky as drops of rain continued to splash against the gray concrete landing apron—like the heavy tears that threatened to spill from her aching eyes. The ambulance was waiting to take Morgan to the navy hospital in Bethesda, Maryland—one of the best in the nation. Laura didn't know what she would do when she saw Morgan. The wait had been agonizingly long—three months since the kidnapping—and now his freedom was at hand. But what condition was he in? How badly had Ramirez tortured him?

Shivering, she felt Jake's arm go around her shoulders and draw her against him. The man was a giant—like Morgan. Morgan was so tall and proud, towering a good eight inches above her petite frame. For just a moment, Laura allowed herself to lean heavily against Jake. He seemed so stalwart and unyielding, and she felt as if the last of her own strength—the wall she'd erected to survive her desperate ordeal—was rapidly crumbling. Maybe it was the fact that it was all over, and she could let down a little of her careful guard. She had her son back. And now her husband, whom she loved with a fierceness that defied description, was returning to her.

"Laura?"

Opening her eyes, she eased away from Jake. "Y-yes,

let's go to the ambulance. I don't want to get in the way when they bring him off the plane.''

He smiled slightly, giving her shoulders a reassuring squeeze. ''Good thinking. Come on....''

Jake held the black umbrella above her as they stepped off their partially sheltered spot on the wet steps. The rain pounded steadily on the taut umbrella. The temperature was barely above freezing, and as they hurried toward the white ambulance marked with an orange stripe, Laura shivered deeply. Her gaze remained pinned on the approaching Lear jet. *Morgan.* Oh, sweet Lord, how she loved him! Her heart ached, tears stung her eyes and she hung her head. She needed so badly to see him, to assess his condition. Would he be glad to see her? Be able to reach out for her hand—and tell her he loved her?

Her heart began skipping beats as she climbed awkwardly into the ambulance. One of the military attendants who rode up front took her hand, smiled a little and helped her. The bright lights in the rear, where a gurney awaited Morgan, made her wince. The paramedic, a young Air Force lieutenant named Bob Martin, guided her into a seat beside him, and Laura was grateful for the heat blowing from the vehicle's front vents.

She watched anxiously as the jet drew closer. Now she could hear the whine of the engines. Jake stood in the rain, the umbrella folded in his left hand, all his attention on the approaching aircraft.

Laura closed her wet fingers into fists in her lap,

starkly aware of all the medical paraphernalia surrounding her. Thank goodness, Dr. Ann Parsons
would be accompanying them to Bethesda and would
be acting as Morgan's primary doctor. Oh, how Laura
ached to see her husband! How many nights had she
lain awake, needing his touch and the comforting
warmth and bulk of his body next to hers? She even
missed those soft snoring sounds he made when he
lay on his back and she had to elbow him gently so
he'd turn on his side. She longed for so many little
things—important things she had never properly appreciated.

"Here they come," Jake said, turning toward her.

The aircraft had stopped, and someone appeared,
seemingly out of nowhere, to put chocks beneath the
tires. The engines were cut, the whine rapidly dissi-
pating even as the rain picked up, bouncing off the
wet glare of the concrete. Jake's hair was soaked, the
tan jacket he wore dark with water as he moved toward the jet's lowering ramp.

Laura's breath became suspended as the two ambulance attendants moved quickly to join him at the
aircraft's opened hatch. A stretcher appeared. Her
heart thudded hard. The still form on it, wrapped
completely in blankets, had to be Morgan. Ann Parsons appeared at the door as the stretcher was lowered
to the ground. Laura's hands tightened almost painfully in her lap.

Lieutenant Martin eased by her, asking her to move
into his unoccupied seat. Her knees weak, Laura got

up, grabbing at anything she could put her trembling hands on to help her make the move. Light-headed with anticipation, she heard voices outside the ambulance. The rain was driving hard now, as if the sky were weeping unabashedly for what Morgan had endured. Instinctively, Laura knew it was a bad sign. Oh, God, how bad? Did Morgan need emergency surgery? Had he suffered cardiac arrest? she wondered with terror. She needed so much just to touch his cheek and let him know that he was finally safe and that she loved him!

Her eyes widened as the stretcher bearing Morgan was hoisted aboard the ambulance by two strong men. Light blue covers swathed his motionless body, protecting him from the cold and rain. Another attendant handed two IV drips to Lieutenant Martin, who hung them on hooks above the gurney. Movement at the opened doors caught her attention: Dr. Ann Parsons.

Laura tore her gaze from the blankets covering Morgan's face as Ann climbed in, her features tight and unreadable. Automatically, Laura's hands went to her chest. The doors slammed shut.

Ann glanced at Laura. ''We've got him home,'' she said a little breathlessly.

The ambulance jerked forward, its lights flashing. At the head of the gurney, Ann quickly pulled the blankets from Morgan's face.

Laura heard someone gasp. Lieutenant Martin worked in tandem with the doctor, very few spoken commands passing between them. The ambulance seemed to move almost drunkenly through the downpour, and Laura's brain leadenly registered that the gasp had come from her, seeing Morgan's face for the first time.

Ann twisted to look at her, then quickly resumed her work, leaning over Morgan, monitoring a blood-pressure cuff around his arm. "He's unconscious, Laura," she said, her voice calm.

Laura fought the panic racing through her as her gaze remained fastened on her husband's slack, grayish face. Shock bolted through her like a lightning strike. This was Morgan? But it couldn't be! This man's face was pathetically thin, his gray skin taut over the sharp bones of his face. Morgan's face was full and strong, not this broken horror. Laura felt terror seep through her skin and muscles to settle into her bones—a coldness leaking to her very soul as she stared at him.

The sounds of the rain pounding on the ambulance roof and Ann's husky orders, the swaying of the vehicle—all ceased to exist in Laura's consciousness. She knew only this man's face—her husband's face—which didn't look familiar at all. Morgan was tall, strong-boned and heavily muscled. This man resembled a prisoner of war starved nearly to death. Morgan had a proud, hawklike nose, but this man's nose was puffy and broken in several places. Her eyes moved to rest on the jet black hair, now peppered with silver at the temples, and those straight, black brows. They, at least, she recognized—remnants of the Morgan she'd laughed with on the night of their seventh wedding anniversary. The night he'd given her a strand of pearls. The night the thugs had broken into their home, shot them with tranquilizer darts and spirited them away to their separate hells.

"Oh, God..." Laura cried softly.

Ann looked up. "He's alive, Laura. Get a hold of yourself."

A lump formed in Laura's throat. Ann's words hit her like icy water—just what she needed to stem the rising tide of hysteria tunneling through her chest. Her fingers curved around her throat as she continued to stare in disbelief at the man on the gurney. Martin changed IVs, and she watched the clear fluid's relentless dripping down the translucent tube into Morgan's arm.

"I-is it him?" she croaked.

Ann handed Martin the blood-pressure cuff and removed the stethoscope from her ears. "Yes, it's Morgan." She reached out, her fingers wrapping firmly around Laura's hand. "He's alive, Laura. Right now, that's what counts."

Nodding jerkily, Laura sat back, still gripping Ann's fingers. The doctor's hands were long and bony, but they were a healer's hands, and Laura was everlastingly grateful that Ann was here with them now. "It doesn't look like him...." she whispered.

"He's been starved," Ann returned quietly. She moved to sit next to Laura. "I've given him a preliminary medical exam, but I'll need to run a lot of tests once we get to the hospital.''

"H-has he asked for me?"

Ann's mouth compressed. "No...he's been moving between unconsciousness and semiconsciousness. He's drugged, Laura. His pupils barely respond to light. My guess is he's shot full of cocaine.''

Pressing her hand against her mouth, Laura stared down at Morgan—a man she no longer recognized. Tears flooded into her eyes. "How could they do this to him?" Her voice broke with emotion.

Ann put an arm around her and squeezed gently. "That's what these men do. They're animals," she said, her voice vibrating with disgust and anger. "Listen to me, though, Laura. We can give Morgan back his lost weight, help him regain his strength. This is temporary.'' Worriedly, she assessed her. "What about you? How are you doing?''

"I'm okay.''

Ann smiled tiredly and patted her on the shoulder. "Sure you are. Have you been taking the tranquilizers I prescribed?''

Laura shook her head. "I tried, but drugs make me feel out of touch, disconnected. I—I couldn't stand the feeling, so I stopped taking them.''

Sighing, Ann nodded. "Damned if you do and damned if you don't.''

"Don't be upset with me, Ann. I did try.''

The doctor's expression gentled to one of understanding. "I'm not upset with you, Laura. I'm just trying to help you through this awful time. Yóu haven't had a chance to work through your own trauma at all. You had to be there for Jason when he was returned to you...." She looked over at Morgan's deathlike pallor. "Now I'm afraid you'll have an even bigger demand on you."

"I'd rather have my family with me," Laura said in a low, broken voice, "whatever the cost." She had been living on tenterhooks for the past three tortured months, not knowing if Jason was alive; fearing Ramirez had killed Morgan. *Hell.* She'd lived in a hell, with no relief, no moments of reprieve to tend the deep wounds suffered during her own kidnapping.

"So Morgan hasn't come out of it at all? Hasn't asked for me...for Jason?"

Ann shook her head. "He's borderline semiconscious at times, Laura. But even then he's so full of cocaine he's not really with us."

"But—he did recognize you, didn't he?"

"No," Ann admitted, "he didn't...."

Laura's stomach began to knot with a terrible foreboding. "Is it normal, when a person's been drugged, not to recognize friends?"

Wearily, Ann pressed her fingers against the bridge of her nose. "Sometimes, in some situations."

Laura looked at this woman who had done so much for all of them. Ann was in her mid-thirties, her dark brown hair glinting with reddish highlights in the ambulance's bright interior. But her skin was taut across the bones of her face, her blue eyes dark and ringed with fatigue. Laura shouldn't be giving her the third degree; the flight surgeon would fight with fierce loyalty through hell itself for Morgan's recovery. It was those very qualities that had led Morgan to actively pursue the Air Force captain for Perseus. Ann's skill not only as a medical doctor but as a psychiatrist specializing in trauma was something he wanted for his employees, who were often caught in life-and-death situations.

No one knew better than Morgan the long-term debilitating effects of trauma. So he'd wooed Captain Parsons away from her prestigious position as one of the Air Force's premier flight surgeons, dealing with field combat and the Post Traumatic Stress Disorder suffered by aviators who had been POWs or had experienced crashes. He'd wanted the best, and Ann had been with Perseus for six of the seven years the company had been in existence. Over the years, Morgan's relationship with Ann had become that of a doting older brother. Ann had grown up without siblings, and Laura knew she considered the Perseus team to be like family.

Reaching out, Laura squeezed her thin hand. "You must be as stressed over Morgan as I am."

Ann returned the grip. "I'm angry, Laura. I'm so angry that, I swear, if I could, I'd put a pistol to Ramirez's head and blow his brains out for what he's done to Morgan." She looked at Morgan and then up at the ambulance ceiling, her voice cracking. "I've seen a lot of PTSD. I'm trained in emergency medicine and trauma. But when I saw Morgan as they took him off that Peruvian helicopter, I cried.'' She grimaced. ''Me, of all people.''

''You love him like a brother,'' Laura reminded her gently.

Ann blinked her eyes and nodded. ''Yes, I do.'' She wiped the tears from her eyes and looked at Laura. ''What Ramirez has done to him is unconscionable, Laura. I'll be glad to get him to Bethesda, where we can monitor him. I'll be glad to get this damned cocaine washed out of his system, too. I want to see what's left of Morgan on a mental and emotional level.''

Laura fought back her own tears. ''Yes…so do I,'' she whispered.

It was still raining. Laura stood at the window of Bethesda's visitors' lounge, watching the gray pall continue to fall, her arms crossed over her breasts. Time crawled by. When they'd arrived, Morgan had been quickly taken away, never regaining consciousness. That had been many hours ago.

Laura felt more than heard someone approaching. Hoping it was Ann, who was working with the chief of internal medicine on Morgan's many tests, she turned. It was Jake, carrying two cups of black coffee. Searching his exhausted features, she mustered a slight smile as she reached for the proffered white plastic cup.

"Thanks, Jake."

He nodded and eased his bulk against the window frame. "How long is this gonna take?"

Laura sipped the hot coffee. She wrinkled her nose, knowing she'd already drunk too much of the stuff. Still, it seemed somehow soothing and familiar, better than nothing. "I don't know." She sighed.

"I wish to hell Ann could come out and tell us something—anything."

"It's nearly four o'clock." Laura felt the acidic liquid eating at her stomach and set the coffee cup on the table next to the window. The lounge was nearly empty. A young navy petty officer paced on the other side of the room, awaiting the birth of his first child. Life. Life instead of death. Laura's mind was groggy with fatigue and she longed for sleep, but knew it would be impossible.

"I remember," she said softly, turning and looking out the window again, "how Morgan hates the rain. He always said it seemed as if the sky was crying. He never did like tears. When I cried, it always upset him terribly. He never knew what to do, or how to help me." The sky was a dismal gray, though the rain had become soft and sporadic compared to this morning's deluge.

Jake snorted. "Most men have trouble with that. Shah tells me it's good for us to feel a woman's tears, to touch them—that absorbing them into our hands will help us get in touch with our own tears and soften us." He smiled a little. "As you know, my wife is part Sioux. She comes from a culture where people believe in showing feelings.''

''Then I wish Morgan had some Indian blood,'' Laura whispered.

''After seven years of marriage, it still bothers him to see you cry?''

''Yes...he's especially sensitive when our children cry. It's almost as if it hurts him physically.''

''Well, Morgan has a lot of tears left inside him, Laura. Maybe that's why.'' Jake sipped the coffee thoughtfully as he gazed out at the gathering dusk. ''Night comes on so fast in the winter,'' he said, more to himself than her. ''There's something about this season that's unsettling. I said that to Shah one time, and she laughed. She said winter was the time of turning deep within, of going on an inner spiritual journey. She compared people to seeds strewn over Mother Earth in the fall. We lie there in the elements, rained on, frozen and snowed on. The seed has to pull inward to survive, waiting for a warmer time to come forth.'' He glanced down at Laura. ''Winter is a time to look at who we are—and aren't. The things it's easy to hide from in the many activities of the warmer seasons—our awareness of what's hurting within us, for example—are revealed in this season when we're trapped indoors.''

''It gives us time to think, to feel,'' Laura agreed softly. ''I'm glad Shah shared that with you. Winter used to be my favorite time of year.''

Jake smiled a little. ''You're introspective by nature, Laura. And shy. Shah is, too. I'm more of an extrovert, but Shah has helped me understand that her quiet depth, her need for silence and time alone, isn't wrong. It's necessary to her survival. I like and need people around me. She doesn't. At first, I didn't fully understand that about her, but after we got married, she helped me appreciate introverts in general.''

"Eighty percent of the world is made up of extroverts,'' Laura said wryly. "Morgan's an introvert like me.''

"Yes—'' Jake sighed "—he is. And maybe that's why he hasn't been able to shed those tears he needs to release.'' He looked at her worriedly. "What about you? Have you been able to cry? To get out what you're holding on to from your own trauma?''

"Now you're sounding like Ann.''

"It's common sense, really,'' Jake told her in a low voice. "You've lost at least twenty pounds you couldn't afford to lose, Laura. You look like hell warmed over and we're all worried about you.''

She reached out and touched his powerful arm. "I'll make it okay, Jake. I've got Morgan back. That's all I need.''

He shook his head. "I'm not so sure, Laura. You haven't had a chance to be by yourself and simply heal. You've been on an emotional roller coaster for three months with no down time. Shah's right, I think.''

"About what?''

"She told me on the phone a while ago that what

you and Morgan need is some quality time together—
alone.''

"Wouldn't that be wonderful?" It would be, but
Laura didn't see how it would be possible.

"It's just a thought," he murmured, sipping the last
of his coffee.

Laura turned toward the lounge entrance, and her
heart banged once, hard, in her breast. Dr. Parsons,
dressed in her white smock, a stethoscope hanging
from her neck like a pendant, came through the doors.
Anxiously, Laura searched the doctor's worn face.

Automatically, Jake moved to Laura's side and settled an arm around her shoulders, as if to steady her
for whatever the doctor had to say.

"Laura, Jake," Ann said in greeting. She put her
hands in the smock pockets and focused on Laura.

"How is he?" Laura managed to ask.

"Right now, he's sleeping," she said. "And that's
a good sign." She gripped Laura's arm and guided
her to one of the vinyl sofas that lined the room.
"Come and sit down," she urged gently.

Anxiety rippled through Laura as she sat down opposite Ann. The doctor pushed several strands of dark
hair from her eyes.

"The bulk of Morgan's blood tests are back. Phys-
iologically speaking, he's severely malnourished, so
we're administering vitamins and minerals via IV."
Ann frowned and her voice lowered as she fought to
keep the emotion from it. "Ramirez broke three fingers on each of Morgan's hands. The fractures have

healed on their own, but two of the six will have to be rebroken and properly set or he'll have trouble with them later. His nose was broken several times, and I'm recommending surgery at a later date to try to undo the damage. His left cheekbone suffered a lateral fracture, but that's healed cleanly. He's lost six teeth, mostly molars—probably from the beatings he took.

"I've got a dentist lined up, and eventually we'll look at bridges to replace the teeth." Ann stopped, took a deep breath, and went on. "Morgan was tortured extensively, Laura. His back is a mass of scars and welts. With antibiotics, all of that should heal pretty much on its own, over time. The scarring will probably be massive, but again, plastic surgery can reduce it."

Ann opened her hands and looked down at them. "There are innumerable cigarette burns on his body."

Laura took in a deep, ragged breath. "My God, Ann—"

"There's more," she warned huskily. "Perhaps the most worrisome is that Morgan so far has no memory—at all. He didn't recognize me. He—he doesn't remember you—"

Laura shot to her feet. "What?"

Jake automatically rose, his hand going to her arm.

Ann looked up at them. "I don't know if it's temporary or permanent, Laura," she admitted. "I've talked to Dr. Williams, the head of psychiatry here, and he says that sometimes, depending on the types of drugs used, the frequency and so on, a person can sustain amnesia...."

Laura felt the hot sting of tears coming to her eyes. "H-he doesn't know me?"

"He doesn't recognize your name," Ann said gently. "Maybe—" she slowly got to her feet "—if he sees you in person, he'll recognize you."

"But he didn't recognize you," she said, her voice terribly off-key.

Ann shrugged. "No...but I'm not his wife, either."

"Morgan's close to you. He loves you like a sister—"

"Laura," Jake cautioned roughly, "let's take this one step at time." He stared at Ann. "Amnesia is usually temporary, isn't it?"

"Yes, but in a case like this, as the drugs slowly leave Morgan's bloodstream, we'll have to see if they've permanently damaged his brain. Once a brain cell is destroyed, it's gone forever. We don't know if the memory portion of his brain has been impaired permanently or not. We're still waiting to do an MRI on him. Right now he's still got too high a level of drugs in his body. In a week or so, we'll do one and see if it shows a decrease in function in that part of the brain."

Laura felt a cold numbness sweeping up from her feet, through her legs and into the center of her body. "I—I thought there would be a lot of physical damage," she babbled, "but I never thought about his brain, his memory.... Oh, my God, what will I do if

he doesn't remember his own children? Or me?
What—"

"Sit down, Laura," Jake entreated gently, guiding
her back to the couch. "Take some deep breaths—
you're going pale on us. Do you feel faint?" He
gripped both her hands.

Blackness rimmed the edges of her vision. She felt
Jake's strong, caring warmth as his huge hands swallowed her small ones. Fear jagged through her, and
she gasped and sank back on the couch. Closing her
eyes, she tried to steady her ragged breathing. Voices
began to swim around her, and she felt Ann's hand
on her head, cool palm pressed to her cheek. She felt
cold. So cold. Morgan's memory was gone. What if
it was permanent? He would have no memory of her
as his wife, of the intensity of their love. He wouldn't
know his own children.

It was too horrible to contemplate, and Laura felt
the icy blackness continuing to sweep upward toward
her head. Ann's and Jake's voices became more distant. In moments, she lost touch with physical reality
and was swallowed up mercifully, by a womblike
darkness that sheltered her from what felt like a near-
lethal blow to her emotions. Of all the scenarios she'd
played out in her waking hours and in her nightmares
over these past terrible months, Laura had never entertained this frightening possibility: Morgan didn't
know her. Didn't know any of them. Somewhere, as
she spiraled even more deeply into the blackness, she
knew that this amnesia wasn't temporary. It was permanent.

Chapter 2

Morgan's world was hazy and filled with nearly unendurable pain. As he drifted in and out of consciousness, torn pieces of voices, faces and experiences shifted in a never-ending kaleidoscope of terror, anxiety and horror. War scenes flashed behind his tightly closed eyes. Sometimes he'd find a moment's rest in a tunnel of light, where he'd stand, looking back toward those horrific scenes.

He felt relief in the white light of the tunnel, a sense of peace that he absorbed like a thirsty sponge and when he walked back toward the twisting, distorted events playing out at the tunnel's end, he felt wrenching pain return on every level of his being. Though he wanted to go toward the opposite end, filled only with the comforting light, something in him said no.

Every once in a while, he'd get a flash of a woman's face—a petite woman with shoulder-length blond hair and the biggest blue eyes he'd ever seen. She looked vaguely familiar, though he didn't know who she was. He did know that when he saw her face amid the clashing pain and suffering, he felt a moment's peace—much like what he experienced in the tunnel of light.

Staring into the depth of this woman's compassionate eyes fed him a sense of serenity and stability that his battered spirit desperately needed. Another woman's face, a younger woman in a naval uniform with short auburn hair, sometimes looked back at him, too. He didn't know her, either, and she didn't bring him the sense of peace the first woman did. And then he'd see a man in his early forties in another uniform—tall, with dark hair. He also saw two very young children, but was at a loss to identify them.

The faces paraded past him, intermixed with the terror and torture of the war scenes that frequently overtook him. He hated it when he gyrated uncontrollably into one of those states because he'd learned to anticipate the pain and anxiety that would come with it—emotions he seemed helpless to fight.

Morgan was exhausted by the cartwheeling sensations and confusing images. He had no idea of time or place. The conviction that he was a prisoner in a nightmarish world that would never end began to wear on him, to the point where he wished he were dead. At least then he could finally rest.

But then the face that gave him solace would return, if only for a moment: the woman with the sunlit hair and sky blue eyes. She made him want to live, to struggle against the scenes that would certainly follow the respite she offered. She made him want to try and hang on, even by bare threads, until her face, her serene presence, would once again fill him with the courage to keep living.

"Ann, you've got to tell me what the MRI results show," Laura quavered. She was standing very still in front of Ann's desk in an office within the Bethesda Naval Hospital. It had been a week, seven horrifying days, since Morgan's return to them. Her hands were damp, knotted tensely in front of her, and she held herself rigidly because if she didn't, she knew her knees would give way.

Dr. Parsons sat behind her large walnut desk scattered with X rays, lab findings and the MRI report. "Please," she entreated gently, "come and sit down."

"I'm tired of waiting for a final answer," Laura whispered, slowly making her way to a chair next to the desk. How many sleepless nights had she endured since arriving at Bethesda? Every night was fragmented with anxiety. Morgan had gone into a coma shortly after arriving at the naval hospital. Ann had said it was due to the high levels of cocaine combined with truth drugs that had been administered in too high a dosage too often during his captivity. They had clashed chemically within his brain and the result had been a war of sorts—with Morgan the casualty, slipping into a coma from the poisonous assault.

With a trembling hand, Laura smoothed a strand of hair away from her eyes. She no longer wore the feminine wool suits that she normally did when out in the world. Wolf Harding, another friend and trusted Perseus employee, had retrieved some more casual clothes from the house for her earlier in the week. Today she'd donned navy slacks, a long-sleeved white blouse and a brightly woven red-and-gold vest, though she felt anything but colorful. Her deep sense of frustration and loss at this point was beyond tears.

Compressing her full lips, Ann fingered the MRI report. Her voice was oddly low and charged with feeling. "It does show some loss of his permanent memory, Laura."

Pressing her hands against her mouth, Laura stared at the doctor. "No..."

With a grimace, Ann put the report aside. "How much, no one knows."

"So we won't know anything more until Morgan comes out of the coma?" *If* he came out of the coma at all, Laura thought worriedly. She knew that some of Ann's esteemed colleagues felt Morgan would remain in the coma, to become little more than a vegetable. Ann, however, felt differently. Perhaps because she was emotionally attached to the case, to

Morgan, she had argued with her psychiatric colleagues that Morgan could rise from the depths he now inhabited. And Laura desperately wanted to believe Ann was right.

Knotting a lacy handkerchief between her fingers, Laura whispered, "What should I do?"

"Keep doing what you're doing," Ann said wearily. "Sit at his bedside, talk to him, read to him, touch him...."

"All right...."

Rubbing her brow tiredly, Ann sat back in the chair and looked up at the ceiling. "I know how awful Morgan looks to you right now. But you've got to overcome your horror at his condition, Laura, and get in there and fight for him. Do you hear me? When I go into Morgan's room, you're sitting six feet away from him. You don't touch him. Your voice is a monotone when you read to him." Sitting up, Ann clasped her hands on the desk and looked across it with sudden intensity. "I know how much you're hurting. I know how much I'm asking of you, Laura. But if you want Morgan to have a reason to come out of that coma, you've got to put some emotion into what you're doing. Get close to him, hold his hand, talk to him as if he were there and awake, listening to you. You know what I'm saying."

Stung, Laura looked down at her clasped hands. "I feel like it's my fault," she whispered after a moment.

"What? That he slipped into the coma?" Ann got up and came around the desk. She leaned over and gripped Laura's slumped shoulders. "No one is blaming you for your reaction to Morgan or his condition. I know he looks terrible. I want to cry every time I visit him on my rounds. And I'm angry because of what Ramirez has done. I'd like to kill the bastard personally." Ann took a deep breath, steadied her own feelings and said, "It isn't fair to you, Laura. I know that better than most. But I believe that if you give your heart to him, regardless of his present condition, Morgan will respond. I know how much he loves you, how desperately he needs you in his world."

Gripping the handkerchief, Laura bowed her head. "Y-you're right, Ann, as always."

Making an exasperated sound, the doctor gently released Laura's shoulders and crouched down, placing her hands over her friend's. "I'm worried for you, too, Laura. You've got so much riding on your shoulders—again."

Laura gave her a small, sad smile. "This reminds me of the time after I was struck by that car at National Airport. I remember waking up blind in the hospital."

"Then recall those feelings and that time," Ann pleaded. "Remember what you felt like when Morgan came to visit that first time. Remember what you felt like when he held your hands."

Laura lifted her chin and felt a momentary trickle of joy. "He was so strong and capable, Ann. I was terrified at the time. Lost. My sight was gone. I felt out of control. Wh-when Morgan came into my hospital room, he was a stranger. But I homed in on his voice, and when he touched me…'' Her voice dropped to a quavering tone. ''I felt as if I could make it. Even if I was blind, I knew that with him at my side, supporting me, I could recover.'' She shrugged. ''It was a silly response, looking back. After all, I didn't know him from Adam. Yet there he was. Larger than life, filling my room with his energy, his light, filling me with hope.''

''So do the same for him now?''

Laura nodded and squeezed her hands gently. ''I understand now, Ann. Thanks…''

It was impossible for Laura to gird herself adequately before entering Morgan's private room. To begin with, she hated hospitals with a passion. As she stepped into the room now, the door quietly closing behind her, she looked over at the bed in the center of all the medical machinery and instruments. At least Morgan wasn't on life-support equipment. Somehow, she had to allow her chaos of emotions to come through no matter what the personal cost to her. Laura forced herself to move forward. She took the chair and moved it next to the bed, within inches of her husband.

Her heart twinged as her gaze moved to his still-swollen face. Morgan was a gaunt shadow of himself. No longer was he larger-than-life, radiating energy much like the summer sun's. Moving almost robotically, she lifted her hand to touch his, but suspended it in midair. All his fingernails had been torn off, and she shivered, unable to imagine the pain he had endured. What kind of monsters would do that to a man?

She sat down and stared at that large, square hand—a hand that had loved her so many times and in so many wonderful ways. Closing her eyes, her fingertips barely an inch from his, Laura allowed those sensations to wash across her, to remind her of their love. Ann was right: she had to allow herself to feel again, regardless of the emotional consequences to herself. Had Morgan abandoned her in her hour of greatest need? No. He'd stuck by her, despite the difficulties presented by her temporary blindness.

Shame wound through Laura as she slowly lifted her lashes and stared down at Morgan's deeply scarred hand. It was the hand of a man who had been forced to walk through hell and had survived it. Now this latest hell could leave him a vegetable. *It isn't fair,* she thought, anger beginning to tinge the depression that had been relentlessly stalking her. Morgan had always fought for the world's underdogs. His company took the dirty little jobs no one in the State Department was willing to take on. He fought for the little people who often didn't have the money, influence or power necessary to rescue their loved ones from some terrifying situation.

A lump formed in her throat as she slid her hand forward until she finally, for the first time, touched

Morgan's hand. How cool his skin was! Alarmed, she leaned closer and wrapped her hands around his. It was an automatic response, she supposed. If one of their children, Katherine or Jason, was cold, she'd do the same thing for them. The muscles of Morgan's forearm were weak from lack of use, but the familiar black hair still covered it, and she allowed herself the luxury of closing her eyes as she gently skimmed his arm to reacquaint herself with the feel of him.

How long she'd ached to touch Morgan this way. What had stopped her? Laura knew she was an emotional wreck right now, in so many ways. She was trying to cope. Her therapist, Dr. Pallas Downey, had cautioned her that due to the trauma she'd undergone, plus carrying the responsibility for her children as well as wrestling with Morgan's uncertain condition, she was literally at the end of her rope. Pallas had helped her see the necessity of living life one hour at a time—minute to minute, and nothing more than that.

Laura's mouth softened as she explored Morgan's limp arm. Her fingers glided slowly up and down his skin, and she allowed herself to experience the emotions that went with touching him, even though, for her, to feel meant to hurt—and to remember the seven wonderful years they'd had together. Oh, how happy she'd been! Her gaze moved to Morgan's slack features. His lips were parted and chapped. Leaning over, she touched his full lower lip with a trembling fingertip. She recalled that mouth, how it could twist into a wry smile or a boyish grin of delight—or flatten into a tight line when he was worried. She recalled the feel of his mouth on hers...remembering....

Dragging in a ragged breath, Laura stroked Morgan's bearded cheek. He needed a shave. She could do that. Yes, she could do small things for him. She felt the first tentative stirrings of hope since Morgan's return. Maybe, if she did such small, insignificant things as shaving him, holding his hand and reading to him from his favorite books, she could help bring him back—for all of them.

Laura laid Morgan's hand across his blanketed belly. "I'll be right back, darling," she whispered. She would go to the nurses' station, get a razor and shaving cream and some towels. Suddenly, she felt some of the dark depression lift from her weighted shoulders. As she hurried toward the door, she felt hope for the first time since the whole horrifying kidnapping ordeal had begun. And for now that was enough. More than enough.

On the morning of Morgan's fourteenth day at Bethesda, Laura had just finished shaving him and was gently drying the unrelenting line of his jaw with a towel, when she saw his eyelashes flutter. She froze. Had it been her imagination? She had spent the past seven days at his side almost nonstop, silently pleading with him to wake up and find her here at his side, touching him, loving him in small, insignificant ways. Morgan's lashes fluttered again.

A gasp escaped her lips, and she placed the towel on the bedside table next to the bowl of warm water she'd been using.

"Morgan?" she quavered, pressing her hands to his cheeks and framing his face. "Morgan, it's Laura. I'm here. Come to me. Please come to me. I love you, darling. We're all waiting for you to come back to us...."

His lashes fluttered a third time.

Laura's breath jammed in her throat as Morgan's eyelids slowly opened to reveal bloodshot grey ones. He stared up at her, as if not really seeing her. But he must!

"Morgan?" she whispered, disbelief in her tone. "Morgan?"

His mouth closed and then slowly opened. A rasping sound issued from his lips.

Anxiously, Laura captured his hand as he weakly tried to lift it. He was conscious! A thrill shattered through her as she stood, gripping his hand in her own. His light gray eyes remained cloudy and unfocused, but again he tried to speak.

"What is it, Morgan?" She leaned forward, her hair spilling across her shoulder as she pressed her ear close to his lips. "Tell me what you want."

But only rasping, animal-like sounds came from him. No words. Laura's heart was pounding with joy even so. Tears stung her eyes, and she allowed her instincts to take over. When Jason was sick and had a fever, he would awake thirsty and wanting water.

Sitting lightly on the edge of the bed, Laura took a glass of water from the table. Dampening a clean washcloth in it, she daubed it gently against his chapped lips. Instantly, he made sucking, drawing sounds.

Trying to still her joy, Laura continued giving Morgan precious drops of water via the cloth. He was so terribly weak! He couldn't so much as lift his hand, and after a few moments, he couldn't move his lips, either. Getting off the bed, she saw his gaze following her. He was still thirsty. Torn between calling Dr. Parsons and remaining at his side, Laura made a decision.

"Here," she whispered, "I'm going to slide my arm under your neck and put the glass to your mouth, Morgan. Then I want you to drink all you want...."

His gaze never left hers. His eyes were bare slits, but Laura could feel him following her movement. Elation made her giddy as she gently slid her arm beneath his neck. Using her own body as a support to raise him just enough to drink from the glass, Laura felt a powerful surge of hope tunnel through her. His head rested wearily against her shoulder and jaw, reminding her more of a newborn baby than a man in control of his own body. But the moment she pressed the edge of the glass to his mouth, he sucked thirstily. As the water flowed to him, he eagerly drank the entire contents. Eight ounces!

Morgan's lashes shuttered closed, as if the effort of drinking had drained what little strength he had, and

Laura eased him back down onto the pillow. With a shaking hand, she put the glass aside. Touching his brow, now furrowed and beaded with sweat, she whispered, "Morgan, I'll be right back. I'm going to get Ann for you. Rest, darling. Just rest. I promise, I'll be right back...."

"He's come out of the coma." Ann Parsons couldn't keep the satisfaction out of her voice as she and three other doctors completed their examination of Morgan, who was staring up at them through barely opened eyes. She looked triumphantly over at Laura, who stood tensely to one side, her hands gripped in front of her. A smile tugged at Ann's mouth as she said, "You did it, Laura. All your love and care brought him back. Congratulations."

Shaking internally with fear that the doctors would say Morgan could slip back into the coma, Laura woodenly moved forward. The other three doctors, all men, nodded in agreement and then, offering congratulations, left the room. Laura moved to the bed and gripped Morgan's hand. It was warmer now, and Ann had adjusted the IVs to deliver more fluids, since Morgan was so thirsty. Laura's heart pounded painfully in her breast as she looked down at her husband. How battered and scarred his face was. His old war wound from Vietnam, the scar that carved his flesh from temple to jaw, remained a constant reminder of Morgan's original life-and-death battle, and it had been joined by more recent cuts and bruises.

"Why won't he speak?" Laura wondered aloud as she held his hand and watched him.

"It may take some time," Ann cautioned, replacing the stethoscope around her neck. "Just stay with him, talk to him and be there for him, Laura." She grinned at her with unabashed pride. "You've done one hell of a job! It's got to feel good."

Laura nodded. "I feel like I'm caught in the updrafts and air pockets of a thunderstorm. One minute I'm elated, the next I'm terrorized. I worry that Morgan will slip away from me again."

"I don't think so." The doctor reached over and gripped her patient's shoulder, smiling at him. "Welcome back, Morgan. You've got a whole bunch of people who love you and want you here with them. I'll be back later to check on you." Releasing her grip, she transferred her smile to Laura. "He's all yours. Just keep doing what you're doing. It's working."

The room fell quiet. Laura released a ragged breath as she lowered herself to perch on the edge of the bed, Morgan's hand resting comfortably in her lap. Facing him, she watched his half-opened eyes train cloudily upon her. A slight smile touched her lips as she whispered, "How tired you must be, Morgan." She reached over and slid her fingertips through his black hair, pushing several errant strands aside. "All this commotion. All this excitement." Laura laughed a little. It came out strained, but it made her feel better. "I'm stressed out, too, by all these doctors. What a bunch of eggheads, huh? Three-fourths of them said you wouldn't come out of the coma. Only Ann, the one woman, said you'd come back to me. Thank God she was right.''

Laura felt a lump rising in her throat. Sudden tears stung her eyes. ''Oh, Morgan, I love you so much...so much it *hurts*.'' Leaning over, she placed her mouth gently against his. His cracked, dry ones. She didn't expect him to kiss her in return. She merely wanted somehow to breathe her life, her energy, into him. Kissing Morgan for the first time felt so right. So fulfilling. How she'd ached to kiss him before, but she had been afraid to—until now. She'd wanted to kiss him when he was conscious and could remember her, knowing the love they shared.

Easing her mouth from his, she smiled down into his gray eyes. ''I want you to rest, Morgan. I love you. I'll be here for you. I'm going to have my bed moved in here. From now on, I'll sleep nearby. Oh, darling, I'm so glad you're back. We all need you so badly—'' Her voice cracked with emotion, and she dashed tears from her eyes.

''Look at me, Morgan. I'm turning into a crybaby. Pallas said it would happen. That I'd have times when the tears would just come, and I should let them. I guess this is one of those times.'' She squeezed his hand gently, leery of causing him pain. His gray eyes remain fixed on her, and she felt a little vulnerable beneath his unblinking gaze.

''Do you hear me, Morgan? Can you nod your head

yes?'' She watched for a reaction, but saw none. Concerned, Laura felt a sudden stab of terror. Gently, she ran her fingers up his hand and across his arm. ''Morgan? Can you feel me touching you?''

There was no response, only that unsettling, unwavering gaze.

Worriedly, Laura captured one of his hands between hers. ''Morgan, I know you're just coming out of the coma. Ann said you might not hear or see everything just yet, that you might drift in and out of consciousness. But, darling, if you hear my voice, please squeeze my hand.'' Her heart rate soared powerfully as she waited precious moments, aching to feel his fingers move against hers. Morgan's stare never changed. His gray eyes appeared so cloudy. *Oh, please, dear God, let him hear me!*

Just as a scream threatened to unknot in her tightened throat, Laura felt Morgan's fingers curve ever so slightly against hers. With a sob of relief, she clutched his hand to her breast. ''Oh, thank God,'' she whispered brokenly. Bowing her head, she pressed small kisses against his injured hand. ''I love you, Morgan. I love you so much. I just want you to get well. That's all. I'd sell my soul to the devil himself to see you get up, walk and talk again, darling.'' Hot tears trickled down her cheeks, dampening not only her fingers, but Morgan's as well.

Gently, Laura pressed his hand against her cheek as she gazed at him through tear-filled eyes. ''I love you with my life, Morgan. The children miss you so much. Your family...your friends. Everyone wants you to be well. Please, darling, keep fighting to come back to us. So many people love you...."

Laura saw his eyes change. It wasn't anything obvious, yet because she was not only sensitive, but intuitive to his emotions after seven years of marriage, she felt the subtle shift. For a split second, it seemed as if the cloudiness in his eyes cleared and he was truly with her. Kissing his fingers, she smiled down at him and pressed his hand back against his blanketed chest. "What?" she whispered, leaning down as he began working his mouth as if to speak. "What is it, Morgan? Tell me. I'll hear you...."

Morgan struggled, his lips seeming to have a life of their own as he tried to shape the words ringing through the nearly empty halls of his mind.

Her smile brightened, and Laura grazed his cheek with her hand. "I'm here, darling. Don't fight so hard. Save your strength. You're getting well. You're back with us. I love you so very, very much...." Her hand stilled on his cheek. Morgan struggled more, and she saw it now, clearly, in eyes. They had sharpened in their focus on her, the pupils larger and black—containing some of their old hawklike intensity.

"What?" she whispered, leaning very close to his lips as sounds began to issue forth.

"...Who..."

"Yes?" Laura prompted, excitement in her voice. She'd actually heard the word! "Who?"

Morgan's breath came raggedly as he tried to capture the fragmented sensations and tie them to the correct words. He felt the warmth of her hands on his, felt the warm silk of her hair against his jaw. He *had* to speak! Beads of perspiration formed on his brow as he struggled to corral the words that danced just out of his gyrating mind's reach. Her laughter was spontaneous. When he saw her lift her head, her clear blue eyes shining with happiness, Morgan absorbed her like sunshine.

"Who…" he managed to say at last, his voice rasping hoarsely, "are you?"

Chapter 3

Morgan watched the blond woman's face, glad he'd finally managed to force out the words. His mind was spongy and shorting out. It had taken every last ounce of his diminishing strength to speak. He had so many questions, but was too weak to ask them.

Collapsing against the bed, his head sinking deeply into the pillow after his efforts, he struggled to stay awake, noting the tears that had come to the woman's huge blue eyes. Why? She was beautiful, with a proud quality to the way she held her shoulders and lifted her small chin. Tiny. She was tiny—like a bird.

His lashes drifted shut and he felt himself spiraling back into the darkness. Felt the return of panic. He didn't want to go back to that nightmarish collage of blood, tortured screams and pain. He couldn't stand it anymore. Fighting to remain awake, he felt a warm, trembling touch on his hand. It was *her*. Momentarily, his world stopped spinning as he used every vestige of his dissolving consciousness to home in on her tentative but tender touch. The touch of a healer. A nurse. Maybe she was a nurse, though she wore no uniform.

Nothing made sense. He opened his mouth to protest against his exhaustion and pain. He wanted so desperately to stay awake—to find out who he was, and where he was! In the end, Morgan couldn't win the battle, and sleep claimed him.

The next time he awoke, it was dark outside. He was relieved to again escape the terror that plagued him. His tortured sleep had left him sweaty, and he could feel rivulets making their way down his temples. Weakly he lifted his hand to wipe them away—and realized he was trussed up with tubes and wires like a Christmas turkey. Awkwardly, he lifted his hand to wipe at the sweat. The gesture caused him immediate pain. Confused, he looked at his hand to see why such a small gesture would cause such agony, and was astounded to see that his fingernails were gone, the flesh darkened and ravaged looking as it healed over to create new nails.

What the hell had happened to him? With minute awareness, he began to assess the rest of his body. No matter where he focused, he was either sore and

aching or became so if he moved slightly. Had he
been in some kind of accident? Opening his eyes
wide, he began to absorb his surroundings. A light
blue room with stainless steel furniture met his bleary
gaze, the venetian blinds open on a night sky.

Sounds began to impinge upon his limited consciousness—muffled voices outside his room. He was
in a hospital; he could see that. His brow furrowed.
Where was the blond woman? He pictured her thick,
golden hair and how it curved to frame her small,
pretty features. Then he recalled the hurt in her expression when he'd asked who she was.

His mouth felt cottony, and he longed for a glass
of icy cold water. What time was it? Where was he?
The questions nagged him as he lay there, needing to
talk to someone. The door quietly opened, and his
heart gave a powerful leap. The blond woman! A
thrill raced through him. Morgan was stymied by his
intense response to this stranger. This time, she wore
a soft pink, cowl-necked angora sweater and black
slacks. The pale shade of the sweater highlighted her
wan features, and Morgan saw the telltale purple circles beneath her glorious eyes. He sensed an incredible sadness around the woman as she closed the door
behind her.

When she turned and saw that he was awake, she
became rooted to the spot. He felt the intensity of her
gaze, saw hope flare in those wonderful eyes of hers
that couldn't hide her feelings. Morgan felt like an
intruder as he clung to that gaze. She wore her vul-

nerability on her sleeve, and he could not only see her emotions register but feel them, too. It was a startling discovery, almost as if he were a mind reader privy to this woman's inner world. Momentarily embarrassed, he tore his gaze from hers.

"Water..." he rasped.

"What?"

Morgan made the effort to look at her again. She moved almost robotically toward him, anxiety plain on her fine features. Working to make his lips move again, he whispered, "Water...please..."

She moved jerkily. "Water. Yes...hold on a moment." She reached for the plastic container and poured him a glass.

Morgan didn't know which he wanted more—her touch or the water. He remembered her tender caress from before. How long ago had that been? Time was meaningless to him. He tried to sit up, but his efforts were short-lived. As she came to his bedside, she leaned over him, and he inhaled deeply, savoring the fragrance of camellia. When she slid her arm beneath his sweaty neck, Morgan groaned. It was a groan of pleasure, but she must not have realized it, because she stopped and stiffened.

"It's...okay...." he assured her gruffly, struggling to rise enough to drink.

"Take it easy," she urged a little breathlessly, continuing to slide her arm around his neck and lift him enough to press the rim of the glass to his lips.

The water was heavenly. He slurped it down like

a man too long in the desert. Wildly aware of her soft, strong body supporting his, Morgan was content to rest his head against her. This woman was soft, yet strong. She gave him three glasses of water before his thirst was sated. As she eased him back down on the bed and nervously fluffed the pillow around his head, he studied her from barely opened eyes.

"You...smell good.... Better than this damned hospital...."

She stopped fluffing his pillow and stared down at him. "It's camellia. Your favorite perfume."

Morgan frowned. "Mine?" His voice was rough from disuse, and words wouldn't flow together like he wanted them to. He saw pain in her eyes, and her soft lips compressed.

"Do you know who I am?" she asked, her voice shaking with emotion.

Morgan watched her steel herself against his answer. Her fingers rested tentatively against the edge of his bed, and she held herself almost rigid, waiting for him to speak. "I...no, I don't know you. I...remember you from another time when you were in here, though. A-are you a nurse?"

"No, I'm not part of the hospital staff," she quavered. "Do you know who you are?"

Morgan scowled and closed his eyes. Who *was* he? Opening his lashes, he stared up at her. "You called me Morgan. I guess I'm Morgan."

"D-do you know your last name?"

He rolled his head slowly from side to side. "I'm

sorry...I don't. And I don't know where I am. Or how I got here.'' He studied her. ''Where am I? And who are you?''

''I'm Laura Trayhern. You're Morgan Trayhern. You're at Bethesda Naval Hospital, in Maryland.''

The information was coming too fast. He tried to digest it but didn't succeed. The obvious hurt in Laura's voice tore at him. He saw tears form in her eyes—saw her battling to keep them from spilling down her pale cheeks. Her beautiful mouth was pulled into a tight line of suffering that touched some deep, unknown chord within him.

His name was Morgan Trayhern. She was Laura Trayhern. He studied her in the tense silence. ''Are you my sister?''

''I—no, I'm not, Morgan. I'm your wife....''

He stared at her, shocked. He saw such anguish in her eyes, and he longed to ease that pain. But how? Nervously, she clasped her hands in front of her and bowed her head. Why couldn't he remember such an important thing? Stunned by the information and feeling her pain, he muttered, ''How long have we been—married?''

Laura lifted her head, fighting the urge to shriek out her grief. She saw the genuine confusion in Morgan's features. ''Seven years, Morgan.'' She watched the information strike him as surely as if she'd hit him with her fist. It was shock, not joy, that registered in his eyes. A sob lodged in her throat, and she swallowed hard. Right now, Morgan didn't need her tears. He needed answers. Maybe Dr. Parsons was right: they should give Morgan the information as he asked for it. Perhaps it would stimulate memories—if any were left undestroyed by the drugs. Oh, what if Morgan *never* remembered who she was or what they'd shared?

Laura felt such a gutting pain surge through her that for a moment she couldn't breathe. Three days ago, Morgan had awakened from his coma and haltingly asked who she was. Now he was fully conscious and able to speak coherently, and she should be grateful—but she was living in a nightmare where her carefully knit strands of hope were unraveling before her eyes. He didn't know her. He didn't remember their love. Or their marriage.

Through a sheer effort of will, she forced herself to put her own suffering aside and focus on Morgan. He was extremely pale, but his strength had improved noticeably, and his gray eyes, once so cloudy, held more of their old sharpness. Laura knew he was still emerging from the drugged state, but at least he was functioning, and for that she had to be grateful. She ached to reach over, caress his shaven features, kiss him and tell him of her great love for him. But she could tell by his stymied expression that he wouldn't accept her gesture. He was staring at her with bewilderment—as if she were a total stranger.

"How did I get here?" he demanded, his voice stronger.

Laura brought over a chair and sat down. Ann had told her to answer whatever questions Morgan had—thoroughly, but slowly, so that the information could be absorbed. "You own Perseus, Morgan. It's a company that hires mercenaries to undertake jobs around the world. Many times you've worked with our government—or with another country's government—to help people who are being held prisoner or in some other kind of danger."

Laura saw his black eyebrows knit as he digested the information, and prayed that something—anything—she told him would spark a latent memory within him. She needed a sign that some remnant of his former life—of her and their children—remained. Her palms were damp as she continued. "You've owned the company for seven years. Three months ago, you and I, and our son, Jason, were kidnapped by a drug lord named Ramirez." Her voice faltered and became strained. "Jake Randolph, one of your employees, took up the reins of Perseus in your absence. With the help of the government, he located us, one by one. I was the first to be rescued, then Jason, and now you."

Morgan stared disbelievingly at her. "A-are you making this up?"

Laura sat very still. Anger lapped at the taut edge of her patience. "How could I be?" Her voice echoed around the room—strident, pain-filled and off-key. Nervously, she touched her brow. "I-I'm sorry, Morgan. No, I'm not making any of this up. I just want you to remember so badly…but you don't…and—"

"It sounds like a James Bond movie," he muttered. Looking away, he stared at the dark void of the window. His conscience pricked him. He heard the hurt in Laura's voice, felt her pain as if it was his own, but dammit, he was hurting too much himself. It took every ounce of his strength to concentrate on her words—and the strange ideas she presented—instead of giving in to the aches of his physical body.

Laura reached out, her fingers curving around his arm. At least he remembered James Bond. That was good. But at what age had he seen those movies? Had his memory been wiped out back to that time? Or was this a meaningless fragment? Instantly, she felt Morgan react, his muscles tightening beneath her fingertips. She released him, and he rolled his head toward her, his eyes dark and angry. Stung by his reaction, she swallowed against the lump in her throat that refused to go away. "You've suffered so much, Morgan," she began in an unsteady voice. "We all have."

"I don't remember anything," he rasped. "I wish I did, but I don't. Hell, if you hadn't told me my name, I wouldn't even know that much."

Standing up despite her weakened knees, Laura whispered, "I know…and it's all right, Morgan. Dr. Parsons said your memory would be influenced by the drugs you were given."

"What drugs?"

Laura took in a deep breath and said in a low voice, "Ramirez wanted to get even with you for damaging his Peruvian cocaine empire. Over the years, you sent many missions to stem the flow of cocaine traffic to the eastern United States. It worked—too well. Ramirez kidnapped the three of us to stop you. To...get even, I guess." Wearily, she touched her brow, a headache lapping at her temples. It was nearly three in the morning, and something had awakened her out of badly needed sleep down in the nurses' quarters, where she'd been spending the nights since Morgan had become conscious and failed to recognize her.

She'd quickly abandoned the idea of bringing a bed into his room. What was the use? He didn't know her from Adam. Laura couldn't stand the thought of him looking at her the way he was now—as if she were some bug under a microscope rather than his devoted wife.

Morgan watched Laura in the stilted silence. Suddenly, he was very tired. And he felt old. Very old. No question, Laura was hurting. She was his wife— of seven years. So why the hell couldn't he remember? He focused on his heart, searching for emotion, but he found no lingering tendrils of love. Frustration ate at him, and his mind whirled with the strange information she'd imparted. He had no reason to disbelieve her. Her face was that of an innocent angel. She seemed incapable of lying.

"Listen," Laura whispered as she came back to his bedside, careful not to touch him this time, "you need to sleep, Morgan. You're still recovering, and it's three in the morning. Dr. Parsons will be here at eight o'clock to see you. You've known her a long time.'' She managed a partial smile. ''I'm glad you're out of the coma. I'm glad you're back with us.''

Closing his eyes, Morgan felt bitterness leaking through him. Who was ''us''? He had a family. He had a son named Jason. Why the hell couldn't he recall that information—or at least feel some emotion? He felt her tug gently at the blanket and sheets, tucking them more snugly around him. Then she left, as quietly as she'd come.

Morgan was not only wide awake at eight, he could hardly wait for this Dr. Parsons to come through the door. He had a lot more questions to ask, and he wanted answers. Despite all the tubes, he'd managed to drag himself into a semi-upright position. Finally the door opened, and a tall dark-haired woman in her thirties entered. Morgan waited to recognize her, but sensed nothing familiar. A name badge on her white coat read Parsons. She carried a clipboard, a stethoscope hung around her neck and a smile of genuine welcome lit up her face.

''Morgan. It's good to see you awake and so alert.''

He scowled. The doctor laid the clipboard on the table and reached out her hand. Weakly, he raised his. Her grip was warm and firm.

''Hmm, you're stronger than I thought you might be,'' she murmured, her voice pleased as she looked intently into his eyes. Releasing his hand, she smiled. "How are you feeling?"

"I'm thirsty as hell, Doctor, and I need to get all these damned tubes out of me."

Laughing, Ann placed the stethoscope in her ears and listened to his heart and lungs. "You're an amazing man, Morgan. But you always were."

Morgan lay impatiently as she examined him thoroughly, from his hands to his back, which smarted like hell itself, to the rest of his body. "I don't know you," he said abruptly when she'd finally stepped back. "Laura said I would know you, but I don't."

Ann sobered and reached forward to pull the covers up over him. "She told you about the drugs Ramirez gave you?"

"Yes." He felt highly impatient. Angry. "Dammit, Doctor, my head is *empty*. I don't remember anything. When the hell is that going to change?"

"I don't know, Morgan. I wish I had an answer for you, but I don't. Damage has occurred to the memory-storage part of your brain because of the cocaine and other drugs Ramirez used on you."

"Ramirez..."

She sat on the edge of the bed, facing him. "Do you remember him?"

"Hell, no! But if I did, I'd like to kill the son of a bitch for erasing my memory."

"He tortured you. Did Laura cover that with you?"

Breathing hard, Morgan shook his head. "No."

Pursing her lips, she said, "I see."

"Well, I'm glad as hell someone does." He glared up at her. "This woman, Laura…"

"What about her?"

"She says she's my wife." He made a frustrated sound and looked away from the doctor's somber features. "If she is, why the hell can't I feel anything for her?"

"You feel nothing, Morgan?"

"Nothing," he said flatly. "And I feel bad, because I can see it hurts her." Working his mouth, he muttered, "I don't want to see her hurt…but dammit, I can't force myself to feel something that isn't there!"

"Of course you can't," Ann said soothingly as she eased off the bed. "First things first, Morgan. I'm going to have a nurse come in and remove these IVs. I think you're ready to try solid food. Later, we'll send some orderlies in to get you on your feet and start working those leg muscles. Right now, you're weak as a newborn lamb."

He tried to steady his breathing. "Isn't there someone I'd remember?"

"You don't remember me at all?" she asked as she picked up her clipboard.

"No."

"This afternoon," she said, "I'm going to ask several of your friends to drop by. They won't stay long, just long enough to see if it jogs something in your memory."

He scowled. "And if nothing jogs? What then?"

"We'll take this one day at a time, Morgan. Some-

374   *Morgan's Marriage*

times, as the drugs wash out of a person's system—
which can take weeks—a memory might return. It
might be something small and insignificant, but it
would be a start to opening the door on all of your
past."

Morgan looked down, feeling completely alone.
"Do you know what it's like to sit here without a
past, Doctor? My memory is a big blank. I've got
nothing!"

Ann reached out and gently touched his gowned
shoulder. "Take it easy, Morgan. I know how upsetting this is. But don't push yourself so hard—don't
try to force the memories." She pointed to the television affixed to the wall opposite his bed. "I suggest
watching some television, and I'll have a nurse bring
you some newspapers and magazines. Anything
might trigger a memory."

Bitterly, he looked around the sterile room. "I hate
hospitals."

A smile turned up the corners of Ann's serious
mouth. "Well," she drawled, "at least that sounds
like the old Morgan speaking."

"What?"

She grinned a little. "You've always hated hospitals—and with good reason."

"Tell me why."

"No," Ann said lightly, "my gut feeling is you'll
remember on your own. It's just a good sign to me
that you might know more than you think you do.
Your responses are those of the Morgan I knew before

this ordeal. Trust your gut feelings, your inner knowing, Morgan. That will help open that door to the past, too.''

"Feeling? Knowing?" He growled the words like a snarling dog. "I'm a man, Doctor. I don't work off feeling and knowing. I go by what I can see, hear, taste or smell."

She chuckled indulgently and patted his arm. "Yup, you're the same old Morgan. Welcome home, my friend. It's good to have you back. I'll send in a nurse shortly to untruss you."

Morgan watched her walk to the door and open it. "Wait."

Ann turned expectedly. "Yes?"

"What—what about Laura?"

"You tell me."

He glared at her. "I don't want to keep hurting her."

Shrugging, Ann murmured, "Neither of you has that choice right now. She loves you. You're her husband."

"But I don't remember her!" he exclaimed, frustrated. "I can't pretend with her, Doctor."

"No, and you shouldn't, Morgan."

"Then what the hell am I to do?"

"Be patient. I know it's not one of your finer attributes. You've never been particularly patient—except with Laura and your children. But you're going to have to try."

"When will I see her?"

"She's sleeping right now. I gave her a sedative that will knock her out for at least eight hours."

Morgan stared down at the light blue bedspread. "She's hurting badly over all this. I can feel it."

Ann shut the door and walked back to his bed, holding her clipboard in front of her. "Morgan, she's very fragile," she warned quietly. "Did she tell you anything of her own kidnapping ordeal?"

"No," he growled impatiently, "only that she and Jason, my son, were kidnapped along with me."

"That's all?"

"That's all."

Ann looked up at the window and then back at him. Her voice was gentle. "She's suffering as much as you, Morgan, for a lot of reasons that I'm going to allow her to tell you when she feels the time is right. Laura is one of the most valiant women I've ever run across in my life, and I've seen a few heroes in my lifetime, believe me. She's been a main support for you, Perseus and everyone connected with these horrible events."

"She's vulnerable," he observed tiredly. "I can feel it around her and see it in her face."

"Yes," Ann agreed.

"So I'm not aiding things by not remembering. Hell," he rasped, "I feel no connection with her! She's a stranger to me, Doctor." His voice cracked with concern. "I can see she needs help but I don't know how to help her. I mean, I feel for her, for whatever she's going through, but I can't make that personal connection that a husband and wife would have. I don't know what the hell to do—'' His voice cracked.

Ann nodded. "I know," she whispered. "It's a painful situation for everyone, and it's not going to go away, Morgan. As a psychiatrist, my response is that you should spend as much time with Laura as you can. It will better your chances of remembering. She was close to you, Morgan, more than anyone else in your life. You trusted her. You didn't let people get very close to you because of—ah—your past. But Laura was able to get beyond your defenses. She knows you best, Morgan. That's why it's so important you allow her to remain in your life.''

An acidic taste stung his mouth as he avoided the doctor's searching look. "All she does is make me feel more pain. I've got enough of my own. I don't want to feel hers, too.''

Sighing, Ann nodded. "Give yourself some time, Morgan. Laura has a lot she's dealing with right now. She can no more hide her pain than you can yours. It's a raw situation with no easy answers.''

Leaning back on the pillows, exhausted, Morgan shut his eyes. "I'm so damned angry and upset," he rasped unsteadily. "I want to cry for myself…for her….''

"That's a good sign, Morgan.''

His eyes snapped open and he looked at her. "What is?''

"The fact that you want to cry for both of you. Stay with your feelings. Stay with Laura. She helped you once. I know she can help you again….''

Chapter 4

Morgan moved restlessly around the hospital room. It had been two weeks since he'd come out of the coma, and he was bored to death. Weak February sunshine filtered between the slats of the venetian blinds. Outside, at least a foot of snow covered the ground. How he longed to be out there! Holding the blinds apart with his healing fingers, he wondered if the *real* Morgan Trayhern also loved the outdoors.

He frowned, and his mind swung back to Laura. She was his wife in name only. No matter what she said or what pictures she showed him of his family, he couldn't find that answering connection within him. He eased his fingers from the blinds and turned around. His level of confusion was almost too much to cope with. Over the weeks, different people—friends and employees from his past, he was told—had visited him. He recognized none of their faces or stories. Not a damn one.

Morgan sighed and ran his fingers through his short black hair sprinkled with silver. Turning, he walked slowly back to the unmade bed. Newspapers, magazines and videos were scattered all over the place. In one way, he supposed, he'd caught up with the world at large. Jake Randolph was continuing to run Perseus for him—and Morgan couldn't imagine trying to run it himself. The Morgan Trayhern they knew evidently had a commanding grasp of military knowledge, but he certainly didn't.

His scowl deepened. On the dresser sat a photograph of his younger sister, Alyssa Cantrell, and her husband, Clay. Another photo showed his brother, Noah, Noah's wife, Kit, and their children. A third photo showed his smiling parents in front of their Clearwater, Florida, home. He recognized none of them.

The door opened.

In relief, Morgan looked up. Who would it be this time? Dr. Parsons had scheduled visitors for him on a daily basis. He got a briefing from Jake at eight o'clock every morning, though he felt foolish that the names, the teams and their objectives meant nothing to him at all.

Jake poked his head around the corner. "Good morning, Morgan," he said in greeting.

"I suppose," Morgan growled. "Come in." Jake was wearing a red flannel shirt and Levi's. For a man running a multimillion-dollar company, he certainly didn't look the part. He looked more like a soldier than an executive. Morgan wondered how he himself had dressed when he'd run Perseus, but decided not to ask. Jake had his briefcase in hand, and he hoisted it up on the bed between them.

"We're switching tactics today," Jake said without preamble as he opened it.

Morgan halted in his tracks. "Oh?"

"Yeah, you and Laura are going deep undercover for a while." Jake eyed him, then handed over a piece of paper. "We picked up a satcom from Peru late yesterday."

Morgan read it. "It's from Guillermo Garcia."

Jake sighed. "That's right, Ramirez's right-hand man. Ramirez may be dead, but Garcia has wasted no time in taking over his cocaine empire." Stabbing one finger at the paper, Jake said worriedly, "He's sending out several professional hit men to get rid of you, Laura and your family."

Morgan studied the paper intently. His mouth hardened. "I wish like hell I could remember, Jake. Garcia's name means nothing to me."

"Doesn't matter," Jake said abruptly. He picked up some photos and handed them to him. "We had a conference this morning, and we feel it best to do two things. This has Dr. Parsons's approval, by the way."

Morgan took the photos. "What's been decided?" One of the pictures was of a ranch in dry, desertlike surroundings. Another showed a small log cabin near a stream lined with pines and white-barked trees.

"Your children, Jason and Katherine, are going with Susannah and Sean Killian. They'll be deep in the woods of Kentucky at a location only I will know about. You and Laura will go into hiding at the Donovan Ranch, in a canyon in central Arizona. You knew Robert Donovan. In fact, his son, Randy, was in your company when it was overrun by the Vietcong. Mr. Donovan and his wife recently died in an auto accident, but his daughters are running the ranch, and they said you and Laura were welcome."

His mouth quirking, Morgan looked up. "Laura is going with me?"

Jake gave him a flat stare. "She's your wife."

Struggling to know how to react, Morgan said nothing.

Exasperated, Jake growled, "She's on Garcia's hit list, too. The son of a bitch is going after all four of you this time. And he's taking no prisoners, Morgan. I don't think you want Laura left behind as a target."

"Of course not," Morgan snapped irritably.

"Look," Jake said, suddenly weary, "I know you're not remembering anything. I can't imagine me not knowing my wife, Shah. I don't know what the hell I'd do, either, but I know if we were under attack, I'd still want her with me."

Angrily, Morgan turned and walked back to the
window. "My marriage isn't any of your business."

"I saw the look on your face," Jake warned, coming over to the window and joining him. He settled
his large hands on his narrow hips as he studied Morgan. "Two other people will go with you," he said
slowly. "They'll stay at the main ranch house, about
fifteen miles from this small cabin on Oak Creek."
Jake jabbed a big finger toward the pictures Morgan
still held. "Dr. Parsons is going, for obvious reasons.
An Army Special Forces officer, Major Mike Houston, who's had a lot of years in Peru chasing Ramirez
and his likes, will accompany you. He's your professional insurance against an attack by these hit men
Garcia's sending stateside."

Morgan inhaled a deep breath, fighting the anger
and frustration roiling within him. "Dammit, Jake, I
wish I could remember!"

"Like Ann said, stop trying to remember specifics.
Trust your feelings. They'll eventually open those
doors."

Glaring at him, Morgan snarled, "Feelings? The
only thing I feel is mountain-sized frustration. How
do you think I feel when Laura comes to visit and I
can read every unhappy emotion on her face?"

"She's wounded, too," Jake reminded him slowly.
"Has she talked to you about her capture by Garcia?"

"Hell, no!"

"Have you asked?"

"No…"

"I think," Jake growled, "you're feeling real sorry for yourself, Morgan, for your plight. Maybe I would, too. But you're being pretty ungrateful about all the help you're getting, if you ask me."

Morgan turned and held Jake's dark stare. "Just what the hell is that supposed to mean?"

"Take the focus off yourself, Morgan. Laura needs you. You're the only one who can help her," Jake said huskily. "I don't care to hear your lament about not remembering her as your wife. Dammit, you have to begin treating her like a *human being*—somebody who cares enough to come daily to this room to see you—rather than as some inconvenient fixture."

His nostrils flaring, Morgan knotted his hands into fists. He took in Jake's implacable expression, the slashed set of his mouth as he held Morgan's gaze. "I suppose she's been running and crying to you."

Jake clenched his teeth. "Morgan, you're being pigheaded, but then, you were always that way, even before the amnesia. No, Laura hasn't run to me or anyone else. That's the problem—she's bottled everything up. Dr. Parsons is really worried about her. Laura has taken too much for too long and has nowhere to safely dump her feelings. You sure as hell haven't been much help."

"She can talk to me if she wants to," Morgan snapped, moving away from the window. Who the hell did Randolph think he was?

Jake followed closely. "Morgan, maybe this quiet

little cabin in a canyon is exactly what both of you need.''

Halting at the bed, Morgan shot a look over his shoulder. "I don't know what you're talking about."

"The old Morgan I know always got back in touch with nature to unwind. The place you're going was a favorite of yours when you were a young officer in the Marine Corps. It's isolated, with a lot of wildlife and trout fishing—no people except the ranch hands and owners. Laura needs a break from all of this." Jake took the photo of the log cabin and studied it. "Right now, we're more worried about her deteriorating condition than about you. You're going to live. You've survived the worst, physically speaking."

"All right," Morgan rasped, "I'll go. I'll try to help Laura, but there's no guarantee."

Jake dropped the photo on the bed and smiled a little. "I have a hunch that this is exactly what you both need. Mike Houston will be around, but you won't see him unless he wants you to. He's a professional soldier, and he'll make sure Garcia's hit men don't get close enough to take a shot at you. Dr. Parsons is coming along more because of Laura's emotional instability than for your health needs, although Laura doesn't know that. I'd appreciate it if you wouldn't say anything to her."

"I'm not the kind of person to deliberately hurt someone," Morgan snapped.

A rueful smile pulled at Jake's mouth. "Morgan, you're a contrary bastard by nature, but I understand why. The only place in your life where you weren't like that was with Laura and your kids. With them, you finally exposed your soft underbelly, and that was the only time you did. Take this time at the cabin and let that side of you surface with Laura. You trusted her more than anyone else in your life...."

"It's beautiful," Laura breathed. She stood beside a muddied Jeep driven by Rachel Donovan, the oldest of the three daughters now running the Donovan cattle ranch. In front of them, at the end of the muddy road, stood a log cabin. It wasn't large, but it was a stone's throw from the rushing waters of Oak Creek.

"We think you'll love it here," Rachel said cheerily. "It's been a favorite hideaway for our friends and family over the years."

Laura looked hopefully up at Morgan, dressed in a white, long-sleeved shirt and Levi's. His face had lost a little of its tension as he looked at the cabin. Their flight to Luke Air Force Base near Phoenix, had been long but uneventful, and for that she was grateful. In her peripheral vision, she saw Rachel pick up their luggage. Days earlier, Major Houston and Dr. Parsons had flown out and were already staying at the main ranch. Laura had met Mike and liked him immensely. She knew he had been instrumental in rescuing Morgan from Ramirez in Peru.

"What do you think?" Laura asked Morgan.

"It's nice," he grunted. Moving forward, he reached to help Rachel with the bags. The ground was covered with pine needles, but the soil was clay, and it stubbornly stuck to his shoes. Rachel had warned them that cowboy boots would be the uniform of the day. Above them, the Arizona sun shone brightly. It was the end of February, and the temperature was already in the high fifties, with no snow in sight. The cabin was located about ten miles north of the small town of Sedona in a huge canyon filled with pine trees and white-barked sycamores. The walls of the canyon, Rachel had told them as she made the drive up the narrow road to the cabin, consisted of red and white sedimentary sandstone, laid down millions of years ago and layered with black basalt—the remains of lava from the volcanic activity that had been a big part of the region's prehistoric past.

Picking up their luggage, Morgan strode into the cabin. It was small—only four rooms. Panic surged within him as he noted that there was only one bedroom. Rachel smiled and pushed some of her reddish brown hair away from her face after hefting two suitcases onto one of the room's twin beds.

"We use this cabin during branding season," she said, sweeping her hand around the room. "The twin beds are all we have."

Morgan stared at them. The room was small, the two beds covered with light pink chenille spreads. The windows were open to allow the clean, pine-fragrant air to circulate. "It'll be fine, Rachel."

"Good," she said with relief. "I'm going to give Laura a quick tour of the kitchen facilities."

Morgan stood alone in the quiet bedroom. At least they'd have separate beds. Still, he was uncomfortable with the idea of Laura being so close to him at night, though he wasn't sure why. Since the day he'd come out of the coma, he'd watched her gradually retreat from him in a number of ways. Could he blame her? He certainly wasn't reaching out to touch her or show her any kind of intimacy a husband might share with his wife. But how could he? Still, her increasing silence spoke louder than words. Maybe Jake was right, and he should pay more attention to his feelings. It was as if an invisible cord was strung between him and Laura—one composed of instinctive responses that he fought daily to ignore.

Turning slowly around, Morgan opened his suitcase and pulled open one of the dresser drawers. Laura kept up a smiling exterior and was excellent at small talk, but he could feel her hiding a lot deep within her. He heard the sudden chatter of chickadees outside the window, joined by the high squeak of a flicker. Going to the screened window, he spotted the rust red underwings of the flicker on a branch of a pine not far from the cabin. Funny, he recognized those sounds, and he'd known automatically what kind of bird made them. Maybe, he ruminated, returning to his unpacking, he shouldn't give up hope yet.

When he'd finished putting his clothes away, he opened Laura's suitcases. His hands stilled as he saw several photos in a plastic bag lying on top of her clothes. Over the weeks, Laura had brought several photos to him in hopes of jogging his memory. These, he knew, were framed photos of his children, and one of their entire family. Fingering them, Morgan felt an odd emotion flow through him—the first of its kind. Holding the photos, he savored the odd feeling.

"Morgan?"

He lifted his head at the sound of Laura's voice. She stood hesitantly in the doorway. Her blond hair had been swept back, captured into a girlish ponytail with tendrils at her temples that emphasized her very readable blue eyes. Morgan noticed she'd changed from the dark green silk shirtdress she'd traveled in, into a bright pink, long-sleeved blouse and jeans. His lower body tightened in appreciation. For a woman who'd had two children, she still had a body that could make any man look twice.

"Yes?" His voice came out off-key, and he saw her eyes become shadowed as she saw him bending over her suitcase, photos in hand. Did she think he was snooping without permission?

She smiled hesitantly and moved to the end of the bed. "I see you found the family photos."

"Yeah," he grunted, handing them to her. As his fingers touched hers briefly in the exchange, that same feeling washed over him again, settling in the region of his heart. Too much was going on, and he needed quiet time to analyze this new twist in his feelings. Maybe Jake had been right after all; maybe he did need quiet and isolation to get in touch with his old, stuck memories.

"You look...different," Laura said, taking the photos and arranging them on top of the dresser. "Are you okay?"

Shrugging, Morgan looked around. "Yeah, I'm fine." He could feel her gaze on him, the question strung between them. "Maybe a little tired," he said. Actually, that wasn't a lie. The trip by Learjet—his company jet, or so they told him—had been long and wearing on him. He twisted to look in her direction. "I just heard the Jeep leave."

"Yes, Rachel's gone." Laura shrugged a little nervously. "It's just you and me now."

Morgan saw the exhaustion in her eyes. "Listen, why don't you rest? I can see you're tired."

"I'll be okay. Just being here is invigorating, isn't it?" She turned, covering her exhaustion with a strained smile.

Morgan had the crazy urge to step up to her, grab her by her small shoulders and give her a shake. She was putting on that cheery-faced routine for him again, and he could sense her retreating deep within herself—as usual. Keeping in mind Jake's warning that it was time to think of someone besides himself, he said gruffly, "When I saw those photos, I felt something...."

Laura's heart thudded once to underscore her reaction. "You did?"

With a shrug, Morgan growled, "I don't know what I felt. Just…something."

Looking around the room, Laura said, "Ann was hoping that if we got off alone, your memory might slowly begin to return."

Sunlight lanced through the western window of the bedroom, and Morgan saw it touch Laura's hair, the strands turning radiant, like a halo across her crown, until a breeze outside the cabin moved the branches of a pine tree and blocked the ray of light. How beautiful Laura was, he realized, beginning to appreciate her on a new, unspoken level. Her skin was translucent, and he could see the small blue veins beneath her eyes. Her mouth was decidedly one of her finest features—full and soft and excruciatingly vulnerable looking. He found himself wondering what it would be like to explore it with his own—and groaned internally at the thought.

The thought was so unbidden, so foreign to him, that Morgan stood very still, assimilating the urge. Scowling, he said, "Rachel mentioned that this used to be an area sacred to the Indians."

"Magic?" Laura said wistfully, beginning to put her clothes in the drawers. "We could use some magic in our lives right now," she added with a gentle laugh.

Morgan moved around the small room, noting that Laura's bed was no more than six feet from his. Beyond this room, a long, rectangular living room held a worn leather couch with a black-white-and-gray Navajo rug thrown over the back, and two overstuffed chairs. Although the cabin had electricity and running water, Oak Creek Canyon was several thousand feet deep, so television reception wasn't possible.

Morgan halted in the bedroom doorway, his hand resting tentatively on the jamb. Funny, he'd never studied Laura as he did now. She had an undeniable grace about her, in the way her small hands moved as she unpacked her clothes. Morgan liked the fact that she didn't wear much makeup or paint her fingernails. No, Laura had a distinctly natural quality. "You belong out here," he said huskily.

"What?" Laura straightened and looked up at him. The expression on Morgan's face was thoughtful, and Laura couldn't quite decipher the emotion banked in his darkened eyes. Her skin prickled pleasantly; a familiar sensation from the old days when he'd often fixed her with that hooded, burning look. Her mouth went dry momentarily, and she froze beneath his gaze.

Morgan watched Laura's eyes widen—beautifully. Could a change of location suddenly make him aware of her on such a new, primal level? He felt his body tighten with need—of her. The sensation was startling, and he wondered obliquely if she realized he wanted her sexually. That would be embarrassing— to her and him. He still didn't remember anything specific, but suddenly, his body was recalling something—something he had to fight. Morgan would no more entertain the thought of taking Laura for sexual reasons than he would any other woman. He had to feel more than raw, sexual chemistry.

"Uh..." He lifted his hand, a little embarrassed. "This place, I guess. I feel different here. How about you?"

Laura felt the invisible cord that had suddenly bound them snap and dissolve just as quickly as it had appeared. That intangible connection was an old, wonderful feeling that had inexplicably established itself between them for the first time since Morgan's return, however briefly. Once they'd shared that sensation twenty-four hours a day. Startled by its unexpected reemergence, Laura's voice was husky with emotion as she said, "Yes, there's a feeling about this place I can't put my finger on—yet."

Morgan saw her hands tremble slightly as she tucked her silky lingerie away in the drawer. What would Laura look like dressed in that pink silk camisole and bikini panties? The image wavered tauntingly before his eyes. With a shake of his head, he forced himself away from the doorway and into the living room. Looking down, he realized his body was responding to her with a will of its own. Damn!

Feeling the need of fresh air, he went outside. A battered four-wheel drive Toyota Land Cruiser sat beside the cabin—their transportation if they needed to go somewhere, though Major Houston had warned them not to go anywhere without checking in with him at ranch headquarters first. The old gray Toyota had seen better days. As Morgan stepped onto the pine needles, still damp from a rain two days earlier, he felt a certain affinity with the vehicle. He was a little beat up and rusty himself.

"Do you mind if I join you?"

Laura's voice intruded gently on his thoughts. It reminded him of the breeze wafting through the pine trees that surrounded the log cabin. He'd jammed his hands into his jeans pockets as he'd stood looking at the Toyota. Now he looked across his shoulder to see her standing tentatively, as if he might banish her with a dark look or irritable wave of his hand. Her face was so easily read, her eyes broadcasting anxiety.

Morgan turned and gestured for her to come closer. "Let's go explore the creek."

"Are—are you sure?"

He studied her flushed face and gazed deeply into her eyes. Maybe this place really was magic, Morgan thought, as he felt Laura's anxiety, and sensed that she didn't want to be left alone—that she needed his company. His or anyone's? Rubbing his mouth with the back of his hand, he turned toward her fully. "Ann said I should try talking more openly to you," he confided in a low tone, "and I know I'm not the world's most talkative person. I feel you're anxious. Over what?"

Laura stood transfixed by his gray gaze. Morgan's face had changed from that frighteningly implacable mask to the familiar expression of the man she had known for so many years. Hungrily, she took in his concern—for her. It was the first time she'd experienced his care since his return, and it left her off balance and feeling suddenly vulnerable in a new way. Just as quickly, Morgan could close up, she knew, striking another wounding blow to her vulnerability. She wasn't sure she could stand too many more of those blows.

Opening her hands, she whispered, "I'm feeling pretty shaky right now, Morgan. I—" she looked up at the towering pine trees behind him "—my heart's beating like a runaway freight train in my chest and my hands are sweaty...."

Scowling, he moved slowly toward her. He not only heard but felt an edge of panic to her voice. Though he wanted to reach out and grip her hands, he stopped about six feet away. Yes, fear was mixed with the anxiety in her eyes. "I'm not too good at this yet," he mumbled, "about talking or trying to talk. What are you afraid of?"

Shrugging, Laura whispered, "I don't know. I really don't know." She rubbed her damp palms self-consciously on the thighs of her Levi's. Her heart continued to pound, and she wondered obliquely if she was having a heart attack. "I have to sit down," she said, and she moved spasmodically toward an old, carved bench along the cabin wall. If she didn't sit down, she feared her knees would buckle.

Without thinking, Morgan gripped her arm and guided her to the bench. Her skin was soft and firm beneath his hand. For a moment, the fragrance of her

camellia perfume beckoned to him. He saw the flash
of surprise in her eyes as he made contact and realized
this was the first time he'd touched her. Once she was
settled on the bench, he released her and crouched in
front of her, a few inches separating them. Laura nervously touched her brow and tried to give him a smile
that said she was going to be all right.

"Were you always like this?" he wondered in a
low voice.

"Like what?" Laura asked, clasping her hands in
her lap. Morgan's very presence was beckoning powerfully to her. Oh, to throw herself into his strong,
capable arms and be held! How many times had she
dreamed he was holding her safe? Holding her tight
against his comforting bulk? Laura fought against
those needs. Morgan had touched her because she was
unsteady on her feet. It meant nothing personally to
him, she realized with renewed agony.

Morgan gestured to her. "You always try to hide
how you're really feeling. I can see you're scared
about something."

Hanging her head, Laura closed her eyes. "It's—
just a reaction. Ann told me they were called anxiety
attacks."

"Why do you have them?"

Her throat closed with tears. She'd gotten so used
to Morgan not caring about her personally that his
unexpected focus was too much for her to cope with
on top of her weakened state. "I—I've had them
since my rescue," she stammered.

Morgan saw her wrestling with very real anxiety. Her hands twisted in her lap and the corners of her mouth pulled inward as if to battle inner demons. "Laura?" He called her name huskily, stunned by the avalanche of feeling behind it. But Morgan didn't have time to analyze his own responses. Right now, what was important was the fact that Laura was hurting.

Compressing her lips, Laura looked up—and nearly melted beneath Morgan's tender gaze. She wanted to fly off that bench and into his arms. Just to feel safe, even for a moment! "Ann calls it PTSD—Post Traumatic Stress Disorder." Her voice broke, and she forced out the rest of the words. "Anxiety attacks are part of it." She shrugged helplessly. "I don't get them very often. I don't know why I had one now. I—I feel safe here." She looked away. "I feel safe because you're here...."

As Morgan continued to crouch before her, he felt a gutting, knifelike sensation pierce his chest and move outward, as if someone were invisibly carving his heart into pieces. He saw Laura's courage in that moment, as she struggled to tame those demons that were strangling the life out of her eyes. "You might look fragile," he rasped, "but you sure as hell have courage." When she turned her head aside to avoid his gaze, Morgan slowly unwound from his position.

"Come on," he ordered huskily, holding out his hand to her. "What do you say we go for a walk and look around our new home?"

Chapter 5

Laura stared in disbelief as Morgan offered her his hand. It was a large, square hand, familiar old scars mingling with frightening new ones. Choking back a sob, she hesitantly lifted her hand and slid it into his. As his calloused fingers curled around hers, she felt his momentary hesitation. He was doing this not because he'd suddenly rediscovered his love for her. No, it was a humane gesture, and she knew she had to be careful not to make anything more of it than that.

Still, as she stood, a thrill arced through her. Morgan's hand was as warm and dry as hers was damp and cool. Just the fact that he had made physical contact with her gave her the strength to stand. Her shaky knees grew stronger. Her heart rate slowed. All the while, her gaze was held by his tender one. It was as if so much of the old Morgan from before the kidnappings had returned to her side! Laura wanted to tell him, but the words wouldn't come.

Starved for the feel of him, she closed her eyes and merely stood there for a moment, savoring Morgan on all levels. The singing of the birds, the rush and tumble of the nearby creek, the soft breeze lifting her hair, all ceased to exist as she centered her heart and soul on his warm fingers curved around her own. She swore she could feel his pulse beat through his fingers, as if he were a lifeline restoring her will to live, feeding her with the desire to fight back for what had been so cruelly torn from her months before. She felt his strength infusing her, halting the terrible downward spiral she'd been inhabiting far too long.

In moments, the anxiety was washed away, replaced by a feeling of serenity that Laura had thought she'd never feel again. Morgan stood near her, mere inches between them as he lightly grasped her hand. He'd reached out to touch her of his own accord, not because she'd begged him to.

Morgan's hand disengaged from hers, and Laura's lashes flew open. To her regret, he moved away from her to follow a small path that led down to the creek bank. Tears welled into her eyes, and a cry lodged in her throat. She swayed, caught herself, then wrestled with the feeling of abandonment he'd created by releasing her. She stared at him, the cotton shirt stretched tautly across his massive shoulders as he picked his way carefully among the rocks and over downed tree limbs toward the creek's pebble-strewn bed. A breeze momentarily wafted several strands of his short, black hair.

Swallowing hard, Laura released a tremulous sigh. Well, what did she expect? Too much, she warned herself as she forced herself to follow him. Her steps seemed wooden and uncoordinated as she tried to recover from his fleeting touch, and her fingers tingled wildly where he'd held them. Heat throbbed moltenly upward through her arm to wrap softly around her aching heart. It was enough. Her heart was no longer bounding, and her anxiety had miraculously dissolved. For that she was more than grateful.

Laura tried to shift her focus and allow the healing beauty of Oak Creek Canyon to soothe her senses. Sunlight danced through pine boughs, dappling the bare, white branches of the gigantic sycamores that followed the curve of the bank. Morgan had found a large, oval sandstone boulder at the water's edge and taken a seat on it. She absorbed his rugged profile as he sat, legs drawn up, his massive arms encircling his knees.

Noting the unhappy line of his mouth, she realized that he, too, was suffering in his own private hell. What had it cost him to reach out to her? No longer did she ask herself each time something happened if an old memory from their past had jogged loose. Her hope on that score had been savagely reduced with every passing minute since his return. The psychiatrists said his memory was gone—forever. Only Dr. Parsons held out a ten-percent chance that some of it might be intact. But which parts? The Marine Corps experiences? The loss of his entire company on that hill in Vietnam? His years in the French Foreign Legion? Or—her fingers curled at her sides as she carefully made her way toward him—his memories of her, their family and their seven wonderful years together?

Life was so tenuous, Laura decided as she halted by the smooth sandstone boulder where Morgan sat. He turned his head, his gaze penetrating her like a laser. Laura felt the scorching quality of his eyes. When he looked at her like that, her entire body responded to him. How she ached to kiss him now that he was conscious. She was sure he didn't remember her kisses when he'd first roused from the coma.

"Sit down," he invited quietly.

Laura didn't sit too close to Morgan, although a healthy part of her cried out to do that very thing. He'd gestured where she should sit, so she did. It would do no good to crowd him. In fact, it might do more harm than good. Laura knew she couldn't make Morgan love her. She had to let him make the moves, no matter how hard it was not to reach out and tousle his hair or throw her arms around him as she would have before the kidnapping.

The boulder was sun-warmed, and Laura enjoyed the feel of it as she sat a foot away from Morgan, her legs crossed, her hands resting on her thighs. In front of them, Oak Creek, about a hundred feet wide and perhaps eight to ten feet deep, flowed strongly. The water was clear and she could see white, red, gray, yellow and black stones shimmering in the depths of the rushing cascade as it funneled, bubbled and frothed around the few larger boulders scattered along the creek bed.

Closing her eyes, she lifted her face to the late-afternoon sun. Soon it would dip behind the canyon walls on its winter orbit, and the boulder would become shaded. For now the sunlight warmed her cold, cold soul, and she reveled in the creek's laughing burble and the chirping of many birds she couldn't identify. For now, she decided, just feeling Morgan's nearness was enough.

Laura was aware of his magnificent bulk; much of the weight he'd lost was quickly returning. Morgan possessed a vibrancy she had always been aware of— and learned to depend on. She wondered if he was aware of his masculine vitality and decided he probably wasn't. So much of Morgan's life revolved around his company—worrying about his mercenary teams and their missions rather than himself or his personal needs.

"What are you thinking about?" he asked.

Laura smiled softly, her eyes remaining closed. Morgan's voice was husky and intimate. "I was thinking of you, of how deeply you care for other people before yourself."

Morgan scowled and played absently with a small

pine branch he'd picked up on his way to the boulder. "How do you mean?"

A breeze caressed her, and her lips parted as she pretended it was Morgan reaching out for her. "You always cared deeply for others, Morgan. I think after you lost your men in Vietnam, you made a promise to yourself to never again allow anyone you had responsibility for to die." She opened her eyes and turned her head in his direction. His eyes were a smoky gray, and she knew he was thinking about what she'd said. "The guilt you felt over the loss of those men's lives has always been with you," she continued gently. "There were nights, after we were married, when you'd be up all night, pacing in our living room, worried about some team you'd sent out on a dangerous mission."

"I'd wake you up?"

Laura turned and faced him, careful to maintain the distance between them. "I pretended to be asleep, but I always woke up when you left my side." She smiled sadly and ran her fingertip across a tiny crevice in the boulder between them. "I knew you didn't want me up with you. You worried about waking me. When we first married, your PTSD symptoms were obvious. You had insomnia and bad nightmares and would toss and turn all night. At first you wouldn't let me sleep with you, but I persisted."

"What happened when I did?"

Laura met his somber gaze. "You started sleeping better."

"I see...."

"Holding someone you love can be healing," Laura said.

"I guess so." Morgan stared bleakly down at the small branch in his hands. He'd been stripping the bark from it systematically. "So, I'd get up and pace all night because I was worried about my employees?"

"Yes. And—" Laura drew up her legs, putting her arms around her knees "—when it was a really bad mission and you were particularly worried, you'd stay at the office. Sometimes I wouldn't see you at home with us for two or three days."

He stared at her. "I can't imagine being away from you for that long." The words came out of nowhere and Morgan stared at Laura, surprised by his own admission. He saw her eyes flare with equal surprise, then grow a misty blue as tears formed. Looking away, he suffered for her. He hadn't slept with her since coming out of the coma. Nor could he.

"I don't know where that came from," he said gruffly, tossing the stick into the stream.

Laura self-consciously dashed away the tears, her heart swelling with incredible joy at what he'd said. "You used to come home after a two- or three-nighter like that, and I'd be in bed. First you'd check on the kids. Then you'd come in, sit on my side of the bed, and..." Her voice faltered. She felt Morgan's gaze burning through her. "And you'd run your fingers through my hair." She fingered strands of hair at her temple. "I used to love your touching my hair like that. It was a wonderful way to wake up. You always loved to touch my hair. Often you'd brush it for me at night before we turned in.

"Sometimes when you came back after being gone for a while, I'd awaken and turn over. You'd put your arm around me and lean over and tell me you were crazy to stay away so long from me...from us...."

"Were you upset when I was gone like that?" Morgan held her dreamy gaze. He ached to reach out and untangle her thick blond hair from its ponytail. Some internal knowing was driving him, and for the first time, he began to understand what Dr. Parsons meant about feeling his way back into his lost memories. Something inside him knew his pleasure in brushing Laura's hair—and hers in having him do it.

"No. I understood your need to be with your people, to keep them safe. I know you would never have forgiven yourself if something happened and you weren't there. Even if a team was half a world away, you wanted to be as close to them as possible when danger threatened." She smiled softly. "That's one of the many things I've loved about you—your loyalty and care for others. I used to worry when you first created Perseus, because you'd go through such angst whenever you sent a team on a mission." She looked down at the boulder. "We had many, many discussions about your fears, your feelings, and how they were affecting us and the children."

Morgan digested Laura's admissions. It was the

first time she'd talked intimately to him about the details of their former life together. Before, she'd limited herself to small talk with no real substance behind it. He dragged in a deep, ragged breath and continued to study Laura's profile as she watched the water rushing over the rocks in front of them. Jake was right: it was time to focus his attention on someone other than himself. Obviously, the old Morgan had attempted that care in a way he wasn't. Morgan wasn't sure what might have caused the change.

"Sitting here with you," he began in a low tone, "and talking like this, feeds me. I feel like I've been missing something. Starving for something I couldn't define—didn't know existed." He shook his head, unable to continue. This was what he'd been missing, he realized. He lifted his head and stared at Laura long and hard. *It was her.*

Laura felt heat tunnel through her like a beam of pure sunlight shafting through her heart at Morgan's words. His eyes were very clear now, a pale gray that told her how deeply he was forging a link with her. She not only saw it, she felt it. Something *was* happening. The old Morgan she knew and loved so fiercely was here now with her, even if he didn't realize that what he missed was her. Did she dare hope some small bit of their connection had survived the trauma he'd endured? That alert, hawklike gaze, that invisible energy that now swirled and danced around her, making her feel as if she was the very center of his universe, like a healing unguent to the psychic wounds she'd sustained throughout the past three months.

And Laura began to understand what had helped forge the link once again between them: her honest sharing of the tiny, daily details that had made up the fabric of their life together. Trying to quell her excitement at the discovery, she said in a husky tone, "There were nights that you'd come home, Morgan, and you'd be completely exhausted. You'd tousle my hair and wake me up, and I could see the dark circles under your eyes. Sometimes you hadn't shaved in days, and sometimes I knew you'd been crying."

Laura hesitated and slowly stroked the boulder's smooth surface with her fingers, fighting the insane urge to reach out and stroke Morgan's skin. "I knew if I awoke and saw your red-rimmed eyes, something had gone very wrong. I'd get up, and we'd go to the kitchen, and I'd make tea. I would watch you wrestle with your pent-up emotions. One part of you wanted to cry out your pain and loss, while the other part, the military part, would try to jam the sorrow and tears deep down inside. I'd ask you about the mission, about what had happened. Little by little, I'd see you stop gripping the mug in front of you, and I'd see the tears start slowly forming in your eyes.

"I would get up, put my cup down on the table and come to your side. Usually, I'd press your head against me, put my arms around you and just hold you. I'd gently touch your hair. Then I'd feel this awful struggle begin within you. I'd feel a sob wanting to tear free, but you'd fight it with everything you had. Finally, you'd trust me enough, and you'd bury your head against me, wrap your arms around me and cry.'' She pressed her lips together and held his gaze. ''You'd cry long and hard because someone you had known, someone you'd wanted to keep safe, had died.''

Laura continued to stroke the stone absently, lost in the memories, closing her eyes as she shared them with him. ''I'd rock you and hold you. You were so strong that sometimes I was afraid you would squeeze me in two, you held me so tightly....''

Taking in a ragged breath, she whispered, ''Afterward, we'd go to the master bathroom. We have a Jacuzzi in there, and I'd take off your clothes and get you in that hot, bubbling water. Water has always had a healing effect on you, Morgan. I would get you in there, sponge you down and we'd...well, we'd relax....''

In that instant, Morgan knew that he'd made love with Laura at those times. He saw the shyness in her face, heard it in her whispered tone as a pink flush stained her cheeks. She was staring down at her hand on the rock, unable to meet his gaze.

An intense, burning sensation began to coil and tighten in his lower body. How he ached to love Laura! But from his perspective, it was a physical attraction he didn't dare indulge. She deserved so much more. Frustrated, he watched the slight, inconstant breeze move tendrils of her blond hair against her flushed cheeks. He wanted to reach out and touch those golden strands, run his scarred fingertips across the slope of her cheek. What did Laura's skin feel like? Was it as soft as her voice, which reminded him of a summer's breeze? Was it as velvet as it looked? Aching to find out, and knowing it would only raise unfair hope in her, he jammed his hands between his crossed legs.

"It sounds," he said, groping to find the right words, "as if we had a pretty close relationship."

Laura smiled brokenly and moved her hand gently across the rock. "Yes—we did."

"And it sounds like I got a hell of a lot from it. But what did I ever do for you?"

Laura smiled to herself. She lifted her head and met his burning, nearly colorless gaze. "When I got hit by that car at National Airport, you were an absolute stranger, and you rode in the ambulance to the hospital and hung around until I became conscious." She opened her hands and gave him a strained smile. "Maybe that's what I love about the military so much, Morgan, I don't know. Maybe that's why I worked within that industry, because my father was a marine. Even though I was adopted, he had a kind of loyalty to my mother and me that I saw didn't often exist out in the civilian world. I grew up feeling very loved and cared for.

"When I awoke in the hospital—blind—and you came in, I knew in my heart everything was going to be all right." She touched her eyes with her fingers.

"I was scared to death not being able to see. Nothing like that had ever happened to me before. My parents were dead by then. I had no one, but suddenly there you were, bigger than life, coming into that room, grabbing my hand and telling me you weren't going to leave me."

Morgan saw the warmth and tenderness in Laura's eyes. He felt it like a glowing fire kindled within him, making his heart swell in some unknown but powerful emotional knowing. Though he had no conscious memory of what she was telling him, he felt a strange sort of inner connection to the incident. "What happened next?"

Laura smiled fondly. "I hate hospitals—like you— and I wanted to leave. The doctor got angry and said I had to remain under observation for at least two days. You saw my need to go home and understood that at home, I'd feel safe and be able to recover more quickly."

"So I took you home." He shook his head. "I'm amazed you'd trust a complete stranger like that."

With a small laugh, Laura dangled her legs over the edge of the boulder. She gave him an impish look. "You still don't get it to this day, Morgan. You didn't at the time, and after we were married, I tried to make you understand, but you just didn't."

"What didn't I understand?" He liked the way her eyes were dancing with a childlike delight. It was good to see her lips curve upward. Something about her laughter, her smile, made him feel damn good about being a man and being with her.

"Your effect on me. On everyone. You're completely oblivious to it, Morgan. You forge an immediate bond of trust with anyone who comes in contact with you, and you don't even realize it. It's the mark of a natural leader. That's why you were so good in the Marine Corps and the French Foreign Legion. People trust you. We instinctively know you'll go through hell and back for us. We sense it, and if we're privileged enough to be around you, we see it in action every day, in large and small ways.

"You didn't abandon me—or take advantage of me—in my darkest hour of need, Morgan. You took me home, nursed me and cared for me. You took care of my baby robin that had fallen from its nest, and you took care of Sasha, my Saint Bernard. To me—" she smiled gently over at him "—you're like a big old teddy bear, the kind you can cuddle up to and hold and feel safe with."

His mouth quirked. "A teddy bear, huh?"

Laughing lightly, Laura nodded. "You gave Jason one shortly after he was born, and when Katherine Alyssa came, she got one, too. Didn't you know? That bears are healers who protect their own?"

"No…" He stared down at his hands. The sun slid slowly past the canyon rim and he felt an immediate drop in temperature. Laura wasn't wearing a jacket, and although he was still comfortable, he wondered

if she was. Rousing himself, he said, "Let's get back
to the cabin. It's going to get dark pretty soon."

Laura swallowed her disappointment. She shivered
and wrapped her arms around herself after she slid
off the rock. Waiting, she watched Morgan move a
lot more slowly from his perch. She knew from Dr.
Parson's examination that he had been so badly tortured that even his joints, especially his knees, were
still healing. He reminded her of a huge football
player who had been in too many games, and never
been given the time or care to recover sufficiently
from all those powerful, bruising hits.

Swallowing hard, Laura decided not to wait for
him. Maybe he would read her waiting the wrong
way. Right now, they'd just forged a link between
them for the first time, and she didn't want it destroyed by some mistake on her part. As she carefully
picked her way through the pebbled area, she hoped
she wouldn't accidentally slam the door shut on what
they'd just achieved. She had no manual to follow on
how to handle this situation, and right now she was
extremely fearful of making a mistake.

The cabin was cool. An earth stove stood in one
corner, and she saw that someone had thoughtfully
placed a box of chopped wood nearby so they could
start a fire. The living room was long and rectangular,
and the dull shine of the pine floor complemented the
brown leather couch and forest green chairs.

"Will you start a fire?" she asked Morgan as he

entered. ''I'll go look in the fridge and see what Rachel left for dinner.''

He nodded. ''Sure, go ahead.'' Closing the door, he watched Laura move to the kitchen. She seemed happier. Or was it his imagination? He felt happier. Why? Because of their intimate conversation on the rock? Possibly. It was the first time they'd been able to sit down and really talk. Moving to the stove, he opened the door and wadded up a bunch of newspapers, deep in thought.

What were they going to do tonight—with one bedroom and two beds less than six feet apart? His sleep had been light and sporadic in the hospital. As he placed wood in the stove, his frown deepened. Part of him, a very primal part, considered Laura's proximity strictly on a physical level. How he wanted to love her! Did she realize how peaceful he felt in her sunny presence? She fed him in some invisible way he couldn't explain. His body knew and was in a constant, aching knot, obviously recalling a great deal more than his damned brain did about Laura and how he felt toward her.

Lighting the fire, Morgan slowly eased upright and watched the tongues of flame lick eagerly at the wood. That was how he felt toward Laura: like a blazing flame wanting to lick and touch every inch of her skin. He wanted to taste her, feel the pressure of her lips against his, tunnel his fingers through her thick blond hair and then...

Making a sound of disgust, Morgan slammed shut

the stove door and jammed his hands into the pockets of his jeans. What the hell was the matter with him? Where was this high-minded concern for others that Laura had spoken so well of? His reasons for wanting Laura were far from high-minded. No, they were strictly selfish.

Chapter 6

Laura emerged from the tiny bathroom in a pink flannel nightgown falling to her ankles, covered by a white chenille robe. She carried her brush. The hot bath had been reviving, and she touched her cheek, which felt warm and flushed, as she padded out into the living room where Morgan was reading.

The cabin was pleasantly warm from the heat thrown out by the stove. A sense of peace filled Laura as she halted in the doorway. Morgan sat on the couch, newspaper in hand, deep in concentration. Little by little, as the evening had passed, he had truly begun to relax, and for that Laura was supremely grateful. Dinner had been somewhat stilted, but afterward, when she took out her needlepoint and sat in the living room, leaving him alone, he'd eventually come in and sat down, too.

A tender smile pulled at her mouth now as she absorbed the sight of him sitting so peacefully. Moving into the room, she lowered herself to sit on a thick sheep's fleece in front of the hearth. Leaning her back against the chair closest to the rug, she slowly began to brush her hair. She felt more than saw Morgan shift his attention to her.

Morgan scowled as he felt Laura's presence. When she walked past him, he automatically inhaled deeply, and the scent of orange blossoms filled his flaring nostrils. Laura looked thin in the nightgown and robe, and the observation struck him hard. Always before, he'd seen her in a dress or suit, bulky winter clothes that disguised her thinness. He frowned.

"You're skinny as a rail," he growled, laying the newspaper aside.

Laura stopped brushing her hair for a moment. Morgan was studying her darkly, his hands clasped between his thighs. "Skinny?"

"Yes."

Smiling slightly, she began to brush her hair again. "I lost twenty pounds or so, as you did," she said softly.

With each stroke of the brush, Morgan felt an aching need grow within him. Laura was so incredibly graceful, her face serene—in sharp contrast with his burgeoning emotions. The little makeup she'd worn was gone, replaced with the fresh-scrubbed look of a

college girl. Morgan found it tough to believe that
Laura had borne two children. His children, he reminded himself awkwardly. Her hair glinted molten
gold in the lamplight, the shadows gently shaping her
clean features. Yes, Laura was beautiful to him.

Forcing his gaze down to his hands, he said grimly,
"You didn't eat enough for a bird tonight at dinner."

"No…"

"Why not?" He'd eaten like a lumberjack. Laura
had prepared steaks, a mountain of fried potatoes,
steamed broccoli, and homemade garlic toast. The
food, his first real meal since being released from the
damn hospital, had tasted delicious. But halfway
through the meal he'd realized she was merely picking at her steak, cutting it into smaller and smaller
pieces but not eating much of consequence. He hadn't
said anything at the time, but seeing now how gaunt
she actually was, he couldn't remain silent.

Placing the brush in her lap, Laura stared down at
it. The tortoise shell object, which had once belonged
to her mother, was smooth and comforting in her
hands. "I—don't know, Morgan."

"People don't eat because they're upset, or something's bothering them."

"I suppose that's true."

"So what's bothering you?"

His abruptness was like a physical blow to her, and
Laura felt herself wince at his question. Nervously,
she turned the brush in her hands. "I really haven't
felt like eating since the kidnappings, Morgan."

"But we're all back now. We're safe. You should be eating more."

Struggling against anger and hurt, Laura lifted her chin and met his flat, searching stare. How like Morgan to address the issue so bluntly, with no preamble. He wasn't known for his diplomacy, and he certainly wasn't showing any here, with her. "*You* might feel safe enough—emotionally stable enough—to resume your normal eating patterns."

"You're saying you don't feel safe?"

Hot tears flooded Laura's eyes, and she looked away from him. Her voice grew strained. "Morgan, you forget that I'm still trapped." She forced herself to look at him. "I don't have a husband. The man who used to love me is still lost to me. I—I'm alone, Morgan, and when I try to eat, I feel nauseous."

Her words carved pain into his chest. He bowed his head, unable to hold her anguished look. The line of Laura's lips told him how much she was fighting not to cry in front of him, and he felt like hell—as if all this was his fault. Angry at hurting her, because she didn't deserve that kind of pain, he abruptly got to his feet.

"Go to bed," he said gruffly, then turned and walked stiffly out of the room toward the bathroom.

"Damn..." Laura whispered tautly, her fingers clenched tightly on the brush. She heard the bathroom door shut a little more loudly than was necessary. What could she have said differently so as not to upset Morgan? She was at a loss. Maybe she should have lied. No, that wasn't right, either. With a sigh, she got to her feet and went into the bedroom.

Laura chose the bed nearest the window. How could she possibly sleep with Morgan so close to her? Placing the brush on the dresser, she eased out of her robe and laid it across the foot of her bed. Fatigue lapped at her, and as she snuggled down beneath the covers, she realized she might fall asleep anyway. The flight had been long, and travel in general always sapped her energy for a day or two.

As her head sunk into the pillow, she closed her eyes. The wool blanket was scratchy against her neck, but she didn't care. Exhaustion stalked her. As she felt herself spiraling downward toward badly needed sleep, she made a mental note to call Susannah Killian tomorrow morning and talk to her, and then to Jason. She worried how he was getting along. Katherine was too young to realize what had happened, so Laura felt easier about her. Vaguely, she heard the shower running. Morgan must be washing up. It was the last coherent thought she had as sleep dragged her deep within its embrace.

Morgan ruefully rubbed his damp hair with a towel as he quietly entered the bedroom. The lukewarm shower had felt good on the healing wounds on his back from whippings he couldn't remember. He'd stood under the shower nearly half an hour, letting the water slough away his anger and frustration. Just being able to bathe so luxuriously was like a gift to him.

The light from the living room cascaded silently into the bedroom. He halted just inside the door, taking in the way the light slid across the pine floor and up and across Laura's bed, making burnished gold of her lightly tousled hair. Dropping the towel on the dresser, Morgan ran his fingers distractedly through his own damp strands. His gaze was focused on Laura—and so was his body.

How beautiful she was, he thought as he quietly padded to the side of her bed. He placed his hands in the pockets of the dark blue terry-cloth robe he wore, afraid of reaching out and touching that thick, cascading hair. Her lips were gently parted, one hand beneath her cheek as she slept, and the covers had slipped down to reveal her small but proud shoulder covered by the pink flannel nightgown.

As he stood looking at her, Morgan began to realize how stress affected Laura. She had beautiful, well-placed cheekbones, but her skin was stretched tautly across them, and bluish purple shadows showed beneath her eyes even in sleep. Her breathing was soft and shallow. Though aching to reach out and touch her hair, to see if it really felt as silky as it looked, Morgan forced himself to step away and take off his robe.

Beneath it he wore only blue-and-white striped pajama bottoms. If he weren't sleeping in the same room with Laura, he'd wear nothing at all. He didn't like clothes binding and twisting around his body as he slept. Wondering if the old Morgan had felt that way, he dropped the robe at the end of his bed. He pulled back the covers, then walked quietly into the living room and shut off the lights.

The darkness was complete, and he stood where he was for a moment, the soft crackle and snap of wood in the stove soothing his tense body. The rush of water in the creek outside the cabin filled him with an odd sense of peace. A feeling of safety wrapped around him as he padded back to the bedroom, his eyes now adjusted to the dark.

Even in the darkness, a thin slice of moon outside glimmered down to reveal the canyon's craggy cliffs. As he sat on the edge of his bed, his hands resting on his thighs, he saw the gentle moonglow envelop like a whitish halo about her still, sleeping form, caressing her features, silhouetting her full, parted lips and the thick lashes resting against her cheekbones. She slept deeply, and for some reason, that made Morgan feel good. Laura had said his presence helped her feel safe.

Warmth threaded through his heart at that realization as he sat watching her take slow, regular breaths. Faintly, he could detect the fragrance of the orange-blossom crystals she'd used in her bath. His mind gyrated back to the fact that Laura was thin. Too damned thin. He hadn't realized the depth of destruction this ordeal had wreaked on her until now—because he'd been too busy feeling sorry for himself and his lost memory, he reminded himself sulkily.

His gaze rested for a moment on the photos Laura had placed on the dresser—of their children and the rest of his family. Everything she was doing was for him, he realized. But what was Laura doing to help herself recover from the kidnapping? Angry that he hadn't even bothered to ask her what had happened during her imprisonment with Guillermo Garcia, Morgan promised her silently that he would try to repair that bridge between them in the next few days.

Hope came on the heels of his realizations. Unconsciously, Morgan rubbed his thickly haired chest. Something was miraculously at work within him that he couldn't quite define—yet. Still, it was there. Intuitively, he knew he had to follow those feelings, retaining an almost blind faith in believing that possibly, just possibly, part of his memory would return with it.

A ragged sigh escaped as he eased himself onto his bed. Hope was such a fragile, tentative thing. He saw it in Laura's eyes, heard it in her voice, all the time. As he pulled up the covers and turned on his side, facing her, he closed his eyes. Morgan had no idea if he'd sleep or not. Having Laura this close to him was a new experience, and he didn't quite trust himself because he wanted her on such a selfish, primal level. It wasn't right, he told himself harshly. She was still recovering from her own terrible trauma. Determined

to ask her about her experience with Garcia tomorrow, Morgan closed his eyes. In moments, he was
asleep.

A whimper awakened Morgan, and he sat up instantly, his heart pounding, adrenaline heightening his
senses. He'd heard a woman cry out. *Laura.* Jerking
his attention to the left, he gazed over at her. She
seemed fine.

He had no idea of the time. The sleep torn from
him, he threw off his covers and sat up, the pine floor
cold under his bare feet. The room was chilly—the
fire in the stove had obviously gone out.

Rubbing his face to get reoriented, Morgan sat rigidly, wondering if he was having another nightmare.
He'd heard Laura's cry—he'd swear he had. Yet she
lay sleeping quietly. Or was she? It took more precious moments for him to come fully awake. His
pulse was bounding. He felt and tasted fear. Why? As
his gaze ruthlessly moved across Laura again, he realized something was wrong.

Her bed covers were twisted around her, and her
nightgown had ridden up above her knees, bunching
between the soft, white curve of her thighs. She was
lying in a fetal position, her hands and arms pressed
tightly against her. Her beautiful hair was tangled, and
as he rose unsteadily to his feet to move to her side,
Morgan realized she must have been thrashing her
head from side to side on her pillow to mess it up so
much.

Without thinking, he leaned over and pressed his

hand lightly to her shoulder. My God, her nightgown was wringing wet! Scowling, he ran his hand down her arm and felt a slight tremble, finally realizing she was sleeping through a nightmare that held her tightly in its grip. The once-soft line of her mouth was compressed, the corners pulled inward with pain.

When Morgan's fingers touched her lower arm, he felt the cool dampness of her skin. She could catch her death of pneumonia! Reaching down, he brought the covers up and over her, tucking them in around her shoulders. It was then he realized her breathing was ragged and shallow, almost as if she were panting. A moan tore from her lips, and she jerked her head to one side.

Morgan eased himself down on the side of the bed, his hip resting against her. He couldn't stand to hear her whimper. Instinctively he stroked her hair and instantly her mouth lost some of its tension. Marveling that something so small as a light touch could have so much effect, he grew bolder. His heart felt as if it was tearing from his chest as he watched Laura wrestle with something he could neither see nor hear. What he could see was its impact on her.

"It's all right, Laura," he rasped, gently tunneling his fingers through her hair. "You're safe...safe...." he crooned as he leaned over, his lips near her small, delicate ear. Her hair felt like fine, strong silk to him. The joy of getting to touch her thrilled him as nothing had since he'd awakened from the coma. Her hair was thick and slightly curly, the strands yielding to his strokes, curving about his exploring fingers.

Morgan watched in amazement as her breathing began to slow and become more regular. He felt her whole body relax as he continued his gentle ministrations. Allowing his hand to move more boldly, he slipped it downward, across her blanketed shoulders. Her lips lost their tense line entirely and slowly parted. Good. How greatly he'd underestimated the importance of touch for a person in pain. Then he recalled Laura's admissions earlier this afternoon on the boulder about how she had held him and allowed him to cry against her.

His eyes glinted with tenderness as he absorbed the sight of her sleeping features. A powerful mixture of joy, gratitude and other, undefined emotions mushroomed through his chest. Just the act—the privilege—of touching Laura was more than enough for him right now, Morgan realized humbly. Before, he'd wanted her sexually. Now, at her bedside, tenderly touching her hair and back, he was filled with such a sense of peace that it shook him deeply.

Morgan loved the way her lips slowly parted to reveal their lush fullness. Trusting his feelings, he leaned over even farther, enough to touch her lips with his own. The moment his mouth met hers, something deep and powerful exploded within him, radiating outward through every inch of his body. Her lips were just as soft as he'd imagined. As he tasted their texture, he felt her move beneath him.

Panicked, he broke contact with her mouth, his hand automatically going back to her hair. He saw her thick eyelashes flutter and barely open, to reveal drowsy blue eyes.

"Go back to sleep, Laura," he rasped huskily. "You're safe…safe…"

Morgan watched her lids droop closed again. What was going on here? Just the guttural tone of his voice, certainly off-key, had soothed her. Laura snuggled her face into the pillow, a sigh slipping from her lips. Afraid to move, afraid she might wake up and discover him with her, Morgan remained sitting next to her for a good five minutes. But it was no longer torture but pure heaven to be here with her, his hand stilled on her thick hair, his hip pressed pleasantly against her now-relaxed body.

If there were such things as miracles—and Morgan didn't really believe in them—then this moment with Laura was as close as he'd probably ever get. It shook him that his touch and voice could have such a profound, healing effect on another human being. Laura was relaxed, her breathing slow and cadenced. Whatever nightmare she'd been inhabiting had fled. Somehow, in his blundering need to help her, he'd chased it away.

Slowly he eased his hand out of the tangle of her hair. He'd kissed her. He'd tasted her lips. Staring down at Laura, he wondered with panic if she would remember him stealing that kiss from her. And it was a stolen thing. Or was it? A part of him had responded to her out of selfish need. But another part had offered the kiss as—what? A healing gesture? With a shake of his head, Morgan cursed himself and slowly eased upward, hoping not to waken Laura. He stood over her a moment, watching her continue to sleep the sleep of angels. Because that was what she was—an angel in human form.

He smiled tenderly at the thought, wishing he had some of her patience, her gentleness and diplomacy. They were diametric opposites, he was beginning to discover, and as he made his way over to his bed, Morgan felt like a lump of hard black coal next to Laura, who shone like a diamond of light in his dark, complex world.

As he lay down and pulled up the covers, he saw the first gray streaks of dawn edging the top of the canyon. It must be around four or five o'clock. Closing his eyes, he centered hotly on the memory of Laura's lips beneath his. He'd kissed her carefully, lightly, their mouths barely touching, but it had been enough—for now. With that thought, he slid into a sleep heated by dreams of Laura, of loving her until she cried out with the unadulterated pleasure that he somehow knew only he could give her.

The smell of bacon frying, of coffee perking, slowly awakened Laura. At first she didn't realize where she was, because the sounds of the creek were so different from those around their Virginia home. She sat up, her hair tumbling in disarray around her face. Pushing several strands out of her eyes, she looked around. Sunlight cascaded through the bedroom window. It took her a long moment to realize she was at the Donovan Ranch, in a log cabin, and—Morgan!

Instantly, Laura looked to her right. The twin bed Morgan had slept in was a tangle of sheets and blankets. He was gone. Panic set in momentarily, and Laura threw off her covers, lowering her bare feet to the cool pine floor. Then, more gradually, she acknowledged the fragrance of breakfast cooking and realized Morgan must be up and making breakfast.

Her panic and anxiety dissolved as she sat running her fingers through her hair and laughing at her groggy state. Exhaustion still lapped at her, but for some reason, she felt better. Happier. Mornings weren't usually her strong point, so she stayed on the edge of the bed, allowing herself the luxury of waking up slowly. In the old days, she would have been out of bed by six, fixing Morgan's breakfast before he left for work. Then Jason would stumble out of his room around seven, his blue security blanket—"blankey"—in tow. He'd rub his little freckled face, his gray eyes sleepily trained on his father, who'd be at the kitchen table eating a healthy breakfast.

So many wonderful memories.... Laura sighed, closed her eyes and allowed them to surface within her. Jason loved to climb into his father's lap, blankey and all, and beg for a piece of bacon from Morgan. There they'd sit, Jason happily ensconced in Mor-

gan's embrace, eating breakfast with Daddy. It was a
precious time between father and son, and Laura had
loved being privy to their bonding....

Somewhere in her groggy state, Laura vaguely recalled Morgan kissing her. He always kissed her after
breakfast, and then Jason would lean forward and
place his own wet kiss on her cheek. It was a breakfast ritual of sorts, Laura supposed. Morgan's kiss
was always warm and tender—how she looked forward to it! She lightly touched her lower lip. The
kiss...had she dreamed it? She frowned, trying to remember. Where did dreams end and reality begin?
Had she dreamed of Morgan tunneling his fingers
through her hair last night and then awakening her
with a kiss? Or was it a wish-fulfillment figment of
her overactive imagination?

Unsure, Laura again grazed her lower lip with her
fingertips, thinking. Was she going crazy? In one part
of her drowsy mind, she was sure Morgan had kissed
her last night! But he wouldn't do that. With a frustrated sound, she decided the whole memory was
nothing more than trying to make her agonizing need
of him a reality—to return to the intimacy of before
the kidnappings.

Easing off the bed, Laura felt depression settling
once again around her shoulders. Maybe she was
slowly going crazy, falling off some unknown precipice deep within herself, and just didn't realize it yet.
Pulling open a dresser drawer, she listlessly chose
some pink lingerie for the day, and added a peach-

colored mohair sweater and dark blue slacks. No, it was her, she decided sadly as she picked up her sensible brown shoes and headed to the bathroom. Her and her overriding need for Morgan to remember his love for her and the two children that was pushing her toward that invisible precipice. Laura wondered bleakly if she could hold on long enough to help Morgan remember his past. She wasn't sure. Not at all.

Chapter 7

Laura was so exhausted by her night's tossing and turning that it was impossible to erect any barriers against Morgan after her hot shower. She walked hesitantly to the kitchen to get some coffee and was surprised to see him looking well-rested, sitting at the round oak table, a mug of coffee in his hand. He wore a yellow-blue-and-purple plaid flannel shirt with his jeans—a definite departure from the old Morgan's preference for conservative colors.

"Good morning," she said, her voice still low with sleepiness.

Morgan watched Laura head for the the coffee-maker. "We survived the night. I think that's important," he said gruffly in greeting. Despite his good intentions, his body tightened with painful awareness of Laura. Her hip-length sweater gently outlined her breasts, slim torso and slightly rounded abdomen, and the slacks, though tapered, revealed her fine, long legs.

Laura poured a cup of coffee, struggling to hide her shaking hands from Morgan. The roughness of his voice grated on her exposed nerves. She noticed a plate of scrambled eggs and bacon sitting in the microwave.

"Is that for me?" she asked, pointing to it.

"Yeah. I can't guarantee they'll be any good, but you need someone around to put some meat on those bones. I'm willing to give it a try if you are."

A slight smile tugged at the corners of her mouth as she heated the breakfast. "This is something new," she murmured, leaning against the counter, the cup of coffee in her hands as she looked across the kitchen at him. "You never made me breakfast before. Maybe there's a positive side to the amnesia I overlooked." It was a poor joke, but she saw him rally—for her sake, she was sure—his lips curving slightly in response.

Her gaze settled on his mouth. Instantly, a flash of a memory sizzled through her. *Had* Morgan kissed her last night? How badly she wanted to ask, yet she didn't dare. Still, the tingling warmth settling in her belly suggested he had. Either that, or her nighttime dream world was becoming disturbingly real during the day. Fortunately, this was a good dream rather than a nightmare, and for that she was grateful.

"Come and sit down," Morgan invited as he slowly stood and pulled out a chair next to his. "You're the one who lost a lot of sleep last night...."

Laura frowned and moved toward him. "I was hoping we'd have separate bedrooms," she murmured, her voice strained.

"Why?" he demanded as she sat. "So I wouldn't know about your nightmares?"

Laura held herself stiffly, conscious of Morgan's bulk and warmth directly behind her chair. His large hands still rested on the chair back, his fingers barely grazing her shoulders. A part of her cried out for his direct touch. If only he could feel her suffering—her need for contact! Shakily, she set the mug of coffee down on the table before she spilled it.

"Dr. Parsons said it was part of the process," she whispered, her mouth going dry.

"Hmph," Morgan said, going to the microwave. He pulled out her breakfast plate and set it down in front of her. "Here, eat it. All of it. I'm making you two pieces of toast to go with it, and I want to see them go down the hatch, too."

Laura smiled tentatively as she looked at the plate, burdened with what must be at least four scrambled eggs. "Morgan," she protested, "there's enough food here for three men!"

He popped two slices of bread into the toaster. "So?" Turning, he saw the bewilderment written across her pale features. In that moment, he realized just how fragile Laura was. Old feelings and awareness moved strongly through him, and though he still couldn't call them memories, he knew the alarm he was experiencing was genuine. Even Laura's hair, barely tamed into some semblance of order, needed a good brushing. She wasn't taking the kind of care of herself she could be, he knew from some far recess deep within him.

"Well—" Laura waved her hands helplessly, looking at the fare "—it's so much!"

"Eat what you can," he said less gruffly, "and then we'll talk."

Talk about what? Laura wondered dully as she forced herself to pick up the fork and swallow some of the eggs. She could barely taste them, though she realized Morgan had gone to some trouble to sprinkle in bits of fresh parsley and chopped red pepper to make them more appealing and palatable. It was a thoughtful gesture on his part.

Just then, Morgan leaned forward and two pieces of thickly buttered toast appeared on her plate. "Eat these, too," he ordered, as he poured himself another cup of coffee and sat down opposite her.

A thread of happiness wound its way into Laura's depression as she force-fed herself at the kitchen table with Morgan looking on, his features unrelenting. A ray of sunlight filtered through the red-and-white checked curtains at the window. Chickadees chirped outside, and the creek was gurgling merrily, the sounds soothing to her frayed composure.

"While you're eating," Morgan continued in a more conversational tone, watching her closely, "I had a couple of fragmented dreams last night I wanted to share with you."

Laura stopped eating. "Have you had dreams before?"

"Not like these." Morgan gestured at the plate. "Keep eating or I don't talk."

She smiled a little. "This is blackmail, Morgan."

"Call it what you want. My heart's in the right place."

Hope rose briefly in her as she saw his clear gray eyes sparkle teasingly. Just the lowering of his voice was like a balm to her taut emotional state, healing her. She continued to eat, not wanting him to clam up. "Tell me about your dreams?" she asked.

He turned the cup slowly in his hands. "Since waking from the coma, I've gotten fragments of things—snatches of a voice saying something, a pair of eyes or a swatch of color of someone's hair." His brows fell. "Last night, after I got you settled from your nightmare, I went back to sleep. It was then I had these dreams. I should say, dream fragments."

Laura stared at him. Her fork halted halfway to her mouth. "I had a nightmare?" She had absolutely no memory of it. A deep caring burned in Morgan's eyes—caring for her—and she felt its healing power sink deep into her wounded spirit.

"Yeah," he muttered, "you had a nightmare, all right. We'll talk about it after you're done eating."

Laura shrugged. "I don't want to talk about it at all."

"You don't have that choice."

Laura's stomach churned. Her mouth went dry. "Why don't you tell me about your dreams?" she whispered, eager to hear about something better than her own rotten nightmares, which had haunted her since the kidnapping.

Opening his hands, Morgan said, "I remember a lot of cardboard boxes in a living room. They were draped with sheets. I saw three kids playing in them."

Laura straightened, her eyes widening. "Yes!"

He gave her a wary look. "Yes?"

Excitedly, Laura said, "When you, Aly and Noah were kids, you used to build cardboard 'cities' out of boxes in the living room." Her voice broke with joy. "Oh, Morgan, that's a wonderful memory to have return! What else did you see?"

He shrugged, feeling her delight, seeing her once-wan cheeks turn bright pink and her blue eyes light up with hope. He grinned a little, elated that the fleeting image was a genuine memory from his past.

"So you didn't recognize the kids as you and your brother and sister?"

"No...it was like a movie, and I was watching it."

"Did you hear them speak?"

"No, I'm afraid not."

Unthinkingly, Laura reached over and gripped his

arm. "Oh, Morgan, it's still wonderful! It's proof that at least part of your memory is intact." She felt his muscles respond instantly to her touch and saw an undefinable emotion pass through Morgan's eyes, leaving her shaken and needy in its wake. Hesitantly, Laura forced herself to release him. Trying to still her burgeoning happiness, she whispered, "What else did you dream?"

"I saw you," he said.

"Me?" Laura sat very still, afraid to breathe. "When?"

"I know you told me you were at an airport—that we met there when a car struck you," Morgan said. "But last night I saw you there and you were wearing a pink raincoat." He studied her intently. "Were you?"

A shattering bolt of joy flowed through her. "Yes, I was wearing a pink raincoat that day." Laura set her fork down and pressed her hands to her mouth, afraid she was going to cry in front of him. She knew how Morgan hated to see her weep. Tears burned in her eyes and she blinked them away.

Morgan saw moisture glimmer in Laura's eyes for just a moment. He saw the utter joy written on her face, now radiant with hope. He felt her hope, too. Deep in his heart, he knew why these fragmented memories had surfaced. It was because of kissing her last night. Somehow, that kiss had unlocked the vault of his past. "I saw one other thing," he said gruffly, his voice emotional. "I was in a battle…bodies were lying all around me.'' His hands tightened around the mug. ''I was on a hill above a jungle.''

Sobering, Laura dropped her hands in her lap. ''I'm sure it was the hill where your company was over-run,'' she whispered, aware of the pain in his voice and face. ''In some ways, I wished certain memories from your past would never resurface, Morgan. They were so terrible...and I'm not sure how you came to grips with the guilt you carried from them. I don't think I could have.'' Reaching out, she placed her hand over his. Tightening her fingers, she said, ''Still, those memories are real, and they are a part of your past. I can hardly wait to tell Dr. Parsons.''

Morgan curved his fingers around her cool, damp ones in return. Laura had eaten barely a quarter of the food on her plate. ''Hold on,'' he ordered, ''let's just wait and see what else happens before we go running to Dr. Parsons.''

Somberly, Laura nodded. Morgan's hand was warm and felt so good to her. She was thrilled he was returning her heartfelt touch. ''Okay, we'll wait.''

''Right now,'' he said, removing the plate from in front of her, ''we need to talk about you...about your nightmare.''

Stiffening, Laura pulled her hand out of his. ''I don't remember it, Morgan.''

Morgan saw the light and hope in her eyes die in-stantly like a candle being snuffed out. Laura was retreating from him. He frowned. Nervously, she clasped her hands in her lap beneath the table, and he saw her eyes go wary, like a wild animal in a cage. Real terror lapped at the edges of her dark blue gaze.

Grimly, he said, "Near dawn, I woke up from hearing you crying out. At first I thought it was one of my fragmented dreams, because I'd heard your voice in them before. This time," he said heavily, holding her frightened gaze, "it was real."

Laura couldn't stand the suffocating feeling stalking her. She'd had it enough times to realize it was the precursor to an anxiety attack. Abruptly, she stood up, nearly tipping over her chair. Turning, she grabbed it before it could fall on the linoleum floor. She had to do something. Anything! Picking up her plate of uneaten food, she walked to the kitchen sink, her motions robotlike.

Morgan's mouth tightened. He saw pure fear in the depths of Laura's eyes as she walked across to the kitchen. "You don't remember your nightmare?" he asked gently.

"N-no," Laura said, as she placed the plate in the sink. Turning, she came back to the table and picked up the flatware and coffee mug. Though she didn't look at Morgan, she could feel his gaze burning into her. It was a relief to turn back to the sink.

"You were trembling, Laura," Morgan began in a low voice that vibrated with concern. "When I went over to check on you, I touched the shoulder of your gown, and it was wet with sweat."

Hanging her head, the mug poised in her hands

over the sink, Laura felt renewed anxiety course through her. "Some nights," she managed to say, "I wake up and find my gown damp." She tried to laugh, but it came out as a choking sound. "It's nothing to be worried about...."

Morgan shook his head. "You were whimpering and moving your head from side to side, as if someone had you pinned, a hand around your throat." He saw her go absolutely still, her lips parting as if in a silent cry. Then a tremor ran through her, as if she'd been physically struck, and the heavy coffee mug slipped from her fingers, shattering into pieces in the sink.

Instantly, Morgan was on his feet, moving swiftly toward her. She was staring in horror at the broken cup, her hands pressed to her lips as she looked down at it. More and more with her, Morgan was discovering he was operating on an instinctive gut level. Settling his hands gently on her rigid shoulders, he felt her tension vibrate through him. He gripped her more tightly, attempting to steady her.

"Laura," he rasped, trying to pull her gently against him. He felt her stiffen, the trembling becoming more pronounced. "Don't fight me," he said, maintaining enough pressure on her shoulders to ask her to let go and trust him—again. Somehow, he knew that Laura always hid her worries from him. Well, this was the wrong time for her to do that. Something so terrifying consumed her that he knew she needed help—his help.

Opening his hands, he spread them flat across her shoulders and, with a light but gentle pressure, continued to ease her back against him. He stifled a groan of pleasure as she surrendered slightly, letting her back, hips and thighs brush against him. "Laura, talk to me—please," he whispered against her ear as her hair tickled his nose and cheek.

Laura quivered in Morgan's grip. How strong he was. Closing her eyes, she felt her terror—all the evil memories—start erupting. He cared. Morgan cared. The same Morgan she loved with quiet desperation was here with her now. The pressure of his hands changed, and she felt herself being turned to face him. Her hands came up automatically to rest against his barrel-like chest. As her palms flattened against his flannel shirt, Laura felt the heavy, slow pounding of his magnificent heart beneath.

His breathing was a solid and steady counterpoint against her quick, ragged breaths.

"Lean on me," he entreated roughly.

Tears burned in her tightly shut eyes as she allowed herself the gift of resting against him. His hands moved in slow circles across her tense shoulders, and with each movement, Laura felt a little more of the tension bleed away.

"That's it," he coaxed thickly, "trust me, Laura. Just trust me. I may not remember a whole hell of a lot, but I do remember feeling some things with you...."

Hope flared sharply within her, and Laura allowed

herself to lean a little more heavily against Morgan. His body was a reassuring presence, shoring up her fragmented state. She felt one of his hands slide around her waist to bring her fully against him. The invisible tie between them was back. She could feel it as surely as she felt each breath he took. How brave he was to step beyond his own wall of pain and suffering to reach out to her. This was the Morgan she knew, the man with the well of endless courage.

"That's better," Morgan whispered, burying his face in her silky hair. "Much better...." And it was. A blazing tenderness moved through him as he held her. He still didn't remember his love for her—at least, in one sense. But in another, he did. Her trembling abated, and he felt her breathing even out, slowing to match his. He felt the rounded softness of her small breasts pressing against his chest, felt the flutter of her smaller heartbeat against his own. She felt so good in his arms. So damn good. He had to remind himself why he was holding her, instead of selfishly absorbing the feel of her to feed his own hungry needs.

"Tell me what happened to you," he ordered thickly. "You've never said anything about your kidnapping. When I've asked Jake or Dr. Parsons, they've gone silent on me. They said I had to get the story from you, Laura." His arms tightened protectively around her slender form. "Well, I'm here, and I'm asking. I want you to tell me what happened."

Shuddering, Laura buried her face deeply in the

soft flannel. "Morgan," she whispered unsteadily, "it's nothing compared to what you went through. I—"

He slid his fingers through her hair and held her captive against him. "No, you don't," he muttered. "I'm realizing just how much you avoid, Laura."

She felt his fingers stroking her hair. "I—I suppose I do," she admitted.

He smiled grimly down at her as he eased her away from him just enough to see her suffering features. "No more running," he rasped, "for either of us. Okay? Last night something happened, Laura. I was so scared when I heard you cry out. Something snapped inside me." His gaze probed her tear-filled blue eyes. "I touched your hair, and then something told me to lean down and kiss you."

Her eyes widened.

Morgan's mouth flattened with the admission. "It was selfish of me. I needed you, Laura. Even without memories, I have feelings for you. I did kiss you until you woke up a little. I told you to go back to sleep, and you did." He raised a hand to touch her flaming cheek. "I'm not proud of what I did, but I'm convinced that kiss was the reason I had those dreams and memories. Hell, maybe it was just my worry for you triggering something in my brain. I don't know. It doesn't matter right now. You do." He gave her a small shake. "I want to know what happened to you."

Anguish squeezed Laura's heart. She absorbed the

feel of his fingers on her cheek, her skin tingling pleasantly in their wake. The care radiating from him filled her with renewed strength, enough to speak. "I'm so afraid to tell you," she quavered. "I've been dreading this moment for so long, Morgan...."

Her painful words tore at him as nothing he could remember had. Whispering her name, he crushed her hard against him, his hand against the side of her head. "It's all right," he rasped unsteadily. "Whatever it is, Laura, we'll take it together. You hear me? Together."

The words fell across her, and Laura felt as if she'd crossed the line between sanity and insanity. How many times had she dreamed that Morgan would say those very words to her with just such fervency? With his fierce tenderness aimed at her alone? No, she wasn't going insane—at least, not yet. This was real. She could feel the strength of Morgan's embrace. The powerful beat of his heart gave her courage where she'd had none. Slowly, she eased her hands downward and slid her arms around his waist. She heard Morgan groan—a deep, almost animal-like sound of absolute pleasure.

"I remember waking," she said brokenly, "in this strange house. It was a bedroom. I was sick and dizzy. A guard came into the room when he heard me moving around. I had worn a silk suit because it was our seventh wedding anniversary, and I wasn't in it. Instead, someone had dressed me in a pink silk nightgown. The guard looked at me and left.

"I was very sick, and I sat on the bed looking at my hands. I had rope burns around my wrists, and I kept trying to think how I'd gotten them." Her voice lowered to a broken whisper. "And then…Garcia came in." She shivered violently and felt Morgan's arms tighten around her in response. Shutting her eyes tightly, Laura said, her voice muffled, "He—he raped me…."

The words escaped, brimming with terror and anguish. Morgan felt tears flood into his eyes. He brushed a kiss against Laura's hair as she began to tremble all over again. A deep longing and tenderness overwhelmed him as he began to rock her gently in his arms. "Let it go," he rasped. "Cry, Laura. Cry…."

A repressed sob jammed Laura's throat. But Morgan's voice was low and husky, and miraculously, the lump dissolved. A cry escaped, tearing violently from her. For an instant, Laura wasn't sure whose sob she'd heard, the sound was so foreign—more animal than human. She felt Morgan's mouth against her temple. He was kissing her, caring for her. Her fingers dug convulsively into his shirtfront, and she struggled to contain the next sob.

"No!" he rasped against her ear. "Let it go! Dammit, Laura, stop trying to run and hide. I'm here. I'll hold you. Just let it go!"

The rawness of his words overran the last remnant of her crumbling defenses. All the months of having to hold herself together—first for Jason, then for herself and finally for the Perseus employees as they frantically tried to locate Morgan—faded away. The last vestiges of her reserve crumbled with a second, tearing sob. Laura buried her face against Morgan's chest and felt his hand in her hair, pressing her face to him. His other arm tightened almost painfully around her waist as he held her as close as possible, as if to absorb her pain into himself.

"Cry for yourself," he growled harshly. "Cry..."

And she did. Laura felt her knees give way, felt him take her entire weight as she collapsed against his stalwart frame and gave in to the horror of her experience. One sob after another tore from her contorted mouth. Hot tears, so long held at bay, spilled from her eyes. Her heart felt as if it was exploding with the grief she'd suppressed. Her body convulsed, as the awful, hurting sounds continued rising out of her. Time stood still, losing all meaning as she clutched frantically at Morgan, her hands opening and closing against his shirt as the choking cries rolled up and out of her.

Laura surrendered to her grief—to the hurt she'd sustained from the ordeal—in every way. For this moment out of time, the real Morgan was back. Even if he never regained another memory, she felt him present with her as never before. The invisible connection was strongly anchored between them, more tangible than she'd ever experienced—and it was a lifeline to her in this moment of grief and searing anger.

A deep terror continued to override the rest of her

suffering. Even now, as she cried in Morgan's arms, she was afraid to tell him the details of her capture—afraid that if he knew the truth, he'd reject her and want her out of his life—forever. Her body ached from the convulsing sobs, and eventually the storm left her. All she could feel in that moment was Morgan's pounding heart, his hand moving gently across her hair, offering solace. Repeatedly, he placed small kisses along her hairline as he held her close and rocked her gently in his arms.

Where did death end and life begin? Was it possible to feel dead inside, yet still be living? Laura wondered bleakly. Opening her eyes, the remnants of tears clinging to her thick lashes, she stared unseeingly, her cheek pressed firmly against his chest. Her arms ached from holding him so tightly and she let them relax a little. She felt Morgan draw in a deep, ragged breath, felt his warm breath near her ear.

"All right?" he asked huskily.

She nodded jerkily, unwilling to let him go just yet. Morgan must have sensed her fear that he would leave her, because he tightened his embrace momentarily, squeezing her reassuringly.

"That was a long time in coming," he said quietly, easing back just enough to look down at her. Laura's blue eyes were wounded holes of grief. Her lips were still contorted with pain, her velvety cheek damp with tears. He raised a hand to gently dry them. Fresh tears started, and he smiled tenderly, slipping his arm back around her.

"I'm sorry," he said gruffly, "so sorry, Laura. I still don't remember Perseus or what started all this. I can only believe what Jake, Wolf and Killian have told me. But it sounds as if I left you and my family open to attack—"

"No!" Laura pushed away enough to meet his ravaged gaze. "No," she whispered less stridently, "don't blame yourself for what happened, Morgan. It was *no one's* fault. Do you hear me?"

He shook his head. "I should have taken steps to ensure your safety, Laura."

"That's ridiculous!" She pushed back farther, her hands gripping his arms. "Don't you think I knew the risks? I'm part and parcel of the military. I knew when you set up Perseus that someone might seek revenge someday. We talked about the possibility many times, Morgan."

"We did?" He searched her pale features.

"Yes, and we agreed enough precautions had been taken." Laura gestured wearily. "I wasn't willing to live behind iron gates followed by guards. When you suggested it, I said no. If there's any fault here, it's mine."

Gently, he framed her face, gazing deeply into her injured eyes. "I don't remember those conversations, Laura, but it doesn't matter."

"I thought," she whispered, clinging to his tender gaze, "the worst time in my life was when I was hit by that car and lost my sight. No one knew if I'd recover from the blindness." She lowered her lashes.

"But this is worse. I—I can't believe what happened to me, sometimes. I have horrible nightmares. I—I was hoping with you near me again, they'd stop." Helplessly, she forced herself to look back up into his eyes. "But they haven't."

"And they shouldn't," Morgan said thickly, using his thumbs to wipe the fresh tears from her cheeks. "I just remembered something from the past that I used to tell you." He gave her an apologetic look. "I remember telling you how safe you were when you were with me." Looking up, suffering deeply, Morgan rasped, "And I didn't keep you safe, Laura. Nor did I keep my family safe...."

Sharp, serrating pain pierced Laura's heart. Laura gripped Morgan's arms tightly. "All we can do," she whispered, "is go on. We can't blame ourselves, Morgan. Dr. Parsons said to live one hour at a time— one day at a time. We have to pick up the pieces of ourselves that way. Otherwise—" she released a ragged sigh "—we'll drive ourselves insane with guilt and pointing fingers. We can't afford to do that. We just can't!"

Hearing the stridency in her voice, he returned his gaze to her. Releasing her, he allowed his hands to settle on her shoulders. "No," he answered heavily, "no finger pointing." Still, Morgan knew without a doubt that this was his fault. Memory or no memory, he'd caused Laura's pain. It was impossible for him to understand yet what the fact of her rape had done to her, but he promised himself he would find out.

Though she had cried long and hard, he could see that she looked a little better now; but he could also feel a deeper, more terrifying wound she was still hiding from him. Somehow, he'd regain her trust. And maybe—if he was the luckiest man in the world—he could help her heal the wound he'd caused.

Guilt bubbled within him as he held Laura lightly in his embrace, but a lot of new feelings rose with it. Somehow, that one innocent kiss last night had cracked open the door on his memory—if not specific recollections, then solid feelings he knew were related to his past.

Forcing a partial smile for Laura's benefit, he stroked her hair. "One hour at a time," he promised thickly. "One day at a time."

She managed a grimace. "I'm more worried about the nights. The darkness scares me—" her voice broke "—because that's when Garcia would stalk me...."

"Then we'll handle the nights together, Laura."

Chapter 8

The sun felt warm and soothing on Laura's back. She had brought one of the folding chairs from the porch of the cabin, along with her needlepoint, to sit along the bank of Oak Creek. In the past seven days the Arizona weather had offered an amazing alternative to the East Coast February she was accustomed to. The temperature was in the high sixties, the sky a blinding blue streaked with long, thin cirrus clouds that reminded her of the soft, downy feathers on a goose's breast.

It was nearly noon, and she languished in the soothing rays while working on an iris design with her needle. One day, it would become a cover for a couch pillow. The work caught and focused her fragmented concentration, and for that she was grateful.

A little farther down the creek's bank stood Morgan, who had borrowed some fly tackle from the Donovan Ranch and was casting endlessly into the cold, flowing water. He'd had no luck yet, but Laura didn't think that mattered much to him. Just getting outdoors, breathing in the clean southwestern air and absorbing the sun's strength was enough.

Morgan. Her heart repeated his name, and her hands stilled over her project. She lifted her chin and watched him. He was at least two hundred feet downstream, dressed in jeans, a blue-and-white flannel shirt, the sleeves rolled carelessly up to his elbows, and hiking boots. The breeze, always present along the creek, lifted errant strands of his black hair.

The tension he'd carried to the cabin seven days ago was gone. His craggy profile had softened. Had it been the miracle that had occurred in the kitchen that first morning after they'd arrived? Laura wondered. Or that kiss she could barely recall, like a hazy strand of fog just out of reach? She wasn't sure. She poked her needle through another hole in the fabric. The week had fled by. Ever since he'd held her in the kitchen and she'd cried out her heart and soul in his arms, those terrible nightmares had ceased stalking her.

In fact, Laura thought as she chose a strand of deep purple thread from the tote bag leaning against the leg of her chair, her sleep had become deep, healing and uninterrupted since then. Six nights of eight hours of sleep had worked miracles on her, too.

As she threaded the purple strand through the needle's eye, she sighed with contentment. Every day, as
she watched, small memories came trickling back to
Morgan. But so far they were all from his childhood.
How she ached for him to remember *their* time, *their*
love. Though they slept only six feet apart, Laura
missed Morgan.

Chiding herself for her impatience, she carefully
inserted the needle again into the fabric across her
lap.

Her heart revolved to Jason and Katy. How she
looked forward to calling her children each night. Jason loved the phone and loved to chat. Katy couldn't,
of course, but Laura eagerly absorbed Susannah's lit-
any of the children's activities each day. Part of her
ached to hold them, to dress them in the morning,
tousle Jason's hair and watch the devilish sparkle
come to his eyes as she played with him. How like
his father he was. And how much Katy was like
her....

Morgan had yet to talk to Jason on the phone, and
that disturbed Laura. He had no memory of his children and was afraid of raising Jason's hopes. Laura
couldn't help but notice how Morgan moved uncom-
fortably around the cabin as she talked to their family,
hidden away in the hills of Kentucky.

What if Morgan's memory was permanently wiped
out regarding her and their children? The question
was simply too brutal to contemplate. Laura knew she
was emotionally unstable and knew it would take

months, perhaps a year or more, to get over the shocks she'd suffered. Ann Parsons had dropped by midweek and talked with them individually in her role as therapist. Laura looked forward to talking to Ann, woman-to-woman. There were certain things she simply couldn't share with Morgan yet. Perhaps she never would be able to, if his memory didn't return. Ann provided a cushion, a friendly ear to listen to her worst fears, without judgment or recrimination.

To give Morgan credit, he was trying desperately to jog memories, Laura knew. He often pored over the photo albums she'd brought. They would sit for hours at a time as she slowly and thoroughly went over each color photo with him. Still, he remembered little beyond fragments of his childhood years. Laura knew his parents were grateful he remembered them; Morgan had phoned them as soon as the memories returned and had reestablished contact....

She heard him give a victorious shout and she looked up. He had caught a trout! A smiled played across her lips as she watched him expertly retrieve the fish and place it in the creel at his feet. His face glowed with triumph, and she couldn't resist him any longer. Putting her needlepoint aside, she walked down the bank to join him.

He grinned widely, crouching over his creel as she sauntered up.

"Dinner tonight," he said proudly, gesturing to the shining rainbow trout in the bottom of the basket.

Laura sighed and crouched down opposite him.

"He's so big and beautiful, Morgan. It's a shame to see him die." She looked up. "Rachel brought T-bone steaks over yesterday. We could grill them for dinner tonight...."

Crestfallen, Morgan watched the trout flop around in the creel, gasping. "He's big, Laura. A good pound and a half. Do you know how hard it is to catch a trout on a fly rod, much less a big one like this?"

Laughing gently, Laura stood. "Hey, it's your decision. You're the one who spent two hours out here casting for him."

Morgan studied her closely. An ache seized him, and he slowly unwound from his crouched position to stand up. Laura was less than a foot away, wearing a denim skirt that fell to her ankles, a feminine, long-sleeved white blouse and a bright red velvet vest, its crimson color accenting the blush in her cheeks. Hungrily, he absorbed the sparkle in her deep blue eyes as she playfully held his gaze. Her lips were softly parted, and he found himself aching even more to kiss her—again. Each night became more and more of a special hell for him. Laura might fall asleep immediately, as soon as her head hit the pillow, but he sure didn't. No, he lay there fantasizing about touching her, loving her and kissing her senseless.

He didn't question Laura's love for him; it was obvious in so many small ways. Not that she had reached out since that morning in the kitchen to hug him or kiss his cheek—or anything obvious. No, she'd circumspectly kept her distance from him. And he knew it was because he still couldn't recall his love for her. Oh, he had emerging feelings for her, some vague recollections, and he'd shared those with her, but he knew that until he could recall the love they had shared, he couldn't—wouldn't—touch her.

Today her hair was plaited into two braids, the ends tied with red threads from her needlepoint kit. How girlish she looked. He had to fight not to reach out and slide his fingers along the soft slope of her cheek. How badly he needed to touch her again, to bury his face in her thick, blond hair and inhale her special womanly fragrance which made him dizzy with need.

He looked down at the trout, then reached into the creel. In one smooth motion he threw the fish back into the creek.

"Morgan!" Laura cried out in surprise.

He grinned mischievously. "You're next!"

Before she could protest, he swept her up into his arms. With a cry of utter surprise, she threw her arms around his neck. She was wildly aware of his strength. Of him. Laughing, she pressed her face against his neck and jaw as he carried her dangerously close to the churning water.

"You save a trout's life and you pay for it," he told her roughly, grinning down at her. How good she felt against him! She was small and featherlight. That familiar fragrance of camellia struck him fully as he stopped near the edge of the bank.

"Morgan! You wouldn't dare throw me in!" Laura

gasped. Her eyes grew round as she watched his own gray eyes sparkle with mischief, and she automatically tightened her arms around his massive neck and shoulders. It was the first time Morgan had done anything so spontaneous and she loved it. She loved him.

"Wouldn't I?" he taunted, threatening to swing her out over the stream.

Laughing wildly, Laura gasped, "The old Morgan wouldn't ever do something this dastardly! He saw himself as a white knight come to the rescue!"

"Maybe the new Morgan would," he threatened teasingly. She was so alive, so fresh and innocent in his arms. He absorbed the feel of her body crushed against him. Laura's eyes danced with such joy that he felt his heart opening powerfully beneath her smile. He made a motion as if to toss her into the rushing water. Instantly she shrieked, grabbed him hard and clung to him, her face pressed against his. Morgan couldn't help himself, nor did he want to.

He closed the scant inches between them in an instant, his mouth covering her smiling lips. Instantly, he felt Laura stiffen in his arms with surprise, but just as quickly, she relaxed against him. Something goaded him to continue the kiss rather than draw away as he knew he should. No, he wanted her. Needed her. Relentlessly, he smothered her mouth with his own. Rocking her lips open, he felt how she surrendered to him. Her mouth tasted of sunlight and the honey she'd had on her toast earlier. He felt unmistakable heat and invitation in her returning kiss as her arms tightened around his neck. Her breasts pressed more fully against his chest, and he felt her moan when he ran his tongue across her full lower lip, then recaptured her mouth with even more intensity than before.

His body hardened instantly as he deepened his exploration of her. His breath was coming in ragged gasps, but so was hers. As hungrily as he took her, she gave back equal pressure and heat. How badly he wanted to plunge himself into her molten depths! But something cautioned him not to go that far. Not yet. Instead, he sent his tongue searching her hot, moist mouth. If he'd ever suspected Laura was weak or shy, he'd been mistaken. Her tongue boldly touched and slid along his, and he found himself staggering beneath her equally fierce onslaught. Fire ignited and exploded through him as her tongue danced with his. Moments melted together, and he felt a fusion of their bodies—and their souls.

Her lips were too luscious, and he couldn't get enough of the feel of her soft, surrendering mouth, which continued to tease and beckon him. But gradually, to his dismay, his mind began to work and again take charge, leaving his body hard and aching with need as he reluctantly ended the kiss. Opening his eyes, he gazed stormily into her lustrous ones, half-open and studying him as the sounds of nature returned around them. Her lips glistened in the wake of his kiss, the lower one slightly swollen, and he was instantly sorry for his powerful, unexpected assault upon her.

Morgan gently eased Laura to the ground, his arms still around her shoulders, holding her close. To his joy, she leaned fully against him, her arms encircling his waist. Her unabashed radiance humbled him as nothing else could. Giving her a shaky, apologetic smile, he lifted his hands to smooth back her hair. "I don't know where the hell that came from...."

"I don't care," she whispered, running her palms across his chest, holding his narrowed gray gaze. And she didn't.

"I was..." Morgan scowled and settled his hands back on her small shoulders. "I made a promise to myself not to touch you until I could remember, Laura."

She frowned. "I'm not sorry it happened, Morgan."

"But you remember your love for me."

"Yes...."

Frustration ate at his euphoria. Morgan looked beyond her, his tone gruff. "I don't think it's fair to you—to us—if I kiss you or...whatever...and I don't remember, Laura."

She placed her hands gently on his massive arms. "And what if you don't ever remember us, Morgan?"

His scowl deepened. "I...don't know."

"That's what scares me," she whispered unsteadily, trying to smile but not succeeding. "I'll take whatever you want to give me, Morgan. I'm not proud. I love you. I'll always love you, no matter how many of your memories come back—or don't.''

He saw the tears glimmering in her eyes. "Don't cry," he rasped, then caught himself. Dr. Parsons had counseled him that crying was often the healthiest thing to do. "Forget I said that."

With a small, choking sound, Laura said, "The old Morgan hated to see me cry, too. Even if you don't remember, you *know,* Morgan."

At the fervency of her voice, he caressed her shoulders tenderly. "I feel as if I'm cheating you—us—if I touch you like this…kiss you…."

"Did you lift me up and kiss me just now because you felt you *had* to?" she asked wryly.

He studied her in the silence. A teasing love shone in her eyes. "No," he admitted unsteadily. "It just sort of happened—in the moment. I wasn't thinking about it," he added awkwardly.

Her smile was tender. "One of the things you used to do—quite frequently, as a matter of fact—was steal me from whatever I was doing, lift me into your arms and take me to our secret garden out back."

He raised his eyebrows. "I did?"

Laura touched his recently shaven cheek. "There's a precocious little boy alive and well inside of you, Morgan Trayhern, and I've been privileged to play with him quite often. So lifting me up the way you did, and kissing me…" She smiled. "It was something I not only enjoyed, but could hardly wait to have happen."

"When I would steal you away like that—we'd do more than...kiss?" He caught her hand and pressed his lips to her palm, watching her eyes turn to the dusky blue that told him she was feeling pleasure at his touch.

"Oh..." Laura sighed. "Yes, much more than kissing...."

He had to stop or he was going to lay her down on the green, grassy bank and take her right here and now. Morgan allowed her to reclaim her hand and gave her a crooked smile. "Memories have a funny way of turning up, don't they?"

"Yes, they do." Laura smoothed her skirt across her thighs. "I always loved your spontaneity, Morgan. I thought it was gone, but I was wrong." Her voice grew husky with tears. "And I'm so glad it's back, because it's such a natural part of who you are and how you express yourself...."

Laura snapped awake. What time was it? Slowly she sat up in bed, the covers falling away. Looking to the left, she realized Morgan was gone. She heard another noise. Her heart pounded hard in her chest as she threw her covers off and stood, the floor offering a cold greeting to her bare feet as she retrieved her chenille robe from the end of the bed. What was wrong? Laura groggily sensed something, though she was unable to put a name to it.

Stumbling sleepily from the bedroom, she moved into the living room. A night-light illuminated the room enough for her to weave among the furniture and head for the kitchen, where she thought the sounds had emanated from. Pushing hair away from her face, she wondered why Morgan was up. The clock on the shelf read three o'clock.

"Morgan?" she called, her voice thick with remnants of sleep. Halting in the doorway, she saw his shadowy form facing the kitchen sink. He was standing tensely, wearing only his pajama bottoms. His hands gripped the counter, and sweat gleamed on his naked back and shoulders.

Biting her lower lip, Laura felt the charged tension in the kitchen and knew instantly it originated from Morgan. What had happened? A nightmare? He'd had so many over the years, but with time, they'd become less frequent and severe. As she slowly approached him from the side, making sure he could see her, she reached out.

"Morgan?" she whispered, tentatively touching his shoulder. One of the dangers of Post Traumatic Stress Disorder was that, caught up in a flashback, a person might not be grounded in reality, unable to disconnect from the violence of the remembered moment. Laura knew from experience not to come up behind Morgan and throw her arms around him. She could be struck by a fist. Although it had never happened, she'd seen Morgan come close to striking her or whoever was near.

She pressed her fingers more surely against his damp skin. He was trembling, his breathing raspy as he hung his head over the sink, leaning against it for support. "It's all right, Morgan," she said soothingly, allowing him to feel her hand more fully against his arm. "It's me, Laura. You're safe, Morgan. Safe. You're here, in the cabin with me. Just listen to my voice, and I'll bring you back home…. Listen to me, Morgan."

She moved inches closer, keeping her hand firmly around his upper arm. She knew from experience what would help Morgan when he was trapped by the virulence of his nightmarish past. She kept her voice husky and low, almost singsong, so that he could struggle internally to tear his attention away from whatever was playing out before his tightly shut eyes and transfer his panicked attention to her. In some ways, not much had changed, Laura thought sadly. It grieved her that Morgan was going to continue to have PTSD symptoms. The one blessing of his amnesia had seemed to be that he would mercifully be allowed to forget his Vietnam War days and the loss of his company—and the horror that had haunted him ever since.

Little by little, as she continued speaking quietly to him, his bunched shoulders began to relax. His breathing evened out, and the sweat began to dry on his skin. Where he'd held the edge of the sink in a white-knuckled grip, his hands began to loosen their hold. Gradually, Laura placed her arm around his torso.

"Come on," she entreated gently. "Come and sit

down, Morgan. I'll make you some hot tea. Come on, darling...." She chastised herself for allowing the endearment slip from her lips. She'd tried to be so careful in not pressuring Morgan with her love, not wanting to frustrate him more or, worse, drive him away from her. What they had was still so tenuous.

Lifting his head, Morgan turned and stared at Laura. He felt her thin but strong arm around his waist, gently tugging at him to move away from the counter. "I..." His voice came out roughened and hoarse. "Laura, I remember Ramirez...Peru...the whole damned thing...."

A shaft of pain pierced Laura as she stood, holding his ravaged, darkened gaze. "All right," she said unsteadily, "then let's go to the living room, Morgan. You need to talk about it." She guided him out of the kitchen and to the couch. While a part of her was thrilled that a huge chunk of his memory had returned, another part grieved for him because he was being forced to reenter a living hell. As Morgan sat tensely on the couch, his legs spread, his hands clasped between his thighs, she saw the devastation etched on his features.

Biting back a cry, she sat down next to him, her hands resting lightly against his arm and thigh. Such agony showed in his eyes and the slash of his mouth that she wanted to let her own tears flow, but she knew it wouldn't help him. Reaching up, she stroked the dampened hair now clinging to his head. "What happened, Morgan? Tell me what you saw...."

Knotting his hands tightly, Morgan shut his eyes. Just the gentle touch of Laura's hand on his hair broke what little defense was left between him and the memories smashing through him. "I went to sleep," he rasped thickly, staring out across the semidarkened living room. "I was happy as I fell asleep." He twisted his head and held her tender, lustrous gaze. "I was replaying that kiss we shared at the creek today. I felt more whole, stronger than I can remember...."

"That's probably why your mind allowed all these memories to surface," she whispered. "You are getting stronger, Morgan, and Ann warned us that as we regained our emotional health, the traumas would probably be released in ways that we could deal with in a positive fashion." She smiled gently and rested her brow momentarily against his shoulder. "It's a good sign in one way."

"Good, hell," he snarled. "I remember the whole damn sequence, Laura. I remember seeing those sons of bitches entering our bedroom and shooting us with dart-tranquilizer rifles. We were like trapped animals—no warning, no way to protect ourselves."

Her heart pounded briefly in her chest and she stared at his suffering profile. "D-do you remember...us?" Afraid of his answer, Laura felt her throat constrict.

"I'm sorry," he rasped, turning and studying her, "I do remember you in the bedroom with me when we got shot. But I don't remember you or the kids in an emotional sense—yet.'' He saw the pain in her expression and reached out to grip her hand tightly. ''I'm sorry, Laura. All I saw after that was the prison, the torture—''

''No,'' she said unsteadily, ''it's enough, Morgan. More than enough. We shouldn't be talking about that, anyway. Talk to me about what you do remember....''

It was dawn by the time Morgan finished recounting his horrifying months in Ramirez's fortress. He felt weakened emotionally from reliving those tortured days. At the same time he experienced a killing rage toward the man who had taken so much away from him. As he'd talked, he'd sat facing Laura, holding her small, warm hands while he grew chilled and tense. Something healing rose out of talking to Laura about his experience. As the pictures and feelings flowed out of him, Morgan saw the anguish in her eyes, in the way her lips parted—for him and what he'd endured.

''I know there's more,'' he told her harshly at last. ''I feel it here, in my gut.''

Laura nodded and whispered unsteadily, ''I'm sure there is, but your mind has given you plenty to assimilate and work through for now, Morgan. More than enough.''

Staring down at her hands, he said, ''You're so small, yet so damned strong. You amaze me, Laura. You always have....'' He had no idea where those words had come from. But he knew now that when things like that came out of him without forethought, it was the old, deep knowing surfacing. He saw her eyes grow warm, shining with unspoken love.

"I wish," he said huskily, "that of all the memories coming back, I'd remember you. Our love..."

"I know," she said quietly, "but in one sense, it will probably be the last thing you'll remember, Morgan."

"Why?"

"Because our love wasn't traumatic to you. Ann has told me many times that your mind and body will work together to rid you first of what can hurt you or perhaps turn into a health problem. The love we had was the healthiest aspect in you and in me." She shrugged painfully. "So we wait."

"It's hurting you," he muttered, watching as she avoided his sharpened gaze. "I see it in a hundred small ways every day, Laura."

She eased her hands from his. Her mouth curved into a bittersweet smile. "I know...but it's all right, Morgan. Really, it is. It's not your fault. I know you're trying to remember."

Hanging his head, he pushed his fingers through his hair. "In some ways, I wonder if I'm not hurting you more by being here with you, Laura."

"*No!*" The word came out filled with anguish—and terror.

Morgan stared at her, seeing her face go pale. "I didn't mean I'd leave," he said quickly, reading her gaze. "I'm not leaving, Laura."

Pressing her hand to her pounding heart, she hung her head. "We're in a catch-22, Morgan. If you walked away and left me, I don't know if I could make it. I hate admitting that to you—or to myself. I've always prided myself on being able to stand on my own two feet, to handle whatever life threw at me." She closed her eyes tightly and her voice became scratchy. "But right now, I'm feeling horribly vulnerable and weak. I'm not as strong as you may think...and I hate myself for feeling that way. I've never had to lean on you...."

Sliding his hand along her clean jawline, Morgan gently made her look at him. "It's always been the other way around, hasn't it, Laura? Because of my past, the PTSD, I've needed you, needed to lean on you and use the resources you've always given me without a thought?"

It hurt Laura to look at the tender, burning light in his eyes. "Y-yes," she whispered painfully. "I never minded, Morgan. Never. I love you, and that's part of loving a person—being there to help them through whatever hell they're going through."

"But it's different this time, isn't it? Something bad happened to both of us. I guess I'm used to leaning on you, using you, but this time it cuts both ways. We don't have a past track record in our marriage for handling this, so I guess we're both floundering a little within ourselves and with each other."

He was right, and for some reason, Laura felt

ashamed of herself, of her inability to be as strong as she always had been before. "I'm sorry, Morgan—"

With a shake of his head, he rasped, "Don't ever be sorry, Laura." His hand stilled against her cheek. "I may not remember my love for you, or all the times we've shared, but my heart tells me marriage is a two-way street. Aren't there times when one partner leans and the other supports, and vice versa?"

The rough gentleness of his voice tore at Laura, and she closed her eyes and choked back a sob. "Y-yes..."

"Then lean on me when you feel like it."

She sniffed and opened her eyes. "Morgan, you're already over the top with your own stuff. I'm not about to add mine to it. You're strong, I know that. But even you have your limits."

His smile was very male and very caring as he studied her in the gray light of dawn filtering through the living room windows. "Let me be the judge of that, Laura."

"Our marriage never worked that way," she argued weakly.

"Then," he said, pushing several tendrils of hair away from her temple, "it's about time for our marriage to change."

Chapter 9

Shortly after he'd finished talking to her about his Peruvian prison memories, Morgan had taken a hot shower and gone back to bed. Laura had remained up, too tense and shaken by their conversation to fall asleep. She tried needlepoint, but her hands trembled too much, and her concentration kept ranging back over Morgan's three months at Ramirez's hands.

When the dawn turned to daylight, she changed from her nightgown and robe into a heavy, rainbow-colored sweater, Levi's and hiking boots. She found a sheepskin coat in the closet, and though it was too big for her, she shrugged it on and left the cabin.

The walk along the bank of Oak Creek, its yellowed grass interspersed with fresh shoots of green,

all thickly coated with frost, helped clear her mind
and emotions—to a degree. Her hands tucked in the
fleece-lined pockets, Laura watched a bald eagle wing
silently down the creek, looking for a fish for its
breakfast. The appearance of the dark brown fishing
eagle with its brilliant white head and tail shook her
out of her own lingering sadness for a moment.

Then she looked up and saw a second eagle circling
a little higher in the sky. She stood on the bank, her
neck craned, realizing vaguely that bald eagles mated
for life. In some ways she was like that loyal eagle,
she realized—it would take death to separate her from
Morgan. Well, that had almost happened, she thought
glumly. Her heart had actually stopped beating on the
deck of that Coast Guard helicopter, though she didn't
remember much of the actual event, except that she'd
been surrounded by brilliant white light. When she'd
regained consciousness, Noah, Morgan's brother, had
been leaning over her, gripping her hand, looking at
her worriedly.

Why couldn't she feel happy about Morgan's returning memory? Laura kicked herself mentally for
being selfish. She should be happy for him, regardless
of what piece of memory it was that came to him.
Resolving to try to find the strength somewhere
within her to remain Morgan's staunch guiding light,
she returned to the cabin.

"What time is it?" Morgan asked thickly as he
moved slowly out of the bedroom, rubbing his face
tiredly.

Laura swallowed hard. "It's noon." Morgan wore only blue-and-white-striped pajama bottoms, and they outlined his magnificent lower body to perfection. As he stood in the living room doorway, looking at her where she sat near the warmth of the wood stove, she savored his drowsy state. He had put on at least ten pounds in the week they'd been at the cabin. He was eating like the proverbial workhorse, and his once-pronounced ribs were fleshed out again, his barrel chest covered with black hair—a chest she'd slid her hands provocatively across so many times before. An ache centered deep in her womb, and she knew she wanted to physically love Morgan. Her mind whispered that it was impossible right now, and she felt the bitter blade of truth cutting into her heart again.

Morgan dropped his hands from his face and hungrily absorbed the vision of Laura's slight form. He thought she looked beautiful in the colorful sweater, which hung halfway down her long, curved thighs. Her hands were clasped in front of her as she sat a few feet from the stove, warming herself. Sunshine lanced through the southern windows, and Morgan noticed a sheepskin coat on the couch. He moved toward her and instantly saw her face change. Or did he?

Still groggy from his exhausted sleep, he moved to within inches of her, facing the fire and holding his own hands toward it. Laura got up and moved away from him until a few feet separated them. "Did you

crash on the couch here after I went back to bed?''
he asked.

Laura shook her head. "No...I was too upset by
what you shared with me. As soon as it got light, I
took a long walk down by the creek."

"That explains the coat," he muttered.

"Oh...yes." Morgan didn't miss much, but then,
he never had. Nervously, she sat down again on one
of the chairs, crossing her legs and folding her hands
in her lap. Being this close to Morgan was torture of
another type. He was so tall and male—and she ached
to touch him, to memorize his body with her hands
and lips. To explore him leisurely with love.

"Did you see my trout?" he asked, a grin edging
his mouth. He rubbed his face, feeling the bristles of
his beard. He needed to shave.

Laura laughed faintly. "No, I didn't see him, but I
saw two beautiful bald eagles flying up the canyon,
looking for breakfast."

"Eagles?" Morgan raised his eyebrows. "I didn't
know Arizona had bald eagles."

She shrugged delicately. "Well, unless I've completely flipped out, I saw them." She managed a half
laugh. "Maybe I was hallucinating. Anymore, I have
a tough time distinguishing reality from...everything
else."

Morgan felt his heart squeeze in response to her
whispered words. He saw the translucence of her features, saw her delicate beauty and her fragile, vulner-

able state. Right now he felt more solid, more sure of himself than she did, he realized. But then, she had been the first to be rescued—had gone through two grueling months alone, wondering if he was alive or dead. She'd taken a more brutal daily beating than he had, in many ways.

Scowling, he draped his hands on his narrow hips and studied the sun-splashed pine floor, shining golden beneath his feet. "Let's do something together today," he began in a low voice. "Something different. Fun."

"What?"

Morgan lifted his head and studied her in the gathering silence that stretched between them. He saw hope suddenly spring to life in her eyes and in the way her lips parted. He'd kissed those beautiful, full lips. He'd tasted Laura's passion, and he wanted a hell of a lot more of it. Tearing his thoughts from his own naked needs, he said, "Remember, Rachel told us about a pretty spot about two miles up Oak Creek? She said it was a nice area for a picnic." He twisted his head and looked out the window. "Looks to me like a nice enough day—blue skies and sunshine." Settling his gaze back on her, he said, "How about it? Are you up to fixing us a picnic lunch? I'll find a blanket, make some coffee, and we'll spend part of the afternoon exploring that area."

"Yes—I'd like that, Morgan."

"We need a break," he muttered, running his fingers through his hair. "We've gone through a lot in such a short amount of time. I'd like to change the pattern and let nature take our attention for a while.''

Laura nodded. "It sounds wonderful, Morgan. Let's do it.''

His grin was uneven but boyish. "Together...''

Laura tried to hide her awe of the place Rachel Donovan called "the pond." It wasn't actually a pond, but rather a place where Oak Creek spilled into a widened area perhaps two hundred feet in diameter. There the rushing water became as smooth and glassy as a lake before narrowing to a bottleneck at the other end and once again becoming a tumbling, rushing creek. The bank where they stood was rocky; on the other side rose a red sandstone cliff capped with a black lava layer a hundred feet thick.

The cliff stood a good two thousand feet high. Trees, most of them smooth, white-barked sycamores interspersed with aspens and evergreens, crowded the water's banks. Luckily, Morgan was good at following the infrequently used trail that paralleled the creek, and they'd managed to discover the beautiful spot.

He stood on the bank now, appreciating the dark, clear pool of water before them. He'd put on a light blue chambray shirt and tan chinos with his leather hiking boots for the day. He turned and smiled as Laura joined him. "Pretty spot, isn't it?"

"Yes," she whispered. "When I think of Arizona, I think of desert, not a mountainous spot like this.''

"Reminds me more of Montana's trout creeks high in the Rockies," he murmured, agreeing with her.

"You did a lot of hunting and fishing with your father, growing up, as your family moved from one Air Force base to another," Laura told him.

Scratching his head, he said, "I don't remember much about that, but I feel it." The breeze was warm and intermittent. As Morgan studied Laura, whose face was flushed from hiking at the six-thousand foot altitude, he smiled. For some reason, she'd left her hair loose and free—the way he liked it—instead of capturing it in a ponytail or braids today. Sunlight danced across her crown, creating a halolike effect.

Reaching out, he gently grazed her hair. "You look like my guardian angel at this moment," he whispered thickly. Allowing his hand to fall back to his side, he saw the surprise in her expression as she turned to look up at him. "Inside me—" he tapped his chest where his heart lay "—I know you've always been an angel looking out for me, haven't you?"

Laughing and embarrassed, Laura turned and took the red plaid blanket and, with his help, laid it out on the creek bank in the sunshine. "Angel? Oh, I don't know, Morgan. I may look like an angel to you, but believe me, I can fall off that pedestal pretty quickly. I have my days," she warned with a smile.

Morgan eased the pack off his back. He'd already rolled up his sleeves. "I can't imagine that even on your worst day you're really all that bad," he teased back. He began taking the food and the thermos of coffee from the knapsack and arranging them on the blanket. The temperature was in the high fifties and the sun made it seem even warmer. He hadn't worn a coat. Though Laura had, she'd shed it halfway to this spot of heaven on earth, because hiking at the high altitude, on a slow, continual upgrade, was enough to heat up anyone.

Settling on the blanket, her legs tucked beneath her, Laura sorted through the bacon-lettuce-and-tomato sandwiches. Morgan sat less than a foot away, legs crossed, a contentment she'd not seen since his kidnapping visible on his features.

''I'm not all sweetness and light,'' she warned again.

''What were you like on your bad days?'' he wondered, slowly unwrapping one of the thick sandwiches.

Laura opened the thermos and poured them each a cup of steaming, black coffee. ''I could get in snits, Morgan.''

''Over what?'' he asked, munching on the salty, tasty fare. He enjoyed watching every movement Laura made. She had such inborn grace, it was like watching a ballerina dance. When he realized she wasn't going to eat, he unwrapped another sandwich and handed it to her. She reluctantly took it, after setting her coffee aside.

''Well?'' he prodded amiably, ''what would set you off? More than likely, I imagine it was something

I did or didn't do. Right?'' He kept his tone light and teasing, sensing that was what she needed right now.

Laura held the sandwich and looked toward the pool, dancing with sparkles of sunlight. The sky above them was such an intense, deep blue that it took her breath away, and the persistent sun warmed her inner coldness. With birds providing a private symphony around them, the spot was, indeed, heaven on earth, as Rachel had promised. Laura wished she could truly absorb the peace and solitude that surrounded them, instead of feeling like a torn-up battlefield inside.

''Laura?''

At the sound of Morgan's deep, thoughtful voice, she roused herself. ''Sorry,'' she murmured.

''Why don't you eat a little something?'' He gestured to the sandwich in her hands. ''Come on, at least half?''

Making a face, she bit into the sandwich and chewed, though it tasted like cardboard to her. Laughing inwardly, she admitted to herself that her five senses had been horribly skewed by the rapes. Not wanting to dwell on those thoughts, she forced herself to swallow, the food becoming a lump in her throat. She reached for the coffee and took several sips.

''Look,'' Morgan said, pointing across the shallow expanse of the pond, ''there's a deer path or something going up that cliff face.''

Peering in the direction he was pointing, Laura saw a small, thin path that appeared frequently. ''Yes, I see it now." She smiled at him. "You're more eagle than you realize."

"The deer must come off the top of that wooded rim." He gestured to the lava crown, thickly forested with pine trees, that topped the cliff. "They probably come down at dawn and dusk, to drink and feed."

Responding to his enthusiasm, Laura said, "Why don't we go over there after lunch and look for prints in the sand? I'll bet you can tell me what animals come down to drink." She wanted desperately to turn the spotlight on Morgan, not herself.

He studied her intently for a moment, watching a blush cover her cheeks as she purposely avoided his stare. Sensing her internal panic, he'd backed off from making her reveal parts of herself. Morgan was a little amazed he could feel her emotions so clearly. Had he always? He wanted to ask, but decided against it. Damn his hungry need to know everything about Laura. He was pushing her, and it was the last thing she needed right now.

"Okay," he murmured, "after you eat your sandwich, we'll find a place to cross above this pond. We'll go over there and test what I think I've forgotten."

"I'd like that." Relief flowed through Laura and she bowed her head, forcing herself to eat the sandwich. She knew Morgan would give her grief if she didn't eat, and she wanted to avoid any kind of confrontation today. Instead, she wanted to pretend their awful past hadn't happened—that they were simply enjoying the day and each other—as they would have before the kidnapping.

"Look at this," Morgan said as he crouched on the bank. "I see raccoon, skunk and deer tracks."

Laura knelt nearby in the thin ribbon of sand along the bank. Everywhere else, pebbles, rocks and boulders followed the twisting, winding creek. They had found a place above the neck of the pool to cross, and her fingers still tingled where Morgan had gripped her hand to help her safely across the wet, slippery stones to the other side.

"What about here?" she said, noticing another, much larger print.

Frowning, Morgan moved around her and in the direction she pointed. "I'll be damned," he whispered, lightly touching the imprint in the sand.

"What?"

"If I'm not mistaken, that's a cougar print."

"You're kidding!"

He shook his head, looking around for more. "No, I'm not. I'm glad we're here together. If this cat was hungry and there was only one of us, he might think he'd found lunch the easy way."

Laura laughed lightly and stood. "He'd take one look at me and think I was far too skinny for a meal."

Morgan grinned and rose to his own full height. In that moment, Laura looked blindingly beautiful to him. The wind had tousled her hair to frame her flushed features, and her dark blue eyes sparkled. Unable to help himself, he walked over and held her face between his palms. Looking deeply into her widening eyes, he said thickly, "You know, I was worried at first when I didn't recognize you, Laura. I remember drawing a blank when you told me your name and that you were my wife." His fingers tightened almost imperceptibly. "But the more I'm around you, the more I share time and space with you, it really doesn't matter anymore to me."

Laura closed her eyes and absorbed his quiet strength, the unexpected touch of his hands upon her, feeling guilty of being so greedy for him. "Wh-what do you mean, Morgan?" she whispered, her hands coming to rest on his arms.

He smiled tenderly. "I mean that even if we don't have a remembered past with each other, it doesn't matter anymore to me." Taking a ragged breath, he murmured, "If today was the first day I'd ever seen you, I know I would learn to care for you...."

Laura opened her eyes, and studied him in the lulling silence. Had she heard correctly? Or, like so many other times, was this some desperate fabrication of her overworked imagination? Morgan had said he cared—about her. She blinked, assimilating his words. He'd not used the word *love*—in reality, he couldn't. He'd only known her three weeks, according to his mind, which refused to divulge their rich, wonderful past together.

It didn't matter to Laura. She was so emotionally unstable that she would take anything Morgan could give her. Right now, she needed him more than he needed her. Perhaps Dr. Parsons was right: once she felt safe, with Morgan back in her life, she would slowly begin to release all the trauma and pressure she'd endured. Ann had warned her she would have a "letdown," and that it could make her feel highly volatile and unstable. She realized she hadn't fully understood the warning—until now.

Still, Morgan's words gave her a badly needed sense of hope in the out-of-control world that was flying apart within her, and Laura was wildly aware of his roughened, scarred hands cupping her face. Her lips parted, and in those moments, she saw the change in his penetrating gray eyes, felt the shift of energy around them. Morgan was going to kiss her. And she wanted to feel his kiss again.

Leaning up on tiptoe, Laura wound her arms around his neck, straining to meet and touch his descending mouth. Nothing had ever seemed so right. Morgan could learn to care for her all over again— whether his memories of them ever returned or not. She would settle for this new caring. But as his lips brushed her, a tiny voice in the back of her head asked her if he was saying these things to ease her anxiety. The old Morgan would never have done that, but Laura had already seen some new, surprising facets to Morgan, completely unlike the man she'd known. Who was the real one? What was important to him now? Was he capable of lying to her to make her feel better?

The thoughts nipped viciously at her as she felt his groan, his mouth plundering hers with fiery intensity. Laura shoved the nagging ideas aside, melting beneath the onslaught of his powerful mouth. She felt the sandpaper quality of his cheek against hers, felt the explosion of moist breath he released as he took her. Her breasts were pressed against his chest, her hips covered by his large hand drawing her insistently against him. Need flowed through her as her pelvis met and melded solidly with his. He felt so strong and good to her, transforming every square inch of her into a caldron of throbbing heat.

She ached to undress him and allow her hands to slide beneath the flannel of his shirt, range across his hairy chest, feeling his muscles tighten beneath her assault. His mouth was searching, and she allowed him deeper entry. Vaguely, she was aware of the hand that had imprisoned her hips moving upward across her sweater to cup her breast.

Her skin pulsed with desire as he caressed her, and she moaned against his mouth. Beyond thinking, she turned, allowing him better access to her yearning breast. If only…oh, if only he would touch her more! His mouth took hers expertly, completely, and she spiraled into the heart of the fire.

A gunshot rang out, echoing through the canyon.

Morgan tore his mouth from Laura's and turned toward the sound of the shot. His arms moved protectively around her, pressing her completely against him, his body a shield. His heart was pounding, his breathing quick as he anxiously searched the surrounding forest. Where had that shot come from? A hunter? Was it Major Houston shooting at a professional hit man sent to hunt them? A hundred thoughts jammed Morgan's mind.

Vaguely he heard Laura gasp, and felt her go on guard, twisting in his arms.

"No," he ordered roughly, remaining positioned between her and the direction from which the shot had come.

"Who's firing?" Laura cried, gripping his arms, her gaze flying from his stony expression to the area across the creek where the shot seemed to have originated.

"I don't know," Morgan answered roughly, suddenly turning and dragging her with him. "Let's go...."

Laura moved quickly as Morgan guided her up the rocky deer trail, which wound steeply upward among the massive, red-sandstone spires. Before too long, Morgan stopped, maneuvering her so that she was fully protected by rock, and surveyed the woods below.

Trying to control her breathing, Laura pressed her hand against her pounding heart. The kiss they'd shared had been incredibly beautiful, freeing. And now, a gunshot. Keeping her voice low, she placed a hand on Morgan's tense shoulder and asked, "Could it be a hunter?"

"In February? I don't know of any hunting season this time of year."

Laura bit down on her lower lip, which was still throbbing with the memory of Morgan's mouth. "A hit man?" She hated to say it. Hated to admit that even here the damnable drug ring could invade, shattering the pieces of their lives they were so desperately trying to fit back together. She felt a white-hot rage at the intrusion.

"It's possible," Morgan growled, frowning as his gaze continued to range across the wooded area. "I don't see anything."

"The shot sounded a long way off...."

"Yes," he grunted, "it did."

"This is a canyon. Sound carries." Laura gulped, her heart beginning to steady a little. No more shots had rung out. "Do you think Mike is on top of it?"

"It could've been Houston in the first place," Morgan said, easing into a crouched position and continuing to watch. "He might have been making his rounds and run into someone."

Shivering, Laura stepped back and wrapped her arms around herself. "Oh, God, Morgan, I thought this was over and done with."

He twisted to look up at her. "It could be nothing," he warned her more gently. The paleness of Laura's features struck him, and he unwound and turned, putting his arms around her. She was trembling like a frightened animal. "Don't jump to conclusions," he said thickly, sweeping her close and holding her tightly. Little by little, he felt Laura's tension dissolve. Kissing her hair and her temple, he divided his attention, his hearing still keyed to the forest below them.

He wondered if it could have been one of Garcia's hit men who had found them. Maybe Houston had intercepted him. Morgan scowled and held Laura firm. Just when they were getting somewhere, just when it seemed they could put their nightmare behind them, their fragile new world had been shattered with a single shot. Damn! The effect on Laura was startling—and frightening. Her blue eyes had turned nearly black, her pupils huge with terror. Her flushed, fair complexion had gone translucent, the skin appearing to stretch across her cheekbones.

"We'll stay here for about half an hour, then we'll take another route back to the cabin," he told her brusquely. "We won't retrace our steps, just in case...."

"And then?" Laura asked, her voice muffled against his chest as she continued to cling tightly to him. "What then?"

"We'll make sure the cabin is safe—then I'll go inside and call the main ranch. Maybe they can tell us what happened."

Squeezing her eyes shut, Laura nodded. She buried her face against him, needing the security of his arms around her. Right now, she felt nakedly vulnerable. The gunshot had stripped her of any pretense of safety. Terror sizzled through her, and it was all she could do to hang on to her sanity. Would their lives ever know peace again?

Chapter 10

Laura sat huddled on the sofa, her gaze riveted on Major Mike Houston as he grimly entered the cabin. Morgan stood near the couch, his hand resting lightly on her shoulder. Somehow, he seemed to know how badly she needed his continued contact. Inside, she was quivering.

If it hadn't been for Morgan's cool, clear thinking, Laura knew she would have become hysterical. But after making it back to the cabin and finding it empty, Morgan had made a phone call to the ranch, contacting Rachel Donovan. She, in turn, had contacted Mike via portable radio, and he'd promised to drive over and tell them what he'd discovered.

Judging by the grim set of the major's mouth,

Laura expected the worst. The Army officer was dressed in gray-and-black tiger fatigues, a pistol riding low on his hip as he walked through the doorway and took off his cap.

"Helluva thing," he said in greeting as he came to a halt just inside the living room. "Someone, a local, was deer hunting."

"Deer hunting?" Laura whispered, looking up at Morgan's fierce countenance.

Mike grinned sheepishly. "That's all it was, so you can both relax. He was hunting out of season and without a license."

"You caught the guy?"

"Yes, I did. The Coconino County sheriff is coming out to pick him up at the ranch." Mike relaxed a little and waved his hand. "You knew the three Donovan daughters run the ranch, didn't you?"

Laura shook her head. "I knew their parents died, but I thought it was only Rachel running the ranch."

"Yes, their parents died in a senseless car crash—a drunk driver hit them head-on. Anyway, the three daughters have all come home from the various parts of the country where they were living. When Rachel heard the gunshot, I was patrolling the area along the creek, and I got lucky. I was probably about a quarter of a mile from the shooter. Rachel thought it was her sister, Kate, who—" he frowned and his voice lowered slightly "—just got out of prison and—"

"Prison?" Morgan demanded tightly. "What was she in for?"

Laura shivered and wrapped her arms more tightly around herself.

Mike held up his hand. "Kate was in prison for three years at a federal facility near Phoenix. She was put there for conspiring to blow up a nuclear power plant. She's an eco-terrorist. Anyway, Rachel thought it was Kate shooting." Shrugging, Mike said, "She called me to say it was probably Kate causing trouble for them—again. It didn't ring true with me because Kate doesn't believe in killing animals, but right now there's a lot of tension at the ranch. Rachel and Jesse are the two younger daughters. They were running things on their own until Kate got out of prison last week."

Morgan scowled. "But it wasn't Kate?"

"No, just a kid about eighteen, trying his luck—out of season." Mike looked at them in the gathering silence. "Are you all right?"

With a sigh, Morgan nodded. "Just spooked, is all."

"Laura?"

"A little hysterical," she jested weakly. "Mike, are we safe with Kate Donovan around? Aren't eco-terrorists fanatical and dangerous?"

"I only met her yesterday," he admitted. "But no, Laura, from what little I got out of her about her prison time, she doesn't strike me as dangerous." He shrugged. "I'll ask Ann—I mean, Dr. Parsons—to keep an eye on Kate since I can't be in two places at once. My main focus is patrolling the area around your cabin, but Dr. Parsons is in constant touch with me via radio, and I'm sure she'll apprise me of anything unusual. As it looks now, Kate's return to the family fold has really put an edge on the two younger daughters.''

"How?" Laura asked, slowly unwinding from her position. Maybe if she got up and moved around, she'd feel less helpless and frightened.

"Let's put it this way: Rachel and Jesse don't exactly get along with Kate. It's obvious they don't share her feelings about eco-terrorism, and they're ashamed of her having been in prison. There's no open hostility, but I gotta tell you, you can cut the air with a knife when those three women are in the ranch house together."

"Mike, would you like a fresh cup of coffee?" Laura asked, pausing at the kitchen doorway. She had to do something to bleed off her nervousness.

He nodded gratefully. "That would be great, Laura. But look, you don't need to put yourself out—"

"I want to do it," she said with a slight smile. "Why don't you come in and relax for a while? How about if you and Morgan sit and talk out here at the kitchen table?"

"Sure," Houston said.

Morgan smiled. "Coffee sounds good, Laura. Thanks."

Laura pulled the coffee can down from the cabinet and put some of the fragrant grounds into the dispenser, part of her tension dissolving under the familiar motions. Her hands trembled, but she ignored them.

"So, how are you getting along at the ranch with Dr. Parsons?" Morgan asked Mike.

Mike flushed and grinned. "It's not exactly tough duty, if you want the truth."

Scratching his head, Morgan said, "I don't have any memory of Ann from before yet, but from what I can see of her now, she's very special."

"You picked a winner when you hired her for Perseus," Mike agreed. "Frankly, since Kate has come home, I'm glad she's at the ranch. The other two women were so uptight about their sister's return that if Ann hadn't corralled them separately and let them talk out their fears, things could have been a lot more rocky than they are right now."

"Pretty tentative?" Laura asked, twisting to look across her shoulder as she flipped on the coffeemaker's switch.

"Ann says Rachel and Jesse are more ashamed of their older sister than anything. But from what I've seen of Kate, she doesn't strike me as a violent person."

"So," Laura said, placing some sugar cookies she'd made a few days earlier on the table, "you don't think she's a problem for us?"

Mike eagerly took a cookie, giving her another grateful look. "Ann...er, Dr. Parsons and I didn't even know about Kate or the situation until she showed up yesterday on the ranch house doorstep.

Rachel and Jesse never mentioned her to us. We think they were hoping she would go somewhere other than 'home' after her release. But Kate doesn't seem the terrorist type.'' He frowned and munched on the cookie. ''Matter of fact, she's real quiet and doesn't say much at all.''

Rubbing his jaw, Morgan said, ''I finally got my memory back from the time spent with Ramirez in the jungle. That was prison to me.''

Houston gave him a sympathetic look. ''That wasn't prison, Morgan, that was hell. There's a difference.''

''The point I'm making,'' Morgan said, ''is that Kate's been behind bars for three years.''

''Yes, she was at a maximum-security women's prison, which meant she was behind bars, with only one hour a day to walk the yard and get a little fresh air and sunshine.''

Laura shook her head. ''I can't imagine that. I'd go insane.''

''That's why I don't think Kate is going to be a problem,'' Houston said. ''She's spending most of her times outdoors and with the horses, riding and staying out in nature. Usually, she only comes in to eat and sleep.''

''Terrorists don't usually operate alone,'' Morgan murmured. ''Do you think some of Kate's buddies will come around now that she's out?''

''I don't know, but it's something I'm looking into. I've got Sean Killian from Perseus working on that angle. He's getting Kate's record from the feds. By the time I get back to the ranch this afternoon, there ought to be a sizable packet of information waiting for me to look through.''

Laura poured fresh coffee into mugs and handed them to the men, who murmured their thanks. Pouring a third cup for herself, she sat down with them.

''What if Kate does have terrorist friends who aren't in prison?''

''There's a chance they could come to the ranch, I suppose,'' Mike said, sipping the coffee with relish. ''This is damn, er, darn good coffee, Laura.''

She smiled gently. ''Thanks.'' Mike Houston was a typical old school military man, she thought. She liked his rugged square face, and alert eyes. In some ways, he was like Morgan, but he had an easygoing, relaxed quality that Morgan didn't possess. Maybe Morgan had been like that at one time, in his days as an eager young Marine Corps officer. If so, it had been destroyed with so much else on that hill in Vietnam.

''Oh,'' Mike said, giving them a look of apology, ''I meant to tell you that Customs in Miami picked up one of Garcia's hit men trying to make it into the States. We believe he was one of two men sent to kill you.''

Laura's hands tightened around the white mug. She frowned and looked at Morgan, whose gaze narrowed thoughtfully over the information. ''What about the other one?''

"They're still looking for him."

"Even if they catch him, there's no guarantee we're safe," Morgan told her. "Garcia could have sent a dozen other men we don't know about."

"I—I know," Laura said faintly. She opened her cold hands briefly. "I just wish this was over. All of it. I wish we could put our lives back together and have a sense of security again, that's all."

Morgan glanced at Houston and back to Laura. He could see the devastation the gunshot scare had wrought. Although it had shaken him up, too, he wasn't traumatized by it as Laura was. "I think Mike will agree with me on this," he told her gruffly. "Once your sense of safety has been compromised, it never truly comes back, Laura. At least, not like before."

Houston finished his coffee. "Unfortunately, you're right," he agreed. "Listen, I gotta saddle up." He grabbed a handful of cookies, nodded deferentially to Laura and stood. "I'll be in touch if there's anything in Kate Donovan's file that I think you'll be interested in knowing."

"Fine," Morgan said, also rising. He saw how tense Laura had become and felt helpless to offer her the safe harbor she longed for. "Come on, Mike, I'll walk you to your vehicle."

Laura pulled herself slowly out of sleep. What had awakened her? She keyed her hearing to Morgan. A week had passed since the rifle incident, and he'd slept soundly every night. Maybe it wasn't him at all that had awakened her. Drowsily, she went over the possibilities. Kate Donovan, according to Mike Houston, wasn't a threat to them. Garcia's second hit man was still on the loose—somewhere. Mike was continuing his patrols. What had awakened her?

A silent alarm was screaming inside her head. The cabin was cool, her blankets drawn cozily around her shoulders. Somehow the gunshot incident seemed to have released a pressure valve within Morgan: he'd been more relaxed since then. But Laura wasn't so lucky, often awakening around three o'clock. She would quietly get up, make some tea and sit in the living room, thumbing through a magazine or something until she felt the fear ebb enough for her to return to her bed and go back to sleep.

As she lay now, keying her hearing to outside noises around the cabin, she caught the far-off hoot of a great horned owl. The rush and bubble of Oak Creek was always soothing, and she loved the sound of it. No, she could hear nothing out of place. Her focus moved back to Morgan. In the past seven days he'd not touched her. That wonderfully melting kiss they'd so hungrily shared by the pool had been the last attempt at intimacy between them.

Closing her eyes, Laura sighed, her hands tightening around her pillow. How many times had she seen that hungry look in Morgan's eyes? Yet, he'd never tried to touch or kiss her again. She could see him seesawing between wanting her and holding himself in iron control. Morgan was a man of principles and integrity, and Laura knew he was wrestling with the devil himself because he'd told her he wouldn't make love to her until he could remember their shared past. He'd said it wasn't fair to her, and he was right. At the same time, Laura thought wearily, feeling the fingers of sleep tugging at her, she needed Morgan's touch, his embrace. Had she communicated that to him? No.

Every day since that gunshot had broken their idyll had been a special hell on earth for her. Gradually, over the past week, Laura realized why. The sound had aroused a blocked memory of her own; Garcia had had one of his guards shot to death in front of her when she was a prisoner at Plantation Paloma. The drug lord had dragged her, dressed in her nightgown, out of her bedroom prison, had hauled her downstairs and behind the huge house and made her watch the man shot by a firing squad. The young soldier's only mistake had been showing up half an hour late for guard duty on the second floor where her bedroom was located.

Laura hadn't known anything about the situation. Her door was always kept locked, and even though she tried to find a way to escape, the windows had had heavy bars across them. She'd had no idea the guards, on duty twenty-four hours a day outside her door, had left her alone for a short time. But when she'd been dragged into the yard, she'd seen the abject terror in the soldier's brown eyes. When she'd tried to cover her face with her hands to avoid seeing him shot, Garcia had yanked them down forcing her to watch the execution.

After trying for a long time to work through those awful memories, Laura felt herself begin to spiral back into sleep. Just as she sighed and surrendered to the process, she heard Morgan scream.

She sat straight up in bed, the covers tumbling away from her. Jerking her head to the left, she saw Morgan's blankets and sheet ripped away, falling to the floor as he flailed about fighting an invisible enemy. With a moan, she quickly got out of bed. Sleep left her completely as she dodged his flying fists.

"Morgan!" she cried. "Morgan, wake up!"

Through the gunfire and explosion of mortars, Morgan heard a woman's voice. He could smell the blood and the sweat of fear, taste the terror and hear the cries of his men around him. In the midst of it, he felt a cool, strong hand grip his shoulder. He heard a woman's low, husky voice calling him away from that hill in Vietnam. With all his strength, he homed in on her voice, knowing on some deep survival level that she could help him. She could save him from the tragedy unfolding before his tightly shut eyes.

His breath was coming in ragged gasps and sweat rolling down his temples, as he shook like the proverbial leaf in a storm. Blindly, he reached out to grab that cool, steadying hand, to cling to that husky-voiced woman who soothed his raw state. With a groan, he buried his face against her breasts, holding her as if to release her would throw him back into his newly remembered hell. Would the nightmare ever end? Morgan had no idea, at once snared in the bloody memories of the past, and yet clutching her small, strong body, which spoke of the present and hope. Even as he pressed his face against her, feeling the soft give of her breasts beneath the silky material of her gown, the memories kept running before his shut eyes like a reel of movie film.

"It's all right, all right," Laura crooned, stroking Morgan's damp hair. She held him tightly with her other arm, which she'd wrapped around his trembling, rigid body. He clung to her, and her ribs ached beneath the tension of his arms. Explosions of breath tore from him, and she knew he was back in Vietnam. Closing her eyes, resting her cheek against his hair, Laura continued her soothing words and began to rock him gently back and forth, as a mother might a frightened child. It had always worked before when Morgan would get caught up in his virulent nightmares, and she could feel it miraculously working now. Little by little, his grip loosened, his breathing softening to gasps, and she could feel him returning to the present, once more escaping his horrific past.

As she sat on his bed, rocking him, she realized more of the memories from Vietnam must have returned. On one level, it was good news—his mind giving up the information, another piece of his life returning. She compressed her lips, kissing his hair, then his sweaty brow. Would Morgan ever remember her? Remember their love? Laura's heart ached for him—and for herself—as she continued talking softly, knowing her voice would lead him out of his nightmare state and back to the present. Even if he had no memory of her similar help in years past, he was responding positively to it, and she was grateful.

Morgan's heart was beating so hard that for a fleeting moment he feared he'd die of a heart attack. But the bloody hill had at last begun to fade. He'd almost died on that hill, had thought he *was* going to, but he hadn't. He felt a woman's lips pressed against his brow. Who...? *Laura.* His mind gyrated between the freshly churned up Vietnam memories and Laura holding him with her woman's strength and tenderness. He'd tasted death that day. He'd been so sure he was going to die like his men around him.

Something in Morgan screamed out for him to prove he was alive. He saw himself in his blood-soaked green utilities, torn and dirty. He saw himself fighting off five Vietcong who had charged through the last lines of defense to attack him. Morgan felt the butt of an AK-47 as it smashed into the side of his face. He felt numbness, then the strong flow of warm blood down his temple and cheek. He was going to die. He saw it in the eyes of his enemies, who wanted him dead.

In one motion, he released Laura enough to capture her soft mouth. He had to live! He had to feel as if he were more alive than dead! Covering her mouth, he took it—hard and deep. He needed to feel her warmth, her body—feel her responding to him. Her fragrance encircled him, its perfumed scent overriding the odors of blood and death. He felt her moan, the sweet sound vibrating through him, erasing some of the nightmarish past that still clutched at him. Oh, God, let him live! Let him survive this! He slid his hand upward, feeling her small ribs, then groaned as his fingers curved around her small, taut breast.

Mindless, acting only out of the instinct to survive, he tugged impatiently at the strap of the silken nightgown, hearing the fabric give way as he frantically searched for and found her exposed breast. Tearing his mouth from her lips, he settled it on her hardened nipple, suckling there. Life instead of death. Love instead of hatred. He heard her cry out—a cry of pure pleasure—and felt her press him.

The past rushed together with the present—the blood of the past mingling with the blood engorging him until he ached for release within her. He pushed the nightgown away from her body, needing to feel her naked, warm skin against him. Laura was alive. She was here, in his arms. He could feel her fingers digging into his bunched shoulder muscles as he continued to suckle her. Nothing had ever felt so right to him. A fierce desire welled up through him, erasing the nightmare once and for all. In its place, he was aware of her lithe body pressed hotly against him, her fingers opening and closing spasmodically against his shoulders, her small cries of pleasure and the fragrant scent that was only her....

Lifting his mouth from her wet nipple, he took her lips again as he laid her across the bed, needing to seek her womanly core, wanting to feel the heat of her life. He slid his hand down across her smooth belly to ease her thighs apart. Her mouth was soft and giving beneath his, fiercely returning his hungry assault, her breath as ragged and demanding as his. As Morgan slipped his fingers between her damp, taut thighs, he relished the moment as no other. It was one thing to kiss Laura, to suckle her, but to touch her this way was to his dizzied senses, even more intimate, more loving.

As his hand moved between her legs, he felt her stiffen. At first he thought it was her enjoyment of his touch contracting her muscles. Then, he heard Laura gasp his name—the single sound holding an edge of terror. Her fear snapped him out of his state instantly. Lifting his head, he felt a new, unfamiliar vibration tremble through Laura. He might not consciously remember loving her before this moment, but instinctively he knew that what he was feeling now between them wasn't right. It was all wrong. But why?

Morgan looked down to see a terror in Laura's eyes he would never have believed possible. She lay stiffly in his arms, her hands shoving frantically against his chest, as if to push him away. Her lips, still glistening from his kisses, were contorted. It took Morgan precious moments to reorient himself. He felt her terror as if it were his own. What had he done wrong?

"Laura?" His voice sounded harsh as he took his

hand away from her thighs and helped her sit up. To his astonishment she crawled away from him, curling into a protective position, her legs against her body, her arms wrapped around herself to hide her naked state from him. She huddled, wildness in her eyes, her back pressed against the pine headboard.

The air was cool. Disgruntled and confused, Morgan pulled the blanket from the floor and wrapped it around her. "Laura? What's wrong? Talk to me. What did I do?"

And as he watched her in the darkness, her face deeply shadowed, her eyes mirroring raw terror, he realized he'd broken his word to her. He'd promised not to touch her—yet he had. Raking his fingers through his hair, Morgan felt ashamed. Caught in the depths of his virulent memories, he'd almost taken her out of selfishness to prove he was more alive than dead inside.

Reaching out slowly, he whispered raggedly, "I'm sorry, Laura...damn, I didn't mean to do this to you.... It was the nightmare, the stuff from Vietnam I was remembering...." His fingers made contact with the edge of the blanket that she gripped so tightly. He wanted to cry over what he'd done to frighten her. Maybe he couldn't recall their love from the past, but dammit, he hadn't meant to scare her like this. He'd never seen Laura look like she did right now.

Wiping his mouth with the back of his hand, he rasped, "I'm sorry, so damn sorry, Laura. I never meant to scare you...."

"It's—not you," Laura gasped out brokenly. "It's me, Morgan. It's me!"

He heard the animal-like sound of her voice and stared at her in the ensuing silence. "What are you talking about? I promised not to touch you until— until I could remember, dammit!" He was angry with himself.

Fighting back a sob, she shook her head. "N-no, you don't understand, Morgan. It's me. It's *my* past that got in the way." A sob tore from her.

Looking at her strangely, he moved closer. "What are you talking about?" He pushed several strands of her hair away from her eyes. "Laura? What is it? I don't understand what you're saying."

Tears burned in Laura's eyes and Morgan's face blurred momentarily before her. She forced out a response. "I don't know what happened, Morgan. I wanted you to kiss me, to touch me...." She shut her eyes, ashamed. "And then...something happened. I was enjoying you, wanting you so badly. But something happened."

"What?" he demanded roughly. "What did I do? Did I hurt you? That's the last thing I'd ever want to do, Laura. You've got to believe me."

Laura gripped the edges of the blanket, feeling so very cold and distraught. Morgan's face mirrored a mix of confusion, concern and anger. She knew the anger was aimed not at her but at himself for some unknown transgression. "The fault," she said unsteadily, "isn't yours. It's mine. You did nothing wrong, Morgan. Absolutely nothing."

"Then..." Morgan shook his head and took her back into his arms. She came without hesitation, huddled against him like a lost, frightened child. "What is it? Talk to me. How can I help you?" He moved his hand up and down her blanketed arm. Laura pressed her face against his chest as if she wanted to hide not only from him, but from herself.

"I—it's the rape, Morgan," she whispered bleakly. "My therapist warned me this might happen, but I didn't believe it. Oh, God, Morgan, I froze when you started to touch me down there. Something inside me just snapped, and I felt myself leaving my body. I felt such terror that I couldn't think. I felt like a cornered animal that was about to die!" She blinked through her tears as she studied his ravaged face in the dim light. "But it was you! I love you! I'm not afraid of you, of your touch." Pressing her hands to her face, she sobbed.

Gently, Morgan held her close, wrapping his arms around her. "Shh," he whispered close to her ear, "it's all right, Laura. It's all right...." It wasn't, but he didn't know what else to say or do. Somehow, Laura's past had been revealed in a way neither had expected. His mind spun with questions, and he felt helpless. And then he felt rage toward Garcia. As he rocked Laura in his arms, whispering words of comfort, renewed fury tunneled through Morgan. At that moment, he wanted to kill the man who had hurt her.

He searched his spotty memory for any knowledge about rape, but he knew nothing about its effects. Damn! As if they didn't have enough to handle, Laura's rape had reared its ugly, controlling head, ruining the one, untouched thing they'd been able to share with each other.

Angrily, Morgan sat there, consumed by his hatred of Garcia. He waited until Laura stopped trembling. When he felt her begin to relax against him, he took her over to her bed and made her lie down.

"I'm going to fix us some tea," he told her huskily. "I'll be right back. Just lie there, Laura. Try to relax."

Laura followed Morgan's shadowy presence with her gaze until he disappeared from the chilly room. Grief overwhelmed her. What had her body done to her? Or had it been her mind? How could she reject Morgan, the man she loved so fiercely? How could his touch, which she had so eagerly dreamed of, suddenly make her feel such terror? Morgan hadn't raped her, Garcia had. Repeatedly.

But that wasn't all, Laura knew it. And Morgan still did not know the rest of what had happened. Her grief turned to a deep, gutting sense of loss. In reality, she'd lost Morgan the night he'd been kidnapped. All his memories were returning except for those of her and their marriage. Bitterness coated her mouth as she lay on her side, clenched into a protective fetal position. Tears dampened her eyes as her mind and emotions spun out of control. How could she have pushed Morgan, of all people, away from her?

Laura felt something deep within her shatter—actually felt the snapping sensation in the region of her solar plexus region—leaving in its wake a spiraling sense of giving up, of no longer having the strength to fight back or to survive all that lay ahead for her and Morgan. Of what use was she? Because of the rapes, she would spurn Morgan in the future. Her therapist had warned her but Laura hadn't wanted to believe it—had gone into denial about it. Morgan's kisses had not brought up these feelings of detachment and terror. On the contrary, she had greedily absorbed them and his touch like sunlight into the frozen ground of her broken heart and mortally wounded soul.

A ragged sigh tore from her lips. She could hear Morgan in the kitchen making tea. He didn't remember her, their marriage or their children. Would he ever? Something warned her he wouldn't. But even if he did, so what? The way she was feeling now, unable to allow him to touch her intimately, what good would it do? The feeling of worthlessness grew within Laura until her life stretched before her, grim and gray. Morgan was a man of great passion. He not only deserved but required a woman who could lie eagerly with him and love him fully. Settling for mere kisses could not be enough. Laura realized sadly she couldn't be the woman he needed.

She was, in the true sense of the word, damaged

merchandise. And Morgan didn't even know the worst of it yet. A sob tore from her throat and she pressed her face into the pillow, wanting to die, wanting to escape the overwhelming pain that had finally broken her. She had no more strength left, no more will to fight back and survive. Garcia had murdered her, she realized, grief stricken by the dawning awareness. He'd taken her physically and killed her emotionally. His evil revenge was still playing itself out.

Sobbing harder, the sounds absorbed by the pillow, Laura realized for the first time the extent of the revenge Garcia had leveled against Morgan. The drug lord had known that by raping her, he was taking her from Morgan. The very thing Morgan loved most in the world—his wife—was gone forever. As Laura tried to stop crying before Morgan came back with the tea, she realized it was probably a lucky thing that he no longer recalled their life together, for it could only cause him greater pain now.

Oh, how could he live with such hurt? She couldn't. She knew that what they'd shared could never again be the same—ever. Why put him through it? Hadn't he suffered enough? Wouldn't it be better if she simply disappeared? A shadow of the past that remained there? That way, Laura thought, he could get on with his life. He could find a woman he could love—who would love him fully in return.

Yes, that was the answer. She had to leave. Who would want her the way she was—frigid, fearing a man's intimate touch? Morgan didn't remember her anyway. And now the terrible, wrenching secret she still carried would stay safe with her. Morgan need never know. To cut out the pain that only grew daily between them, Laura became increasingly convinced that she must leave as soon as possible. Somehow, she would disappear. No one, not even her children, must know where she'd gone, though just the thought of never seeing Jason and Katherine again made her sob even harder.

Still, Laura convinced herself, Susannah Killian would care for them, would be a wonderful surrogate mother until Morgan could find another woman to love him without the baggage of the past overwhelming their present. Yes, her children were young; they would adjust. But could she? Laura wasn't certain. But she was sure she had to leave. It would be best this way—for all involved.

Chapter 11

Sunlight lanced brightly into the bedroom, eventually wakening Morgan. He raised his head, blinking, and pushed his covers off. What time was it? Disgruntled, he sat up, feeling exhausted. Leaning over, his hands covering his face, he allowed the memories of the night before to return. Shame intertwined with guilt as he thought about his selfish, almost instinctive actions with Laura. Where the hell was his head? Why hadn't he placed her rape squarely in front of him instead of behind him, practically denying it had happened?

Sourly, Morgan lifted his head and rubbed his hands along his thighs as he stared at the sunshine spilling through the east window. Laura's bed was empty. She usually got up and moved about sooner than he did of late. He heard the short, sharp exchanges of chickadees outside, and the soothing sounds of the nearby creek. A momentary peace settled over him. He liked being so near water. Maybe he should move the family to the ocean. He wondered what Laura would say to that idea.

Hell, he didn't even remember if Laura liked the ocean. Today he was going to drop by and talk to Dr. Parsons—see if he could cultivate an understanding of what rape did to a woman and how to handle it. He wasn't about to put Laura through that kind of anguish again—at least, not knowingly.

As he sat thinking about her, Morgan began to realize that what he felt toward Laura was far more than caring. Something alive and healthy remained between them despite the terrible circumstances that now engulfed them. Morgan felt that vibration of certainty in his heart, which seemed to expand with absolute joy. Though his mind might refuse to release the memory of loving her, he knew now, sitting on the edge of his bed, that he loved her anyway.

The feeling exploded through him, flooding him with a wonderful sensation. Yes, he loved her. When had it happened? Morgan couldn't honestly pinpoint a day or an hour when his feelings had shifted from care to love. Excitement thrummed through him. It didn't matter now whether he recalled their past love, because it had somehow been transferred from his past into his present. It had just happened.

Gratefully, he closed his eyes, resting his hands on his thighs as he savored his discovery. Up until this moment, he'd been careful not to say the word *love* to Laura. He hadn't wanted to hurt her or raise false hopes. Now Morgan realized he could honestly get up, leave this room and go tell Laura, to her face, that he loved her.

The corners of his mouth tipped upward as he savored that forthcoming duty. What would she do? Would her deep blue eyes sparkle with those flecks of gold? She had such a soft mouth. He would watch the joy shimmer through her and absorb the beauty of her tremulous smile. With this latest revelation, they were freed from the past. Laura had told him she loved him, but he hadn't reciprocated. Now he could!

Eagerly, Morgan got to his feet. He didn't hear Laura stirring in the cabin, but that wasn't unusual. She would often wake up before him, take her bath, dress and go for a walk, then come back and make breakfast for them. By that time, he'd be up, showered, shaved and ready to start his day—with her. Hope tunneled through him as he retrieved some clean clothes from the drawer and padded through the warm living room to the bathroom. Stopping, he poked his head into the kitchen. Laura wasn't there, but he smelled the coffee she'd made earlier, and it made his mouth water. First, he'd shower and dress.

Glancing at his watch after he'd showered and shaved, Morgan saw it was nearly nine o'clock. Today he'd chosen a dark blue chamois shirt, fresh jeans and his usual hiking boots. Glancing in the mirror, still ringed with humidity from his shower, he quickly combed his short, black hair into place. A smile tugged at his mouth as he studied himself. What an ugly-looking bastard he was, with that scar running the length of one side of his face. Yet Laura loved him. Unequivocally. Forever. The feeling in his heart, that newly pulsing warmth, hadn't stopped since he'd realized his love for her. If anything, it was even stronger now, more anticipatory, because Morgan wanted so badly to share it with her.

After last night's fiasco, when he'd wounded her by his ignorant, selfish actions, Morgan wanted to make her happy, to take away the terror he'd seen in her eyes and replace it with wonder. Humming to himself, he stepped out of the bathroom, his boots echoing down the short hall. He halted in the living room doorway. The radio wasn't on. They picked up a great FM station out of Prescott, which Laura usually turned on when she returned from her walk. The living room remained quiet.

Morgan scowled, feeling uneasy without knowing why. Maybe Laura was back in the bedroom, lying down, still shattered by last night's experience. Worry began to edge into the joy thrumming through him as he walked back to their bedroom. His hands resting against the doorframe, Morgan looked around the room. It was empty. Laura had to be in the kitchen, though he didn't pick up the normal sounds of her making breakfast. Shoving away his growing anxiety, he walked into the kitchen.

A glance told him it, too, was empty. His gaze swept the small area, catching something out of place on the table. A piece of paper was propped up between the salt and pepper shakers. His anxiety heightened savagely as he walked over to the table. Reaching for the paper, he saw Laura's flowery handwriting and gave the note his full attention.

My Darling Morgan,
I don't know how to begin or end this letter. It's so painful to write. Anymore, I don't seem to know what I'm doing. I used to think I knew right from wrong, day from night, black from white, but I don't. Darling, please forgive me for what I've done. Last night I felt something so intrinsic within me break that I feel disconnected. Perhaps I've gone insane. I truly don't know.

When you awoke out of your Vietnam nightmare, I knew that more of your past had come back. No one could be happier than I was when you took me in your arms and started to make love to me. I couldn't believe it was happening, because in the past, we often made love after you came out of those nightmares. For you, it was a way to prove you were alive, and I understood that and *wanted* you to love me.

But suddenly, last night, I didn't want you loving me. I couldn't stand the thought of being touched—even by you. Images of being raped flashed before me, and I couldn't make them go away. I couldn't concentrate enough on the fact that it was you loving me. Oh, Morgan, I'm so sorry. I feel so horrible, so out of control. I left my body at some point—was completely disconnected from you—and that's never happened before. I felt violated. I knew you weren't my rapist, yet my body and emotions responded as if you were.

I can't go on this way, Morgan. God knows, you don't deserve it. Right now, I can't stand the agony. I thought I knew what hurt was, but I didn't. I thought I was in pain during my captivity with Garcia, or after I was rescued and we tried to find Jason. Then I thought getting our son back would ease the pain, but it didn't. It just multiplied because I didn't know if you were alive. But the children kept me going. They needed a parent, and I clung to that fact.

When Perseus found you, I went through the pain of waiting. I lived moment to moment, more uncertain than ever before. How badly I wanted what we had to come back! And what if you were dead? When Culver and Pilar rescued you, and we received the call that you were alive, I felt a joy that made me faint for a moment. And I thought that finally the pain would leave. But when Ann told me that you had suffered damage to your memory, the pain was worse than ever.

These past few weeks with you at the cabin have been heaven and hell for me, Morgan. I've tried so hard to do the right thing, say the right thing, but little by little, whatever strength I had has slowly oozed out of me. Last night broke me. I realized then that nothing I did or didn't do was going to help you. Morgan, I'm not the Laura you knew and can't remember. I'm broken inside. I don't know who I am any longer. I can't look to you for help because you're struggling so hard to heal yourself. You don't need me around, causing you pain. Right now, I feel crazed. The hurt is so horrible that I feel insane with it.

I've decided to leave. It is the hardest thing I've ever done, but I believe I'm doing it for the right reasons—or at least I think I am. I'm not really sure about much these days. It's a relief to me that you don't remember our past, because I've changed so much since my kidnapping and rapes. You need a warm, loving, giving woman to help you through your trauma, and I no longer have the strength to be that for you. If I stayed, Morgan, I'd become an albatross around your neck—just another responsibility and liability to carry while you're trying to heal. I love you too much to do that to you.

Worse, I never told you the full truth about

the rapes. I was afraid to tell you that the doctor examined me and told me I could never have another child; the damage done to me was too great. For me, that was the ultimate sentence, Morgan. I love children so much, and we had wanted at least four. Before the kidnapping, we were planning our third baby. We even had names picked out. I'd be useless to you in that way—frigid and sterile. What man in his right mind wants a woman like me around?

It's early in the morning, and I'm leaving. Please ask Susannah to continue to take care of Jason and Katherine. I cried so much at the thought of never seeing them again. But I know my decision is for the best. I don't want our children ever to know the hell inside me. I'm afraid I'd lose control, and I don't want to hurt them or you. None of you deserve this. Please don't try to find me, Morgan. Let me go. I hope that my leaving will ultimately help everyone.

I don't know what I'm going to do or where I'll go. Please forgive me, Morgan. I don't know what else to do. I love you. I love Jason and Katherine. I pray that someday your memory will return and you'll love them as much as you did before. You were a wonderful father to them, and I know you can be again.

Goodbye...

Love, Laura

"Son of a bitch!" Violently, Morgan spun on his heel. The paper fluttered to the table as he reached for the phone on the wall, his heart pounding with unrivaled pain. The joy he'd felt was destroyed, in its place raw, primal agony. No! Laura didn't know what she was doing! He grabbed the phone, his hand shaking as he dialed the ranch.

"Rachel? This is Morgan. Let me talk to Ann. It's an emergency."

The next few minutes were an unfolding nightmare as he stood tensely in the kitchen, telling Ann about the letter Laura had left.

"What the hell's going on?" he demanded tightly.

"She's had a temporary break from reality," Ann said worriedly. "I was afraid something like this might happen. Laura's therapist said she wasn't getting anywhere with her, that Laura had gone into deep denial over the rapes. It's typical of her to push her own problems and feelings aside in favor of her family's needs. She hasn't been taking care of herself first, Morgan, and this is the result. It's a highly codependent response, and Laura isn't the only woman who has that problem, believe me."

His hand tightened on the phone receiver until his knuckles whitened. "Is she going to kill herself?"

"It doesn't sound like it—at least, not yet. Right now she's trying to run away from the pain. Later, when she discovers she can't outrun it, is when the suicidal impulse could set in."

"Dammit!" he rasped. "Why didn't I realize all this? Why didn't I—"

"Morgan, you're both hurting. It's especially hard when both parties are at a survival level and trying to put the pieces of their lives back together. It's impossible for either of you be there fully for your partner. My hunch is that Laura tried to do that, to be everything for you, and in doing so, she used up the extra hope, love and energy she needed for her own recovery. She was on the edge, anyway. That's why I kept coming by to check on you two—I was more concerned about her than you."

"I was stable because she was feeding me with her attention, love and care," he growled angrily. Why the hell hadn't he realized that? In effect, Laura had been transfusing him with her lifeblood: he grew stronger, she was slowly dying right before his eyes— and he hadn't seen it. He knotted his fist, agony exploding through his chest. He heard Ann's voice— and tried to focus on what she was saying.

"Got to find her. Do you have any idea where she might have gone? Did she have a favorite place here?"

"I—I don't know," he answered, looking around the kitchen. "Her coat is gone. She has a couple hundred bucks. That's enough to get to a bus and head for God knows where."

"Sedona's the closest town," Ann said. "Still, she has to walk out of this place, Morgan. Let me get Mike on the radio. We need to start a search. I'll call the sheriff. They can begin looking for hitchhikers along Route 89, which heads into Sedona and Flagstaff.''

Suddenly, an idea struck him. ''Wait!'' he exclaimed. ''I think I know where she might have gone. It would be one way of getting off the ranch and to the highway.'' Quickly telling Ann his idea, he hung up the phone and ran through the cabin. He jerked the door open and began racing along the creek.

The morning was cool and his breath came in white explosions as he paralleled the stream, dodging the rocks and boulders that seemed determined to slow his progress. Breathing harshly, his heart pounding, he tried to calm down and think clearly. Two days ago, it had rained. The soil here was clay, still damp and impressionable. He stopped momentarily and looked around at the muddy ground, trying to control his agony and fear for Laura. She didn't wear hiking boots, which would have left deep impressions in the soil. No, even though she had boots, she favored an old pair of plain leather oxfords that she'd laughingly told him were more comfortable—''like old friends.''

Morgan stopped and rubbed his brow. The shoes were specially made, with an emblem carved into the sole though they had no tread to speak of. Breathing hard, he shut his eyes and brought that symbol forward. All he could remember was that it was circular. Opening his eyes, he crouched down. Everywhere Morgan looked, he saw the hoofprints of cattle that roamed along the creek in search of grass and water.

He could find no evidence of Laura's shoe print, but perhaps she had taken a diagonal route instead of the path they'd trod previously.

The sun beating down was making Morgan sweat as he checked his watch. It was eleven o'clock. He wiped his mouth with the back of his hand and looked around the scenic area. The red and white cliffs with their black lava caps rose thousands of feet around him, the dark trees standing out against them in brilliant splash of greens. The sky, a deep blue, reminded him of Laura's wide, innocent eyes.

Morgan began to run again, feeling his own strength diminishing with each stride. He knew with a gut feeling where Laura had gone: to that pool. Vividly, he remembered showing her on a map, after they'd returned from their picnic, that the deer path that wound up the cliff on the far side of the pool eventually led to Route 89A. She must have taken it.

Praying he was right, Morgan pushed himself as never before. He had everything to lose; his weakening body had to respond! He loved Laura. He wanted her back. She had to know that! As he ran, his arms pumping, Morgan stumbled on some loose rocks and felt tears streaming down his cheeks. My God, he couldn't lose Laura now. Not after all they'd endured together! A scream began to uncurl deep in his gut, a scream of fury at the turn of events that had been thrown at them. Nothing mattered anymore to

Morgan. Nothing but Laura, and getting her back, safe and sound, in his arms.

His heart felt as if it were going to burst in his chest as he ran, drunkenly now, toward the pool. Breathing raggedly in gasps, he stumbled to a halt, anxiously looking around. He'd run three miles, and he was trembling with exhaustion. His lower legs cramped, the pain floating up to his awareness, but not stopping him. As he stood rigidly on the bank, anxiously looking around the pool, he choked.

His eyes narrowed and his heart slammed hard into his ribs. There, across the pool, halfway up the steepest part of the deer trail, lay Laura, apparently unconscious. In those split seconds, a tremendous amount of the past flashed back to Morgan, overwhelming him. His cry echoed through the area. Plunging into the cold, icy water, he lunged forward, his hands stretched toward her. Laura lay unmoving, like a broken rag doll, half on the trail, the rest of her body hidden in the thick, green manzanita bushes that lined it.

Morgan never felt the water's icy temperature. He lunged roughly through the sometimes waist-deep pool to reach the other side, his cry of pure terror echoing and re-echoing around him. As he thrashed the pool, memories of Laura avalanched through him. Pictures and fragments of the past—how they'd met, fallen in love—overwhelmed his panicked senses. As he reached the other side, he stumbled, falling to his hands and knees. He crawled out of the water as the memories of their children sheared back upon him.

As he staggered to his feet, the water rushing down his pant legs and squishing in his hiking boots, Morgan vividly recalled the agonizing hours when Laura had nearly died in labor with Jason. She'd hemorrhaged unexpectedly after the birth. Morgan had been there, had gone into shock as all hell broke loose in the delivery room. He'd stood with a newly blanketed Jason in his hands, watching Laura's face go waxen within moments, due to the heavy loss of blood.

Oh, God, that's how she looked to him now! She was a quarter of a mile up the narrow, steep trail, unmoving. Even as he scrambled, clawing at anything he could get his hands on to reach her faster, Morgan thought she was dead.

Another vignette sheared through him, leaving him sobbing. Morgan remembered how anxious and worried he'd been while Laura carried Katherine. How many nightmares he'd had about her dying during the delivery of their second child. Worse, Laura had gone into premature labor with her. Morgan remembered the pain of thinking he might lose them as he'd paced the hospital's visitor area. Laura had refused a cesarean, though her doctor wanted to perform the operation to keep Laura safe from the possibility of hemorrhaging again. This time they might not be so lucky. This time she could die.

Morgan gasped. Only a few yards to go! Memories overlapped the present, and he remembered Dr. Jane

Holly smiling triumphantly as she came out of the delivery room. Little Katherine Alyssa was fine, despite being a month early. Even better, this second birthing process had gone without a hitch, and Laura was not only fine, but asking for him.

Oh! Morgan recalled how he'd run to that delivery room and seen his baby daughter resting on Laura's belly. He remembered Laura's eyes filled with tears of joy as he leaned down to slide his arm beneath her and hold her. They'd cried together—he out of relief that she was alive, and she because Katherine was so perfect and beautiful.

Morgan shook his head, forcing away the wave of memories. He could see now that several rocks had evidently loosened as Laura had tried to scramble up the trail. She had slipped in her smooth-bottomed shoes. As he climbed to where she lay, his gaze riveted on her. Was she dead? She couldn't be! What a horrible way to end such a beautiful, wonderful life. He loved her so much that it hurt him to breathe in that moment.

As he fell to his knees beside Laura and reached out with a shaking hand, Morgan knew she was dead. Her skin was waxen, with a grayish cast. Her lips were parted, her arms hanging lifelessly, her legs tangled in the red branches of the thick manzanita that had stopped her plunge to the bottom of the cliff.

As Morgan felt for a pulse, he sobbed in grief. He would do anything—*anything*—to have Laura alive!

Chapter 12

"I love you, Laura. Do you hear me? I love you...."

Groggily, Laura opened her eyes. Morgan's tense face hovered close to hers, and she felt the strength and warmth of his body surrounding her, supporting her. What had happened? Almost as soon as she asked the question, the information filtered through her shorted-out senses. Her head aching abominably, she struggled to sit up. Morgan eased her upward, using his body to support her back, his arm around her shoulders.

"Are you all right?" he demanded, breathing raggedly. Pushing several strands of muddied hair off her face, he searched her pale features. "Laura?"

"Y-yes, I'm okay...." On one level, she was. On many others, she wasn't. Weakly, she raised her hand and rubbed the back of her head. "I—I must have fallen—"

"You fell, all right," Morgan rasped, glancing down the dangerous trail. He saw where she'd slipped on the slick red clay. Devoting all his attention to her, he said unsteadily, "My God, you could have been killed, Laura."

She hung her head as hot tears pressed at her closed eyelids. The terror in Morgan's voice ripped through her. No longer did she have the strength to stop anything from wounding her further.

"Any broken bones?" he asked hoarsely, running his hands gently over her extremities. "Anything pulled?"

Laura sat in the harbor of his embrace, dazed and unable to think as quickly as he did. But the mere touch of Morgan's hands helped soothe her chaotic state. Bitterly, she realized she couldn't even run away successfully. She vaguely remembered a branch sticking out on the steep deer trail. She'd seen it, but had disregarded it and stepped on it. The stick had rolled and so had she. The last thing she remembered was having her feet fly out from beneath her and landing hard on her back.

Opening her eyes, Laura laughed a little hysterically. "The only thing broken in me is my mind...."

Worriedly, Morgan assessed her eyes, which appeared dark and lifeless. "Hold on," he growled, then picked her up as if she weighed nothing. Steadying himself on the narrow path, he got his bearings, holding her tightly against him. He heard her gasp, her arms going around his neck, but within moments, she relaxed against him, trusting him totally. Well, this time, Morgan decided, he wasn't going to let her down. Gingerly, he picked his way back down the path to the edge of the pool.

"Hang on, you're going for a ride," he warned huskily. She clung to him like a frightened child now, her face buried against his neck. Carefully, he moved through the water, bringing her safely to the other side. It would take another forty minutes to reach the cabin, and he knew his arms would ache like hell itself from carrying Laura that distance, but he sensed she had given up and wouldn't have the strength to walk on her own.

He struck out on the trail that led back to the cabin. "Listen to me," he said roughly near her ear, "listen to what I have to say, Laura." His hand tightened around her thin form. "I remember. I remember us." His voice was unsteady with feelings. "After I read your letter, I thought you might have gone back to the pool where we'd picnicked. As I ran up to the pool and saw you, everything started coming back about us, Laura. Do you hear me? I remember how we met, what happened. Dammit, I remember my love for you!"

Blinking through her tears, Laura lifted her face and looked up at Morgan. Each step he took jarred her, increasing the pain in her head. But miraculously, with his shocking words, the pain left momentarily as she homed in on his raggedly given admission. ''Y-you remember?'' she asked, afraid to believe what she'd heard. He cut a glance at her, his stride shortening.

''Yes, I remember. *Everything,* Laura.'' The corners of his mouth turned downward and his voice roughened. ''All I want is for you to stay with me. Don't try to run off again. Do you hear me? All these months you've had to be strong for everyone else. Well, that's changed now. I'm going to be strong for *you.* Do you understand what I'm saying? You need some care and support. Dammit, I didn't mean to take from you the way I did. I didn't realize...honest to God, I didn't. But it won't happen again, and that's a promise, Laura. Looking back over the past seven years, I can see that I've always taken from you and depended on you—without giving you back half of what I got.'' His mouth compressed. ''Well, all that's changing. Right now.''

Laura sighed and rested her brow wearily against his jaw. Was she dreaming? Hallucinating? She knew she'd crossed the line somewhere in that unmarked territory between what was real and what wasn't. What could she trust? Tears dribbled down her cheeks, she tasted the salt of them as they followed the outline of her lips.

''Y-you read the letter I left?'' she asked, her voice scratchy. Laura felt completely unable to protect herself from whatever Morgan might think about that letter. By rights, he should be angry.

. "I read it," he said, his eyes narrowing as he paid strict attention to where he was placing his feet along the trail. Sunlight cascaded down among the branches of the tall pines, and shadows and light danced across Laura as Morgan carried her rapidly toward their cabin. "I read it," he repeated harshly, "and you know what? I don't care if you can't have any more children. We already have two beautiful children. We should count our blessings for what we have, Laura." He risked a glance down at her and for the first time saw a glimmer of hope in her dark blue eyes.

Morgan could tell Laura was waiting for his anger, but he felt none toward her. "I could kill Garcia with my bare hands," he rasped. "If I ever get the chance, he's a dead man. I'm so damned sorry about what happened to you, Laura." His voice broke. "So damned sorry."

Laura tightened her hold around his neck and powerful shoulders. "I was so afraid, Morgan...so afraid to tell you...."

"I wish you had told me," he said thickly. "But I know why you didn't, too, and it doesn't matter anymore, Laura." He cast another quick glance down at her. "What matters is you. That's all. Everything else in our lives can go to hell." His arms tightened briefly around her, and he watched more of the tension dissolve from her eyes. How he loved her! The powerful, unfolding feelings in his chest were still hitting him in tidal wave proportions as nuances of old memories kept returning, one on top of another. But sorting through all of them was of minor importance in comparison to Laura and her mental and emotional condition. All he wanted in the world in that moment was to get her back to the cabin, call Dr. Parsons and get Laura some help.

"Well?" Morgan demanded in a low tone after Dr. Parsons quietly shut the door to the bedroom, where Laura was resting.

Ann smiled gently and guided Morgan to the living room couch, where she sat down with him. Mike Houston had brought her to the cabin, and he stood worriedly in the kitchen doorway, a cup of coffee in hand.

"I gave her a tranquilizer, Morgan. She's already asleep. She's exhausted from everything that's happened."

"What did happen?"

Ann picked up the note. "Basically, in layperson's terms, she gave up. I'm sorry, I didn't know she hadn't told you about her physical complications from the rapes. I thought you knew."

He shook his head and folded his hands between his thighs. "She said she was afraid to tell me."

"I can understand why," Ann murmured as she set the note aside. "But the worst is out in the open now. No more skeletons remain in either of your closets, so to speak. You're finally sharing a level playing field. You remember your past with Laura, your marriage and your children, so that's a very healthy start toward healing all that's happened to both of you.''

Worriedly, Morgan rasped, ''What about Laura, though? I know she hates to take any kind of drugs. I hate to see her on antidepressants or tranquilizers—even if she'll take them.''

Reaching out, Ann patted his shoulder. ''It's only temporary, Morgan. Right now, you're Laura's antidepressant.''

''What do you mean?''

''When she wakes up, which probably won't be for a good eight hours, let her talk. You just sit and listen. When she needs reassurance, give it to her. But keep in mind that she felt abandoned, out there all alone with this big, bad world looming over her, slowly crushing the life out of her. Try to be more aware of when you're placing demands on her, and try not to. She's given too much to too many people for too long. It's time she came first, not second or last.''

''That was my gut feeling about all this,'' he admitted harshly, angry all over again at his role in putting Laura in such a position in the first place. ''Damn,'' he growled, running his fingers distractedly through his hair, ''I'm one selfish son of a bitch.''

Laughing gently, Ann got up. ''A healthy response, Morgan. And yes, you've been pretty demanding on Laura over the years. She always came second to Perseus, too.''

His eyes narrowed on the physician. "You're right," he said finally.

Ann's smile increased as she put her medical items back into her black leather bag. "I've never accused you of being slow, Morgan. I think you've got the big picture now. You know what needs to be done to help Laura through this, so she can put her life back together. Mike's going to take me back to the ranch, but I'll leave some sleeping pills and a few tranquilizers, in case Laura needs them. She probably won't touch them, but they're here, just in case."

Mike came over and picked up Ann's bag for her.

"I prescribe R and R for both of you in the next week," Ann added. "If you or Laura want me to come back out, call. Otherwise, I'm keeping a low profile."

Morgan nodded. "Thanks, Ann—for everything." And he meant that—she'd been a steady light in their darkness. "You're one hell of a flight surgeon. Did I ever tell you that?" He saw Ann's face flush and pleasure come to her eyes as Mike opened the door for her.

"No, but it's nice to hear it—finally. We'll see you later...."

Morgan sat in the silence of the cabin after Ann and Mike had left. Harshly, he rubbed his face. He'd come so close to losing the one thing he loved most in the world. Getting up, stiff from the extreme exercise of the morning, he went into the kitchen to pour himself some coffee. Memories and emotions were continuing to roll over him, more than ever now that his focus wasn't needed elsewhere.

How long he sat at the kitchen table, the cup of coffee growing cold between his hands, Morgan didn't know. Most of the emotions he experienced during those hours were good ones. Rich ones filled with happiness, hope and laughter. They'd shared some bad times, too—especially when Laura had nearly died in childbirth. Morgan felt a bitter taste in his mouth. Damn, he'd nearly lost her again—in a different way.

A lot had to change, he realized. And he had to be the one to do it—for Laura, for himself and for their family. First, though, he had to reestablish that broken connection with Laura. She had to believe he remembered and fully felt his love for her. Would she? Morgan was no longer sure of anything. He could only wait and see.

When Laura awoke, it was dark outside. The cabin was warm, and she noticed the door to the bedroom was open, the heat from the earth stove filtering into the room. Oddly, she felt not only warm, but safe and even happy. Happy? As she rubbed her face and drowsily sat up to push the covers away, she remembered what had happened, and her small flicker of happiness died. Fear replaced it—and anxiety. Where was Morgan? Laura didn't hear anything except the soft music of the Prescott FM station she loved. The music helped soothe her anxiety to a degree as she forced herself to get up.

Pulling on her chenille robe, she slowly made her way into the living room. Morgan was sitting on the couch near the stove, one of the family photo albums spread open across his lap. The light from the nearby floor lamp deepened and emphasized the ruggedness of his features. How much she loved him! Her heart pounded with the knowledge as she stood absorbing his strong, powerful presence back into her life.

He must have sensed she was up because suddenly his chin lifted and his gray eyes narrowed on her. Laura managed a broken smile. Almost instantly, he was on his feet, striding toward her, an anxious look replacing the intent concentration of moments before. Without speaking, he gripped her by her upper arms and assessed her.

"How are you feeling?" he asked huskily after a few moments' study.

"A little out of sorts," Laura whispered, allowing her hands to rest on his arms. "Is it true, Morgan? Or did I make it up or dream it?"

"What?" Morgan saw the fragility in her eyes and heard it in her low, husky voice.

"That you remember...us? The children?"

He smiled a little. "Yeah, everything came back this morning when I was looking for you, Little Swan."

Laura swayed. Closing her eyes, she felt his grip tighten on her arms. "Little Swan" was Morgan's special endearment for her. Tears threatened to choke her. "Oh," she whispered unsteadily, smiling up at him, "you do remember. You really do...."

Whispering her name, Morgan brought Laura into his arms and held her gently against him, kissing her mussed hair. "I really do," he assured her gruffly. "You're my Little Swan with the long, beautiful neck and the grace of a ballerina." He buried his face in her hair. "God," he rasped, "I love you so much, Laura. So much it hurts." His embrace tightened, and he felt her tremble violently, once, at his admission. He managed a choked laugh. "In fact, I'm afraid you're going to get sick and tired of me telling you how much I love you."

"N-no," Laura quavered, sliding her arms around his waist, "I'll never get enough of you telling me that, Morgan. Not ever..."

Gently, he placed his hand against the clean line of her jaw and guided her lips to his. It was so natural, so easy between them, to cover her lips and feel the softness that had always been her—to feel her tentative response to his mouth taking hers. But Morgan was aware of her fragile state more than ever. Even the way she returned his kiss was hesitant. Because of the rape? Because she thought he was Garcia and was unable to separate them? Right now, it didn't matter to Morgan. All Laura had to understand was that he was back. He was home, finally—for her and their children.

Easing his mouth from her lips, he smiled deeply

into her lustrous eyes. "I love you," he said thickly. "And no matter what's happened, Laura, I'll always love you." He threaded his fingers through her tangled blond hair. "That's never going to change, Little Swan, so no matter what you're feeling, or what hell we still have to walk through together, never let go of that fact. All right?"

Laura nodded, her hands resting against his massive chest. "All right."

"Do you believe me?"

She smiled a little. "I believe you, Morgan."

"Good," he said, satisfied. "Then let's get you a bath. From here on out, you're number one in this marriage, not number two. That's changing as of this moment."

Laura had no idea what Morgan was talking about, but she found out soon enough. Not only did he draw her a tub of hot water with her favorite orange crystals in it, he washed her hair for her. When they had first been married, Morgan had done that for her from time to time, and Laura had loved it. She had luxuriated in his care of her—and now she got to do so again. Completely surprised by the change in him, she reeled a little in shock from it all. But Morgan pressed on, making her a late dinner of T-bone steak, mashed potatoes and salad. Though she didn't feel very hungry, he sat with her, cajoling each bite of food into her mouth and not allowing her to leave the table until at least half of it had been consumed.

Later, as she lay on the huge sheepskin rug, her

back to the warmth of the stove and only the flickering of the flames lighting the cabin, Laura felt hope trickling back into her heart. Morgan had provided a pillow for her head, and it felt good just to lie on the rug and be warm and safe—and loved. He was washing the dishes, and the pleasant sounds emanating from the kitchen lulled her into a light sleep.

She felt more than heard him coming into the living room. Sleepily, she opened her eyes and saw him sit down, his long legs spread out parallel to her, a piece of chocolate cake with two scoops of vanilla ice cream in hand. A smile played across her lips as she eased into a sitting position.

"There's no secret to you," she teased huskily, pushing her hair away from her face and crossing her legs.

"Any secrets I ever carried, you know about," Morgan said seriously. He dipped the spoon into the ice cream. "Here, have some."

Laura was about to protest, but seeing the glint in his dark eyes she thought better of it. Instead she opened her mouth and allowed Morgan to slide the spoon between her lips. The ice cream was sweet and soothing.

"Mmm, that's good," she admitted gratefully.

He smiled a little. "You need to gain back that twenty pounds you've lost, Laura. You look too much like a prisoner of war."

Moving slowly, Laura propped herself next to him, her back against the couch, her shoulder and hip touching his. The silence was soft and without incrimination as Morgan shared his cake and ice cream with her—a sensual, delicious and unexpected experience for Laura. Sighing softly afterward, she was contented and let Morgan place his arm around her and draw her against him.

"This is heaven," she whispered, sliding her arm around him in return.

"It doesn't get better than this," he agreed thickly, placing a kiss on her hair.

With a shake of her head, Laura said hesitantly, "I feel as if we're starting all over again, Morgan."

Taking her hand and placing it against his thigh, he gently caressed her skin. "In a way we are, Little Swan."

"I'm so scared...."

"So am I." Morgan studied her in the warming silence. "So we'll be scared together, okay?" He was relieved to see the hope burning in her eyes once more. One thing about Laura: she might be strong, and God knew she was a warrior of the first order when it came to fighting for her family, but when she crashed, it was complete. He'd seen her surrender once before, when she'd nearly died after Jason was born. With his help and care, a miracle had taken place within her: she'd rallied, flourishing remarkably well in a short time.

He didn't really expect her to rally so quickly this time, but already he was seeing signs of her responding to him—just as before. Grateful beyond words,

Morgan cupped her face and held her tear-filled gaze. "We have a lot to work through, sweetheart. I know the rapes stand between us, but with therapy for both of us, and working together, we'll one day make all of that a part of our past, too. I've talked to Ann about what rape does to a woman, and she made me see clearly how it affects not only you, but me."

"And our marriage," Laura murmured softly, her fingers digging into the fabric of his shirt.

"Yes. Rape affects everyone." He caressed her flushed cheek. "And neither of us is going to go into denial about it. Ann said it often takes at least a year to get over the worst effects, and time slowly takes care of the rest. I know," he told her somberly, "that I can't make love with you right now. It's impossible for you to emotionally separate what happened from our being together. But one day, Ann said, we will be able to enjoy making love together again, Laura, and it's a day I know will come. I don't care how long it takes. You've got to believe me on that, Little Swan. I didn't marry you just to have you in my bed."

"No?" Her smile was broken and fragile.

"No. Although—" Morgan whispered, kissing her lips tenderly, "it's a natural way to express our love for each other. But there are plenty of other ways I can show my love for you, and vice versa. I see this as an opportunity to explore those other ways."

"I—I don't like separate beds, Morgan."

His smile was very male and very gentle. "No?"

Laura shook her ahead adamantly. "I hated sleeping apart from you. I need you to hold me at night. If you could do that—"

"You just tell me whatever you need, and I'll provide it, Laura," he vowed fiercely. "Ann says we've got to talk, to communicate like never before. I know I haven't been very good at it the past seven years, but I'm going to get good at it now." He brushed the tears from her cheeks. "You know what this whole thing has taught me, Little Swan?"

"No...what?"

"Well, for one thing, that you and our children are more important to me than my work." He shook his head apologetically. "I didn't realize until now how much. I put work before you and our family. But all that's coming to a roaring halt, Laura."

Startled, she studied him in the warm darkness. "What are you talking about?" she whispered unsteadily.

Pressing her against him, Morgan rested his jaw lightly against her hair. "While you were sleeping, I made a lot of decisions, Little Swan. Among them is that I'm going to sell Perseus to the government. They've wanted to buy in as a partner before, but now I'm going to sell them the whole thing. I know I can wrangle a financially sound deal for us, and I'll write operation manuals for them, but beyond that I'm taking a back seat for now.

"We need time to heal. Our children need us, and we need them. When you're ready, we're going to

Jake Randolph's place. He's already agreed to act as liaison between the CIA, which will be purchasing Perseus, and myself. You and I will go up to Oregon, to the Cascade Mountains, and the kids will join us there. We're going to spend the next three months living there—Jake figures it will take at least that long to perform the transition work between the company and the CIA, and he'll stay in D.C. doing it. His Oregon home is big and has plenty of bedrooms. We'll have the privacy we need, too.''

Laura lay against Morgan, almost unable to believe what she was hearing. The gruff emotional quality of Morgan's voice felt like a thick, protective blanket over her rawness. ''I never thought you'd give up Perseus,'' she said finally, after a hushed silence.

''In a way I won't. The government will use my knowledge, tactics and strategies in the manuals I'll continue to write and refine. But most importantly, this change will remove us as a target, and that's what I want.''

Laura could hear Morgan's commitment to her and their family in his fervent voice. She tightened her arms around him briefly. ''I miss the children so much,'' she whispered.

''So do I,'' he rasped. ''I want to hold that little tiger of a son of mine in my arms again, and I want to smell Katherine's fresh, clean scent as I carry her.''

Hope exploded into Laura's heart. The sensation of warmth that followed it was completely unexpected, yet she savored the feeling, greedily absorbing it. ''I like your decisions,'' she said faintly. "I feel like I'm in a waking dream. You don't know how many times I wished you would put your work aside for our family.''

Grimly, Morgan stared out into the darkness, taking in her painful admission. "This is no dream. It's for real, Laura. I've learned my lesson. I can have everything taken away from me: my career, my company, my money. But you know what? The two things I can't live without are you and the children. I'm nothing without you, Little Swan.'' Morgan caressed her cheek and held her luminous gaze, which radiated with a love for him he really didn't feel he deserved.

"I'm the luckiest man in the world, and I didn't know it, Laura. I took advantage of you and the family. I got in over my head, and I went to extremes— and you and the kids paid the price for me. God, what an awful price it was, too....''

Laura closed her eyes, content to be held and protected by Morgan. She knew without saying it, that the work that still lay ahead of them was not going to be easy. She wasn't going to try to fool herself or lie to herself ever again. Too much that was important to her was at stake, and she was willing to make the commitment to work through any amount of pain in order to have a better, more complete life with Morgan and her children.

Easing away from him, she reached out and caressed his scarred face. "What about me not being able to have more children?''

Morgan felt tears fill his eyes as he studied her softly shadowed face and saw the grief there. With his thumb, he gently caressed her cheek. "It doesn't matter," he said thickly. "We're lucky to have a son and daughter, and that's enough for me, Little Swan."

"But...you wanted at least four children. So did I...."

Helplessly, Morgan shrugged. "If that becomes important to us again, Laura, we can always adopt, can't we?" Making a sound of frustration, he sat up and framed her face with his hands. "Listen to me, will you? I love *you*. I need you. I don't need you because you can have my children, all right? I didn't marry you or fall in love with you because you could have children, Laura. That happened to be a nice by-product of what we shared, and I'm thankful for our family, but I'm content with two children. We love them with our lives, and I'm the luckiest bastard in the world right now, Laura. I've got you, Jason and Katherine. I'm more than fulfilled. I've got it all."

Laura believed him. She felt the truth of his words to the depths of her soul. Sliding her hands across his, she managed a tremulous smile. "I like the two we have, too, darling. And no, I don't need four children. I just thought you wanted them...."

"Partly because I didn't talk clearly with you about it," he growled unhappily. "But you see? Talking is already removing some of the barriers between us, Laura. So maybe now things don't seem as bad to you as they once did? We have the two best kids in the world already, as far as I'm concerned.''

Smiling, she nodded. ''I believe you. I really do.''

Relieved, Morgan grinned. ''Good. What do you say we go to bed? I don't know about you, but I'm beat to hell. This is one day I'm glad is behind us. All I want to do,'' he said thickly as he caressed her hair, ''is to lie in that narrow bed with you in my arms. What do you say, Little Swan? Does that sound good to you, too?''

Did it ever. Smiling tenderly, Laura allowed him to help her rise to her bare feet. She relaxed in his arms, a contentment she never thought possible filling her as he held her in a tight embrace.

''I love you, Morgan,'' she murmured.

Seeking and finding her lips, he kissed her hotly, letting her know just how fiercely he loved her in return. This time, Laura responded in kind, and he felt the strength of her mouth, the fire of her as a woman. Tearing his mouth from hers, his breathing ragged and his heart pounding like a sledgehammer in his chest, he rasped against her ear, ''And I'll love you forever, Laura.''

Chapter 13

The next morning, Laura awoke to the sound of the cabin door opening and closing several times. She lay alone in their bed, hearing Mike Houston's low voice, then Morgan's responding. Their footsteps echoed hollowly on the pine floor, and she wondered why there was so much activity. Sitting up, she was shocked to see it was nearly eleven o'clock. She'd overslept!

As she hurriedly got out of bed and donned her robe, she heard the door close once more. Quiet descended on the cabin again. As she opened the door to the living room, she saw Morgan carrying something to the kitchen in his arms. Peripherally aware of the fragrant smells of coffee perking and bacon frying, she realized she actually felt hungry as she followed Morgan into the kitchen. He was busy cooking, and a huge pile of magazines was stacked on the table near her waiting plate. Standing in the doorway, she saw him turn in surprise.

"You're up."

She smiled a little drowsily and pushed several strands of hair off her brow. "Finally."

Morgan came over and slid his arms around her, pulling her gently against him. He kissed her silken hair and her temple, then inhaled her womanly fragrance. "Mmm, you not only smell good, but I wonder how you taste?"

Laura smiled beneath his lips as they came to rest against hers. The gentle strength of Morgan's mouth was more healing than he could ever realize. She kissed him back, sliding her arms around his neck. As they eased out of the kiss, she smiled up into his smoky gray eyes, which burned with obvious desire for her.

"What was all that noise about? I know I heard Mike's voice. Is something wrong?"

Morgan led her to the kitchen table and sat her down where he'd laid out a sunflower place mat, a plate and flatware earlier. "No," he replied as he returned to the stove, "it was just an idea whose time was way overdue." He quickly scooped scrambled eggs and bacon from two different skillets and placed them on her plate. Popping two slices of bread into the toaster, he gave her a triumphant smile.

Laura began to eat, surprised to find she felt ravenous. Morgan had that devilish look glinting in his eyes, and she knew he was up to something. He came and sat next to her, his elbows propped on the table. ''What idea?'' she asked suspiciously.

He pointed to the huge stack of magazines. ''I had Mike go into Sedona and buy a lot of different magazines this morning and bring them out for us.'' He frowned, suddenly serious, and held her gaze. ''I remember when we were first married and you told me how you'd been adopted by your Marine Corps father and mother. You told me he'd been born in the Colorado Rockies and that you'd always wanted to live there someday. You told me how, as a child, you bought a scrapbook with your allowance and called it your 'Book of Dreams.' You would cut out pictures from magazines and paste them in the scrapbook— pictures of the mountains and log cabins, in hopes of someday making your dreams come true.''

Laura sipped the coffee. She set it down and smiled softly. ''Yes, I remember telling you about my 'Book of Dreams.'''

''You put all kinds of things into that scrapbook over the years.''

Laughing lightly, Laura nodded. ''I certainly did. I don't know how many times I toted it out and sat with my mother or father, talking over what my future husband would look like, how many kids we'd have and what they'd look like or where we were going to live.'' With a shake of her head, she murmured, ''I wonder if they ever got tired of me going over and over those things I'd pasted in that scrapbook.''

"I doubt it, Little Swan." Morgan reached out and captured her hand briefly. "And neither will I. Because that's what we're going to do for the next few days. You're going to create a new 'Book of Dreams' and tell me about everything you put in it." Triumphantly, he set a bottle of glue and a pair of scissors in front of her plate. "After you're done eating and have had a chance to shower and dress, you and I are going to sit here and do it. Together."

Tears flooded Laura's eyes as she looked at the raw hope on Morgan's face, heard his voice waver with deep feeling. "Oh, Morgan, that's such a beautiful idea...."

"It's more than that," he told her gruffly, squeezing her hand a little more tightly. "It's going to be my SOP—standard operating procedures—with you. It's time your dreams got explored, don't you think?"

Shaken, Laura was momentarily unable to speak. Her life had always centered around making Morgan and the children happy, not herself. But all that seemed to be changing—radically and suddenly. "Well," she stuttered, "but—but what are you going to do with whatever dreams I might put into this scrapbook?"

Morgan's smile was very confident and filled with love as he said, "I'm going to make them come true."

* * *

At the end of three days, Laura's new "Book of Dreams" was completed to her satisfaction. As she and Morgan sat at the kitchen table, the radio playing softly in the background, she watched him for a reaction. He'd said very little during the past days, except to occasionally nod his head or make sure she had more magazines if she needed them. Now, as they sat down in the late afternoon, coffee in hand, to discuss what she'd cut out, she felt an unbidden excitement.

"Okay, let's take a look at the final product," he murmured as he pulled the scrapbook to him. Opening it, he studied the first page. On it was a huge, beautiful, cedar-log home. Laura had also found some pine trees from another magazine and glued them in around it.

"There's more to this landscape," she said tentatively. "I just ran out of room on the first page."

He smiled a little and turned the page. On the second spread was a huge vegetable path and next to it, a wildflower garden. On the third page, he saw the rugged Rocky Mountains as a backdrop to two children playing happily by a stream, surrounded by tall rushes and wildflowers. On the next page two people, a man and woman, stood arm-in-arm on a grassy knoll watching a peach-colored sunset.

Laura sat very still, her hands clasped tightly in her lap, watching every emotion register clearly on Morgan's battered face as he slowly leafed through page after page. She could literally feel him digesting the dreams she'd cut out and pasted on those pages. Why was she so nervous? So afraid? Deep down, she had come to realize that Morgan was right: after seven years of living for him and their children, she'd never really learned to live for herself. In the wake of their latest revelations, Laura had realized more each day how much she needed time and creative expression to live out her life according to her own inner, spiritual needs. Morgan had told her repeatedly that the balance of power had shifted in their marriage—to her. But how was he going to accomplish that, beyond selling Perseus?

"All right," he said gruffly, "I think I've got a fair idea of what you need." He looked up and studied her shadowed blue gaze, seeing the tension around her mouth. He knew Laura was still wary of his promises to change, and he didn't blame her. "Rachel was telling me of a woman architect who lives here, in Oak Creek. She's world famous for the homes she designs. What do you say we make an appointment to see her and discuss the building of this cedar home for us?"

Laura's mouth fell open and she gaped at him. "But...where?"

Giving a lazy shrug, Morgan let a sliver of a grin leak through his serious demeanor. Taking her hand and holding it in his, he said, "What you didn't know is that I've been in touch with Wolf Harding. You know he owns Blue Mountain up in Philipsburg, Montana. Sarah, his wife, mines sapphires, and they

live on one side of it.'' His grip tightened. ''Wolf and
Sarah are willing to sell us half of Blue Mountain, so
we can build that Rocky Mountain dream home of
yours. What do you think of that?''

Again, Laura was rocked by Morgan's decisions.
She could only stare, but her heart was racing with
joy. His gray eyes looked so grave, but she saw the
glint in them, too, that proved he meant what he was
saying. ''Oh…'' she whispered, touching her throat
with her fingertips.

''*Oh?* As in, oh, that's a great idea? Or, oh, Morgan, that's a terrible idea?''

Laura felt the sunlight of his smile radiating upon
her, and she offered him a full-wattage grin in return.
''It's a wonderful idea, Morgan! You really bought a
mountain in Montana?''

''Yes.'' At the incredible pleasure in Laura's eyes,
Morgan's heart expanded like a flower opening.
Never had he felt as good as he did right now. The
new life in Laura's eyes was something to behold,
and the hope clearly written there rocked him as little
else could. Finally, he was beginning to grasp just
how much of her life had been given to him at the
expense of herself. But now that they were truly becoming equal partners in the relationship, Morgan
found it far more satisfying than what they'd shared
before.

''Oh,'' Laura whispered, tears filling her eyes. ''A
real mountain.''

''Yup, just like the one in here.'' And he opened

to the page in her "Book of Dreams" that pictured a white-topped mountain swathed in the green of fir trees. "Wolf and Sarah understood what we needed. They didn't have to sell us the other half of their mountain, but they did."

"But Sarah makes their living off the sapphires. Won't we be taking away half their ability to make money by buying half their property?"

Morgan shook his head. "No. What you don't know is that Sarah just found an incredible deposit of cornflower blue sapphires—the biggest one is some fifty carats—and basically, they're set for life with this find."

"Wonderful!" Laura whispered, meaning it. She knew how hard Wolf and Sarah had struggled to make ends meet—Wolf working as a forest ranger and Sarah continuing her sapphire mining, faceting her finds and selling them to jewelry distributors. "They really deserve this kind of a break."

"Yes," Morgan agreed, "they do. Now maybe they can focus on other important things in their marriage."

"I know they both wanted children," Laura said. She rallied gamely, though reminded that she could never have them again herself. "They deserve every happiness."

Leaning over, Morgan kissed the back of her hand. "No question about that. So, how do think you'll like your new home, Mrs. Trayhern? Will a Philipsburg, Montana, address help fulfill your dreams?"

Her lower lip quivered. "Yes," she whispered, "it's a dream come true, Morgan. I just don't believe it. I never thought—"

"Good," he rumbled, satisfied. "Let me call this woman architect. We've got some designing to do. If we're lucky, we'll get things set in motion. In a couple of days, we can fly to the Cascades and set up temporary housekeeping at Jake's cabin. Then we'll have the kids flown out to be with us."

Laura nodded, overwhelmed. Finally, she managed to say in a broken whisper, "We'll be a family again...."

Morgan lay in bed with Laura in his arms. It was barely dawn at Jake's cabin in the pristine wilderness of the Cascade Range of central Oregon. Laura's warmth felt damn good to him. How he looked forward each night to sharing this bed with her. Had three months fled by already? He keyed his hearing to the room next door, where the children were sleeping soundly. Jason would wake up around seven, he knew, and little Katherine would follow shortly. Then the day's chaotic but fulfilling events would begin. But right now, it was only five-thirty, plenty of time to savor the silence—and Laura.

A sweet longing filled Morgan, as it always did when he awoke at this time of morning. In some ways the past three months had been like a visit to hell, in other ways, heaven. The children had finally settled in, and Morgan was amazed at their resiliency, con-

sidering the toll that had been taken. Even more profound was the fact that Jason, who'd been showing
hyperactive symptoms, was calming down, and it was
now that Morgan honestly began to see the cost to
his family. Jason was reacting to the stress Morgan
had always brought home with him from Perseus. The
little boy picked up on his worries like all-terrain radar.

Little Katherine, who'd been still being breast-fed
at the time of the kidnapping, was sleeping much better, too. She had been through nights where she'd
wake up screaming—for no reason. Here at the cabin,
Katherine was finally sleeping soundly through the
nights, and Morgan knew Laura was especially grateful, since she was usually the one to get up and go
to her.

Chickadees began chirping outside the window,
and somewhere, far off, the high, warning shriek of
a blue jay could he heard. Morgan thought it was
probably reacting to the old cougar that lived about
ten miles from the cabin, high in the cliffs where there
was a cave. He and Laura hadn't been able to do
much hiking yet, because of the weather, but with
winter's hold on the mountains finally breaking,
spring flowers were beginning to dot the surrounding
landscape.

Laura… A pain filled him, along with a fear. They
still hadn't been able to make love—because of the
damnable rapes. Morgan found himself hating Garcia
more every day. Dr. Parsons had warned him about

Laura's on-again, off-again ability to be touched, kissed, held or loved. With the children underfoot, the possibility of lovemaking had become strictly a nighttime affair, and Laura was still recovering from the trauma, desperately needing all the sleep she could get.

Morgan tried to take on some of the mothering role so Laura didn't have the pressure of caring for the children twenty-four hours a day. He was learning in no uncertain terms that being a housewife was a damned demanding and drudgery-filled job—and his admiration for Laura had increased tenfold as a result. His taking over half the family duties had brought them all much closer together as a unit, too, in a way that wouldn't have happened if he hadn't sold his business. In a perverse way, Morgan liked the change. He'd never realized the extent of the toll on him, until he'd gotten far away from the intense demands of Perseus.

Laura moved in his arms, her brow resting against his jaw. Her breathing was soft and shallow, and he could feel her stirring from sleep. Moving his hand along her slender arm, he felt the softness of her skin, the curve of her body fitting against his. The silk of her hair tickled his lips, and he smiled lazily as she pressed her full length against him like a cat stretching languidly. A part of him was scared to death of her rejection—once again—should he try to love her. But Ann had said to remain intimate with Laura on as deep a level as she could tolerate.

That was the frustration, he thought, as he eased Laura onto her back, his arm beneath her neck and cradling her shoulders. Neither he nor Laura knew when her rape trauma would rear its ugly head. Sometimes it was when he was kissing her. Other times, when he caressed her breast. Or, if he became too aggressive, she would instantly freeze and push him away. The worst was the look of terror in her eyes. It made Morgan feel like a bastard, and his emotions would flash to an overriding anger—toward Garcia. It was as if the drug kingpin was here, standing between them at their most intimate times together, and Morgan could taste his hatred for the evil man and what he'd done to Laura.

So he'd learned to go slow and easy, which wasn't all that hard for him. Morgan missed those times of passionate spontaneity he'd once shared with Laura. But if he grieved silently for that aspect of their old relationship, he never told her, because he didn't want to hurt or worry her.

Still, Morgan had seen progress in the intimacy they'd gradually established. The first month he'd learned not to play the rejected husband. Laura could no more help her flashbacks, or that out-of-body sensation that sometimes drove a wedge between them, than he could his occasional nightmares where he relived the horrors of that Vietnam hill. He watched now as Laura sleepily lifted her lashes to reveal smoky blue eyes. Smiling, he leaned over and caressed her parted lips. She tasted sweet and soft beneath his exploration, and he felt her moan, her arms sliding around his shoulders in invitation.

Her lips parted even more, and, feeling her hips move against his hardness, he groaned. Her silky hair swirled across her shoulder as he lifted the thick strands, easing his fingers across the top of her head in a gentle, kneading motion. Nothing relaxed her more than his combing her hair or gently massaging her scalp, he'd discovered. Another part of him waited with bated breath to be shoved away, or to feel her stiffen awkwardly in his arms—her nonverbal request, asking him to stop. How he wanted to love her completely! The ache in his loins burned through him as he allowed his hand to range tentatively down her arm to her waist.

Her skin was soft and giving as he cupped her hip and brought her against him. It was then that he felt her stiffen. It was nothing obvious, but mentally he cursed, placing a tight rein on his own raging needs. As he eased his mouth from hers, he opened his eyes and looked into hers. They were wide again—with fear. Dammit, anyway!

"Morgan," Laura began softly, "I'm—"

"Don't say it," he exclaimed harshly, easing away from her and sitting up. "You don't have to apologize, Laura." And she didn't. It wasn't her fault. He saw her crestfallen look, disappointment joining the guilt in her expression. He couldn't be impatient or angry under these circumstances, and he didn't want her to think he was upset with her. "Come here," he murmured, pulling her gently against him.

She came without a word, resting against his naked form, her head against his shoulder, her arm around his waist.

"That's better," Morgan murmured against her hair. He pressed a kiss to it and held her a little tighter for a moment.

"It was so wonderful, like before," Laura said in a whisper. "And when you touched my hip, I had this awful flashback, Morgan." She squeezed her eyes shut and pressed her cheek against his warm, strong shoulder. Biting back the words of apology, knowing they would only upset Morgan, she concentrated instead on the sensation of his hand moving slowly up and down the curve of her arm. The massive pounding of his heart told her how badly he wanted her. And she wanted him, too! At least, her heart did, though her mind seemed to control everything—including the flashbacks that came between them, chilling her ardor, preventing her from loving him physically.

"Listen," Morgan said gruffly, "I'm beginning to realize that rape is like war. They're one and the same." He caressed her slender jaw and looked deeply into her worried eyes. "You remember how many times when we were making love I'd have a PTSD flashback to Vietnam?"

"Yes," Laura said with a grimace.

"And how those flashbacks interrupted our love-making?"

"You're right, they did. I hadn't thought about it."

"Because," Morgan said gently, "over the years the flashbacks diminished, intruding less and less on us."

Laura felt hope spring up in her breast. "Yes, that's right, they did."

"So," he whispered, caressing her hair and placing a kiss on her brow, "this is no different. You didn't get angry with me for my flashback."

"No, but you felt bad about it coming between us."

"Yes," he admitted heavily, "I did. You went un-fulfilled."

"So did you," she noted wryly, content to be held by him forever. Did Morgan realize how strong he was for her? It was more than just his physical size and strength—it was the strength of his heart, and his support of her.

The phone rang.

Morgan groaned and reluctantly released Laura. The phone didn't ring often, and when it did, he made a point to answer it, because it was usually Mike Houston with information they needed. Had they found that second hit man? He fervently hoped so as he shrugged on his terry-cloth robe and moved quickly into the living room to the phone.

Laura sat up in bed, ran her fingers through her mussed hair and decided she might as well get up, too. The mood had been spoiled anyway. She heard Morgan answer the phone tersely, followed by the usual grunts of ''yes'' or ''no'' that she'd heard so many times before. Retrieving her robe, she slipped it on over her silky pink nightgown and went to the bathroom.

She was filling the tub with water when Morgan entered the bathroom, an odd expression on his face as he shut the door behind him.

''Who was calling?'' she asked, taking the jar of orange-scented crystals from the vanity.

''It was Mike.''

Laura opened the jar and sprinkled a handful of crystals into the water. ''What's up?''

Morgan leaned against the door, his hands in the pockets of his robe as he watched her. ''Good news.''

''Oh?'' She set the jar back on the vanity and gathered up her hair with a pink ribbon so it would be off her neck.

''Yeah, the CIA just called Mike. Garcia was flying to Bogotá, Colombia, with thirty other powerful drug lords from around South America for a big meeting.'' He smiled a little. ''The plane carrying them blew up in midair halfway to their destination.'' Morgan saw Laura's eyes go wide with shock, and she stood very still.

''Then—''

''He's dead. The whole lot of them are dead. There were no survivors, according to Colombian officials.'' Morgan snapped his fingers. ''Just like that, all those bastards went up in a puff of smoke.'' His smile was savage and filled with satisfaction.

A chill went through Laura as she stood considering the news. "He's dead...." Garcia, her rapist, was dead. Somehow, the idea was liberating, and for a moment she felt guilty that she was glad he was no longer alive. It wasn't like her to wish anyone dead. Ever. At times, in sessions with Dr. Downey, she'd confided with great guilt that she'd like to kill Garcia herself for what he'd done to her. Laura hadn't felt good about admitting it, but Pallas had assured her it was a healthy, normal reaction.

Morgan moved over to Laura and pulled her into his arms. "You okay? You're a little pale."

She closed her eyes and sank willingly against him. His arms were strong and supportive, and right now, she needed that sensation. Slipping her own arms around him, she pressed her face against his robed chest. "I'm okay...just...in shock, I guess."

"It couldn't have happened to a nicer bunch," he growled, easing his fingers across her jaw. "Mike also said they caught the second hit man in New Orleans. He's in jail now, awaiting deportation."

"Thank God," Laura whispered, feeling even more weight falling from her shoulders. She hadn't realized until now how much tension she still carried in them. As if sensing her thoughts, Morgan began running his large hand slowly across her shoulders.

"We're free," he told her. "Really free, now. With all the major drug lords dead, the underlings will be scrambling to take over and rebuild their empires. They're going to be too busy in their own backyards to come after us again.''

''You really think that, Morgan?''

''Yes, I do.'' He eased her away, dropping a quick kiss on her parted lips, and smiled down at her. ''The CIA will take advantage of this shift of power. Mike said he's going to fly back down to Peru and help them create continued chaos in the drug industry—to try to stop it from re-forming, or at least from re-forming too quickly.''

''But,'' she protested, ''what about Ann? They're in love with each other! What will she do?''

''Mike said Ann's going down with him. She's submitting her resignation to the CIA and quitting Perseus.'' He smiled a little. ''Mike's head over heels in love with her, and they're going to set up house-keeping in Lima, Peru. He'll be working with the Peruvian government at the capital, and Ann's going to start working with the city's poor, because doctors are always needed there.''

''Will they be in danger, though?''

''Some,'' Morgan admitted, gently tracing the outline of one of her arched eyebrows. ''They know the risks, Little Swan. They'll take steps to protect themselves.''

''I'm so happy for them,'' she murmured. ''Ann deserves someone like Mike. He's a neat guy—'' she looked up at him, smiling ''—like you.''

Morgan cherished her lips, and felt her returning

ardor as he absorbed her feminine form against him. The air was moist and filled with the fragrance of orange blossoms. "There's just something about us old, battered warriors, eh?" he teased as she moved from his embrace to shut off the water in the tub.

Laura removed her robe and hung it on a hook. "Yes, there's something very sexy, dangerous and provocative about you warriors," she teased in return, meeting his very male smile. She saw the desire smoldering in his eyes as she eased the nightgown over her head.

"Come on," she entreated, stepping into the oversize tub. "Join me?"

Morgan groaned. "The water smells like perfume."

With a lilting laugh, Laura held out her hand. "Oh? Big, bad old warriors can't stand a little perfumed water every once in a while? Really, Morgan, being a man doesn't mean you can't smell good."

"There's a difference between man smells and woman smells," he muttered defiantly, shedding his robe. He saw the impish quality dancing in Laura's eyes as he gripped her outstretched hand.

"Who knows?" she said, baiting him. "Something good might happen when we take a bath together. It's a new experience—why not try it? I thought you warriors were always up for new adventures."

Stepping into the warm water, Morgan grinned. A decided difference had come into Laura after hearing the news about Garcia. Maybe, just maybe, it would help her continue to get well—to know that the person who had victimized her had gotten his just reward. The gold flecks were back in her eyes, and for that Morgan was grateful. It was the first time he'd seen those shining sunlit flecks in far too long.

As they lowered themselves into the steamy, scented water, Morgan held Laura's returning smile as she picked up the soap. Life was getting better— one day at a time, one hour at a time—just as Dr. Parsons had promised. Right now, their new home was being built by contractors on Blue Mountain in Montana. By June, they would be moved in. The future seemed suddenly brighter and happier than ever before to Morgan, and a fierce love swept through him as Laura moved to his side and began to provocatively slide the lathered soap across his shoulders and chest. In that moment, he knew without doubt that his marriage was whole again, and there would be no other woman for him ever but Laura.

Epilogue

"Look, Morgan!" Laura called from where she crouched in her wildflower garden. "Come and look."

He stood on the sun deck of their Montana home, his hands deep in the pockets of his Levi's. Jason and Katherine were helping their mother weed the garden, which bloomed in colorful profusion on the eastern side of their new home. Laura's face shone with joy, her once-pale skin turned a golden tan from her many hours in the sun spent working not only on her huge, oval flower garden, but on an even bigger vegetable patch.

Where had the past fifteen months fled since the fateful day when he'd found her unconscious on that trail? Morgan hesitated a moment on the deck, simply enjoying the sight of his family busily working together on a project they all loved. Since that day at the Donovan Ranch, Morgan had never regretted a single one of the major, life-altering decisions he'd made. His love for Laura and his children and their safety was more important to him than anything else in the world.

The warmth of the wood railing felt good beneath his callused palms as he leaned over to watch his family. Jason, the very active seven-year-old that he now was, rushed up and down the rows, picking at a weed here and a weed there, unconcerned about being thorough. Meanwhile, Katherine worked at Laura's side as they eliminated every last little weed among the brilliant, blooming flowers.

The straw hat Laura wore to protect her face made her look like an old Victorian print, Morgan thought. She wore a loose, summery white blouse and baggy, light blue trousers that had seen better days. But it was the smile always hovering around her lips that sent his heart pounding and made his lower body tighten instantly every time. Katherine liked coveralls, bright-colored ones, especially, and her blond hair was in tiny braids, the red ribbons matching the flush on her cheeks. Yes, Katherine decidedly took after Laura, while Jason was the spitting image of himself.

Running his hand distractedly across the smooth cedar rail, Morgan sighed. Nothing had made him happier in his life than seeing Laura cry with absolute joy when he'd flown her to Montana, and then driven her and the children to Blue Mountain to see their newly designed home. Stately Douglas firs rose nearly a hundred feet high all around them, and they'd walked the pine-scented land for many days, planning the details for her gardens. It was there that the final miracle had occurred, and Morgan had seen the last of the depression and terror lift from Laura.

He continued to write operation manuals for the government based on the exploits of Perseus teams over the years. To his own surprise, impressed by the accuracy of the manuals, twenty-five other democratic countries had signed up to make use of his world-class knowledge, and the price he charged as a consultant was high. High enough to give Laura her dream home, put money away for their children's college education and never have to worry about their golden years again.

Because of Laura's background as a military and technical writer, she'd easily fallen into helping him almost daily on the writing and rewriting of the manuals. They'd become a good team in so many new and satisfying ways that he'd never even dreamed of before. No longer was he an absentee parent, either. He was home every day, sharing the child-raising duties and house-related chores with Laura.

Morgan straightened and rubbed his hands on his jeans. The laughter and joy drifting up from the garden made him smile. In fifteen months there had been such a positive change in all of them. Looking up at the fir trees that embraced the house from a distance, he inhaled the fresh air into his lungs.

They were safe now. No longer would a drug cartel come after them. As a matter of fact, it had been Culver Lachlan, the Peruvian government and Major Mike Houston who had combined resources to eradicate the scrambling drug underlings to such a degree that their iron-fisted hold on Peru had been destroyed.

The other good news was that Mike Houston had married Ann Parsons a year ago. Now Ann was pregnant with their first child while she continued to work with Lima's poor in setting up free medical clinics. They were one happy couple, and Morgan wanted only the best for them.

With a shake of his head, he walked down the steps. His family was healing finally, and for the first time since his days in Vietnam, he was happier than he could ever recall. The sound of a car engine caught his attention and he looked up to see a blue Chevy Blazer driving slowly up their road. It was Wolf and Sarah Harding, come to take the children to Wolf's favorite swimming hole. Morgan lifted his hand in greeting as the couple pulled into the driveway. He'd never seen Wolf happier, either; Sarah was decidedly pregnant, and the homeopathic doctor from Philipsburg, Michaela, had told her she was going to have twins!

Morgan watched Laura stand when she saw Wolf and Sarah walking toward them. He felt warm inside as her smile blossomed. She raised her hand as the children raced to the gate, then past it toward their honorary "aunt" and "uncle." Having good friends on the other side of the mountain had helped all of them enormously, too, Morgan acknowledged.

Jason picked up a nearby knapsack packed with their swimming suits, towels and a lunch, and continued toward the Blazer. Katherine was a little more circumspect, running on her short, spindly legs, her hands opened wide. Sarah laughed and crouched down to hug the little girl while Jason got swept up by Wolf, who settled the boy on his shoulders.

It was a weekly tradition now, and Morgan was grateful to Wolf and Sarah. Without them playing baby-sitter, he and Laura would have been hard put to make the time they needed to sort out the deep, emotional problems created by Laura's rapes. Sarah had single-handedly come in and laid down the law to them very early on, telling them that under no circumstances were they going to heal properly without some quality time alone together.

So once a week, Wolf and she came and picked up the kids, planning a day with numerous activities such as swimming, hiking, going to Anaconda or in some way making healthy, educational fun for them. Jason and Katherine would stay overnight with the Hardings and return home the next afternoon.

It was good for the kids, too, Morgan realized as he continued to walk slowly toward Laura, at the gate blowing kisses to the children, who had already climbed into the Blazer, raring to go on their next adventure. Jason and Katherine were being taught independence from their parents at an early age, learning how to be flexible and get along with other people who loved and cared for them. And Wolf and Sarah got to practice their child-rearing skills. It was a plan that had worked well for everyone concerned.

As Morgan reached the gate where Laura stood, he saw her lift her chin. The straw hat shaded her face but didn't hide the flush across her cheeks. Her blond hair, although gathered in a ponytail, had escaped in tendrils that clung damply to her golden skin. The temperature was in the eighties today—hot for this part of the Rockies.

"I don't know who's more excited by these once-a-week adventures," Morgan said with a chuckle, watching Wolf back the Blazer out of the driveway.

Laura slid her arm around Morgan's waist. She smiled softly and leaned against his tall, proud frame. "Me, neither."

He removed her hat and kissed her brow. "Are you ready for your surprise?"

Her eyes shone as she turned in his arms. "I love these times," she said huskily, absorbing his male smile. "And I love you, too...."

Morgan leaned down and pressed a quick kiss to her mouth. He wanted more. So much more. "Come on," he rasped, "I've got everything packed. All I need is you."

Blue Mountain was more a dream manifested into reality than anything else, Morgan had decided a long time ago. They walked hand in hand down a deer trail that cut diagonally across the mountain. Laura had changed into a pale pink blouse and long navy rayon skirt dotted with tiny pink rosebuds. She wore sandals, since Morgan had told her the surprise wasn't far away and hiking boots wouldn't be necessary, though he carried a large pack on his shoulders.

Once a week, he planned these "surprises," all of them designed to get Laura and him away where they could be alone and intimate. Over the past year, the rape issue had remained between them like an insurmountable wall, but gradually, as Dr. Parsons had promised, with intensive therapy and Morgan's help and understanding, the wall had been dissolving. It hadn't been easy on either of them. Morgan hadn't realized the pervasive and murderous effects of the rape not only on Laura, but on him, as well. What had been taken from Laura had also been taken from him, and he'd had to deal with the rage and helplessness of that knowledge.

Now Laura looked forward to these times as much as he did. If they felt like making love, they would— to the extent that Laura's flashbacks would allow. Morgan had been taught that intimacy was more than just sex. It was about talking, caring and being sensitive to Laura's needs. It was about touching and holding, too. He'd had to work a lot on that angle of himself, and he was admittedly far better off with these new aspects of himself, because they allowed him to appreciate and enjoy Laura more fully than ever before.

"Okay," he said, tugging gently on her hand and drawing her to a halt, "we have to stop here, and I need to blindfold you."

Laura laughed gaily. "Oh, Morgan, I'll keep my eyes shut. I promise!"

He grinned and shook his head. "No way. Last week," he said, pulling a scarf from his pocket, "you said you wouldn't look and you did." He gestured for her to turn around. They stood on a small knoll, surrounded by firs.

Pouting playfully, Laura turned obediently, her laughter breathy and filled with excitement. "I tripped, Morgan! I had to open my eyes. It was a natural thing to do."

Chuckling, he slipped the scarf across her eyes and knotted it carefully behind her head. "Well, there are no rocks on the path, so you can't use that excuse this time." He caught her small hand in his. "Come on, I'll help you." Unable to keep the excitement out of his voice, he guided her down the trail.

"You said I've never been where we're going?"

"That's right," he said, leading her carefully, watching the steep trail in front of him as it wound sharply downward. "Now, it's pretty steep here, Laura, so don't hurry." She was like an excited child, reminding him of Jason at the moment, barely able to contain her joy.

"Oh, Morgan!" She burst into laughter. "We

aren't very far from our house. I must have been here!''

"No," he growled. "You think you know Blue Mountain, but this is one place I discovered when you and the kids were shopping in Anaconda for school clothes.''

"Hmm," Laura whispered, taking small steps down the trail. "I hear water!"

"Ears like a wolf, eyes like an owl," he teased. At the bottom of the path, he eased around her and whispered, "All right, I'm going to take the scarf off. Are you ready?"

"Oh, hurry, Morgan! I can hear water, and to tell the truth, I need a bath!"

"Now—" he grinned "—I wouldn't say that." He unknotted the scarf, enjoying touching the thick tendrils of her blond hair in the process.

"You need one, too," she reminded him archly, shifting from foot to foot.

"Thanks," he retorted, laughing fully as he removed the blindfold.

Laura's eyes widened enormously and her hands flew to her lips. "Oh!" A small stream meandered around the base of Blue Mountain, and in one spot it widened to create the perfect swimming hole, with a meadow filled with wildflowers on the opposite bank. The meadow was small by Montana standards, but to Laura it was like a fairy-tale painting from a children's book, nearly knee-deep with grass and colorful blossoms.

"It's so beautiful," she exclaimed as she turned and looked up at Morgan. She saw the pleased look in his eyes and felt herself respond effortlessly to his powerful masculine presence. He stood with his hands draped casually on his narrow hips, a proud smile playing at the corners of his mouth.

"It's like you, Little Swan," he whispered, taking her into his arms and pressing her against him. She relaxed instantly, her head resting on his shoulder as he enclosed her in his arms.

"I feel like this meadow," she confided, her voice quavering with emotion. "I feel abundant, blossoming...." She twisted to look up at him. "I suppose you're going to say something like, yes, you are a blooming idiot."

Chuckling, he pressed a kiss to her temple. "You hurt my feelings, Little Swan."

"I saw that teasing look in your eyes," she said, elbowing him gently in the ribs. "Don't forget, I can almost read your mind at times, Morgan Trayhern. Eight and a half years of marriage gives me that ability."

Morgan couldn't argue. He was always amazed at Laura's intuitive ability, not only with him, but with their children as well. Grinning, he nipped her earlobe. She dodged away, laughing, but he kept her captive within his embrace.

Turning around in his arms, Laura smiled up at him as she slid her arms around his neck. "Let's go for a swim! I'm so sweaty, and so are you."

Arching his eyebrows, he murmured, "I didn't bring any swimming suits."

Hitting him playfully in the shoulder, Laura said, "Of course you wouldn't. You men are all alike."

Pretending hurt, he released her. Laura found a nice grassy place a few feet away from him and began to undress. "I can't remember everything," he said, unbuttoning his shirt, his gaze never leaving her. Everything Laura did was graceful. He would never tire of watching her. Her blouse dropped away and he was pleased to see she wasn't wearing a bra beneath it. The skirt was next. In seconds she stood proudly naked before him, her eyes half-closed, a sultry, teasing smile on her lips.

"I may have forgotten the swimsuits," Morgan said, his voice husky as he dropped his shirt in the grass, "but I think you forgot a few things, too."

Laughing impishly, she raised her arms toward the dark, turquoise sky, languishing in the rays of the sun as it struck her naked skin. "Not that you mind," she said, pirouetting toward him like a ballerina. She enjoyed watching Morgan undress. His old weight had returned, his strength and vitality with it. It hurt her every time she saw those awful scars across his back, but even they were fading with time, for which she was glad.

"Did you bring towels?" she taunted as he, too, stood naked, a burning look in his eyes.

"Sure," he muttered, gesturing to the knapsack. "Towels, a blanket to lie on, wine to drink—later, and food. Besides you, what else is there?'' His mouth curved teasingly as he walked toward her. At that moment, Laura loosened her hair so that it flowed down across her shoulders. Her hair was long now, much longer than he'd ever seen it. The golden strands curled provocatively around her breasts. Something seemed different about her body, but he couldn't quite place what it was. She had lovely breasts, the kind a man could cup, hold and suckle. And even after two children, her waist was small. One of his favorite places to touch was Laura's slightly rounded abdomen. It had a pearlescent quality, and he loved to run his large hand across it, spanning it, feeling the softness and reminding himself that she'd carried two children made from the pure love between them.

"No, you don't!'' Laura cried as she dodged his outstretched hand. With a yell, she leapt into the clear blue water.

Morgan watched her dive, her golden hair darkening and flowing behind her like a ribbon. She came up for air on the opposite bank. Slicking the water from her face, she gestured for him to come in. Did she know how beautiful she was? Morgan wondered as he dived in after her.

The water was icy cold, and it took his breath away. He met Laura on the other side, and she scooped up a handful of sand, then another, rubbing it against his shoulders, back and hips. He did the same for her. There was nothing like sand to clean the sweat and freshen the skin to a bright, pink hue.

Laura danced away from him as he tried to wash the front of her with the sand. She quickly did the chore herself. Her hair lay wet against her head, wrapped like a thick scarf around her long, beautiful neck and breasts. He ached to have her, and he saw the desire in her dark blue eyes for him. But instead of chasing her, he was content to continue to bathe.

Climbing out, Laura went to the knapsack and drew out the red plaid blanket, spreading it out across the thick, deep grass near the bank. She lay down on her back, stretching her arms above her head, allowing the sun and breeze to dry the water from her body.

Laura felt Morgan come to her side. A few drops of water splashed across her, and she lifted her lashes. Smiling, because he was sitting facing her, his arm across her body so she couldn't escape, she saw that he was going to kiss her and her lower body ached with need of him as she relished the sensation as never before. The rape had taken so much from her, and only in the past three months had she felt the return of her old sensual, sexual self. It had been wonderful discovering that it hadn't been entirely taken from her forever.

As Laura reached up, sliding her damp arms around Morgan's wet shoulders, gleaming in the sunlight, she felt as if she was drowning in the burning dark gray of his eyes. Automatically, her lashes swept downward, and she stretched forward to meet Morgan's mouth. She wasn't disappointed as she felt his arms go around her, sweeping her against him, their bodies meeting and melding slickly against each other.

The warmth of the sunlight and the cooling dance of air across Laura's sensitized skin combined with her dizzied senses as Morgan's mouth settled commandingly on hers. She tasted the sunlight on his lips, inhaled the pine scent that encircled him, mingling with the clean, male fragrance that was distinctively his. Easing her fingers through his wet hair, she opened her mouth farther, inviting him in, her breathing ragged and her heart pulsing with need.

As he kissed her more deeply, she felt Morgan's hand range downward to cup her breast. Molten heat sizzled through her, and she arched against him, a moan vibrating softly in her throat. He tore his mouth from hers, and she waited those exquisite seconds before his lips settled over the hardened peak begging for his attention. Fire seemed to jolt from her breast down to her very core. Helplessly, she arched within his arms and felt herself being placed on the blanket.

Sliding her fingers down across his massive chest, following the hard curve of his narrow hips, she wrapped her fingers provocatively around him. Instantly, he groaned, stiffening against her, his eyes snapping open, their dark, stormy look making her sigh with joy. At that moment, he was more animal than man, and she thrilled to his masculine strength covering her body, taking her, his hand moving her thighs apart to receive him.

The water provided a slick lubricant between them, and the heat of the sunlight combined with the heat they were generating made her feel as if they were fusing like hot metal. She threw back her head, a small cry escaping as she felt Morgan ease his hand between her straining thighs. A new, molten warmth flowed from her, and she felt his fingers move provocatively within the confines of her womanhood. Each movement made her arch harder and sigh with need for his touch. Her lashes swept closed, and she surrendered herself to him in every way. The fire of the sun, the chill of the water, the playful dance of the breeze all conspired to heighten her senses.

Somewhere in her spinning, delicious state, Laura felt Morgan slide between her thighs. How she'd waited for this exquisite moment! She felt his hands settle on her hips, lifting her slightly, and she arched willingly into those large, scarred hands. The moment she felt him sheath into her, a cry tore from her—a cry of utter pleasure combined with acknowledgment of their union, of their becoming one again.

No longer did Laura see their union as something to take for granted. No, the rapes had taught them differently. Now each time she was able to stay connected, in her body, and focus on the fact that it was Morgan touching her and loving her, she experienced a miracle.

Laura felt Morgan move powerfully within her, taking her, claiming her for his own. He was strong as he surged into her, and she held him with all her woman's strength and tenderness as he began to rock her hips in a rhythm as ancient as the world that now embraced them. She gave herself freely, fully to Morgan, matching his rhythm, pulling him even more deeply into the confines of her sacred place, which burned with molten fire. They moved in a unison born of years of loving—and months of careful relearning. Laura was forever amazed and grateful that each time they loved was better than the last—more sacred in a way that not only touched her heart, but grazed her very soul. At eighteen, she hadn't known lovemaking could have this deeply spiritual aspect, but now, as a mature woman, she knew and appreciated this new awareness—this new level of exquisite pleasure.

An explosion of heat rushed through her lower body, and Laura felt Morgan stiffen in almost the same instant. She felt a wonderful joy in climaxing together, at the same moment, for it didn't always happen that way. She wrapped her legs around his, heightening his pleasure, even as she relished his powerful arms around her, holding her so tightly that her skin seemed to dissolve and become his. Intense waves of pleasure washed over her, and she sighed, clinging to him and reveling in the golden moment they shared.

Little by little, Laura became aware of the sunlight warming her once more, the breeze dancing over them as they lay on the blanket, on their sides, still holding each other. The gurgle of the creek entered her consciousness, and slowly she opened her eyes.

Morgan was slightly above her, propped on his elbow, studying her in the silence. His gray eyes were half-closed, thoughtful, still banked with coals of desire. She smiled tenderly and turned onto her back, content just to be close to him. Reaching up, she threaded her fingers through his drying hair. Despite the horrors and hardships Morgan had endured in his forty-some years of living, he looked stronger and more hand-some to her now than ever before.

And Laura knew it was because of the decisions he had made fifteen months ago. No one was more grate-ful than she for his unselfish choices. It had taken that kind of dramatic change and commitment from him to help her overcome the rapes. Without that, she wondered if she would have healed as well as she now had.

"I love you," she quavered, sliding her fingers across his scarred cheek.

Morgan leaned down and cherished her smiling lips. "And I love you with my life, Little Swan," he rasped, sliding his hand down her ribs to rest on her hip.

Laura reached up, framing his face with her hands, mere inches separating them. "I have a wonderful surprise for you, Morgan."

He frowned at the undisguised, raw emotion in her voice, then smiled a little. "What is it?"

Laura smiled tenderly and took his hand, placing it against her belly. "Haven't you noticed something different about me?"

Morgan frowned again. His eyes widened. He gave Laura a shaken look, then stared down at his darkly suntanned hand spanning her abdomen and back into her radiant blue eyes. *"You're pregnant?"* The words came out in an explosion of disbelief. The gynecologist in Fairfax, Virginia, had told Morgan in no uncertain terms that Laura would never conceive again.

Laura laughed softly and sat up, throwing her arms around his neck and burying her face against his neck. "Oh, Morgan, I'm three months along! That first time we were able to truly make love, I conceived! It's been killing me to wait until today to tell you!" She laughed freely and kissed him repeatedly all over his face like a happy puppy.

"But," Morgan growled, gripping her by the arms, staring at her flushed features, "the doctor said—"

"What do doctors know?" She laughed, throwing her arms around his neck. "Morgan, I'm pregnant! Isn't it wonderful? Michaela said the pregnancy is fine. I'm fine!"

Stunned, Morgan continued staring at her. One of the things Laura had done shortly after moving to Philipsburg was to visit Dr. Michaela, the homeopathic physician who served the small community. Sarah had gone to her for help from time to time, and their smoke-jumper friend, Pepper Sinclair-Woodward, swore by Michaela's magic with alternative medicine.

"B-but—" he stammered, "how? I—I don't understand."

Trying to contain her joy, Laura knelt in front of him, her hands on his shoulders. "First of all, are you happy about it, darling?"

"Well...of course I am," he rasped, sliding his hand along her jaw and drowning in the joy in her eyes. "But I'm worried, too."

Laura shrugged. "I went to Michaela for a homeopathic constitutional treatment right after we moved here, Morgan. You remember that."

"Yes. Sarah said it might help you with the emotional problems resulting from the rape."

"Exactly," Laura said, smiling. "And it did. Well, what I didn't know but learned from Michaela is that homeopathic treatments not only works on a person mentally and emotionally, but physically, too." She shook her head and reached out to take both his hands. "I didn't tell you about one conversation Michaela had with me quite a while back. She examined me as any other doctor would, and she said that with homeopathic treatment, there might be a chance I could have children again."

"This isn't making sense," Morgan muttered. "How could conventional medical treatment say one thing and this alternative method another?"

"Proof's in the pudding, isn't it?" she teased, laughing. "Michaela said that scar tissue sometimes could, with homeopathic treatment, be dissolved. I didn't believe it, either, Morgan, but over the months, it was happening. And at that point—" she sighed, brushing several strands of hair away from her eyes

"—I really began to believe what Michaela was saying all along—that I could have children again. I didn't tell you because I didn't want to get your hopes up, Morgan. I didn't want us to fail at this. I kept it to myself and hoped it would work." Her hands tightened around his and she shrugged. "It did!"

Morgan shook his head, stunned. "I'll be damned."

"Are you happy?"

"Of course I am, Little Swan." He pulled her back into his arms and they sat looking out over the mirrorlike surface of the deep blue water. He kissed her cheek. "Does Michaela think you can carry this baby to term?" he asked, recalling the trouble they'd had with Katherine coming early.

"Yes, she does. You know, half her homeopathic practice is mommies-to-be, babies and children. Michaela has fifteen years of experience, and I trust what she knows, Morgan. She feels I can deliver our baby to term, healthy and without labor problems."

"Because of your homeopathic treatments?" he wondered aloud.

"Yes. But Michaela isn't going to take any chances. I see her monthly for examinations and checkups. She gives me different remedies." Laura eased her head to the left and looked up at him. "I didn't even have morning sickness this time, Morgan, because she gave me a remedy that stopped it. Isn't that wonderful?"

Amazed, Morgan nodded. Gently, he covered her

abdomen with his hands. "A baby," he whispered unsteadily.

"Our baby, rising out of the ashes of our love for each other," she reminded him softly. "She's like the fable about the phoenix—the bird that's destroyed by fire, burned to ashes and arises even more beautiful and strong into a new phoenix.

"Our love has gone through those fires, darling. We were both destroyed and reduced to ashes ourselves. We've risen out of that horrifying past—and look at us now! We're better and happier than before. Yes, this little girl is definitely our phoenix child, a gift for having the courage to fight back, to survive and put our love back together." Her voice trembled. "She is about our redefined, newly discovered love, Morgan. I've never felt happier or more at peace with myself, with you and our family than now. I have my hope back, and life looks like such a rich, unfolding adventure to me now—thanks to you helping me survive and climb back on my feet...."

Morgan saw the tears in Laura's eyes and knew he had matching tears in his. Running his hands gently over her swelling abdomen, he felt too emotional to speak. Laura sighed softly, leaning back against him. The pond, the green grass and bright flowers blurred before his eyes. "I had my dreams torn from me so many times in the past," he whispered raggedly against her ear, "that eventually I quit dreaming. Then you walked into my life like a lightning bolt out of the blue, and my whole life was upended—in a positive way.''

He pressed small kisses along Laura's neck and jaw, feeling her quiver with joy. His heart felt as if it would explode with the intense happiness he was experiencing. No one deserved the joy he felt, Morgan thought. Especially not him. Yet somehow the universe had given him a third chance. And he was taking it, come hell or high water. With Laura and their children, he could do anything it took to survive. Anything.

''A Christmas baby, huh?'' he rasped, smiling and enjoying the feel of her lounging against him.

''Yes—'' Laura sighed ''—a Christmas baby.''

''We couldn't ask for a better gift, could we?''

''No,'' she whispered softly.

''A baby girl, eh?''

''Katherine Alyssa will have that sister she always wanted. And Jason will learn to be a big brother all over again.''

Gently, Morgan turned Laura so that she lay in his arms, her face inches from his own as he probed her radiant blue gaze, his voice thick with raw emotion. ''I love you, Little Swan. Forever and beyond eternity.''

*   *   *   *   *

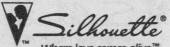

LINDSAY McKENNA

Silhouette ®

Where love comes alive™

Visit Silhouette at www.eHarlequin.com

PSLM0204BL

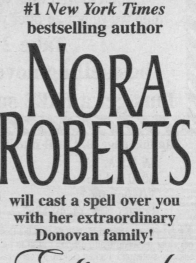

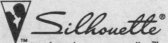

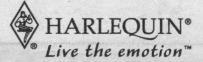

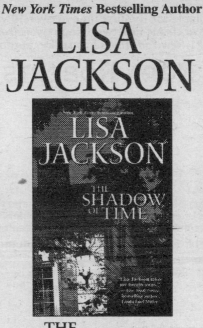
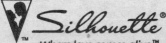